MW01092504

A Whispering Castell Anthology

TALES
OF THE
DRAGON

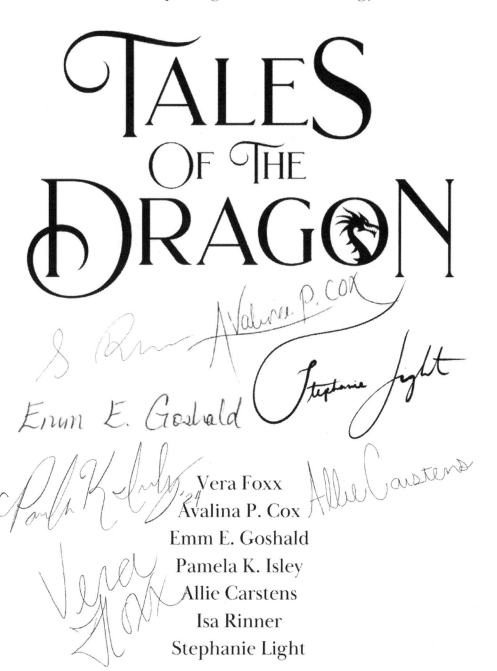

Vera Foxx

Avalina P. Cox

Emm E. Goshald

Pamela K. Isley

Allie Carstens

Isa Rinner

Stephanie Light

To all the princesses who fell for the dragon and not the knight in shining armor

Contents

Note from the Authors

Tales of the Dragon is a collection of stories all focusing on dragons and is rated 18+. There are explicit and descriptive scenes of a sexual nature and references to slavery, mistreatment, and a range of sexual relationships.

You can expect seven individual stories that are not interrelated and can be read as standalone. Each story has its own myths, rules, and possibilities and are based entirely in fictional lands.

Dark themes include but are not limited to Slavery, murder, vengeance, and betrayal.

Possible Triggers:
Attempted Rape
Descriptive Violence
Death
Slavery
Sexual Assault

THE LOST
DRAGON KING

ISA RINNER

Blurb

In a mechanical city, driven by steam engines and its dystopian society, the only protection from the 'deadly' outside conditions is a barrier, which the 'maidens' project with their powers.

For the people living in the outer circle, if you were pretty enough, you worked in the brothel. If not, you became a tinker, made to brave the wasteland, in order to sift 'the trash' – detritus left in the destruction caused by the flying monsters.

Estelle is a tinker, and a 'maiden'. The only maiden ever to have been born in the outermost circle. She loves her fellow tinkers and every day strives to help them, by excelling in her role as a maiden.

Until, one fateful day when Estelle and her uncle dig out a stranger from the trash…

Chapter 1 - The Maidens of the Blue Light

Estelle

I glance at my pocket watch, a skeleton pocket watch my father made for me before he passed away. He retrieved it from the wasteland right next to our city where all the trash collects. We inhabitants of the fifth, the outer circle, make our living by collecting and upgrading it. The nice inhabitants of the upper circles call us the tinkers. The not-so-nice ones—waste.

One glance at my watch tells me I am running late. Not good. I hurry to freshen up in the bathroom before dressing in my uniform. Us maidens of the Blue Light are supposed to dress appropriately. I wear an off-white petticoat dress with frillies but otherwise looks modest. It ends right at my knees, and over it a steel-boned over-bust corset. It's in the colors of the temple I serve in...deep azure blue. It has a sweetheart neckline and a belt with gold metal accents. I braided my blonde hair overnight and can tie it up now with a curled section going over my shoulders.

The headpiece is a small azure blue hat, I pin to my hair.

Done.

I grab my boots before hurrying downstairs.

"Stella, honey," Maude greets me. "Have breakfast before you leave."

"I'm running late," I tell her.

"Have something on your way," Maude says, handing me a tartlet.

"Thank you," I say, hugging her swiftly.

Maude is the boss of the establishment I'm staying in. She was a friend of my father and started as an orphan in this brothel before she rose through the ranks and took the reins over it. Most orphaned tinkers are either sent to work in the brothel or work to supply the guards and inner circles with the trash they find. Maude, however, doesn't let any girl or boy below the age of sixteen offer any services to the men and women coming here. They are all only allowed to clean and cook, but nothing else. She watches over them like a hawk.

I am an exception because the light reacted to me, and I was chosen to serve it and our high priest as a maiden. But Maude still let me stay with them.

I love her and the girls and boys working here. We are like our own little family. As if on cue, my two best friends appear. Ned and Winnie are twins who are both working in the brothel. They are eighteen, rather delicately built, and both with dark-brown hair. Ned, in particular, is a favorite here. Sometimes he and Winnie get booked together, and they jokingly compare their body counts.

Winnie is wearing a red frilly dress with a tight corset that shows off her tiny waist. "How do I look, Maude? I added some accessories to it to make it look more exclusive. I thought I could wear it for the special event on Saturday. We will have a lot of guests then."

"Beautiful," Maude says. "Do you have a fitting hair piece?"

"No, but I can make one."

"I have one from my active times," Maude says. "You can have it."

Meanwhile, Ned gives me a swift hug. "My favorite maiden looks beautiful," he says, a smile curling his lips. He always looks a bit melancholic with his soft features and big eyes. "You are our pride," he whispers. "The proof that the outer circle isn't *waste*."

I grab his face between my hands. "Don't ever call yourself or anyone else of the outer circle, waste," I say. "We are so much more than that."

I kiss the tip of his nose, and he smiles at me.

"May the light be with you," he says.

"And with you," I reply.

I grab my things and hurry out of the building. The paths to the elevator leading me to the inner circles are narrow. Metal and engines cover the paths, and little houses and shady bars line them with men and women working on the narrow streets to sort through the trash. The buildings here are small but are raking high into the air. Steam from the engines covers everything. I can't even spot what's above me. The tinkers are all really nice people, though a bit gruff and rough sometimes, but we stick together.

Most of them greet me and wave at me. The owner of the little bar waves a bottle of beer in my direction. "I wish my favorite maiden would grace me with a visit," he says.

I laugh. He was a friend of my father's, too, and keeps watching out for me. "Maybe later, Uncle Arthur."

I can't halt and chat with anyone, though. Instead, I make it right to the elevator. It's guarded as usual, but the guards know me and let me pass. Only with the correct permit can we leave our circle and travel to one of the higher ones.

The whole city is built like a clock...or perhaps, a tower. Most of us are on the lower floors, so those are broader, while the higher we go, the smaller the circles get, the more private and the more beautiful.

The city is built out of five circles, or rather, five floors. The lowest floor, the outer circle, where I and the other tinkers live, is the lowest in the hierarchy.

The next floor, called the fourth circle, is where the mechanics reside. They work on the engines that keep the city running, but there are not only mechanics. The fourth circle has a lot of guilds and even a detective bureau. Some of them even get hired by the higher circles. They are called the activists.

The regulars inhabit the third circle. They work for the two highest circles but don't belong to them. They live more comfortably than us lower ones. They are called the proletariat.

The second circle is where the nobles reside. As a maiden, I sometimes get to see the second circle. It's beautiful, with breathtaking buildings...and they can see the sky above them instead of steam and dust. Mostly it's clouded, but sometimes when it's really early and I'm not running late, I can see a few sun rays.

How nice must it be to see the sun, every day.

I shake the thought off and hurry to the next elevator, which brings me to the temple. The highest floor and the innermost circle is the sacred one where the temple of the blue light resides. Once I reach my destination, a well-known view greets me. Other maidens are walking around in the same uniform as I am wearing; some of them have their heads buried in a book, others are chatting.

I make my way to the guard overseeing our duties today to register my name as proof that I am present. He checks me over shortly. "You have worked on your clothes, I see."

"Yes, Master," I say. "You said I should try to make it look better so that I will be worthy of the light."

He nods contentedly. "You listen well and are fast at getting to work." He furrows his brows while he looks at a group of girls from the proletariat. "Unlike them."

I don't tell him that it doesn't surprise me. Tinkers are used to working from a young age, and especially to be self-sufficient. The moment my family and friends in the outer circle knew I was having a hard time, due to my clothes not being as fancy as the others, they all worked together to help me upscale what I am wearing.

The overseeing guard waves me off, and I join a group I have somewhat befriended. There are no quarrels and arguments allowed here, but clearly, the maidens that come from higher circles don't really want to spend time with me. However, there are very few activists within the maidens, and they have been nice to me from the first moment on.

Evelyn, a sweet redhead who is the sister of the owner of the detective bureau, is my closest friend here. She appears shy and quiet at first glance, but once I befriended her, she turned into a little chatterbox. We clicked right away. "What's our schedule today?" I ask her.

"We are attending to the gardens later, but first the high priest is coming to watch us doing our prayers."

"They are hoping for us to raise our arcane powers," I muse. It's our arcane power the blue light reacts to, after all. The magic we have inside us. The blue light comes from a gemstone, and every girl born is brought to it. Only if it reacts and eludes its glow will it mean you are a chosen one.

"I cannot wait for us to ascend," she whispers, brushing over her clothes to smooth them. She looks beautiful, but I know she hates dressing up. The only thing she likes wearing is her favorite brooch.

"I wish we would know what it means, though," I point out.

"Well, we need to finish our studies first and then pass the test...only then we can ascend." She smiles. "Probably means that we will finally have reached our powers. That would be amazing. We could further protect the town like that."

"You are not wrong," I muse. "Everything around us is wasteland. The tinkers who go out to dig through the trash and waste keep saying how hot the air is, and how there are no shadows looming anywhere. They say there is barely any sun anymore."

"I've heard something similar from one of the girls from the nobles. She said the sky is always covered in clouds or darkness. That's what they need us for," she says. "We are the barrier."

The barrier.

It's such a foreign concept to me. Something I can't see, but something that's apparently around our city, preventing the darkness from swallowing us. That's what us maidens are for. Our magic is strengthening the barrier and keeping it up. To keep the darkness outside—and the monsters. I have never seen one, but my father once had. He said they are huge, with wings like a massive lizard. And they fly.

The high priest calls them winged monsters.

All that matters to me is to keep my fellow tinkers safe. They are who I am doing this for. "By the way," Evelyn's voice is just a low whisper. She gazes around so that no one can hear her. "My brother had a new customer."

"Oh?"

"Yes, his detective agency is booming," she says, sounding genuinely happy for him. "The new customer is looking for his brother. Seems like he disappeared. He was so cute."

Her secretive behavior makes sense now. "Oh no."

"Oh yes. He even smiled at me, and we talked," she says, her cheeks flushed.

"Evelyn," I whisper. "We are not allowed to—"

"I know, we are maidens," she sighs. "But, a girl can dream."

"You are right," I mutter, thinking about Ned for a moment. I think if I weren't a maiden, he would have asked me out a while ago. I'm not sure if I would have ended up with him, though. He feels like a brother to me. My sweet Ned. Recently he looks tired.

There is no use dwelling on the what-ifs. Evelyn's and my fate are bound to the barrier now. We are serving this city.

A gong echoes through the whole floor. Evelyn and I stop our little chat and follow our peers to the vast hall where we are supposed to meditate. We do this daily, gathered around the little pedestal with the blue orb floating above it, and us maidens sitting around it on our pillows while saying our spells. The goal is to be in sync with everyone and instead of acting as individuals become one. This time the high priest is present too, sitting a bit further away to watch us.

He is a bit older. A silver fox, as Evelyn said once, and hot. I'm not sure if I agree with that, but he is indeed handsome. His name is Alistair, and he is the head of the temple and our leader. I ignore him for now and settle down in my assigned place. It's always the same, so we get used to it and our surroundings. Soon, the shuffling and chatting dies down, and the room becomes silent. The master who has the supervision today hits the gong once more. The sound of it filling the room, vibrating slightly.

Murmurs fill the room as we chant the spells we have learned over and over again. It takes a while for us to be in sync, but once we do, it feels like the room is vibrating. Then, one after another, one of the maidens steps forward, a flower in her hand while she sings. I'm the last one due to being the lowest in hierarchy. I walk forward, the white lily in my hand, the murmurs around me filling the room. It's almost like the air around me is vibrating. I take a breath before I start to sing. It's an old melody we have all learned by heart. It's beautiful but feels melancholic, in a language I don't know.

It's about a looming danger surrounding the world, sacrifices having to be made, and the maidens protecting the barrier surrounding us. That's how long this system has existed already, I realize. There have been dozens of maidens before me, all of them going through this school like I do. All of them trying to channel their arcane powers. It's about the flying monsters who have burned the world to the ground; the waste filling our lands and making it almost impossible to live anywhere, and how important it is to keep the engines of our city moving and working.

About how humans are part of this engine.

I imagine them merging with the motors and engines, and turning to steam themselves as they work and work, day and night.

I think of my fellow tinkers who leave the city, risking their lives in the wastelands to retrieve objects they believe could be useful. I think of Ned and Winnie, and how Winnie cried when she had to join the active girls in the brothel. How scared she was when her first customer bought her for the night, and how she pretends for it to be fun now.

Something about this makes me feel sad.

When I open my eyes again, I notice that the murmurs around me have stopped entirely. The orb in front of me is radiating, and its shining beams falling on me. The lily in my hand has grown into a full flower.

Chapter - 2 The High Priest
Estelle

"That was amazing!" Evelyn exclaims when we leave the hall. The other maidens eye me with a mixture of curiosity and respect now, but Evelyn remains unfazed and joyful. "The blue orb just started to radiate when you sang. It was unbelievable. How did you do it?"

"I don't know," I admit. "I just...sang."

"I wish I could be that amazing!"

I'm not sure what to answer her. Before I can come up with something, the overseeing master approaches me. "Maiden Estelle," he says. "Follow me. The high priest demands your presence."

Evelyn's mouth drops open in shock, while I stare at him in disbelief. "What...me?" I mutter. "Are you sure? I'm just...a tinker."

The man's gaze softens. "Yes, you. I am very sure. You do not need to be afraid, Maiden Estelle."

"I will see you later," Evelyn promises. She looks a bit worried, but still gives me an encouraging nod. "I can visit you if you want. We are allowed to do that, aren't we?" She looks at our overseeing master now, and he nods.

"There's no reason you can't, especially with the current development." He pauses, looking guilty, almost as if he was caught saying something he shouldn't.

Well, he got me curious for sure, and there is no way I can not meet the high priest if he summoned me. I'm not that reckless to endanger my life that way. I wave Evelyn off and then follow the guard. To my surprise, he leads me past the school and temple grounds and through a heavily guarded fence. I have never been here. That's only for the high priest and those working for him. He and his subordinates form the committee that rules over the city. It consists of a few members of the innermost circle and some nobles.

They are the only ones allowed to step onto these grounds.

"Are you," I pause, "are you sure I am allowed to be here?"

"Yes," the man reassures me.

I am spellbound, to say the least. The innermost circle is breathtaking, but stepping onto these forbidden grounds is an adventure. Flowers are everywhere, beautiful intricate statues, and a skillfully set up path. It leads directly to the enormous building I can usually spot from the scholar's garden.

Evelyn and I have always gossiped about what it is like to be inside. I can't believe I will see it now. There are huge glass windows, no steam surrounding anything, not even machines are visible. It's a mansion in light colors instead of the common dark ones. It's like from a different world.

The guard leads me through the main entrance and then through a hallway. A few people pass us, casting me curious glances, but not minding me otherwise. Our goal is a beautiful office. High Priest Alistair expects me already. He has put his robe away and is dressed in a well-tailored suit with a long-tailored coat with multiple buckles. Evelyn always calls him handsome, and I'm starting to see why.

"Maiden Estelle." He approaches me and shakes my hand, much to my surprise. "Please come in." He nods at the guard. "You can leave now."

He leads me towards a desk with two chairs where we sit down. In front of us, a plate with the finest pastries, tartlets, and a wonderfully scented tea. I've never smelled anything like it. He seems to catch my curiosity. "This is a rare blend," he says. "I thought you might want to try it."

I am completely caught off-guard by his hospitality. "I would love to," I say, unsure how to act in front of him. Maidens are generally supposed to be well-mannered, but we don't learn etiquette. We are not supposed to mingle with the nobles and the high priest.

High Priest Alistair hands me a cup before offering me some pastries. My anxiety is growing now. He certainly wouldn't set this all up if he doesn't want something from me? I clear my throat. "High Priest A—"

"Alistair," he tells me. "You may call me by my first name when we aren't on the temple grounds."

I stare at him, shocked. I am supposed to address him so informally. That's just wrong, isn't it?

"So, what did you want to ask, Maiden Estelle?"

"Estelle," I hear myself say, blushing when he looks at me. "I mean, it's only the right thing to do if...you know...if—"

"I understand." He smiles. It's the first time I have ever seen him smile. It doesn't quite reach his eyes, but he looks friendlier. "Estelle, what did you want to ask?"

"I would like to know why you summoned me?" I dare to ask.

"Well, isn't it obvious?" When I don't answer, he continues, "It's been many, many years since there has been a maiden with your talent," he says. "The last one to make the orb light up in front of her died of high age two years ago."

"But I didn't do anything," I say.

"She always said the same."

There was an old maiden here who could do something like that? How come I have never seen her? Most maidens are really young. I don't know what they do once they reach their thirties, but I assume they just retire. An old maiden would have certainly caught my attention. "Who was she?" I ask.

"She had different duties than you young maidens," he explains evasively. "She mostly resided here. She was the former high priest's wife."

"I see," I say, although I don't understand a thing, but being a tinker has taught me to go with the flow; to watch, listen and then put the pieces together.

"Estelle, I want you to polish these powers of yours. For that reason, I want you to take some special classes."

Learning something new sounds amazing, so I smile at him. "I would love that."

"You can attend these classes here," he says. "I will make sure you have good teachers. I have a handful of capable subordinates well versed in arcane magic."

"And my duties as a maiden?" I ask. "I don't want to keep the others hanging."

"I like your diligence," he says. "You can do both."

I'm surprised by the prospect of so many new things approaching me. "Thank you, high pr...Alistair," I say.

"There is something else, Estelle," he says. "Your talent isn't the only reason I called you here."

I look at him curiously.

"I wonder if you would allow me to visit you."

"Visit me?" I'm completely flabbergasted at his suggestion. "Visit me...in the outer circle? In the brothel?"

"Having you stay with the waste..." He clears his throat. "With the tinkers is a waste of potential, Estelle," he says.

"But, they are my friends and family," I say. "They are good people."

"I know." He smiles at me again. "Which is why I want to visit them to see where you live and introduce myself." He looks at me through his thoughtful eyes. "And, I hope you will accompany me on a dinner."

He wants me to dine with him? I'm more than taken aback at his suggestion. I'm not sure I feel comfortable meeting him in private.

"And I forgot to mention," Alistair says. "Of course, I will lift the usual restrictions from you. As my...acquaintance you are free to go anywhere in the city without regulations." He hands me a card. "This is proof that you have access anywhere you like, even here."

That's the third...fourth...or fifth shocking thing he says today. I have barely any chance to put my thoughts into order. I just know that there is no way I can turn him down. "Thank you," I say. "I am free of my duties in two days."

"Then, it's set," he says. "I will pay you a visit then."

Maude looks at me in complete shock. I returned home and told her, Ned and Winnie what happened today. My friends are already in their working attire for today. Ned is clad in a white satin shirt with puffy sleeves and a waistcoat above it, paired with dark brown high-waist plaid pants. Meanwhile, Winnie is wearing a long, layered skirt, and a dark brown corset, with a flowery blouse underneath.

"The high priest wants to visit?" Winnie asks once more.

I nod. "I don't know why...it's...I don't think I can reject his wish."

"You can't," Maude mutters. "And I don't like that."

"He just wants to visit though, right?" Ned wants to know. He shakes his head when I offer him something to eat. "I-I can't sleep with anyone with my belly full," he says quietly.

"You are still so nervous," Winnie says, wrapping her arms around her twin brother while he leans his head against hers.

"Just a habit," he admits.

Maude squeezes the two of them, but is still caught in her thoughts. "I don't like it," she repeats once more.

"You mean Estelle's high priest?" Ned asks.

Maude sighs. "He is a lot older than Estelle," she says. "If I know one thing, a man of his status and age doesn't just invite a young girl out."

"Wait, you think he has an interest in me?" I say, laughing. But the look on Maude's face makes the laughter die in my throat. "No, he...he never noticed me before."

"You are young, beautiful, and apparently have a very rare power," Maude says. "And he is a man of power." She takes my hands. "Estelle, if he starts courting you, keep in mind that you don't need to say yes to him. If he wants to bed you, don't let him. By all means if you like him, if you truly do, then make him announce you as his, officially, before you give yourself to him."

"I don't even know him," I whisper. "Let alone like him that way."

"I think Maude is right," Winnie says all of a sudden. "He is going to court you."

"How old is he?" Ned wants to know.

"He is thirty-eight," Maude answers. "He is not old by any means, but a lot older than Estelle." She looks worried yet puts up a smile for me. "Don't worry, Stella, we won't leave you alone." She pauses. "Why don't you accompany Uncle Arthur today?" she offers.

"Oh!" I beam. "Is he going outside?"

"Yes, he said he wants to see if he can find something interesting in the waste," Maude says. "With your rank changing and the higher-ups having their eyes on you, you won't be able to do that much in the future."

"It's been forever since I joined him." My mood rising instantly. "You're right. I should go while I still can." I pause. "Oh, I forgot. A friend might visit me later. You know, Evelyn. I told you about her. I might show her around and then go to the activists."

"Are you allowed to roam the fourth circle freely?" Maude asks.

"I-I don't have any limitations anymore," I tell her. "That's what the high priest said."

Maude looks worried again but doesn't say anything. Instead, we get interrupted by Uncle Arthur peeking inside. "I heard I have a beautiful maiden accompanying me this afternoon."

I am on my feet instantly. "I will just change swiftly," I say. "Then we can leave."

Chapter - 3 The Stranger
Estelle

I haven't been out in a while. The landscape outside of town is truly mind-boggling. Behind us is the town with its five floors. It looks like a tower from the outside, like a pyramid. Seeing it from this angle makes it look fascinating with all the elevators and jagged buildings. There is even one zeppelin above the temple. Dust covers the lower area, and the buildings there are more crooked, but it still looks like a piece of art.

"What are you thinking?" Uncle Arthur asks.

"That our city is beautiful," I say.

"Really?" he chuckles. "It's just technology and engines. When I was a child, there were still a few trees here and there, but they all died out."

"Still, it's vibrant," I say. "It's home."

I turn my attention back to him. He talked about trees, but the only remaining trees are in the innermost circle. Other than that, there are no trees or bushes anymore, and only the royals and the temple still grow flowers.

I think that's why we maidens are supposed to sing with a flower or plant in our hands, in hope that they won't die down completely.

Even here, away from the city, thick clouds cover the sky. "I can't imagine that there was once a time that the sun was constantly shining," I admit.

Uncle Arthur smiles, a nostalgic look in his eyes. "The night sky, Estelle. The night sky was the most beautiful." He shakes his head, looking sad, while he leads me through a small path. Around us there is metal garbage, broken engines, and rocks.

"Where is all this waste coming from?" I ask. "Is it all of us?"

"I doubt it," Uncle Arthur says. "I think for many years the waste from all the surroundings was dropped here." I watch him dig up a piece of brown, rusty metal. "That's a music box," he says.

"No way!"

"Yes." He smiles. "You see the crooked figurine? That used to be a ballerina. And inside…" He opens it, where there are a few screws and plates. "This used to be the inner case." He puts it in his bag. "I will make sure to restore it for my favorite maiden."

"You need to show me how you do that," I say. "Maybe I can make a present for Ned and Winnie too."

"How about this," he offers, digging out a small rusty chain. "We can make a necklace out of this for Winnie. And here…" He searches for something else. "Cufflinks for Ned."

"Is this really okay?" I ask. "We are here because you are looking for decoration for your bar, aren't we?"

"Ah," he laughs. "I just like to see you and the other kids happy."

We spend the next hours that way. I am trying to be helpful, but I doubt I'm of any use to Uncle Arthur. He doesn't complain though, and instead seems to enjoy being out here with me. I tell him a bit about my work as a maiden, but keep the details about High Priest Alistair out. Something tells me I should not talk about him.

Maude thinks he will court me, but I bet I am just a child in his eyes. He is tall, imposing…and important. If he is looking for a suitable woman, why would it be me? I absent-mindedly dig through some of the metal waste, poking it with a stick Uncle Arthur gave me when I feel something soft beneath it.

The waste here is mostly metal junk, old engines, and machines, sometimes pieces of clothing. The men and women going out here regularly tend to bring back whatever clothing they find for everyone in the brothel, but also for me sometimes. It's fascinating how they find pieces of clothing here and there…almost like someone keeps tossing it away regularly.

Maybe that's the royals?

I poke the soft spot again, feeling how something moves. "Uncle Arthur!" I blurt out.

"What happened?" he asks, hurrying to me and shoving me behind him.

"There is something in there.".

He turns his head to stare at me. "What?"

I know it sounds silly. There are no animals living here; nothing can remain and stay here in this environment. Still, Uncle Arthur humors me and carefully pulls some of the metal aside. A gasp leaves his lips, and I curiously peek past him, my eyes widening at the view in front of me.

"A…man?" I whisper.

He is naked, covered in wounds and scars. His face is smothered in dirt, so is his hair.

"By the light," Uncle Arthur mutters.

"Is he alive?" I ask breathlessly.

Uncle Arthur kneels down next to him, checking his pulse. "He is still breathing," he says. "But he must have been hurt severely."

"We need to do something."

"Estelle, sweetheart," Uncle Arthur looks uncertain. "Visitors are strictly prohibited in the city."

"But is he truly a visitor?" I mutter.

Uncle Arthur looks from me to the young man. He looks conflicted. "I swore to never hurt a living creature," he mutters. "Leaving him here would kill him."

"We can't leave him here," I say quietly. "I'll take the responsibility in case someone asks."

"The hell I will let my best friend's daughter take the blame," Uncle Arthur grumbles. "Help me tie this blanket around him. Let's wrap him up tightly."

It takes us almost an hour to retrieve the young man, and I try my best not to stare at his naked frame. I have never seen a naked man before, and I don't want to hurt his privacy further by staring. Uncle Arthur and I manage to wrap him in the blanket, and then carry him back to the city. Fortunately, night has approached us, and it's getting darker every minute.

"How are we going to pass the guards?" Uncle Arthur asks.

"Can you carry him by yourself? I could distract them."

Uncle Arthur shifts his weight until the man is draped over his shoulder, and I make sure to hurry to the entrance of the city. It's always heavily guarded, unfortunately. The guards are shocked to see me. "A maiden?" they ask, stunned. "What are you doing out here?"

"I was looking for something," I say, innocently. "I think it may have dropped from a higher level." I pause, showing them my new papers. "High Priest Alistair assured me there are no restrictions for me anymore. I wasn't aware that I shouldn't leave...I am so sorry—"

"The High Priest?" the guards exchange a gaze. "Well, I'm sure he didn't mean you should stroll around at night," they say, but their expression gets a lot more polite. "Maiden Estelle."

"I understand," I say, noticing how Uncle Arthur uses the distraction to sneak past us. "I...this is still new to me. I will make sure not to repeat this mistake."

"Don't mention it," one of the guards hurries to reassure me.

"Thank you for your kindness." I show them a dazzling smile before walking past them. I can hear them whisper behind me something about the high priest. Their curious gazes follow me, and I am once more reminded of Maude's worried expression.

"What a handsome young man," Maude mutters.

Uncle Arthur snuck the young man we found to the brothel, mainly because Maude is a bit like everyone's mom here for the tinkers, and the brothel is the biggest establishment. It's easy to hide someone here.

Uncle Arthur disappeared to call one of his best friends for help, a woman who is our emergency nurse here. None of us tinkers can afford to visit an actual doctor, and she is our to-go person. Also, I think Uncle Arthur has a little crush on her, which is just adorable.

Alice indeed comes immediately, helping us with the young man. He has a lot of cuts and bruises, and Alice thinks his wrist might be sprained. After she checks him, Ned and one of the other boys clean his body and dress him. Once they leave the room, I grab a towel to wash his face and comb his hair.

Cleaned up now, it's obvious how handsome he is. His face resembles one from a painting, and his hair is long and colored a light brown. Next to him I almost feel invisible with my dark blonde hair that's neither really blonde nor brown. The only notable thing about me is my rank as a maiden.

Maude leaves shortly, and Winnie and I take over watching him.

"Do you think he will be a danger to us?" Winnie asks.

I shake my head. "I don't think so."

"How do you know?" she asks.

I put a hand on my chest. "A feeling," I say. "I can't explain it, but something about him calls out to me, and I know he won't hurt us."

"He certainly is a fresh wind here," Winnie says. "Things are dull."

I look up at her words, a bit surprised. Winnie always acts happy and joyful. "Are you alright?" I ask carefully.

She just shrugs. "I...have no time to think about being alright," she admits.

I grab her hand, pulling her towards me. "What's wrong, Winnie?"

"Sometimes I just feel dirty," she admits.

My heart breaks at her words. We never talk about work here in the brothel. If I hadn't become a maiden, I would have been one of them too. And sometimes guilt eats me up for living a better life than they do. I love these people more than anything else, and hate watching them sell their bodies to the rich dealers, mercenaries or nobles.

I hug Winnie tightly. "I wish I could help you. I wish I could take you and Ned and run away."

"We can't run, Estelle," she says, hugging me back. "There is nowhere for us. Here at least we have Maude, who steps in if one of our customers oversteps." She draws back, smiling slightly. "Some days are good. And not all customers are bad."

I don't know what to say to her. There is nothing to say, I guess. However, her words struck something in me, and I think back to High Priest Alistair and to what Maude told me. If he wants to court me, should I maybe say yes? Maybe I can make things better that way for my beloved tinkers?

Winnie's gaze moves back to the young man we found. "I am curious about him," she says. "Where did he come from? Why was he hurt?"

"Hopefully, he will answer once he is awake."

Maude returns to the room with a fresh bowl of water. She has heard my last words and nods now. "Let's hope he will wake up soon," she says. "Poor thing. Who hurt him like that?"

"Where is he going to stay?" Winnie says.

"The room next to mine is vacant," I say.

Maude frowns. "Your room is further away from the other girls and boys," she mutters. "I don't like letting a stranger sleep beside you."

"But that's exactly why it's the best place," I say. "Because it's further away, no one will look here."

"She isn't wrong," Winnie agrees.

Maude sighs before rummaging in her pockets and handing me a bell. "If he tries something, ring it, and I will come."

"Thank you." Before I can say anything else one of the girls peeks into the room.

"Estelle," she says. "Your friend is here. The other maiden. I made sure to make her come through the back entrance and wait in our private dining room."

"Oh, Evelyn! I almost forgot."

"Go," Maude nudges me. "Winnie and I will watch over him."

"But I have to work?" Winnie mutters.

"You can take the evening off," Maude says nonchalantly.

"I can't leave you here," I say. "Not after it was me who convinced Uncle Arthur to drag this man into town."

"Your rank as a maiden is very important to us," Maude says. "And your friendship with the other maidens is too. You are our only hope, Estelle. Be a maiden with all you can."

Be a maiden.

Kind, thoughtful, well-educated, and selfless.

That's our dogma.

Be a good maiden.

Chapter - 4 Just a Girl
Estelle

Evelyn hugs me the moment she sees me. Her cheeks are flushed, and she looks so happy. "You won't believe what happened," she exclaims.

I smile at her excitement. "Let me introduce you to everyone before you tell me everything."

"Oh!" Evelyn clasps her mouth. "I'm sorry. My manners! I am a bad maiden."

"You are a very cute maiden," Ned reassures her, making her giggle.

I take advantage of the moment, pulling Ned closer. "This is one of my best friends. He is like a brother to me," I tell her. "Ned." I proceed to introduce everyone else, including Maude and Winnie, who peek into the room before they return to our mysterious guest. "This is my family," I end the introduction.

Evelyn is letting her gaze wander over everyone, clearly noticing their attire and what they work at. Her eyes are sad for a moment, but soon she smiles brightly at everyone. "I am so happy to meet all of you. Estelle always talks about you."

I smile when Ned hugs me briefly from behind and squeezes me. "Estelle is our hope," he says.

"My brother and friends say the same about me," Evelyn admits. "There are only three maidens from my circle."

"I thought it was four?" I ask.

"No, one of them ascended," Evelyn beams.

"Oh, I didn't know! Is she back at home?"

"Not yet," Evelyn says. "I think they offered her to stay at the private residence of the high priest and the committee."

Weird. When I visited it today, I was sure I didn't see any other maiden or young women around, but then I didn't check everywhere.

I know my friends are supposed to go back to work, and I don't want any of them to feel uncomfortable, so I offer to show Evelyn around. I am not ashamed of being a tinker and living in the outermost circle. However, most people react with disdain and disgust when I reveal where I am from. Evelyn is different, though. She seems rather curious and interested. When I lead her through the narrow paths, she asks question after question, and I make sure to lead her to Uncle Arthur, to meet him too.

I don't know what I expected. I've always liked Evelyn and considered her a potential friend, but seeing her now makes me realize that she truly is a friend to me.

"Thank you," I say when I have shown her everything.

"What for?" she asks curiously. "You were the one showing me around. I should be thanking you."

"For being so open-minded. And not judging me. I love the people here, so it means a lot to me."

"There is nothing embarrassing or shameful about the tinkers," she says. "My brother says the same. He is actually happy that I befriended you. You are so nice, Estelle. I don't have many friends because I am so loud and unladylike...but you never minded."

"You are nice too, Evelyn," I say. "And now I am curious about your brother."

"Oh! Why don't we head to the elevators and take a ride to the fourth circle?" she asks. "We need to sneak you in, though."

"Not anymore," I say, showing her my new papers.

"No way!" she squeals. "I know a celebrity now."

"I doubt it's like that," I mutter. "Evy, please keep it to yourself, okay? I am not sure this is a good thing..."

"I promise," she says, locking our arms as we walk to the elevators. "Meanwhile, I can tell you a secret in exchange."

"What kind of secret?"

"You know the guy I told you about?" she asks, and I vaguely remember her mentioning a handsome guy who visited her brother's office.

"Yes."

"He visited again," she whispers, giggling slightly. "He kept looking at me all the time and smiled. He is super sweet. Not one of these stuck-up guys. He is...just funny and kind. He has a bit of a belly, but it's cute."

I grab her hand to stop her. "Evelyn," I whisper. "What are you telling me here?"

"He asked me on a date," she tells me shyly. "And I think...I might have said yes."

"By the light," I mutter. "Evy, no one can know this."

"That's why it's a secret," she whispers.

"I promise I will keep it," I reassure her. "But you need to promise me to be careful,l and not to tell anyone else."

Maidens are not allowed to have any relationships. It's only because I'm a tinker that they didn't mind me staying in the brothel, but they also know I'm not working there. It's why my room is the furthest away from anything else. And Maude has regular checkups from our overseeing guards.

I don't know why Evelyn's revelation makes me so nervous. I just did something forbidden too by dragging this stranger into town, and I have the high priest apparently courting me. But still, that's all different. A feeling deep inside me is making me worried.

But Evelyn doesn't let me linger on this thought. "Come," she says with a giggle. "Time to show you around the fourth circle."

I've only caught a few glances at the fourth circle when I pass through to get to the upper level for my maiden work, but now I can finally look at everything. One glance at my new papers and the guard easily lets me through, even changing his grumpy demeanor to something much more polite.

"You are turning into a celebrity," Evelyn teases.

"Please, no," I mutter.

She takes my hand, dashing ahead and tugging me behind her. I pick up my pace and run with her, laughing at her antics. I can't remember the last time I let loose like this. "Come," Evelyn exclaims, eagerly showing me around.

The activists live similarly to us tinkers, just that it's cleaner and less narrow. The houses are small but in better shape and look less butchered, yet I can still see spare parts and materials retrieved by the tinkers from the wasteland. It makes me happy to see how their work pays off, and how the materials they find are being used accordingly in another circle.

The air is a bit cleaner too. "It's homely here," I tell Evelyn.

"Right? I bet it's the best circle," she exclaims. It makes me realize that she is like me. She loves her home and people so much. "I will introduce you to my brother," she says. "He is already so curious about you."

"I'm curious too," I admit.

She seems happy about my words and tugs me along to the detective bureau of her brother. I know her brother is her only family, and they are really close. She told me so much about him and his co-workers, yet the reality surprises me even more because she forgot to mention how handsome this man is. "That's Perceval," Evelyn exclaims, letting go of my hand to grab her brother's arm and pulling him closer.

Perceval is tall, athletic, with a kind face and beautiful curly blonde hair framing it. He smiles at his sister, patting her head, before reaching out his hand to shake mine. "It's an honor to finally meet you, Maiden Estelle."

"Just Estelle, please, or Stella," I say.

"Then, it's just Perceval for you too," he says with a smile.

Evelyn proceeds to introduce all the other people in the room, who all greet me politely and engage with Evelyn, teasing and joking with her. It's obvious how loved she is, and it makes me happy that she has a family. The others might look down on the activists and the tinkers, but it doesn't matter because we are loved.

After I've recovered from the shock of Perceval being so handsome, I find my confidence again and dare to ask him questions about his work. He is truly amazing, even getting commissions from the upper circles sometimes, and he has also helped some tinkers. "Our biggest issue is of young men and women going missing," he explains. "I've brought this to the upper circle already, but they don't see it as a pressing issue yet."

"Yeah, because it doesn't involve them, but just us lowly scum," Evelyn says.

"Don't say that too loud," Perceval warns her. "Someone might hear you."

"She isn't wrong, though," one of the others defends her.

"I know," Perceval mutters. "Still—"

He doesn't get to finish his sentence because the door opens, and a young man enters. He looks kind and gentle, and he immediately turns to Perceval. "Any news, Perce?"

"No, I'm sorry, Chester," Perceval says. "But, it's my top priority to find your brother."

I don't need any special powers to notice that he is the one. He is the one Evelyn talked about. The description fits, but also the way he smiles at her when he thinks no one is looking and how she beams at him.

I'm not sure if Perceval notices, but I can see a hint of worry crossing his features. It reminds me of Maude...she wants me to be happy, and I think part of her wishes I could be with Ned, but at the same time, she is scared of what the higher-ups will do if they find out I might engage in indecent behavior with a man.

"How about we eat something?" One of Perceval's co-workers offers. "I made some pastries yesterday. It's rare to have two maidens in the house."

With her suggestion, I can feel the tension subsiding, and Perceval looks more relaxed. Chester joins us, too, but Evelyn makes sure not to engage too openly with him. At least she is trying to be subtle.

Later that day, Perceval joins Evelyn and me on a walk so that I can see more of their circle, and we stumble over a huge gathering. "What's going on?" Evelyn asks. "Why are there so many people?"

"We have a high visitor," Perceval says, a hint of annoyance in his voice. "The higher-ups are gracing us with their presence."

I glance over the crowd of people, noting that Perceval was right. There are two men I know are from the nobles, and there is...

"The High Priest is here too," Evelyn whispers.

Alistair looks up, gazing over the crowd until his eyes meet mine. He looks surprised for a moment, then his lips tug into a smile. My instincts tell me to run, but then I remember Ned, Winnie, and Maude and how much I could improve their lives.

I return his smile.

Evelyn

"Thank you for helping me," Chester says. "You are always so kind, Evelyn."

"I'm doing this for everyone I like," I say.

He just smiles. Chester is such a nice person, so kind and gentle but also protective. I feel like he could be the perfect shoulder to rely on.

"Did you mean it?" I ask him. "Yesterday, when you said you wish you could take me out for dinner."

His smile falters. "We know that's not possible."

"But you want to?" I ask.

"You are a maiden," he points out. "I don't know what they would do to you or me if—"

"But, you want to take me out?" I ask once more.

Chester is silent for a moment before he nods. "Of course. How could I not want to? Every time I visit your brother, I hope you will be there."

"And if we are subtle?" I muse. "Everyone will think we are just friends."

Chester looks at me, his soft, warm eyes lighting up when he reaches out his hand. I take it, squeezing it slightly and letting him tug me closer. My heart skips a beat when I lean my head against his chest. Some people make fun of him for being on the softer side, but he is so strong, and I feel safe with him.

"What do you even see in me?" he mutters. "You are a maiden, and I'm a nobody."

"I'm a nobody too," I say. "I was chosen as a maiden out of pure luck. But even within the maidens, I'm not special. It's all relative."

"I'm just a guy," he says.

"And I'm just a girl."

He smiles at me. "You caught my attention immediately. You were so full of smiles and laughter and kind to everyone around you. It was impossible not to notice you."

"So?" I ask him hopefully.

"How can I reject such a special young woman." He chuckles.

"I just want to tell Perceval," I say. "I don't want to betray my brother by lying to him."

"Truth to be told," he admits. "I asked him if he would let me court you."

I look at him hopefully. "And?"

"He wasn't happy, but thinks I'm better than one of the douchebags from the higher circles. He is just worried, Eve, because of your position, so let's be careful."

"At least don't hold her hand while I am here," Perceval groans. "It's gross."

"He is only holding my hand," I laugh. "Not kissing me."

Perceval crosses his arms in front of his body, glaring at Chester. "Just because I gave my okay to this relationship doesn't mean I have to like it."

"Come on." I beam. "I bet secretly you are happy that I went for such a sweet guy."

Perceval still looks scandalized, but I can see his lips tugging into a slight smile. "You aren't wrong," he says. "Just be careful, Eve. I'm not sure what will happen if you get found out."

"I'm worried about that, too," Chester admits. "We need a plan."

"Maybe I could talk to the overseeing master," I say. "Maybe there is a way to stop working as a maiden. I can offer them my mana."

"That's an option," Perceval says. "But we need to think this through. For now, try not to attract too much attention."

I promise him I'll be careful. During the last couple of days, we all tried to find a new routine to help me sneak around. I pretend to help out in my brother's detective office and to run errands, and since Chester is a customer, my path leads me to him...naturally so. Chester and Perceval also have made sure to announce their deep friendship and hang out with each other regularly.

Chester and I can't go on dates, but I stay the nights with him. I know as a maiden I need to remain pure, but I love him so much. He is worth it to give up my work as a maiden. This is happiness and the kind of life I want to lead. I want to be with the man I love and eventually have children.

As usual, we spend the night together. During the very early morning hours, I wake up to make it back home while it's dark outside. I rest my hand on his chest. "If only I wasn't a maiden," I say. "Then I would work in my brother's detective office, and we could date openly."

"We will find a way, my angel," Chester reassures me.

I leave his house while it's still dark, quietly returning to my brother's place, still feeling giddy and happy. There is the hint of a breeze, which feels amazing. Usually, the air is pretty still here, and to actually feel the wind is a miracle.

A shiver goes down my spine, and I feel goosebumps on my arms. My skin suddenly seems to crawl. I turn around, gazing into the darkness. Is someone here?

Is someone watching me?

Nah, I'm probably just imagining things.

I pick up my pace and hurry home, but the eerie feeling of being watched doesn't leave.

Chapter 5 Alistair
Estelle

I brush through the stranger's hair gently. His wounds seem to be healing, but he is still deeply asleep. His skin feels warm, though. Whenever I accidentally touch him, I feel little tingles.

"Now you look somewhat decent again," I say after cleaning his hair. Ned and some other boys have washed him already, but forgot to scrub the dirt off his hair. While combing it, I figured it's not enough, deciding to use water to clean it properly. Now he is clean, I notice his hair isn't brown but white-blonde, and he wears it long.

He is truly handsome, tall and muscular, with a face that looks like it was chiseled. He looks like a piece of art.

"What is such a handsome man like you doing in the wasteland?" I ask. "Did someone hurt you?"

I pause, eyeing his wounds that have begun to heal.

"Of course, someone hurt you. I'm so stupid. But you are safe here," I reassure him, although I'm unsure if he can even hear me. "No one will hurt you because Maude and I, and all the other tinkers, we will protect you. We know how it is to be treated like dirt, which is why we always stick together." I pause. "I'm Estelle, by the way. Everyone calls me Stella. Oh, and I'm a maiden."

I keep telling him more about myself, my work as a maiden, and the tinkers and our city. The time passes so fast, and to my surprise Maude suddenly peeks into the room. "Stella, honey, you need to get ready. I will send Winnie to you to help you." She looks torn. "I wish you wouldn't do it."

"High Priest Alistair asked me out. I can't reject him," I say.

Earlier today, during the morning hours, I went to my first scheduled special class where I trained with two tutors who began teaching me how to channel my arcana power, my mana, more effectively. After my lessons, the high priest told me to join him in his office. When he asked me if he was allowed to pick me up for dinner today, I had no way to decline.

I'm scared for my fellow tinkers if I do.

"Remember, you always have a choice," Maude says. "The tinkers won't let anyone hurt one of theirs."

"That's why I'm so worried," I say quietly. "What if I reject him, and he takes it out on you?"

"It wouldn't be the first time," she says.

"But it's the first time it would be against the high priest," I point out. "And maybe...it would help all of you if I agreed to an alliance with him. Well, that is, if he truly wants to court me. Maybe he will lose interest."

"You are a beautiful girl, Estelle," Maude says.

"I'm just normal."

"No, there is something about you, something only you have. A spark. And it draws everyone to you."

"The high priest is only in it for my powers."

"Yes, it's a logical decision for him," Maude agrees. "But, you are also pleasing to the eye and have that special charisma. I'm scared he will truly want you."

"Maybe that's not bad," I say, but unconvinced myself. "Maybe...it will be good for all of us."

Maude stays silent for a while. "I hope so, Stella. Just be careful."

"You look so beautiful," Winnie exclaims, helping me fix a small hat to my hair. My attire this time is way more official and elegant. Winnie and Maude gathered some dark-violet fabric and combined it with an intricate corsage with small flowers sewn into it and a couple of buckles as a lighter contrast.

"It's only thanks to you," I admit.

"Are you happy?" Winnie asks me.

I turn to look at her. "Where does that come from all of a sudden?"

"I've just been wondering about life and all that," she admits. "About the future."

"Are you not happy?" I ask her quietly.

"On some days it's better than others," she admits before smiling at me. "I need to be strong for Ned. He is such a softie, and sometimes I'm scared that this work here will break him. But, you know, I love all my fellow tinkers. This is what makes it worth it to keep fighting."

"I will do anything to improve your lives," I say quietly, my resolve only strengthening. If it means giving myself to Alistair to help everyone here have a better life, then so be it.

"You shouldn't sacrifice yourself for us," Winnie says, sounding more resolute than usual. "I mean it, Stella. You are one of us; being a maiden doesn't change that. And we don't sacrifice one of us. If this high priest ends up being a creep...just don't do it."

I stay quiet.

"Please promise me," she begs. "I can't live with the knowledge that you would give yourself to a sleazy man who will hurt you. There will be ways to improve our situation, but this isn't it."

"What kind of ways?"

"I don't know, but I don't think you getting with the high priest will change it. We need more drastic changes. And we don't know if the high priest's intentions are good...we don't know what he will do to you or to us. Maybe being with him will open a whole new can of problems."

Maybe she is right. Truth be told, I don't know what I should do, but I don't have time to think anyway because soon I can hear the bell in my room ring. It's a communication device Maude and I have built if she wants to reach me.

"He's here," I whisper. "Let's go." I take a deep breath before following Winnie out of my room, through the corridor, and down several staircases. Maude has ensured that most of the girls and boys here are either in their rooms or at their most presentable. She doesn't want anyone to accidentally upset the high priest.

Once downstairs, I notice how Ned has dressed particularly beautifully today and is serving cups of wine to Maude and Alistair. Both of them look up when they see me. While Winnie bows in front of Alistair and steps aside, I approach him. My heart beats so fast, I'm scared I might actually faint. The high priest is here, in the brothel where I live, in the outer circle.

Suddenly, Winnie's words come back to me. How having him court me might not be a solution to anything...how it might be dangerous. My body feels warm all of a sudden, like a surge of power flows through me. It feels like a couple of days ago when I made the flower bloom. Is this my mana?

There is no time to linger on any thoughts because Alistair takes my hand, kissing the back of it like he is picking up a lady. "You look beautiful," he says. "As expected from the most promising maiden." He turns to smile at Maude, but his eyes still look cold. "You raised this flower well."

Maude returns the smile, equally icy. "She is our precious fellow tinker. We all love and protect her."

"Well." Alistair turns to me and offers me his arm, ignoring Maude. "Shall we leave?"

I take it, nodding at him. "Thank you for picking me up, High Priest."

"I told you," he says while staring into my eyes. "It's Alistair for you."

Alistair takes me to the second circle, to the nobles, where he has booked a place in a beautiful restaurant. I have never seen anything alike. While I did pass through the second circle sometimes, I was never allowed to look about, stroll around, or enter any buildings.

Everything here is so vast and light. Even the colors are softer. There is no steam clouding the area, no dirt. The restaurant we visit specializes in poultry dishes, which is a rarity here and very expensive. I'm so stunned about everything I don't manage to utter a word.

"Your astonishment is beautiful," Alistair says, while he takes my jacket like a gentleman and offers me a seat.

I feel my cheeks warm up in embarrassment. "I apologize," I say. "I've never been to this circle, not as a guest at least."

"Do you like it here?"

"It's beautiful," I say.

"As a member of the temple, you would be able to pass through here as you please," Alistair says, while a waiter brings us wine.

I'm usually not allowed to drink. "I don't know how to say this," I mutter. "But the wine...I am a maiden..."

"It's okay when you are with me," he tells me.

It is? I thought it would hurt my mana if I drink. I want to ask him but don't quite dare to. Maybe it's okay when it's occasional. I will make sure to only have one glass of wine. I am so focused on the alcohol that it takes me a while to catch on to what he said previously. "A member of the temple?" I ask, stunned.

Alistair just leans back and smiles at me. "You don't need to decide anything immediately, Estelle," he says. "But you have potential and could do great things."

"Does this mean I could become a member of the inner circle?" I ask.

"It's an option if you want that." He pauses. "However..."

I knew there was a catch.

"You can only do so as the wife of one of the members."

"Oh," I say.

"Don't worry," he says, smiling again. Something about it sends goosebumps over my skin. "I'm here. We will find a solution."

I don't know what to say. Maude's worried expression and Winnie's words are coming to my mind again. Can Alistair be genuinely up to any good? If he is, why have I never seen the former maiden that lived in the inner circle? I have never heard of her. He thinks

I'm naïve because I'm a tinker and come from the lowest social rank, but I'm not stupid. He gets something out of this, but I don't know yet what it is.

It's certainly not my looks because there are many beautiful maidens from higher social standings. It must be about my mana...but what does he want me to do with it? What's in it for him?

I try not to look upset or uncomfortable and just smile at his words. As long as I don't know what he wants, I must keep him at arm's length without being too impolite. I feel like whatever step I take is going to be horrendous for my friends and me.

Fortunately, Alistair doesn't push our date too much. After dinner, he walks me through the second circle and shows me everything. Once it gets colder, however, he escorts me back to the brothel.

"You really shouldn't live here," he mutters while we walk through the narrow and now empty paths of the outer circle.

"I'm used to it," I say honestly. "And...there is a lot of good here."

He looks at me, surprised. "And what's that?"

"Well, the people are very kind and watch out for each other. If someone needs help, they are always there." I smile. "Isn't that beautiful?"

He looks at me for a while. "You have a very peculiar way of seeing the world, Estelle." He halts in front of the brothel. "Well, we are here." For a moment, he looks like he wants to touch me or hug me, but then he resorts to kissing the back of my hand. "May we repeat this?"

I want to decline so badly, but I know it's impossible. "Yes, I'd love to," I say, forcing a smile to my lips.

Alistair looks content, waiting for me to disappear through the door before he takes his leave. The brothel is in full business, so I make sure to take the employee's staircase up to my room, only briefly saying hello to Maude, who is relieved to see me.

"Have you eaten?" she asks.

"Yes," I say. "But maybe I should bring something upstairs to the stranger. See if he is awake."

Maude looks like she wants to ask questions, but then drops them. "Yes, take a piece of pie upstairs."

I'm relieved that I don't need to answer any questions for now and take the plate before I hurry upstairs. The stranger is still lying in the guest room, looking peaceful. His wounds are healing very well; surprisingly so. I've never seen someone heal that fast. I carefully pull the blanket over his frame in case he feels cold. When my hand touches his skin, I feel it again...the warmth and the light tingles.

Shaking the feeling off, I put the plate to the side and sit on the chair next to his bed, covering my head in my palms. I didn't even realize how tense I was, but now that I'm in the safety of my home, I feel how my body trembles slightly. I want to help the tinkers so badly, but I'm scared of Alistair.

I tried to shake the feeling off when I first met him, but I can't lie to myself anymore. I feel so uncomfortable around him. He doesn't elicit any warmth. There is nothing that feels like he cares about me, truly cares.

I don't trust him. And compared to him, I'm a nobody while he is everything. One snip of his fingers and he will destroy everything dear to me.

"What am I going to do?" I whisper, feeling tears filling my eyes.

Suddenly I feel something warm against my back, a hand gently stroking it. I startle, my eyes snapping up; just to look at the stranger sitting in his bed now, blue eyes looking at me in curiosity and worry while he keeps gently brushing my back.

Chapter - 6 Ascension
Estelle

Maude inspects the stranger from head to toe, furrowing her brows. "You are awake," she states the obvious.

The handsome stranger is standing tall now, composed and dignified. He nods at her words. "I am," he says, his voice deep and calm. "But talking is straining."

"Probably due to the shock," Maude says.

The stranger looks at us. "You saved me, thank you."

"Estelle saved you," Maude verifies.

When the stranger looks at me, I swear I see something in his eyes. Something that pulls me in, and it seems for a moment his eyes darken. He puts his hand on his chest, bowing his head.

"You are welcome," I say with a smile. "Allow me to introduce us properly. I am Estelle, and these are my friends and chosen family. Maude, mom to us all, Ned, and Winnie."

"It's a pleasure," the stranger says politely. His manners are top-notch, and so is the way he carries himself. With so much dignity. Where does he come from? Who is this man?

"You need to hide here until we know what to do with you," Maude says. "They can't see you in the city."

"Do you remember anything?" Winnie asks. "How you ended up in the wasteland, and who hurt you?"

The stranger shakes his head. "I'm sorry, my mind is completely blank. I just remember being attacked...then everything turns black."

"Do you know who you are?" I ask.

"No, not even my name."

"But you need a name," Winnie points out.

"How about Zepherin?" I suggest. "It means west wind...and wind brings change."

Again, the stranger smiles at me. His expression is stoic whenever he faces the others, but softer when he looks at me. He turns to Maude now. "I can help around until my memory returns. With whatever you need me for."

"Actually," she says reluctantly, obviously unsure if she can trust him. I understand her, but Zeph is here now, and we can't do anything about it. "There are some repair jobs that need to be done. My girls and boys here are busy all the time, and I hate to bother them on their days off work."

Zeph looks at her, nodding firmly. It's strange because despite him not having his memories, he oozes so much confidence. Calm and stoic confidence. When he looks at me, I could swear there is a hint of something else...something more primal, longing, and hopeful. I have never seen that look in a man's eyes before.

"I can help him find his way around here," I offer Maude. "I need to be careful here too, and know how to sneak around."

Zeph looks at me now, his gaze curious.

"I am a maiden," I explain. "I have to follow specific rules in our city. I work for the inner circle."

"Estelle has mana in her," Ned explains further. "Arcane power that keeps our barrier up and helps to keep our city alive."

Zeph keeps looking at me, his gaze curious, as if he is searching for something in me. I wonder what it is he is trying to find. A smile curls his lips. "That's interesting," he mutters. "Mana..." He doesn't say anymore, fortunately, because Maude is already eyeing him skeptically.

Maude gazes at the clock. "It's almost time for the second wave of customers to come," she says.

"Oh," Winnie says. "I need to change."

"Me too," Ned agrees.

"Hurry, you two," Maude says gently before turning to me and Zeph. "Be careful, Stella. May the light be with you."

"And with you," I answer.

Zeph stares at us, furrowing his brows but not saying anything. Since my friends have to return to work, I take it upon myself to show Zeph around and explain our city's social structure to him.

"And your work as a maiden?" he asks me. "Your friend Ned said you are supposed to keep the barrier up.".

"All maidens are," I say and briefly explain to him how we are chosen and what our work entails.

"The blue light?" he asks. "Chanting songs, abiding by these strict rules, and having a high priest as a leader...it sounds like a cult."

"It's not a cult," I argue. "It's necessary to keep up the barrier, or the waste will swallow our city. And the flying monsters would attack us."

He halts, eyeing me all of a sudden. "Flying monsters?"

"They are said to be reptiles with wings, evil. Swallowing and burning down everything in their way. The barrier is to keep us safe."

"From them?" he asks.

I look at him, wondering why he is asking so many questions. I swear there is a hint of pity and also anger in his eyes. "We need to use our mana to keep the barrier up."

"Alright, I get that," he says. "But what about the weird rules; your lack of freedom?" He pauses. "And isn't this a brothel, and you are lowest classed citizens?"

"They call us waste," I admit, quietly. "But it's not a cult. Maidens can leave by ascending."

"Ascending?" he asks, sounding astonished. "What does that mean?"

"I think it means pouring our mana out," I say.

"You think?" he asks. "But you don't know?"

"Well—"

"And weren't you crying because that creepy high priest is preying on you?" he continues to ask. "And you know he is using his rank and his power to threaten you to give in to him."

I stay silent. I wasn't aware he heard all that. I thought I was pouring my heart out to a silent stranger who couldn't hear me.

"You don't know this city like I do," I say defensively.

"That's true," he admits. "But do you? There are an awful lot of questions you don't have an answer to, Estelle."

Something about the way he says my name sends chills down my spine, but unlike with Alistair, it's not a bad feeling. It's rather...exciting. Before I can stop it, I find myself answering honestly. "Asking too many questions is dangerous," I say.

He looks at me like someone well aware he made a huge point. "Exactly," he says.

It was a very short night thanks to Zeph waking up and me showing him around, but I don't mind. It was one of the most fun experiences of my life...that alone makes me sound so pathetic, but I can't help it. When I hurry downstairs, Zeph is already in the kitchen, repairing the sink and oven.

Even Maude looks pleased.

"When you said you would help around, I didn't expect you to be that efficient," she says.

Zeph looks amused. "Why? Do I look like a man who can't hold a hammer?"

"Hm." Maude rubs her chin. "You look more sophisticated than most men I know. If I didn't know better and knew you were an outsider, I would expect you as someone to inhabit the second circle."

"That's the nobles, right?"

"Yes," she says.

"No, thank you," he says. "Judging by what Estelle told me and explained, I rather prefer the realness of the tinkers."

Maude and I both chuckle. He looks up, his eyes lighting up when he sees me. Maude must have noticed it too because she gazes from him to me and back to him, but to my surprise, she doesn't say anything. She is very vocal about Alistair courting me, so I thought she would be about the stranger having an interest in me...a potential interest.

"Are you on your way to your maiden work?" Zeph asks.

"Yes. It's going to be a long day," I admit. "I have private classes too."

"I wish I could come with you to keep guard and keep the sleazy high priest off you," Zeph says.

Maude frowns. "I was about to say the same."

"I'm so busy today, I doubt I will see him."

Or rather, I hope I won't see him.

"If only the land wasn't all wasteland." Maude sighs. "I would grab you kids and just run with you."

Zeph looks at us with a frown but doesn't say anything. "I will think of a good disguise," he says, changing the subject. "Then I could walk around at nighttime and help some of your friends."

"That would be a good idea," Maude says. "Also, it means you could get out for a bit and not be stuck here."

"Plan it, and I can show you around later tonight," I offer. "But for now, I need to run."

"Bye, darling," Maude says.

Winnie and Ned poke their heads into the room at that moment. "May the light be with you," they call out.

I wave at them and smile before racing off. I'm not running late this time, so I can walk and look around while making my way to the elevators. I spot Uncle Arthur and briefly inform him that our guest is awake but has lost this memory, and he promises to pay Maude a visit to check on how he is doing.

When I make it to the fourth circle, Evelyn is waiting for me, and we walk the rest of the path together. She looks nervous and giddy. "Eve," I mutter. "What's wrong?"

"Can you keep a secret?" she whispers, once we are in the elevator and no one can hear us.

"Yes, of course."

"Chester and I are dating now, and I'm sleeping with him."

"WHAT!?" I exclaim.

"I'm so in love," she tells me, squeezing my hand. "Perceval helps us sneak around. We are trying to think of a plan for me to leave the maidens."

I look at her, taking in her rosy cheeks and the smile on her lips. She looks so happy, and despite my fear of her having broken the rules, I'm glad for her. "He really seems such a nice guy," I say.

She nods. "I'm just nervous."

"What for?"

"Last night, when I returned home from Chester's, I had the feeling someone was watching me," she admits.

I turn around to look at her, shocked. "Evelyn, are you sure?"

"No, I'm not sure, but...it's a feeling, you know?" she says quietly.

"Why didn't you say something earlier?" I blurt out. "We are in the last elevator, heading right up to the inner circle. We could have found a way to—"

"It's okay," she reassures me. "I've been thinking. If they truly discovered what I was up to, I will offer them to step back from my work as a maiden."

"Is this even possible?" I ask.

"Well, I can ascend," she says. "And offer them my mana. I won't have powers anymore then, but that's okay if I'm happy."

The alarm bells in my head go off, and I remember my talk with Zeph last night. He was right. There are so many answers missing, so many questions, so many facts in the open. "Eve—"

"It's okay," she reassures me the moment the elevator door opens. We step outside just to be greeted by two overseeing masters.

I can feel Evelyn tense next to me, so I take her hand.

"Maiden Estelle," they tell me. "Please proceed to join the other maidens. Maiden Evelyn, the committee wants to talk to you."

I turn to her. "I will accompany you," I say firmly.

Evelyn takes a deep breath before smiling at me bravely. "It's really alright, Stella," she says softly, hugging me. "Nothing bad will happen. They just want to ask some questions. They want to talk."

She lets go of my hand and gestures towards the men to lead the way. I can see anxiety in her eyes but also hope. With a sinking feeling, I watch how she leaves.

The next couple of hours feel like they are dragging on forever. I have my lessons with the other maidens, we chant our songs, and I have an additional private class with one of the tutors Alistair assigned me to.

All his creepiness aside, this is the only upside of his interest in me. I can actually learn something.

I can barely focus, though. Not being sure what's happening to Evelyn. When I'm about to finish my work and reluctantly leave for the elevator, I finally spot her running toward me. The other maidens left long ago and went home, so it's just the both of us.

"Evelyn!" I blurt out, running towards her and meeting her midway. I pull her into a hug.

"I told you I would be okay." She beams at me. "Nothing bad happened. I don't have much time, though."

I draw back a bit. "What do you mean?"

"I'm just gathering some things and then heading back. The committee was very understanding," she says. "Chester was there too."

"What...really?"

"Yes, it surprised me to see him at first, but he was a great moral support. I think he knows one of the committee members."

"So, they saw the both of you together?"

"Yes, they had an inkling about me being in a relationship. You know, due to my impurity, my mana was diminishing, so they researched and saw me," she explains.

"And then?"

"I explained my situation to them." Evelyn looks excited. "It's top secret," she whispers to me. "But...but they understood. And they said they will let me ascend. Apparently, it will put me in a bit of a longer sleep, and I will give my arcane power, my mana, to the barrier, and then once that's done, I'm free to leave."

I feel stunned by her words. I should be happy, overjoyed even, but I have a weird feeling in my chest. Evelyn hugs me once more and kisses my forehead. "I need to leave now. I'll see you once everything is done."

Chapter 7 Nothing Hurts Like The Truth
Estelle

D ays pass in which I don't see Evelyn. I visit her brother twice to check if she's back and talk to him. He is worried too, but since Evelyn announced it would take a while until she returns, he is holding up well.

I also went on a date with Alistair once, unable to avoid him.

Meanwhile, I go through the motions of my maiden work, but something doesn't feel right anymore. Despite my negative feelings, I bring the light forward a couple of times and make more flowers bloom. Alistair even voiced how overjoyed he is about my progress.

Maidens should always have a positive mindset. They should never complain or have bad thoughts. If that's true, how come I still manage to get my mana flowing?

"Okay, little maiden," Zeph peeks into my room. I have left the door open and am sitting on the floor, facing the wall gloomily. "We need to do something about that awful mood of yours."

"I'm not in a bad mood," I say quietly while he sits down next to me. "Just...sad."

"I know." He looks worried when our eyes meet.

"I've been thinking so much," I admit. "About what you said on your first night here. How there are so many things I don't know, because no one has ever asked the right questions."

"I didn't mean to be condescending and to make it sound like it's your fault. It's theirs...it's..." he says, his voice trailing off slightly.

"Just say it," I beg. "I can take it."

"It's a cult," he says bluntly. "The hierarchy, the whole systematic discrimination against the lower ranks and circles, the way they use a certain group of people...the maidens...to enslave them and strip them of their basic rights. A cult brainwashes people."

"How come you know so much about these things?" I ask.

He smiles. "See, you are able to ask the right questions." He pauses. "I've forgotten a lot of things about myself. I don't know what role I play in this world or how I ended up here, but I didn't lose my memory about essential things. I know how this world runs. I know about magic and, for example, how this barrier works. It's just my own person that seems to have been wiped from my memory."

"Thank you for being honest," I say. "I know you don't need to..."

"I'm not being that honest," he mutters.

"What do you mean?" I ask him.

"I feel like if I dump all I know on you, you would go crazy."

At his words, I have to chuckle. "Aren't you underestimating me?"

"Maybe I am," he admits. He reaches out his hand, and I put mine into his. I don't even question why I do it. There is just a pull to him that I can't explain. His hand feels warm and there are these soft tingles again.

"Touching you feels weird," I say into the silence.

"In a bad way?" he wants to know.

"No, just...different," I admit, while I gaze into his deep blue eyes. "I can't explain it."

He smiles at me. "You are a beautiful person, Stella," he says.

"I'm so plain."

"No, there is a light in you," he says. "It's strong and powerful. I'm not surprised the higher-ups have their eyes on you."

"I wish they wouldn't have," I admit, a tremble going through my body. "They...it feels off. I'm scared of Alistair. I don't know what to do if he starts pushing for more."

"He wants to use you, clearly," Zeph says, anger flashing in his eyes. "Didn't you say there was another maiden living there? And that she passed?"

"Yes," I say, furrowing my brows. "But, I don't know anything about her."

"If she lived there, there needs to be traces," he muses.

I look at him as an idea catches me. "I can snoop around," I say. "I'm there for lessons constantly, and can use the library." When Zeph looks worried, I just smile. "I'm going to be careful, I promise. But I need to do something, or I will remain in Alistair's clutches."

"I wish I could do something," he grumbles.

Before we can continue our talk, I can hear footsteps and reluctantly let go of Zeph's hand. It's Winnie and Ned. "Are we interrupting something?" Winnie asks.

"No, come in," I say, though I'm not sure about the interrupting part.

Ned looks exhausted. "That was a long shift," he mutters.

"Yeah, we had a lot of customers," Winnie says. "Oh, but two of my nice regulars came. They are always very generous with their tips."

Zeph and I let them talk about their evening. Judging Zeph's expression, he has similarly mixed feelings about this as I do. Winnie and Ned are my best friends; I love them like they are my siblings. I can't stand by and do nothing while they get exploited in this brothel and have to sell their bodies to strangers. I know Maude does everything to protect her girls and boys, but she can only do so much, and she is still bound to the rules of the higher-ups. The moment she reduces someone's workload, she has to report the reasons.

It's tiring and almost like there is no use in fighting.

Zeph's words about the cult come to my mind again. The city is the perfect machine...running on our backs while burning us out, just for our leaders to live comfortably. But then, there is the barrier as well, and the dangers from outside. So at least we are safe from that.

Winnie sits down next to me, and I gently brush her hair, braiding it so it will be curly when she wakes up tomorrow morning. She loves it that way.

"How does she look?" I ask Ned and Zeph once I'm done.

"Beautiful," Zeph says with a smile.

"It suits you so well, Winnie," Ned agrees.

"Really?" She beams, turning her head to look into my mirror.

"And the best part is, if you open the braids tomorrow, your hair will be curly," I say. "Or you could leave them in the braids for a day."

"You should do Zeph's hair, too," Winnie says.

Zeph looks amused. "I wouldn't mind."

I shake my head, but still slip over and sit behind him. I make sure to brush his hair, noticing how silky yet thick it is. Wow, he has amazing hair. I tie it back while braiding two strands of hair into the ponytail.

Winnie and Ned have gone back to discussing their day, while Zeph is completely silent. I can feel his body moving against mine when he stirs; that's how close we sit together. Something about this warms my heart, and at the same time it strikes me how intimate what I'm doing is. I can't bring myself to stop, though. Instead, I put extra effort into doing his hair so that we can sit like that for a bit longer.

By now, Zeph has learned to mingle with the tinkers, dress like them, and make sure he doesn't stick out. He is eager to help them, claiming they were so generous in saving his life, all of them sticking together with no one telling on him. He wants to pay them back.

He even went to the wasteland once to help some of the workers there. The guards didn't notice him even though he is taller than the others. That's how little attention they pay to us. In this case, it isn't too bad. Today he is out with Uncle Arthur, both of them hoping to find some things for the brothel, and the girls and boys working there.

I have the day off too, so I help Maude cook and spend some time with Ned and Winnie.

"Do you think I will ever find someone who loves me?" Winnie asks us out of the blue.

Ned looks up in surprise. "Why wouldn't you find such a person? You are the best!"

"But I'm a tinker," she says quietly. "And this here"—she gestures at the brothel—"is my job."

"Nothing of that will matter to the right person," Ned says with finality.

"I think you are wonderful," I tell Winnie. "You are kind, funny, and helpful. And you are so beautiful too. Every man would be lucky to have you."

Tears swim in Winnie's eyes, and she hugs me out of the blue. "Do you really think that?"

"Yes! And whoever it is," I say firmly. "No one should ever disrespect you!"

When Winnie draws back, she looks so relieved. "Thank you," she says. "I thought I could never talk to anyone about this."

"You can tell Ned and me anything," I reassure her.

"She is right," Ned agrees.

"What about you?" she asks me. "You and our handsome stranger?"

"What?" I squeal.

"Ned thinks the same," Winnie says, elbowing Ned. "Right?"

"You kind of have something between you," he admits.

"You know I'm a maiden," I say, not sure how to answer them. I have never believed in love at first sight, nor have I ever been in love, but when Zeph opened his eyes, there was a pull to him that I can't deny.

"You can still love," Winnie says. "Despite being a maiden."

"And if someone disrespects you, we will kick their ass," Ned adds.

I smile, about to say something to them, when the door opens and Uncle Arthur and Zeph return. They carry a lot of gadgets. "Wow," I exclaim.

"Amazing!" Winnie squeals. "You found so much."

"Zeph, my boy, here." Arthur smiles brightly at Zeph. "You were such a great help." He turns to us and gestures for us to come closer. "Look what we found, everyone!"

Maude peeks into the room as well, and we gather around the two men, who show us what they found. They truly had a successful hunt today. There are things we can use for the brothel, but also for Arthur and some of the other tinkers. They will even be able to restore and revive some items and sell them to the higher circles.

"Oh," Uncle Arthur angles for something in his pocket. "We also found something else. Particularly beautiful and well-crafted, and it doesn't even need any touching up. We thought it would be something for Estelle to wear during her maiden work."

He pulls out a beautiful blue brooch, sparkling when the light hits it. I can hear the others gape and ask questions, while I can just take the item and stare at it. My stomach starts sinking, a cold hand seemingly grabbing my lungs and squeezing the air out of them.

I tried to have hope, I tried not to believe in my gut feeling, I tried telling myself that everything was well, that I shouldn't be worried.

I tried lying to myself and forcing myself to feel a fake sense of safety.

Technically I could still do that, but I can't bring myself to believe in my own lies anymore. Tears fill my eyes.

The others look confused when I clutch the item to my chest. "That's Evelyn's," I whisper.

Chapter 8 Witches
Estelle

The moment realization hits, I run to my room, dropping onto the ground. I feel numb first before violent sobs start shaking my body. Why? Why? Why? This can't be true! Not Evelyn, my kind-hearted, joyful friend, who never once looked down on me. She was so innocent and warm.

I register the others coming to my room but can't bring myself to look at them.

"Stella," Maude says in worry. "What's wrong?"

Zeph kneels down next to me and pats my head awkwardly.

"This is Evelyn's," I sob.

"Yes, you said that," Uncle Arthur mutters.

"She...she must have lost it," Ned mutters.

"NO!" I yell. "It was her mom's. She cherished it like nothing else." I sob. "That's what happens to the maidens who disappear."

Maude stares at me as understanding settles in, and I know I am right. This is the eerie feeling I got. Like the mana in me was trying to tell me what was happening, but I didn't listen to it. I didn't listen to my own gut feeling. "They die," I whisper. "Once their services aren't needed anymore, they get tossed away, like waste. When they want to quit, they get sacrificed and drained of their powers. Evelyn had a boyfriend. She was in love and wanted to live a normal life. And they promised her she could. They told her she could *ascend*. People constantly disappear in this city, and we always say it's because of illnesses, the atmosphere, the dirt...but...but...is it really true? The maidens are waste, not the tinkers. The maidens are waste."

"But, I don't understand..." Ned mutters, completely taken aback. "This is...it can't be."

"It's like Stella said," Winnie says, all joy and hope deprived from her voice. She just sounds bland and fed up with everything. "It's all a scheme. They suck the power from the maidens and then toss them away. Probably burn the remains, and throw their belongings into the waste. They come to us for their sexual pleasure and then kick us and hurt us, saying we are the dirty ones. No one is going to save us. No one can. There is no hope."

"There is," Ned argues. "There always is."

Winnie kneels down to hug me from behind. "I'm so sorry for your friend," she says sadly. "So sorry."

"Come, everyone," Maude mutters, her voice sounding strained. "Let's leave Stella alone for a moment." She pauses. "Zeph, are you coming?"

"No," he says shortly.

"I thought so," she says. "Promise me to protect her."

Zeph says nothing, but I can feel him move against my body. Eventually, silence engulfs us, and someone closes the door to give us privacy. Zeph pulls me into his arms fully, and I just can't help but break down, crying into his chest.

Zeph keeps consoling me, rubbing my back and letting me cry as much as I want. Eventually, I have no tears left, and the wish to understand what's going on in this city, with the maidens, to understand what happened to Evelyn starts to come forward.

I pull away from Zeph and look at him. I must look ridiculous with my swollen face, but he doesn't seem disgusted.

"Tell me what I refused to see," I beg Zeph. "You said while you forgot your past, you can remember the world, the outside, and everything else."

He looks reluctant. "I don't know...I don't want to hurt you further."

"You know what's happening, don't you?"

"I don't have any proof," he admits. "It's just experience and a gut feeling."

"Tell me. I promise I will listen. I promise I won't dismiss you."

He takes a deep breath. "I know for certain that no one can extract their magic, or their mana and arcane powers, as you call it. It's impossible to do it, and to pour your mana out...unless you die," he says after a while. "You are witches, not maidens. You are born with a gift, which is amazing."

"Witches," I repeat.

"Magical beings. I don't know why this city has so many witches. I assume your history is buried somewhere in the highest circle. They just hide it from you. Maybe a powerful witch coven once merged with the humans here. And over the years, they got exploited."

I nod. "Okay," I say. When he looks surprised, I shake my head. "I told you I wouldn't dismiss you." I pause. "The barrier?"

"Unnecessary," he says quietly. "If you ask me, it's to keep everyone locked inside. It's true that the air outside is polluted, but it's not everywhere. I don't know what happened to me, but I remember green forest and lush meadows."

"The winged monster?"

"They don't care for normal humans," he says.

"But what are they?"

"Dragons," he says. "Humans who can change their form, and turn into dragons if they want. This world is full of mysteries, Stella, but not all of them are out to kill you."

"They are not our enemies?" I ask.

"No, why would they be? They live within their own lands and have their own problems. If they wanted to, they could easily come and destroy this city. With so many witches, it should be impossible to do, but the higher-ups have manipulated you into just using your basic powers. You don't even know what you can do. You have never learned."

I stay silent, trying to grasp what he just told me.

"What do you think?" he asks me. "Too much?"

"I need to sleep on it," I admit. "And then think about what I'm going to do from here on."

When he is about to get up to leave my room, I grab his hand. "Stay," I beg.

A smile lights up his handsome face. "If that's what you want," he says.

I still feel devastated when I crawl into my bed. I feel horrified for the lies I've heard growing up; for the many people who died; for the many maidens who were sacrificed, and probably their loved ones too when they started to ask too many questions. I don't know what to do or how to save anyone, let alone myself, but when I feel Zeph wrapping his arms around me and pulling me against his chest, I feel a blanket of calmness over me.

The next day, I'm just running through the motions. I know I can't quit; I have to play it smart. So, I do everything dutifully. I do my work, talk to my friends, and go to my maiden duties. I try not to think about Evelyn when I'm there and instead focus on the way I felt in Zeph's arms.

The way his touch calms me down.

But deep inside, I can feel a storm brewing. I need to find out more of the truth, and I need to pick my allies wisely, and most importantly...I can't show my hatred and disgust for Alistair and his minions. Funnily, my heightened emotions seem to further push my mana, or rather magic, as Zeph called it, and it's getting easier for me to reach out to it.

My worst task of the day, however, is still ahead of me. And after my excruciatingly long lessons, I find myself dragging my feet to the fourth circle, to the activists, and Perceval's detective office in particular. I don't know if this is a mistake, but I know that Perceval loves Evelyn more than anything else, and that she is the light in his life.

"Estelle." Perceval looks up when he sees me, smiling at me. "Such a nice surprise. Evelyn still isn't back, though."

"I know," I say quietly, my hand in my pocket, clutching around Evelyn's brooch. I gaze through the room, seeing their mutual friends. Stepping closer to Perceval, I pretend to drop something and pick it up so no one will notice. "Send everyone away," I whisper.

Perceval looks at me, his face falling and an expression of dread filling his eyes. He does as I tell him, however, successfully sending everyone out to run errands and do some tasks. "We are alone," he mutters. "What happened? I'm sure it's nothing bad, is it?"

He is begging me to say everything is okay, but I can't.

I take out the brooch and hand it to him, unable to form the words. "My friends found it in the waste," I whisper. "Outside, in the wasteland."

Perceval takes the brooch, and I can see how realization settles in. He doesn't ask or say anything; he just clutches the brooch while tears fill his eyes. Both anger and sadness are all over his face, the first one winning over the second...just like it did with me.

"Tell me everything," he spits out. "Tell me who I need to slaughter."

"You can't," I say. "Because it will end you, and me, if you do. I told you because Eve was your only family, and she loved you so much."

"But, we can't not do anything!" he blurts out.

"I know," I say. "But, we need to be smart about it. I know how dangerous it is by now. If we run headfirst into this, we will die, and our friends might too."

Perceval takes a deep breath. "Alright," he says. "You are right. We need to keep our cool."

For a split second, I wonder if I can trust him, but then I don't have many other options. I need a strong ally, and Perceval has customers through all circles. So, I tell him what I know, keeping Zeph out of it as much as possible and only referring to him as my secret informant.

Perceval's expression changes from anger to horror to disbelief and then back to deep grief. "I was so proud when she was chosen as a maiden...all the while, she was just a lamb being fed until she was ready to be sacrificed."

"We all are lambs," I whisper.

"You need to be really careful," Perceval says.

"I want to learn more about the former maiden, the one before me, who was wedded to the former high priest."

"Yes, but be careful, and the truth you find might be crushing," he warns me.

"I'm prepared," I mutter. When silence engulfs us, I remember something else. "Is Chester okay?" I ask him.

"Ches? Yes, why are you asking?"

"Well, when Evelyn said goodbye to me, she told me he was there when she was called to the committee. He was with them." I pause. "I don't think she would be happy if he got hurt."

Perceval stares at me for a long while, making me wonder if I said something wrong. Then, however, he turns around, stalks into his separate office, and out of nowhere, he starts punching the wall, screaming while doing so.

"Perceval!" I gasp.

"That fucker," he yells, punching the wall so hard I'm scared he will break his hand.

I hurry to his side, clinging to his arm. "Stop it," I beg.

"Chester…" he sneers. "…recently got a pretty huge donation, and was invited to work for the third circle, even move there. I thought, oh, that's amazing; he will be able to give Eve a good life that way."

I stop. "What?"

"A donation!" Perceval laughs bitterly, his face contorting with fury.

Realization settles in again, hitting me with full force. Another truth I didn't expect or was too blind to see. "He sold her out?" I whisper. "She…she loved him so much. She was so happy."

"I will kill him!" Perceval spits. "I will go there now and—"

"No," I exclaim, grabbing his arm again. "Calm down! You can't, not now!"

Perceval takes a deep breath. "Alright," he says, his voice calming down, but the anger in his eyes is still evident. "I will help you in every way you need. But once everything is done, I will get my hands on Chester, and no one will stop me."

I nod. "Please promise me one thing."

"What?"

"If something happens to me," I say shakily. "Please make sure to warn my friends."

"I promise," he says. "I might start visiting the brothel," he suddenly adds. "You know, a man sometimes has his needs."

I look at him, relief filling me. "We are happy to host a renowned detective like you."

Chapter 9 The Former Maiden
Estelle

Alistair's gaze follows me when I pass his office in between two of my private lessons. His door is open, and he calls out to me. I make sure to play along, and act like the naïve dumb maiden he expects me to be.

"Alistair," I say shyly. "I'm sorry I couldn't visit you today."

"I appreciate how diligent you are with your studies," he says with a smile.

"I just want to become the best maiden possible," I say, gazing around. "And this place is so wonderful. I can truly feel my mana getting stronger here."

He seems to like what I say. "I'm happy you like it here. Why don't you look around more to get accustomed to this place?"

Ick! I believe he wants me to get accustomed so I can spend my life here...with him. I'd rather *ascend* than do that, but for now, it plays into my plan. "I...is this really okay? I don't want to take advantage of your hospitality," I mutter awkwardly. "You are so generous to me."

My words seem to stroke his ego because he just smiles. "I insist," he says. "Nothing here should be off-limits to you."

I nod, bowing my head submissively and flashing him a shy smile. Then I make my way to my next lesson. Afterward, however, I finally do what he asked me to...and roam the area. My goal is to find something, anything, about the former maiden. She must have had a room here somewhere. I make sure not to rush, so I won't raise any suspicions. Only a couple of rooms each day I'm here. I don't want Alistair to know I'm snooping.

In the meantime, Perceval visits us regularly. He always makes sure to enter with a grim expression and comment on which girl he wants for the night so that no one would grow suspicious of him being here. Obviously, he doesn't buy any services when he visits.

We also both make sure not to engage when we coincidentally meet outside, and I don't visit him in his office anymore. The less attention we have on us, the better.

"It's just so weird," I tell Perceval and Zeph, who I've introduced to each other. Perceval doesn't know that Zeph is from the outside and that he is my contact person. But I think he is making his own guesses. Maude, Ned, and Winnie know the truth too now, and what I'm planning. I trust them with my life, and I'm sure they won't backstab me.

"Still no luck?" Perceval asks.

"No, I'm continuously snooping around, but I don't find any traces of the old maiden," I say.

"Are you sure she even had a room there?" Ned asks.

"She had to have one," Winnie and Maude answer in unison.

"I don't want to pull out all those clichés," Winnie mutters. "But she had to be able to dress somewhere, have some comfort, anything. Even if she had to stay with the former high priest at night, I'm sure she had to have her own place."

"Also, to control her," Perceval adds. "No one ever saw her roaming around. We are sure they didn't kill her, aren't we?"

"I don't think they did," I say. "I see it with Alistair's interaction with me. He is way too interested. If he wanted to, he could have forced me to ascend already."

"He knows you are powerful," Zeph says all of a sudden. "Maybe he even knows the truth, because I'm sure someone has to."

"What truth?" Perceval asks.

Zeph and I exchange a gaze, and he gestures for me to continue. "Zeph said I' witch," I say. "No, actually, that all maidens are."

"The blue light is bullshit," Zeph says. "It's probably just a crystal that resonates with a witch's magic if it's strong enough." He shakes his head. "A whole nation, brainwashed and manipulated, for centuries; forced to follow this cult that's only use is to control and have everyone submit."

The others stay quiet, just staring at him in shock. When they gaze at me, I shrug. "I believe it's true."

"How do you know that stuff, Zeph?" Perceval asks. "I thought you lost your memory."

Again, Zeph and I exchange a gaze, and this time it's me who gestures for him to continue.

"It's true. I lost the memory of myself," he says. "I don't know who I am, where I came from, and how I ended up in the wasteland, but I didn't lose any memory about the outside world."

"What?" Maude exclaims.

"Estelle is a witch," he continues mercilessly. "I don't know the history of this city, so I can't tell how witches ended up living here, but she is. I know for certain. Evelyn was too, albeit not as powerful."

"Evelyn is my sister," Perceval mutters. "How can it be...how..."

"You are probably a warlock," Perceval says. "A male witch. Your power differs from a female witch's, which doesn't make you as interesting to the high priest as your sister."

"It's all a lie," Maude mutters.

"You believe what Zeph is saying?" Ned asks.

"I do," she says. "I've always known something felt off. I can't even wrap my mind around the fact that they let the orphans work here to be exploited and further exploit the maidens." Her face saddens. "It has to end."

"I want to know what the old maiden knew," I say. "Maybe it can help us."

"Perceval mentioned that they needed to control the old maiden," Zeph says. "I think he is right. That can only mean one thing."

[...] at him curiously. "And what's that?"

[...] ivate room was either at the highest place or the lowest. The basement or a [...]ays. "I know that's where I would lock a prisoner in. Make sure they can't [...] a window or break through a door easily."

[...] vords stun me, but at the same time, he looks surprised too. "Don't ask me [...]hat from," he says, a deep frown on his face.

"The building has no tower," I say.

"A basement?" Ned asks.

"I haven't checked on that," I mutter. "Don't you think it will be weird to be down there?"

"Play into the dumb girl act. They will buy it," Perceval says.

"How about we make cookies," Winnie says. "You can take them along, walk around like a dunce, and pretend to look for the kitchen. Where else can the kitchen be but downstairs?"

"Good idea, Winnie." Ned chuckles and hugs his sister.

"It's really not bad," Zeph mutters. "You can play dumb then."

"Yes, Alistair, I wanted to warm up these cookies for you," Perceval says, grimacing slightly.

At the mention of Alistair's name, something in Zeph's eyes flashes, something angry and possessive. I reach out my hand to touch his arm; not sure why I do it, but it's like an instinct that pushes me into it. "Don't worry, I will be careful," I promise.

I sleep in Zeph's arms again, like every night after I found out about Evelyn. We do nothing but sleep next to each other, but I can feel a longing in me whenever he is close, and even when he isn't, I think of him. It's like he has invaded every part of my mind.

Ned has prepared cookies for me to take to the inner circle with me. "I made sure that they aren't fully done," he says. "They still need some baking in the oven. It's going to make your lie more believable."

"You are amazing, Ned!" I exclaim.

He chuckles. "Anything for my family," he promises. "You are like a sister to me, and I need to make sure to protect you and Winnie." He pauses. "You like Zeph, don't you?"

"Would it be weird if I said yes?" I ask.

"No," he chuckles. "It's pretty obvious. Winnie saw it too, and Maude. I didn't know what to think about him at first, but he seems a decent man. He treats us with respect despite our profession and helps us so much." He pauses. "I think by now he could have left and returned to the outside world, but he is still here."

"You are right. I haven't even considered that he could have left," I say.

"He is obviously staying for a reason." Ned chuckles, patting my head. "Be careful out there, okay?"

"I promise. May the light be—" I stop myself. "Forget it. See you later, Ned."

He grins and nods. "See you later."

I'm almost running late again, so I make sure to race to the elevators without stopping to take me up to the innermost circle. When I pass the fourth one, one of Perceval's co-workers calls out to me. "Have you heard anything about Eve, Maiden Estelle?" she asks.

A guard is nearby, so I play the dumb idiot, though my heart secretly breaks. "Not yet, but I will tell you once I hear from her," I say with a beam and wave at her.

The woman nods and smiles brightly, waving back at me.

Feeling like the biggest fraud ever, I finally make it to my lessons, as usual, just going through the motions until I'm alone again. Then I start my mission, holding the basket tightly in my hand, even making sure to peek into it and take a lungful of the heavenly scent and then start strolling around.

I peek through several doors, but none of them lead downstairs. Not ready to give up, I take one of the paths that leads me outside, circle the building and keep my eyes open on any path that might lead me to a door I haven't spotted yet. I almost think it's useless and Zeph's suggestion is wrong when I spot a strong metal door surrounded by ivy.

My heart makes a nervous leap when I step closer. Deciding not to look around so I can keep my innocent image, I step inside, finally met with a staircase leading me downstairs. From the outside it looks rustic, but once down it's actually a beautiful hallway. There are murals on the walls of forests, animals, and the sky above us. My heart starts to sink when I realize that this is where they kept her...the murals probably only there to give her a feeling of the outside world.

How cruel.

To my surprise, I find a kitchen and place the cookies there before roaming around. It's a dungeon, a beautiful one, yet a dungeon.

How lonely did she feel here? Locked in, most likely all alone. My heart sinks as I realize this was supposed to be my fate too. Stay here, be used for my magic, and probably have to bed Alistair. A shiver goes down my spine, but I push forward and continue searching.

The biggest room is a bedroom. There are pictures here, one of them is a wedding picture. A young woman is in it with dark-brown hair and a gentle smile, and next to her an older man who looks stoic. I guess it was her, the former maiden, with the former high priest.

Again, I swallow nervously. This is what Alistair wants. Zeph and Percival are right. He is a dangerous man. I decide to hurry up before someone spots me and I get in trouble. There are books on the shelves, some card games, and even more books. And it looks like she was crafting and drawing a lot. Some jewelry and clothes, and...in a far corner of the shelf, I find a dusty box. Opening it, it reveals a beautiful notebook, with little birds drawn on it, and inside there are drawings and pages where someone has written something.

I blink. It's her diary. Before I can overthink it, I grab it, hurry back to the kitchen, and put it safely at the bottom of my basket. Not one second too soon, because I can hear sudden noises at the door.

"Estelle?"

I grab the cookies and switch on the oven before taking a deep breath. Putting up my sweetest smile, I turn to peek out of the corridor. "Oh, Alistair, I'm in the kitchen."

When Alistair joins me, he looks guarded, but I make sure to pretend I don't notice anything. "I made cookies at home," I tell him. "As a thank you for you being so helpful towards me, but I need to finish them here."

"And why here exactly?" he asks.

"Oh, I was looking for the kitchen," I explain. "And looked through most of the ground floor. Then I found this place." I look at him wide-eyed, pretending to be worried. "Did I do something wrong?"

"Not at all," he says. "This place is private, though. We have a kitchen on the third floor."

I clasp my mouth. "I wasn't aware! The kitchens in the fifth circle are always in the basement or the ground floors."

Alistair relaxes visibly. "Next time, just ask when you are looking for something. I will help you anytime." He looks around. "Are you done here?"

"Sure." I open the oven and take out the cookies again, neatly placing them in my basket. "Say," I look around curiously, pretending to be dumb. "Who lives here?"

"Oh, it used to be my mother's," he says.

That liar! As if I'd buy that. To keep my cover, I nod. "I'm sorry for sullying her place by coming here."

"Don't mention it," he offers me his arm. "Let's go to my office and have some tea with your cookies."

Chapter 10 Winnie
Estelle

Perceval skims through the diary. "This poor woman," he mutters. "She was locked in the building like we assumed."

"Is there something interesting in it?" Zeph asks before shaking his head. "Not saying that anything she wrote is uninteresting, just..."

"Relevant?" I help him.

"It's exactly what we assumed. They forced her to marry Alistair's predecessor. And it seems they sucked her out of her power."

I turn to Zeph. "Is that possible?"

"No, not like you think it is," he tells me. "They locked her in, and it took a toll on her mental health. That's what happened. They probably used her to do spells."

"They did. She confirms it," Perceval mutters. "She also describes that..." He swallows, looking pained all of a sudden. "What Estelle said when she told me about my sweet Evelyn. The ascension is a sacrifice. They kill the maiden's off to get ahold of their powers." He closes the book. "I wish I could have protected her," he whispers. "My sweet sister."

"We will make sure her passing wasn't in vain," I say, anger filling me.

"Yes," Zeph agrees. "We—"

We get interrupted by the heavy footsteps and Maude running into my room. "ES-TELLE!"

I was so engrossed by my task, so full of motivation to do something and happy not to feel helpless anymore that I didn't expect anything bad could happen. And if something happened, I thought it would be to me, maybe even to Zeph or Perceval. No one else is in danger for now, only us as the main plotters against Alistair.

I felt safe and almost a bit happy, that nothing could have prepared me for what was to come.

"Maude?" I get up immediately. "What happened? Why are you looking so—"

Her eyes fill with tears, and she pulls me into a hug immediately. Instant dread settles in me. Maude never cries. I have never seen her break down. She is always strong and a shoulder to lie on for us. "It's Winnie," she sobs. "Our sweet Winnie..."

I draw back instantly. My hands are turning sweaty, while shiver over shiver runs down my spine, an unknown fear and panic filling me. "What's with Winnie? Is she sick? Did she get hurt?" When Maude stays quiet, I grab her arms. "Maude, what's with Winnie?"

"She is..." Maude swallows. "She is...I'm so sorry..."

Some truths hit so hard, so spontaneously, it's almost impossible to grasp them, let alone understand them.

I let go of her and dash out of the room, my body moving on its own while my heart keeps hammering against my chest in cold fear. I can hear Zeph calling my name and running after me, but I make it to Winnie's room first. I didn't know what to expect. I was still hoping for...I don't know what, while I ran to her. Nothing prepared me for it, nothing. I can't grasp it. I don't understand. I just didn't see it coming, not able to understand what's happening here.

Why didn't I see it coming?

Time stops spinning for a moment, everything still and painful, like a cold hand is gripping my heart. I sink onto my knees, not able to look at anything else but Ned, who is cradling his sister in his arms. He sobs silently, his body shaking with every heavy sob that goes through it.

Why?

I was just sitting with Zeph and Perceval, plotting something. Only yesterday I talked to Winnie, and she smiled at me like always. We even cuddled and joked around.

My best friend and surrogate sister, my family.

Every day I lose some more. How much will this city keep taking from me?

I feel warm arms wrapping themselves around me from behind, and just like that, I feel like a dam is broken; the tears flow out of me while I scream out my pain.

It's late at night when I wake up again, for a split second, hoping that I dreamed everything. A nightmare. I'm nestled against Zeph's chest. Raising my gaze, I meet his eyes and immediately know it wasn't a dream. It's a nightmare I'm still living through.

"Winnie," I whisper, my throat sore.

"She is...I'm so sorry..." Zeph mutters, tightening his embrace around me.

"Tell me what happened," I beg. "I...I left Ned there. Poor Ned. And Winnie, Winnie...why?"

"She took a high overdose of drugs," he tells me. "Maude found them. She said that some of the royals use these in small doses to get high. It looks like Winnie stole them from one of her customers, and well..."

I bury my head in Zeph's chest. "I didn't know," I whisper. "I didn't know she couldn't bear it anymore. I know she was unhappy because everyone is, but I didn't know...I failed her as her best friend and sister. I should have known. I should have seen it and stopped her."

"No, Estelle," he mutters into my hair. "No one could tell. We can't explain what happened logically; we can't explain what she felt. She was desperate and deeply hurt by this city. It's the cult's fault, not yours or Ned's."

"Ned," I blurt out. "How is he..."

"Arthur and Maude are with him," he reassures me.

"I can't stay here," I whisper.

"You need to rest," he urges. "Estelle, you literally collapsed."

"You don't understand," I interrupt him. "I mean, I can't stay here in this city. I lost so much here. This place holds no joy and hope for me anymore. Nothing."

Zeph looks surprised. "I...I was hoping you would say this. Actually, we all were."

"What do you mean?"

"Arthur and Maude came to check on you. They begged me to take you away, but I said I can't do it against your will."

I look up at him. "But you can do it?"

"Yes," he says shortly. "But you don't know anything about me. I might be dangerous. I—"

I sit up abruptly and grab his face between my hands before pressing my lips against his. Something seems to shift in him, and with a passion I didn't know he possessed, he presses me against him, kissing me back. I forget my first fumbled attempts at kissing the moment he pushes his tongue past my lips. I have no idea what I'm doing, but he doesn't seem to mind, and I find myself suddenly not caring either.

Something unknown urges me forward toward him; a sudden pull, and I find myself tugging at his shirt.

He draws back slightly. "You are not in the right mind," he pants. "You are grieving. You—"

"I am in my right mind," I tell him. "Actually, I have never seen clearer. This place is doomed, and the only thing that feels real is the bond I feel with you."

"You can feel it..." he mutters.

"Yes. I assume it's something you haven't told me about, but I guess you have your reasons."

"My reasons are not to scare you away," he admits.

"I accept that, for now," I say.

"I feel like you should ask more questions," he mutters.

"I feel the same, but at the same time, I don't care who or what you are, or what you are hiding," I say. "I lost Winnie and Evelyn, and I will be damned if I lose someone else in my life."

Something in his eyes seems to flash. He looks vulnerable all of a sudden. "Estelle," he whispers, bending forward to kiss me gently. "You are the light, but not the weird twisted thing they made out of it here in this city. You are a beautiful star, shining brightly and healing those around you."

Yes, a light that shines on everyone, yet I couldn't save my friends. One after another fell into a dark pit of doom. "I couldn't heal Winnie, though," I say bitterly.

"Maybe the reason she held on for so long was because you were there," he retorts.

I wrap my arms around his neck, burying my head in his chest. "I want to feel something real," I beg. "Make me feel, Zeph."

He draws back, finally removing his shirt, before helping me out of my clothes. I can't remember the last time anyone saw me naked. I should feel vulnerable and embarrassed, but I don't. Zeph's warm hands glide over my body before he bends down to add kisses to all his touches. His fingers find their way to my breasts, squeezing them until my nipples harden.

All these sensations are so new and different from what I'm used to feeling, but I find myself getting lost in them. Zeph is so gentle, and every time he moves further downward, he gives me time to adapt to what he is doing.

"You are so beautiful, Estelle," he mutters while he spreads my legs gently, his tongue gliding over my folds.

I feel a sensation I've never felt before. It starts with a tingle and burns more with every move and touch of Zeph's tongue and thumb. His thumb spreads me open for his tongue to push into me. I gasp, clutching my hands over my mouth to remain silent.

Zeph stops what he is doing and is suddenly hovering above me.

"Don't hide your moans from me," he says, pulling my hands away. There is a glint in his eyes that intensifies the fire I feel burning inside of me.

I wrap my arms around his neck immediately, not able to let him go again. Zeph seems to want to give me all I want, exactly the way I want, because he keeps me in his arms.

"How do you feel, my love?" he asks me.

I grab his face between my hands. "I will feel even better if I get to feel all of you."

"What my queen wishes shall be hers," he says, but something in his voice has shifted. He sounds different, darker, but equally alluring as before.

I don't have time to think about what he just said, and instead, I close my eyes to feel everything more intensely. I spread my legs for Zeph to settle between them, feeling his cock pushing against my vagina. His careful preparations have made me wet, but I still feel like something is tearing me apart when he pushes into me.

Winnie told me all about how it feels, so I'm prepared. Or so I think. My chest heaves as I feel my muscles tense, then Zeph's hands brush over my face gently. He plasters my face with light kisses until I find myself relaxing. I didn't know sleeping with a man would feel this way. It's nothing like I expected. My body longs for him, and there is this tingly sensation of want, but it also feels weird and different.

Zeph starts thrusting into me with more intent now. The burn subsides, and instead it's replaced by a warm feeling that soon spreads into that tingly sensation I had before.

"Estelle, are you okay?"

"It feels good, Zeph," I pant. "Just continue."

A shiver goes through his body. "You are so beautiful."

I find myself getting bolder and more confident now that my tension has subsided, deciding to move my hips against his and meet him halfway. It surprises him because a guttural growl leaves his lips, and his eyes glint again.

I don't know what it is or why, but it's like it dawns on me all of a sudden. I just *know*. I wrap my arms around him. "I know what you are," I say quietly. "Your fears are unfounded., I'm not scared."

He stops his movements, his eyes snapping open.

"I'm not scared," I repeat.

His expression is so full of relief and joy that I can only bask in it for a minute. "The true monsters are here in this city," I whisper.

Without saying anything, he pulls me up into his arms with inhuman strength, his hips snapping forward as if he decided to claim me for eternity. His cock pulsates inside me. With one hand, he keeps holding me while the other moves between our bodies and starts massaging my clit.

Every time I think I've adapted to what Zeph's doing, he changes the pace or strengths of his thrusts. My body shakes from the intensity of everything I feel.

"This is..." I moan. "I can't anymore. Zeph."

"Mine," he groans before I feel my walls clenching around him. I'm not sure what's happening to my body; it's like a bundle of nerves suddenly lets loose and shakes me to my core. It should feel scary, but it's incredible.

It takes a while for my body and mind to calm down. When my senses return, I am resting against Zeph's chest. He is playing with my hair and keeps gently touching my back.

I look at his face, taking in his handsome features. "Now, I'm a maiden no more. Not that I ever was."

"I fell in love with you, Estelle," he says suddenly. "From the first moment I heard your voice, when I was still in and out of consciousness."

"I don't understand this," I admit. "But I feel the same."

I bury my head in his neck before I burst into tears. I have lost Evelyn and Winnie. They are never going to come back to me.

Now I need to make sure not to lose Zeph or Ned either.

Chapter 11 The Disgraced Maiden
Estelle

After my night with Zeph, I had another breakdown and cried in his arms for hours. In the early morning, I finally met Ned, both of us wordlessly hugging each other. Losing Winnie broke him, and I know I have to get us out of here somehow. I feel like my heart is hardening by what just happened, not allowing me to grieve or cry anymore. I want to hurt someone and get back at those responsible for all the suffering.

I turn to gaze around the now familiar building I'm taking my private lessons in. They can't know, but this will be the last time I'm going to be here. I'm impure. I have slept with a man, but no one notices. I go to the inner circle as usual. I do my prayers like usual, and nothing happens out of the ordinary. Nothing changes. It's a hoax, and it always has been. Evelyn got murdered for nothing.

It was for nothing.

I am about to pack my things when a sudden shadow hovers over me. I know who it is even without having to turn around. I take a shaky breath, steadying myself before turning to look at him. "Alistair," I say. "What a surprise."

He smiles at me. "Why don't you come and dine with me, Estelle?"

My heart sinks. I was hoping to avoid having to go on a date with him. I'm too scared he will start pushing for an answer.

He seems to catch my indecisiveness. "Do you have an appointment?" he asks.

"It's just I promised to help Maude with some chores," I say, cursing myself for not having a better excuse.

"Well then, how about we just have tea instead?"

"Yes." I smile. "I'd like that. We can dine together next time," I promise, well aware that there won't be a next time.

As usual, Alistair serves me the best possible tea with some tasty-looking pralines. They have a creamy, crunchy filling, just overflowing my taste buds. I have never tasted anything alike. "These taste wonderful," I admit, completely stunned.

"They do, don't they?" he says, tilting his head. He smiles at me again, his creepy, dreadful smile. "Estelle," he says after a while. "I have been patient, haven't I?"

"Yes, very patient," I mutter.

"Good," he entwines his fingers and looks at me. "I would like an answer now. I have told you I'd like to court you. Surely by now you have made up your mind."

It's not a question; it's a command. "I...I don't know, Alistair," I say, the wheels in my head turning to find a way to stall time. "I don't feel like I am ready yet."

He gets up, walks around the table, and bends down to look into my eyes. I have to suppress the urge to flinch away. "Oh, Estelle, you are so modest. Of course, you are ready. You are a wonderful maiden."

I can barely catch up with what is happening because suddenly, he grasps my face and kisses me. I'm so mortified I go entirely still before pushing him away. I know it is the wrong decision the moment I look into his face. "Well then," he snarls, all the fake kindness gone from his face. "We'll need to do this my way."

"What...no—"

He leaves me no time to act. Grabbing my arm and tugging me up, he drags me across his room. And with a simple button, he moves the bookshelves away, revealing a staircase that leads downwards. He tugs me towards him and grabs me by my shoulders. "It's the waste, isn't it? Your fellow *tinkers*. They have poisoned your mind together with that brothel. I will have them all eradicated from this city."

"No," I scream. "Please, no. They didn't do anything!"

"They are keeping you from me," he says coldly. "I will make sure every one of that forsaken brothel will be locked away."

"It's not their fault…it's…I'm in love," I blurt out, not sure what else to tell him. I just don't want him to hurt my family and friends. I don't care if he hurts me.

"You think I will let another man have you?" he snarls.

"You killed Evelyn," I yell at him. "Do you think I could ever be with a man who disposes of his maidens like they are waste!"

"But, you are waste," he snarls. "Your bodies are waste. Only your powers are valuable. And with every maiden being sacrificed, we find a new one." There is a glint in his eyes. "Maybe we need a bigger sacrifice this time," he says. "Our barriers are weak, aren't they?"

"What are you talking about?" I whisper.

"Nothing that concerns you," he says, pushing me down the stairs and closing the door firmly in front of me.

Regaining my senses, I realize I'm there…in the old maiden's basement.

Zeph

The moment my body united with my mate's, it's like a door opened up, and step by step, the memories are trickling in like a dripping tap. Estelle has left for her maiden work, not wanting to raise suspicions until I take her out of this city.

I grab my head, groaning.

"Are you not feeling well?" Maude asks me. She looks exhausted and broken after losing Winnie.

"I'm okay," I mutter. "How is Ned doing?"

"Perceval is with him," Maude says. "And Estelle spent the morning at his side. I don't think either of them will be able to move on from this anytime soon."

"Estelle said she was like a sister to her, her family."

"Yes," Maude says sadly. "Promise me, you will watch out for Estelle," she says all of a sudden. "You need to take her away from here."

"She wants to leave too," I say. "But I don't know if she truly can leave you all behind."

"Actually, I wanted to ask you something," Maude starts, but right at that moment a new wave of memories hit me. "Zeph?" She calls out. "Are you sure you are alright?"

"Just my head," I breathe out. "It's just..."

I feel something cold being pressed against my forehead. "Wait here," she says. "I will see if I can find a medicine for you."

She is kind, even to me, a literal stranger. She has to send these poor girls and boys to sell their bodies every night. I'm sure deep inside it's tearing her apart. Another wave of pain hits me, making me groan.

My dragon clan has been under attack, and my brother, the traitor, stopped at nothing to try to kill me.

My clan. I am leading them. I feel the beast inside me stir, like it did when I slept with Estelle. She made our memories return and woke him up again.

Our battle led us far away from the dragon lands, where I killed him. But I almost succumbed to my wounds.

This is where Estelle found me, where fate led her to me. My mate, I found my mate. I knew what I was when I woke up without my memories, and I knew the beautiful blonde maiden was my mate the instant our eyes met. Even dormant, my beast was able to recognize her as his.

My mind and body hurt at the memories returning to me, but I have to push through it. There is no turning back now. From what seems far away, I hear noises, unsure if they are in my head or truly there. It almost sounds like metal hitting metal...and there are screams.

I force my eyes open slightly, noticing I'm curled up in a corner of the kitchen, barely able to see anything through the pain. "You stay here, Zeph," one of the boys working here yells. "We'll handle it."

Handle what?

"Zeph is hurt and can't defend himself!" One girl calls out. "Make sure no one comes into the kitchen."

"Take the knives, everything you can find." Maude's voice comes through the doorway. "We are not going to make this easy!"

What the fuck is even happening?

I drop down on my back, closing my eyes again. It's all here now, every piece I was missing, but I'm relieved whatever returned didn't change what I've become and felt here. I still care for these people. They had nothing, yet they saved me and protected me when I was vulnerable.

I dive deep into my mind until I finally find him, my majestic beast that had to retreat into the depths of our mind to protect the both of us. His silver scales are shimmering slightly; he is tall and strong like the king he is.

What do you say? I ask him.

He raises his head, his yellow eyes meeting mine, while he starts getting up on his feet.

I agree. I reach out my hand to touch him. *Our clan is strong, and our warriors have defended it. I still feel our bond to them going strong. But here? We are not done here!*

Chapter 12 The Fall of the Maidens

Zeph

I get up with a groan, my headache subsiding to a simple dull ache at the back of my head. My palms feel sweaty, and I'm annoyingly wobbly on my legs, but I can feel my strength returning, and my beast becoming more dominant again. Finally.

Around me there are still screams. So, I didn't dream or imagine it. Something is happening. I follow the voices outside, passing young girls and boys hiding in the brothel. "You are feeling better, Zeph?" one of the girls whispers. She is only fourteen and not working here yet, but she will be eventually.

It's heartbreaking.

"Yes, I'm feeling better and ready to help," I say. "Stay here, everyone!"

I hurry forward until I finally find myself outside. The view in front of me takes my breath away for a moment. There are guards everywhere, trying to tug the tinkers with them. But these brave folks are putting up a fight the guards didn't expect.

I see Perceval and some faces I haven't met trying to push back against the guards. More and more soldiers are pooling in. Maude, Ned, and Arthur are right at the front, trying to protect the brothel from being overrun.

I lunge forward with only a couple of steps, coming right in time when a guard is about to pull out his gun to shoot at the crowd, at Ned in particular. "Be gone," I growl, kicking him so hard he falls back against a group of soldiers behind him, knocking them all over.

"Zeph!" Ned calls out.

"I'm fine now, and ready to end this," I mutter.

"They are going to open fire soon," Arthur calls out. "They are set out to either imprison us or kill us!"

"Like the dirt you are," one of the guards yells.

"Let's clean this city of them!"

I furrow my brows, feeling a well-known knot of anger forming in my chest, its threads of fury reaching out through my body. There it is! With my power in my hands again, I let my aura come forward. "Quiet!" I snarl, noticing with contempt how some guards drop to their knees. They are weak, so weak.

"How did you do that?" Ned whispers.

I ignore him for now and turn to Arthur. "Do you have anything to defend yourself with?"

"Yes," Arthur nods.

"You have a minute to gather everything. Make sure everyone here is equipped." I turn to Maude. "You too. Use whatever you can."

"Got you," she says grimly.

"And now," I turn to the guards again, my eyes scanning for one higher in command. I notice him by his differing clothes and stalk forward to grab him and tug him upwards. I let my aura come through again, making him whimper. "Where is Estelle!?" I growl.

He shivers but keeps silent. "Talk, or I will rip your useless tongue out of your mouth," I snarl.

"She is in the inner circle," he blurts out. "We are just following orders!"

Following orders? They look way too happy to get *rid of the waste* to be just following orders. I toss him onto the ground, noticing with grim satisfaction how his head knocks against the street. Before I can say something, I see a white light appear at the top of the city, directed right to their barrier. It's a strong bundle of light.

"These fools," I hiss.

"What are they doing?" Perceval asks.

"That's arcane power," I say. "I know exactly what they are doing."

"Zeph!" Maude calls out as she comes running back. I can see her holding an axe in her hands, and a bunch of her older proteges are following her, equipped with knives and other weapons they found. "You need to leave and get Estelle! We can defend ourselves now. Help the maidens; they are innocent."

Arthur appears at the same time with his friends, all of them wearing guns. I wasn't aware of how well-prepared the tinkers are. He must have noticed my surprise, because a sly smile curls his lips. "The good thing about being waste, and forced to dig through the wasteland, is that we are tough."

"You are warriors," I say. "Fighters." I think about my clan and those with lower ranks who aren't warriors. I will make sure they get the respect they deserve, and if I see anyone of my warriors looking down on them, they will get their ass kicked by me personally.

"You bet," Arthur says. "And I'm ready to defend my fellow tinkers."

"And you are?" Ned asks me. "What are you?"

"A winged monster," I say without hesitation.

For a split second they all stare at me, but to my utmost shock they react nothing like I expected. "I don't care what you are," Arthur says. "I had a feeling something was different about you."

"You helped us when we needed it," Maude agrees. "Now it's time for us to change our own history. And for you to save Estelle. Take her away from here, like you promised."

"Please take me with you," Ned says to my surprise. "I want to help Estelle too. She is the only remaining family I have."

"And take me," Perceval says. "I have nothing here anymore. Evelyn...is gone. She is gone."

Taking humans into the dragon clan is new and unheard of, but I couldn't care less. These are good people. They helped me when I needed it. They proved to be loyal to my future queen, and they are her friends. It eases my mind that she will have friends with her.

"It doesn't feel right to leave you behind," I say to Maud and Arthur.

"You are not leaving us behind," Arthur says. "This is our city and our battle. We will win this and enter a new stage of history, but it will take time."

"I will reach out to a witch coven," I tell them. "To come here and help the maidens with their powers."

"Make sure Estelle is safe, and you are good to her," Maude warns me.

"I will give her everything and do everything to make her happy," I promise.

Maude hugs Ned tightly. "Watch out for yourself and for Estelle."

"Let's go," I say, turning to Ned and Perceval. "It's time to leave. But, it's not a goodbye forever."

Estelle

I've searched through the whole basement for an escape, but there is none. They truly built this prison well. What makes matters worse is that I hear yells and screams through the tiny window in the former maiden's bedroom. I don't know what's going on, but something is wrong, terribly wrong.

I recall what Alistair said when he tossed me in here...how the maidens are disposable. What's he doing now? Is he truly going to imprison my fellow tinkers? Is he going to hurt the maidens? It's like a cold hand has gripped my heart again, making it difficult to breathe.

How can he do that? Why is a living being so disposable to him? Not just to him, but to everyone from the inner and second circle. The people they want to dispose of have families and friends, dreams and hopes. They are kind and hardworking, and they have a right to live here like everyone else.

My fear and worry about what's going on makes me get up again and search once more for an exit. I don't mind if it's hopeless; I have to do something. I have to find a way. I rush up the staircase leading me to Alistair's office, cursing myself that I didn't find it the first time when I was snooping around here, and hammer against the door.

I don't know for how long I scream and hit the door. Eventually, I drop down to my knees, exhausted. I'm so shaken, I can't even cry. I've lost Evelyn and Winnie already, and who knows what else I will lose today. My friends, my fellow maidens, my freedom.

Zeph says I have magic in me, but I can't do anything with it. The way I am now is so useless. I lean my forehead against the door, taking a few shaky breaths. What am I going to do now? How can I help anyone like this?

A rustling sound from the other side of the basement startles me. Raising my head, I listen closer. Are those voices? Someone is at the door, the one that leads outside the building. It's the one I came through the first time I found this place. I jump up again, not sure what to expect. My gut feeling tells me that nothing good will come through this door, but at the same time, I'm well aware I can't stay here. I need to play along. Maybe it's Alistair...maybe I can manipulate him.

I wait at the bottom of the stairs, my eyes catching three men coming downwards. I recognize one of them as the overseeing master who commended me for my choice of clothes a while back.

"Maiden Estelle, you will have to accompany us," one of the other guards sneers. He looks like he is enjoying this.

The overseeing master has a grim expression, trying to look everywhere but at me, almost like he feels torn.

"Where to?" I ask.

"To your fellow stupid maidens," one of the guys laughs.

That asshole. They brainwash those poor girls, treat them like disposable trash, and have the audacity to laugh about them. It would probably be safer for me to resist now, to try to stay here, but there is no way I'm going to do that. I won't sit here while everyone else's life is on the line, while the maidens are in danger.

"Then take me to them, you imbecile," I snarl.

The guy stops laughing, glaring at me now, but before he can do something, the overseeing master takes my arm. "Come," he says, leading me upstairs. He casts me a glance, almost looking apologetic. "It's time for the maidens to ascend."

Chapter 13 The Winged Monster
Estelle

I feel my head getting dizzy. My heart is beating so fast, hammering against my chest, not in the least bit able to calm down. With every step I take, I feel more and more dread settling in. I can hear their cries.

They are crying, desperate, and probably completely lost as to what's going on.

Guards surround the whole inner circle, locking the maidens into our main hall, where we usually pray. I don't know what exactly Alistair and his guards did to them, there are crystals surrounding them, illuminating them in their glow, and one by one, light leaves the maidens, leading upwards toward the barrier. Some girls are crying, some are lying on the ground, motionless.

"So, this is your version of humanity?" I ask without addressing it to anyone.

The man leading me doesn't answer, but one of the other guards just snorts. "Whatever," he grumbles.

It's like an out-of-body experience. I know what's happening, but I still can't wrap my mind around it. The guards push me into the circle as well, the glow of the crystal enveloping me. So, this is it. Something seems to be invading my whole presence, sucking the life out of me. To my right is a young maiden kneeling next to me and reaching for my hand. I take it gently, hugging her while I feel her body going limp and all life leaving her.

One by one, the maidens fall, their light switched off forever. If only I knew what to do. What am I supposed to do!? They are dying...and some of them already passed on forever. If I don't do anything, they will all die. I let my gaze wander around, my eyes falling on the guards, who keep watching, shooting at every maiden who wants to leave the circle, until I find *him*.

Alistair, that monster. He, who lures the maidens into false safety just to exploit them. Who keeps up this system because it gives him power and wealth. Winnie killed herself because she couldn't live in this reality anymore, where night after night she was forced to go to bed with strangers. Evelyn died because she loved a man who betrayed her.

Sudden rage fills me while I keep my eyes locked on Alistair. Something in my chest tightens, just to be released with full fury. A stream of light leaves my hands, hitting one of the crystals first. So that's how I do it. I collect my anger and pain again, directing it towards Alistair. He is too surprised to move, letting me knock him off his feet.

"Maidens!" I yell. "Keep your composure. Stay focused."

"Should we sing the song?" one maiden asks with a weak voice.

"Forget the fucking song," I snarl. "It's just a hoax. What they are doing now is letting us *ascend*."

By now, it has pretty much dawned on them that they are supposed to die here, but it took me mentioning ascension for them to truly grasp what's going on.

"They have lied to us," I yell, shooting another crystal with my power. "We are witches, not maidens. They are lying scum who think we are disposable trash. Gather all the fear and anger you feel, and let's show them who is the trash!"

Zeph

Ned, Perceval, and I make it to the uppermost circle with ease. The lower circles helped us go further, and the higher ones just aren't made to fight. Now we're here, the severity of what's going on hits me. There are dead maidens everywhere, yet there is a whole group of them surrounding Estelle, my beautiful mate, and fighting back.

"Let's end this farce," I yell. "The guards need to go down. Let's make sure they won't be able to harass the population anymore."

"Got you," Ned says grimly, tightening the gun he got from Arthur. He is ready to draw blood. I feel for him; he lost his sister, the most important person in his world.

Meanwhile, Perceval dashes forward toward a man I don't recognize. "You!" he snarls. "Chester! You killed her!"

The man can barely react, just stammering something, before Perceval knocks him off his feet, pointing a gun to his head. "All for money. You even betrayed your probably very dead brother."

"For the hope of a better future!" The man yells.

"And for that you took Evelyn's," Perceval screams, fury and pain in his voice. "She was an angel."

"She was stupid," Chester grunts. "She believed I loved her, that stupid cunt."

Perceval pulls the trigger without hesitation, followed by Chester's lifeless body dropping to the ground. I didn't think Perceval had it in him. I didn't think any human had in them to do what they are doing, to do what the tinkers are doing. They are fighting for their freedom, and I shall be damned if I don't help them. It's the least I can do.

Now is a good time. Never has there been a better moment. I fly forward, allowing my beast to come forward. He has been waiting for this, eager to burn this place down. With a loud screech, he takes over as we shift to our dragon form.

Ned pauses, his eyes following me as I fly upwards. "Wow," he mutters.

I will give them the show they deserve. Picking up my pace, I dash upwards, breaking through the barrier easily and destroying it for good. I hear screams from the inner circle and guards shooting at me with their feeble weapons. As if that's enough to get through a dragon's scales. I snarl angrily, dashing down and letting my breath of fire out on the guards who have dared to hurt my mate.

My tunnel vision easily spots her. She stands amidst the maidens, proud and beautiful, and not with an ounce of fear when she sees me.

"Don't worry," she yells at the maidens. "He is on our side. There is no winged monster. There is no barrier. There is just us and a dragon, and them." She points at Alistair. "Who exploited and lied to us."

One of the guards tries to attack Ned, pulling my attention away from Estelle and back to the battle. I dash downwards again, grabbing him and flying upward before dropping him to the ground.

"Zeph!" Perceval yells. "We have it under control. Go and help the tinkers."

My gaze returns to my mate, who nods at me before turning her attention to the man she hates so much. Alistair faces no chance against her. With a well-formed stream of light, she cuts through his head. Pride fills me at seeing her fight. She wouldn't be a king's mate if she needed me to save her. In fact, she was the one who saved me.

I circle the city, amazed by how it looks from above. The steam, the metallic buildings, the wheels. Everything looks fascinating and oddly beautiful. I fly downwards again to where the tinkers are still getting at it, screeching loudly when I fly past them.

"Down!" Maude yells. "That's Zeph."

Letting my breath of fire out again, I let it rain down onto the men attacking them. Then I move further, destroying one watch tower after another. Lastly, with grim satisfaction, I move to the inner circle, the secret mansion, where they kept the old maiden and also wanted to keep Estelle.

I let my claws dig into the roof, tearing it apart and destroying as much of it as possible. I don't burn it down, as there are documents Maude and Arthur might be interested in.

"Zeph!" Estelle calls out to me and waves. I turn around, finally allowing myself to land on the ground next to her. The fight around us is still going on, but the maidens and the tinkers together with the activists are getting the upper hand. Some of the regulars, and even a few royals from the third and second circles are joining them. For a split second I wonder why, but then I figure that the maidens who were killed today probably were their daughters, sisters, or friends.

I feel Estelle's warm hand against the scales of my neck and turn my head to look at her. "You are amazing," she whispers.

"Estelle," Ned calls out while he runs to her with Perceval hot on his heels. "We are done here. They have it under control."

I lower myself to the ground for them to climb onto my back. "Maude and Arthur?" Estelle asks anxiously.

"Can you show her, Zeph?" Perceval asks.

Instead of an answer, I lift us up in the air and fly another round of the city for Estelle to see what's going on, and how her fellow tinkers are so bravely fighting. They have successfully freed the outer circle and have moved to the others now. I spot Arthur in the third one. He stops briefly and waves at us. "Make sure to keep in contact." He laughs. "Don't worry; we have it under control."

Maude is currently making her way through the second circle, her reaction similar to Arthur's. I make sure to land close to her. "Maude," Estelle sobs.

"Don't cry, sweetheart," Maude smiles at her. "I promise I will watch out for the maidens. No one will be exploited anymore. And no one will be forced to work in the brothel." She chuckles. "Your boyfriend is a dragon. I'm sure he can fly you here occasionally."

"I love you, Maude," Estelle blurts out.

"Me too," Ned says.

"And that's why you have to get out of here and start a new life," she says, gazing towards me. "With the dragon king."

The Village

Avalina P Cox

Blurb

Elsie, orphaned and living alone in the mountains, knew she was different and that being different she would never be accepted by the rest of the realm.

Living a secret and sheltered life meant she would survive.

Santos, lead warrior of the Village, an isolated settlement in the mountains, has the difficult task of organising its protection from bandits and thieves.

Taking refuge from a powerful storm while out scouting, Santos meets Elsie, also sheltering in the cave. Sparks fly, however, when he takes her with him back to the Village everything changes.

Does the conflict of their relationship mean the end for them? Or does their destiny have other ideas?

Prologue

Mount Kalika sat prominently at the furthermost point on the eastern side of the human realm and had been named after the ancient Goddess of Destruction. The mountain was known for its formidable terrain, steep embankments, jutting ledges, sheer drops, unstable passes and thick unyielding forests. All of the villages that resided on the mountain, except for the village of Wyrmvern, had been deserted for safer ground. The inhabitants of this isolated village continued to endure the harsh conditions of Mount Kalika as they had done since the beginning of time.

Village life on Mount Kalika had always been tough, but in recent times, the traffic on the mountain that threatened the community had intensified, due to the vast influx of outlaws trying to escape their sentencing. With a new king in power, many lives had become fragmented. Unlike his mother, the new king, Marius, was disillusioned with the people of his realm. He implemented strict laws, forbidding many previously accepted practices, causing a surge of numbers within the prisons.

To deal with the overcrowding, King Marius ensured punishments were much more harsh than in his mother's time, often cruel beyond necessary, hoping to ensure law and order would be restored. Instead, finding the king's new regime to be a violation of their human rights, many people of the land soon found themselves on the run to escape the infliction of the king's wrath; leading Mount Kalika to be inundated with more outlaws than it had ever known.

The people of Wyrmvern had become progressively more vulnerable, becoming targets for outlaws. The mountain on which they lived was free from those who policed the borders, due to its treacherous terrain and belief that anyone foolish enough to try and conquer the mountain would surely die. However, being on the coast of the island's peninsula, it became a thoroughfare for those trying to escape the realm in a bid to seek asylum in distant lands that remained unknown to their kind.

Wyrmvern's village elder had become increasingly concerned about the safety of his people, and had instructed that more warriors needed to be trained and for the training schedule to be increased. More guards protected the village borders, and an increase in patrols in the surrounding areas was put in place, to ward off danger before it came too close to those vulnerable inside the village walls. It was the only way the village elder could see a future for them on the mountain. He feared if it became too unsafe, they would be forced off the mountain and their home, like the other villages, and neither he nor his people wanted that.

The village elder prayed to his God for a miracle. His God had always answered his prayers and the prayers of his people. However, the answers given weren't always in the way some may have expected. The village elder had forgotten that important part of his faith. Their God's help could come in many ways. If facilitated correctly, all would be well, but if abused or ignored, then the outcome would be out of his control. A miracle came, but with it so did a startling and unexpected outcome, which the elder did not see coming.

Chapter 1
Elsie

Being alone in the woodlands that surrounded the mountain, unable to show myself for fear of capture or death, I had always been a lonely soul. I didn't always dislike the peace being alone gave me, but there were times I craved company, someone to talk to, a friend, a companion. Occasionally, I would daydream an afternoon away thinking a knight in shining armour would sweep me off my feet, and save me from my lifetime punishment of being destitute and alone.

Having lived in the deepest part of the thickest and most dangerous forest my entire life, I had managed to stay completely off the radar. Beneath the mountain side forest, the sheer cliff edge dropped into the unrelenting and vicious sea below. No human would be foolish enough to come here.

Born in the human realm, Maryst, I had no place amongst those heathens, and they had no understanding of our kind. I was nothing like them, and for that, I could only be grateful. However, it also meant I was destined to spend my entire existence alone.

My parents didn't tell me much about their past or how we had come to be here. In fact, their love story always made me believe I may have a chance of finding love myself.

They had both been brought up in Maryst, as humans and with human families. Neither one was aware of their true species until they reached twenty-one. When they met, it had been love at first sight; they were unable to stay away from one another.

One day, not long after they met, they went out on a date to a remote meadow for a picnic. They hadn't realised they were in the middle of an area dense with hungry bears until one came to attack them, and they both unexpectedly shifted into dragons. The bear made a hasty retreat but it left my parents in complete confusion and panic. They spent the next few days researching everything they could about the species, but there was very little to discover. When they asked their parents about the mythical creatures, they were laughed at.

Neither one of my parents had the courage to tell their own what they were for fear of rejection and backlash. They had never been made aware they were adopted, but it seemed abundantly clear the notion of dragon shifters existing was not something their families could take seriously. Unable to control their shifting, or the abilities they had discovered when in dragon form, they had become a danger to all those they loved.

They had never been caught out, but they couldn't risk it, and so they left to live their lives out together in the forest of Mount Kalika, certain no one would find them. They vowed not to have children and inflict the life they led on a child. However, it transpired that my mother was already pregnant, and when I was born, I would be their first and only child. I understood their decision, but it didn't make it any easier for me. They had always been open and honest with me about everything, yet I longed to be with other children my own age.

In an attempt to normalise my life a little, they tried to enrol me in one of the village schools. However, too many questions were asked about where I had come from, and my school days were over before they had begun. Nothing about growing up for me had been easy or straightforward, but I loved my parents, and while I knew I could be demanding and moody about being so far away from civilization, deep down, I accepted it and appreciated their decision.

When I had not long turned sixteen, and winter was at its harshest, we were struggling to find food to sustain us. It had always been difficult in the winter, so we prepared in the summer months with stocks; however, that winter, our supplies had been plundered by a bear, who thought his big oafish self could take it all and leave without incident. Instead, he took our provisions, unable to see his footing clearly, slipped on some shale and fell to his death in the sea below, our food stocks tumbling behind him.

My parents made the risky decision to hunt in dragon form at night. In the cover of darkness, they had gone once a week for several weeks without incident. The last time I saw them leaving for their weekly trip, they never returned, and I barely survived the remaining winter. With no idea what happened to them, or where to even start looking for them, I grieved their loss and began trying to live my life in solitude, accepting they would never be coming back.

I missed human contact. Talking, conversation, laughter, touch.

When I reached twenty-one and my own dragon came to me, I spent hours perfecting my skills in the secrecy of the forest. However, flying scared me. I had nowhere safe to practise, and the fear of my life coming to an end, like my parents, had stopped me from even trying in the beginning. Yet, the urge to attempt it continued to compel me to know what it felt like to fly, soar and dive in the sky with the wind blowing the cobwebs away. After weeks of restraint, I couldn't hold back any longer.

Standing on the edge of the cliff with nothing but the crashing waves and swell of the sea below, I closed my eyes, jumped off and hoped for the best. When I didn't plummet into the freezing water, I opened my eyes. As if my body knew what to do, I found myself sailing through the wind just above the surface of the sea; I had never felt freer. There was nothing more thrilling than the exhilaration of being at one with the birds.

Knowing my parents took to the skies and failed to return, I kept my nighttime sea flights to a minimum. However, I couldn't bring myself to stop altogether. It felt like home. Unfortunately, as the realm made way for the new King Marius, things became much more difficult for me.

More and more people trying to escape the tirade of his ruthless leadership were escaping to the mountain. I heard them talking while out searching for food and found myself having to hide more than once. They were encroaching closer and closer to my safe haven, forcing me to become even more vigilant than I had become accustomed to.

It had been a little over a month since I had a night-time flight, and I found myself itching to get out. I knew it was risky, but I couldn't stop myself. I flew further out to sea than I normally would, knowing it may be some time before I would be able to go out again. When the winds picked up and the clouds rolled dark and ominous, I turned to head for land. The swell in the sea became rough and turbulent, so I flew higher to avoid the oversized waves.

The rain started to fall in earnest, causing my sight to become compromised, and I cursed myself for having not anticipated such a storm before setting off. I had always been more aware of these things. Having lived by the sea all my life, I could usually tell when a storm was brewing, but I missed all the signs. Perhaps for my own selfish need to fly. Whatever the reason, as the lighting struck and the thunder bellowed, I knew I was in trouble.

Not much further. I willed myself to make it to the forest safely. I could see the land mass in front of me and pushed myself through the increasingly strong winds. However, with the torrential rain blurring my sight and catastrophic gale throwing me off course, it was becoming increasingly difficult to stay on course. Another huge gust made me veer to the right, and I knew I had to try and steer myself back on track, but I could no longer see where I was. Confused, tired and battling the elements, panic set in.

The forest was large and usually easily seen even in difficult weather, but I struggled to identify where I was, and began to think I had gone even further off course than I had realised. I tried to circle back to find my home. However, flying into the wind and not with it proved even more strenuous than I had anticipated. Rain turned to hail, and the large pellets started to pound on my already battered scales, as I lowered myself, knowing I would simply have to find somewhere to hunker down until the storm settled.

Scared and alone, I knew being out in the elements would be dangerous in my human form, but, even more so in my dragon form. I didn't have a choice. I cursed myself once again before coming to a less than delicate stop mid-way up Mount Kalika, where several caves were carved into the mountainside. Anyone and anything could be lurking in the deep open caverns, but being sheltered from the elements would be my only way to survive the night as a human. It was the least dangerous of the two options for me. If I was caught as a dragon, I would be killed immediately.

Shifting, I slowly walked into the cave, trying to make as little noise as possible. I could hear the bats shuffling around one another and darting in and out of the entrance to catch their fill of insects. I didn't sense any other beings near and hoped the howling winds and battering rain hadn't messed with my heightened senses.

When dragons shift and return to their human form, we have on the clothes we wore before the shift. I didn't have much, and my clothes were thin and worn. They had been my mothers. Wet through, shivering beyond control, and exhausted, I curled up into a ball.Thankfully out of the elements, I tried to rest.

Sleep must have come, because bleary eyed and a little warmer, I woke to the sounds of the birds, the sun shining and the warmth of a blanket over me.

*Huh...a blanket...that...*jumping up in surprise, I cleared the sleep from my eyes to find a handsome man sitting close to the entrance of the cave. Had he wanted to kill me, he could have already, but it didn't stop me from being cautious and on guard.

"I'm sorry if I startled you." His deep voice was a little rough. "I didn't mean to scare you, but you looked cold, and for a short while, I wasn't sure if you were going to be okay. I haven't been here long, but you were sleeping, and I didn't want to wake you. Are you okay?" He spoke softly and with kindness.

"I, um, thank you. I got caught in the storm. I'm okay," I replied uneasily.

"My name is Santi." He smiled. "I haven't seen you before. Are you travelling with others? It isn't safe for you to be out here alone even when the weather doesn't turn."

Gazing at him with caution, I tried to guess his angle. Was he genuinely worried for my safety? Checking if I was alone so he could harm me? Or wondering if he should be worried about a group of bandits looking for me. He didn't give me the impression of some of the thieves and scoundrels I had seen crossing the mountain, when I had ventured out of the forest. I had always kept myself hidden, but I had seen enough of them to know this well dressed and clean-cut man didn't fit the type. I gave him the benefit of the doubt while keeping my distance.

"Elsie," I blurted out my name. "My name is Elsie," I added for clarification.

"It's nice to meet you, Elsie. You don't seem the usual type of person I encounter when travelling from the village," he said, explaining he was indeed not an outlaw but a local.

Usually, no good came from the people that dared to try and cross the treacherous terrain. Even the locals of the villages that resided on the mountain. I hadn't met any of them in person, but I had seen the way they carried their bows and arrows, ready to attack anyone they didn't know. I had seen them in action a few times, and it had never ended well. I didn't want to believe this beautiful man to be bad. He seemed kind and he hadn't tried to hurt me. In fact, he had given me a blanket when I was sleeping, and surely, that had to count for something. Plus he was the only human to ever engage in conversation with me.

"My parents died," I announced as if that explained everything. "We didn't go with our village when they left the mountain. We should have. When they died, I didn't know where to go, so I stayed. I have been living out here alone for a while. I am not a fugitive."

It wasn't a complete lie. More truth than not. It at least explained my situation a little better. At least, I hoped it did. I found myself unable to look away from the enigmatic man. He looked empathetic, and I could see he saw the vulnerability and tenderness of my lost soul, as I spoke for the first time aloud about the loss of my parents and my lonely existence.

"I'm so sorry for your loss. You must be an incredible person to have been able to survive out here alone for so long. It is a testament to your strength and courage," he said with reverence. "I have water and food. Would you like to sit and share it with me?" he asked kindly. "I would like to know more about you, Elsie."

Having given each other the benefit of the doubt, I regretted nothing as we spent the next several hours together. Santi told me about his village, the people there and the way they lived off the land. I sat and listened, enjoying every tale he told, wishing I had been able to live a life with laughter, playing, music, people. I told him about my parents and my childhood. A little about life on my own. I tried to stick with simple things that wouldn't create more questions. With each passing minute, I felt the connection I was building with Santi grow and I didn't want our time to end. When he got up to leave, my heart started to race. I didn't want him to leave.

"I wondered, perhaps maybe you would like to come back to my village with me?" His offer surprised me. "I know it seems a little out there, and if you really like living out here alone, I won't even mention I met you, but...if you wanted to stay on the mountain as part of our village, I could speak to Elder Johan. I'm sure if I explained your story, he would welcome you."

My eyes bugged a little at his offer. Having listened to the proposal Santi had made, I couldn't help but feel a little excited at the thought of seeing more of him and being included in a village for the first time of my life. I tried not to get excited or seem too eager. Especially as he would have to speak to the village elder first. If I wasn't accepted, then not only would I have exposed myself to these people, but I would never be able to meet Santi again, either.

The thought of not seeing his bright hazel eyes, jet black hair and smooth brown skin again filled me with a sadness that I felt in my heart. I wasn't sure if I could ever accept never hearing his deep silky voice, or seeing his broad smile and eyes light up when he spoke about the things he loved. Going with him could offer me a daily dose of Santi, but it could also lead me to never seeing him again, and the decision felt like it was crushing me.

The way my emotions seemed to soar and dive when I was with Santi seemed insane. I had to wonder if I craved attention and human contact so much that at the first sight of someone being kind, I had leapt in too quickly. However, I couldn't control the way my heart fluttered every time he glanced my way or brushed his hand over mine. I had never met a man that wasn't my father before, and I couldn't be certain if the way I felt towards him was normal or not. I had no idea if he felt the same way or if my mind had been playing tricks on me; seeing things that weren't there in his looks, his words, and his eyes. *Oh boy, those eyes.*

"Okay," I said before my brain had engaged in the reality of the words I had spoken. "I would like that."

Inwardly, I cursed myself for my inability to think or speak straight around the man, who had somehow captured my heart just a little more than would be deemed normal or accepted, after only hours of being in each other's company. However, the way his smile broadened and his eyes sparkled at my response made my heart flutter even more; if that could have been at all possible. I knew then that whatever happened, Santi would always have a piece of my heart, even if the village didn't accept me and I would never see him again.

Chapter 2
Santi

The storm had been far worse than we had anticipated. As one of Wyrmvern's most respected and skilled warriors, I had been sent out at the break of dawn, at the end of the storm, to check the caves closest to our village that were a known hot spot for those travelling to take a break. Having only checked them hours before the storm kicked off, I had not anticipated anyone foolish enough to have come this high in such treacherous conditions. Especially, as the caves were well hidden, and not an obvious place of shelter to those who didn't know the lands, but I didn't question the order.

To my complete surprise, I saw a young woman curled into a ball, sleeping just out of sight of the entrance to the smaller of the two caves. She wore a thin veil of fabric that hugged her slim but perfectly curved body. Her long, wavy, blonde hair looked like it had golden threads running through it and covered her face. She shivered a little in the cool morning air, and when I got closer, I could see she must have been caught out in the rain, her hair and clothes still a little damp, and she looked like she'd had a rough night.

She had no belongings with her, which was unusual for those travelling such a distance. She didn't seem like a threat, so I delved into my rucksack and took out a small blanket

I had, and put it over her. Not wanting to wake her before she was well rested, I sat at the entrance of the cave and waited. I didn't have to wait long for her to wake, and when I faced her, the startled expression on her face made me quick to speak and let her know I wasn't going to harm her. She replied in almost a whisper with somewhat of an explanation of being caught in the storm, but her unease radiated from her in waves.

Her eyes were the colour of liquid amber with a hint of green to their outer edges. I had never seen eyes quite as unique or beautiful before in my entire twenty-seven years. She looked wary of me, and my heart skipped a beat at the thought she may think I wished her harm. She was clearly considering what course of action to take, and I hoped beyond hope that she wouldn't try and fight me. I didn't want to hurt her, but my orders were clear, and I took my job seriously. Eliminate all threats.

Whenever possible, we tried to help those that came this far up the mountain. If they had made it this far to the crest of the mountain, then they surely deserved a medal and could likely manage well in our village. However, many didn't want to be helped, or saw us as another threat. Encounters like that rarely ended well. I wasn't proud of how many people had died at my hands, but I was proud of keeping my village safe from the threat of the bandits that tried to pillage us.

Still unsure quite how she came to be here, I gave her my name and pushed a little further in questioning her. I hoped to gain some information about the intriguing young woman while not scaring her off. Her pale skin seemed to lack lustre, perhaps from malnutrition, lack of sunlight, dehydration or maybe all three, but it didn't take away from her beauty. I struggled to tear my eyes away from her and worried she would think me some kind of lech. I forced myself to move and look away. When I did, she spoke, and I almost laughed as she barked out her name in response.

Turning to face her, her cheeks pinked just a fraction. I couldn't hide the smile that took over my face. Elsie. '*A beautiful name for a beautiful woman,*' I thought to myself, careful not to repeat the words aloud. For a woman alone, slight in figure and average in stature, she had a strong aura, but she continued to eye me warily and with great apprehension. Wanting to put her a little more at ease, I tried to reassure her that I didn't see her as a threat, and I simply wanted to make sure she didn't see me as one, so we could move forward.

When she blurted out about her parents dying with more confidence than she had said anything else thus far, I found myself both further fascinated by her and equally wanting to comfort and protect her, even though, having told me she had survived on the mountain alone for years, I had no doubt she could look after herself and didn't need my protection. Every morsel of information she gave me had me desperate to know more about her. Anything she would give me. I had never found myself quite so enamoured by another person before. No other woman had caught my interest in that way before.

For years it had been expected that I would settle down and marry, have children and all that jazz. However, I had simply never found anyone I had wanted that with. Living in the village made it much harder. Had I not met anyone I was willing to marry in Wyrmvern, then I was unlikely to meet anyone at all. Not unless I left the village. Some folks did and returned to the village or set up home elsewhere. I had no intention of doing either.

Wyrmvern wasn't only my home, but my livelihood. I belonged. I had always felt it was my destiny and duty to stay. Unfortunately, there were many single women vying for my attention and many parents, mine included, tried to set me up. As a bachelor and respected warrior, apparently I was deemed a catch. I had never seen myself as anything special, but many of my friends and other warriors teased me about being too good looking for my own good. I didn't see it, yet they continued to jest.

Elsie was like no other. I simply needed to know more about her, and when she agreed to sit and chat with me, as we shared some water and food, I found myself internally fist pumping the air, like I had won gold. She was so easy to talk to. I chatted for far too long about my boring life, yet she seemed completely engaged, listening intently as if hanging onto my every word. I wanted to know more about her, and when I asked questions in return, she always responded openly, if somewhat guarded.

I could hardly be surprised that she regarded me with caution. I was much larger than her, a warrior, and had been known to intimidate people, but I hoped that wasn't the case with her. From what I knew, she had led a very lonely existence since her parents died, and I could see the sadness etched deep in her soul. I wanted her to feel alive again, to laugh, make friends and be happy. Maybe, even I could do those things for her. I had never wanted to make someone laugh and be happier, more, than I did Elsie in that moment.

It seemed ridiculous that after only a few hours I felt so connected and in need of this woman's company. Despite this, I found words leaving my lips inviting her to come to the village and stay, just so I could be near her. Had she known the real reason, she probably would have run a country mile, but even should she just consider it, I would take that as a win. I would worry about Elder Johan if she actually said yes.

"Okay," she responded, looking like she hadn't expected that word to escape her own lips. She took a deep breath and with more confidence, added, "I would like that."

Unable to hide my sheer delight at her agreeing to come, it took all my strength not to grab her and pull her into my arms. I didn't need to scare her away after she had just agreed to come to the village. My mind felt like a squirrel on speed, thinking ten thousand things at once; darting in different directions before starting something new. I would see her every day, be near her, get to know her. She would need somewhere to stay, a job, clothes. We would need Elder Johan to agree to her staying of course, but he would. He had to. It was all I could do not to jump with excitement on the spot.

Reigning myself in and trying not to act like a child with a new toy, I took some slow, steady breaths to try and regulate my insanely overactive brain. This entire situation was completely new to me. Not only did I have no control over it, but I was struggling to maintain any decorum. She had done nothing to make me feel like she even remotely liked me in any other way than gratitude. I couldn't even consider we were friends yet. So, why did I feel like my heart would break into a thousand pieces if she didn't choose me to be hers, and chose another instead?

I suddenly found myself inwardly panicking about all the single men at the village, who would most likely take no time at all trying to court Elsie. She was stunning, yes, but also the most enigmatic woman I had ever encountered. While I had no claim on her; absolutely no right to stop her from seeing whomever she pleased, the thought made my stomach curdle, and I knew then I was in trouble.

Never had I felt possessive of anything or anyone. I didn't even know I had a possessive bone in my body. However, there was no mistaking it at that moment. I couldn't be certain I wouldn't try and kill a man, even a friend, should they make an advance at her. Taking her to the village could very well be a huge mistake, and I would only have myself to blame, yet I couldn't go back on my word. Or wouldn't.

Finding myself incredibly close to her as we walked and talked for the next hour, to the crest of Mount Kalika and eventually on to Wyrmvern to meet Elder Johan. I began to wonder if the slight blush to her cheeks, extended glances and longing in her eyes were all in my head. Part of me was desperate to ask her if she felt the same strange and intense connection between us, but what if my mind had been playing tricks on me and I embarrassed myself.

Once or twice, I tried to test the waters and find out if she would be willing to get to know me better and spend more time with me. However, either she was being coy, or I wasn't being blunt enough. Perhaps both were true because her answers were vague, and I found myself in no better understanding whether she wanted me the way I wanted her.

It could be called nothing less than shameless, the way my mind wandered and my body responded to her. We hadn't even so much as shaken hands or touched each other, yet, she made me go weak at the knees.

I despised men who leered over women and treated them less than the equal and fellow humans that they were. And, while I neither leered nor thought Elsie anything less than my equal, I had still fallen into the trap of lusting over her and wanting more of her mind, body and soul. By the time we reached the village gates, my mouth felt dry, my palms were sweaty, and my dick ached.

Leto and Iago were manning the gates, with watchmen in the towers that surrounded the ten-foot wooden panels topped with metal spikes and barbed wire that encased Wyrmvern. Anyone who even attempted to breach the village would have to have a death wish. No army was coming this far up a mountain to pillage a village they had little inside knowledge about. It would be risky not only for their lives but for the possibility of walking away empty-handed. For all they knew, we had nothing of value worth their trouble. It was far too risky. However, bandits often found one another and once Elder Johan took his position, he increased security and added the watchtowers, metal spikes and barbed wire to the panelling. It was a move we were all happy about, more notably the woman and children, who could walk freely around the village knowing they were safe.

Both Iago and Leto nodded when they saw me. They gave Elsie a curious glance that lasted far longer than I liked, but said nothing until they gave the command to open the gate and allow us through. When inside the gates, I watched Elsie's face with my own curiosity.

"Was your village like this?" I asked, having few details of the place she once called home. "What did you say it was called?"

"Oh, I didn't." She smiled, her eyes wide with wonder and excitement. "I've never seen anything quite like this place," she said in awe. "It's beautiful."

My intention had been to take her directly to Elder Johan, but Elsie had other ideas. She wandered off towards the wild grasses and mountain flowers that grew on the edges of the wooden wall. She inhaled their scent, touching the flowers and smiling so brightly I didn't want to drag her away just yet. We had always allowed the natural beauty of the wild growth to remain along the wall borders. It fed the few insects and birds that ventured this high up the mountain, all while softening the harshness of the wooden panels that kept us enclosed. We were safe but confined, nevertheless.

The children also painted murals on the walls in bright colours to keep it cheerful and less intimidating from the inside. It stopped them from seeing it as scary and allowed them to have some fun. The houses were made from wood and stone, mainly from the mountain. Occasionally, we would have supply runs, but these could take weeks, sometimes months, and were dangerous. However simple the buildings were, they were well insulated, had running water and a hearth with plenty of firewood for cooking and warmth.

Most of the homes had small gardens, but in the centre of the village was a large open space with a good-sized playground in one corner, and enough room for older kids to play outdoor sports, families to picnic and friends to enjoy good conversation away from the confinements of their homes. The space was used by everyone. I thought Elsie would love the communal area the most, but before I took her to see it, I steered her away from walking through the houses and the eager prying eyes of the villagers, straight to Elder Johan's home.

When we arrived, I could feel the intense nervous energy flow through Elsie, like a tidal wave. I wanted to reassure her that he was a fair man and once he knew her story he would welcome her with open arms, but before I had the chance, the door opened and Elder Johan was standing in front of us; his eyes sweeping over us both with great interest in them.

"Santi, you have brought a guest," he said keenly. "Please, come in."

He took us through to his meeting room, and I offered Elsie a seat. Once she was seated, Elder Johan and I took our places. I spoke, explaining to Elder Johan Elsie's situation, and while he didn't once interrupt me, his eyes didn't venture from glaring at Elsie with intense curiosity. I knew he had questions about her. Questions I couldn't answer, because I held them myself. She had not been overly open about her former life; avoiding to answer even the most basic of things, and for the first time since I met her, I felt worried.

Chapter 3
Elsie

Sitting in Elder Johan's home, under his powerful glare, I found myself feeling under intense scrutiny. Did he already know my secret? I had no idea what I had been thinking about, agreeing to come to this place. Well, in truth, I did. Santi. His lush brown skin, thick black hair, hazel eyes that sparkled in the light. He was handsome, yes, but the strong connection I felt towards him found me not wanting to part from him, in fear of never seeing him again. Just the thought made me shudder with angst.

None of that comforted me while I worried about how I would explain the truth about me, should Elder Johan know. Equally, I couldn't be remotely certain that pretending to be a human, and never letting my dragon out would be something I could do. A myriad of thoughts rushed through my mind, while Elder Johan and Santi continued to chat as if I wasn't present.

I had always wanted to settle down and have children, but how would I ever explain to Santi that our child or children would be a hybrid half breed that no one could ever know about. Children. Santi. What on earth had I been thinking? He hadn't even said he liked me, never mind anything more. He simply offered an olive branch because it was his duty.

"Miss Elsie?" Elder Johan's voice cut through my thoughts.

"Sorry, yes, your honour," I replied, not in the least bit sure what to call him or what he had said.

"Elder Johan is fine, Elise. I am not a judge." He laughed lightly, making me feel a little more at ease. "I simply asked if you had any papers with you? We offer solace to most, but should you have committed a heinous crime, then we would have to reconsider and discuss with the villagers. It is their home and their safety after all." He smiled softly, but there was a hidden curiosity behind his eyes.

"Oh. Right. No, I don't have papers. I haven't committed a crime. I lived on the mountain with my parents my entire life. I don't know any differently," I explained.

Far simpler to tell as much of the truth as possible. I knew managing on my own in such harsh conditions would raise questions, but these questions were far easier to answer than any that would involve sharing that I was in fact a beast.

"Santi says your parents passed away some time ago, having decided to stay on the mountain when your village left it. You have lived on your own since then," he stated. "What happened? If you don't mind me asking."

"Bandits. They kept me well hidden. I was old enough to listen when they told me to hide but too young to help. I am not proud of my cowardice," I admitted.

"Not at all cowardly. Smart and brave, I would say," Santi soothed.

"Outlaws had never come our way before. We were ill prepared." I sighed.

"And you survived alone all this time?" he pushed. "How many years have you lived alone?"

"Eight years," I lied.

It had actually been seven, but I didn't want him to put two and two together had he and his men been the ones to kill my parents. Had Santi been one of the warriors that helped? It hadn't crossed my mind before, but he was older than me by at least 5 years. He would have been a warrior then. I didn't even know if they had been killed by humans. If they had, then the secret of dragons existing, or at least my parents' existence, wasn't such a secret after all.

"Hmmmm. Eight years you say?" he pushed.

"Yes."

"That's a long time to survive out there alone for anyone. Never mind a young woman." He eyed me with suspicion.

"My parents taught me well. I am a capable hunter, cook and warrior," I said with a little more sass than intended.

He looked at me, irritated at my retort. As I shifted uncomfortably in my seat, Santi looked between us, mildly curious about the line of questioning. Elder Johan clearly had his own opinion and thoughts, on me and my past. Surely, he didn't know I was a dragon. How could he possibly know that? Yet the more he interrogated me, the more uncomfortable and uncertain I became.

"Age?" he barked, looking down at a clipboard, which had some papers attached, that he had begun to scribble on.

"Twenty-three," I responded.

"Good. Well, Santi will take you to your allocated home. It is only small, but I'm sure more than you have had before, so it should be comfortable for you. We will have some supplies brought to your accommodation, and someone will arrive first thing in the morning to show you around the village and let you know what jobs would be available for you to do to earn your keep. It is how it works here," he said, a little less agitation in his tone.

Smiling with as much enthusiasm as I could muster under the man's continuous stare, I tried not to seem unappreciative. After all, he was right, I had never had anything like the comfort he was offering me, and if he was just cautious for the sake of his people, then he had every right to be. I wasn't an open book, and he would be taking a chance on me.

Santi escorted me out of Elder Johan's home and back out into the fresh village air. Cool and crisp, being higher up the mountain, the breeze had a sharper edge to it than I was used to, having been sheltered by the thick forest canopy. I shivered, and he offered me his jacket. I took it and thanked him, and when we were a short distance from the Elder's home, he paused.

"Elsie, I am sorry about your reception. Elder Johan can be...cautious," he said quietly.

"He has every right to be." I placated.

"Yes, but even so, he was quite harsh. It just takes him a little time to warm up to people," he said apologetically.

"I understand. He really knows nothing about me." I smiled softly, avoiding his eyes.

Santi didn't really know anything about me either. Lying to him had begun to feel like a burden. I wanted to tell him, but I knew deep down I couldn't weigh him down with my secret. He would feel obligated to tell Elder Johan, and I couldn't risk it. I planned to keep my head down, work hard and earn my place in the village, like everyone else.

The sun was beginning to set by the time we reached the small cottage that would become my home. Santi stood on the doorstep, allowing me to open the door and go inside to look around my new residence. I was in awe of the place, having never had the option to live in such a secure and homely environment. As I stepped inside and took in my surroundings, Santi remained on the doorstep.

"Aren't you coming in?" I asked, curious as to why he hadn't followed me inside.

"Only if I am invited." He smiled sweetly. "You are a single woman, Elsie, and I am a single man. It would be quite unethical of me to assume you would want me in your home."

"Oh." My mouth went dry. I hadn't even considered that. "I'm sorry, I didn't know; please, come inside," I said, hoping my lack of understanding of the village ways wouldn't offend him.

"It's quite alright, Elsie. Thank you for allowing me to share this moment with you. What do you think of the place?" he asked.

"I've never been blessed with such stability," I admitted. "There isn't anyone else I would want to share this with than you," I said softly.

My stomach felt jittery, as if a party of fireflies were dancing in my belly. The more time I spent with Santi, the more I felt a connection between us. His eyes lingered on me a little longer than they had before, and when I caught his eye, he looked away and cleared his throat. Having had very minimal human contact, I couldn't be certain if he felt something for me or if he was simply doing his duty. I wanted to ask, but I wasn't brave enough. I didn't want to ruin our friendship over a misunderstanding on my first night.

"Well," he said gruffly, "then I am glad I am here with you." He swallowed hard and averted his gaze once again.

"Would you like a drink?" I asked, looking through all the cupboards in the small but perfectly efficient kitchen to keep myself busy.

"That would be lovely," he said, a mild stiffness in his tone.

The air between us had somehow become awkward, and I couldn't be certain when it had changed from the open friendship we had established to this more uncomfortable situation. I managed to find two glasses and poured us both a glass of water. Having running water alone was a novelty for me, but I tried not to get over excited about the things I was sure the villagers took for granted. I didn't want to seem foolish. Not in front of Santi, anyway. Handing him a glass, I sat with my own, and he followed suit.

"Is something wrong?" I finally asked after a few long minutes of silence.

"Wrong?" he questioned. "No, what makes you think that?" he asked, abashed.

"You seem uncomfortable. Did I do something to make you feel uncomfortable?" I asked, worried.

"Not at all." He sighed, his cheeks flushing with a hint of colour that hadn't been there before. "I, um, I was just thinking about tomorrow. I should prepare you. You will be introduced to the rest of the village people in a welcome ceremony in the morning. It will happen before you are shown around the village and choose a job," he stated.

"Oh. Right." I took a sip of my water, shifting uncomfortably in my seat. "I hadn't realised I would be introduced in front of the entire village. Not like that anyway. I just thought I would get a job and meet people as I went about my day."

"The villagers will be talking the moment they realise you are here. We are not used to visitors and rarely have newcomers. It sounds scary, but it is better this way. Less gossip and the people will see you are not a threat." His small and uncertain smile made my heart skip a beat. "There will be many eligible men who will vie for your attention. We don't have many single women of age," he continued, sounding rational. "You may not be interested in finding a partner, but if you are, you will have plenty of choices."

"Choices. Sure," I said, trying to hide my disappointment.

The more time I spent with Santi, I knew my heart was slowly becoming his. I didn't want choices. It seemed ridiculous having only known him for such a short time, but my parents knew they were destined to be with one another the moment they met each other. Somehow, I knew that was how I felt about Santi. However, he was offering me options, other men. He told me his role as lead warrior meant he didn't have time to settle down, and as much as it pained me to let him go, I knew I had to.

"Well, if it's all the same to them, I am not looking for choices. I would like to earn my keep, fit in with village life and keep to myself." My voice cracked a little at the loss of the man I didn't even know I wanted until only moments ago.

"Very well," he said, sounding disappointed.

"Is that why you brought me here?" I snapped angrily as I stood from my seated position.

The feeling of incredible rage embodied me at the thought he only wanted me to join the village because I was an eligible female for one of the single men. I shuddered at the thought, feeling sick to my stomach.

"What?" Santi sounded confused. "What do you mean?"

"You wanted me here to palm me off with one of your single men?" I pushed; the upset was no longer hidden from my tone.

"Oh, Elsie. No!" He exclaimed. "No! I just wanted you to be aware. I…I like you, and I did hope you may like me too. I was scared to say anything because I didn't want you to feel like you…" He sighed. "I am not very good at this. I am making everything worse. I just didn't want you to feel like you had to say you liked me too. Especially as you don't really know me, or anyone else. But if I didn't tell you, then you would never know and it all came out wrong, and…" He slumped back into his chair, a look of utter defeat in his eyes.

"Santi," I said softly, "I don't want choices because I want you. I feel a connection between us that grows stronger every second we are together. I can't explain it. It just feels like…"

"We were meant to be together," he said quietly, hopeful.

"Exactly." I smiled.

Reaching my hands across the table to meet his, he took them firmly. Slowly lifting them to meet his lips, he kissed them one at a time. Relief seemed to flow through him as his body relaxed. I allowed myself a moment to drink in the man who I had just admitted my feelings for. As rushed and strange as these feelings were, they had been reciprocated, and I had never felt more at peace. I knew I would have to tell him my secret, having declared our intentions to one another, but I couldn't do it then.

The little my parents told me about the history of dragons in this realm did little to reassure me in any way that I would be seen as anything other than a threat. Even if they did know me in my human form. Dragons were believed to have been banished and extinct from these parts a long time ago. Maimed, captured, tortured and killed without ever being given the opportunity to show the good in themselves. Perhaps long ago their battle for survival didn't allow for that, but times had changed, and I wasn't like that. I just couldn't be certain the village, or Santi, would give me the option to prove it.

After all, my parents had gone out one night to hunt and never came home. It could have been a freak accident, but something deep in my soul told me that wasn't the case, but that someone knew dragons still existed, and while Santi had never mentioned specifically what the other threats that he protected his people from. I had a feeling that dragons were amongst the *wild animals* that he had been trained to defend the village against.

Allowing myself to have just that moment may have been selfish; in fact, I knew it was. Yet I couldn't stop myself from having it. Scared my truth would see him banishing me from his life, I couldn't bear the thought of telling him. I knew I needed to have more faith in him, but it was all so new, and I had never had anything of my own. I wasn't ready to lose him before I had the chance to really have him. If he knew what I was and believed me to be a dangerous beast, something he had sworn to protect his people from, it would all be over before it had really begun.

As the continual thoughts of my predicament swirled around my head, I wondered if I should confess before anything further happened between us, but I didn't have time to overthink the situation as he stood up, swiftly moving himself around the small table and pulling me into his arms. As his face inched closer to mine, my breath hitched. He waited for a moment to allow me to back away, but I couldn't. I was frozen to the spot, wanting nothing more than for him to kiss me.

Taking my unmoving stance as the green light that it was, he leant in and brushed his lips across mine, and I sunk into the kiss as sparks between us lit me on fire. Even if I had wanted to move away from him after that, I knew I wouldn't be able to. My feelings for him had gone from tentative but wanting to certain and desperately needing.

Chapter 4
Santi

The strangest sense of feeling, like I had known Elsie my entire life, had been waiting for her, yet had no idea who she really was or that she even existed, embodied me. Knowing she felt the same way sent relief flowing through my veins, and I couldn't stop my feet from moving towards her, desperate to have her in my arms, to hold her, kiss her.

Many marriages in our village happened out of convenience, sometimes lifelong friendships, occasionally love, but I had never known anyone to fall for someone so instantaneously as I had done for Elsie. I couldn't put my finger on what it was about her, but she was everything I didn't know I needed or wanted in my life.

Pressing my lips gently to hers, the affirmation of our bond seemed to solidify. I felt a surge of electricity pulse through me, blazing heat igniting a passion I didn't even know possible. Elsie deepened the kiss, taking some control. Her actions showed me she wanted this as much as I did. I liked that she had the confidence of knowing what she wanted, and that what she wanted was me.

She tugged gently on my lower lip with her teeth, and a guttural groan escaped my lips at the quiet and assertive dominance she showed. I had never felt passion and desire quite like it. As soon as my lips parted, her tongue swiped the inside of my mouth, and I had trouble believing she had never done this before. We hadn't discussed it, but having spent her entire adult life in solitude on the mountain side suggested it.

Either way, I didn't care. Whatever her past may have been, Elsie chose me. Our tongues danced in each other's mouths, exploring the unknown and becoming familiar with one another. My hands encased her, moving of their own accord up and down her back and in her soft golden waves of hair; she clung around my neck, as if willing me to stay. I had no intention of leaving. Eventually, our lips parted, our breaths heavy and panting, our lips swollen and pink.

"Santi," Elsie said in barely a whisper.

"Elsie," I responded equally breathlessly.

"Stay with me," she asked, her nerves evident.

"Are you sure?" I asked, not entirely certain what she was asking of me but prepared to give her whatever she wanted or needed.

"I am. Are you...allowed?" she asked, knowing there were many rules within the village she had yet to be familiar with.

"I am not on duty tonight," I stated. "There are no steadfast rules, but it wouldn't look good if I was seen sneaking out of here in the morning before we have had a chance to declare our status to the village. The older generation can be...judgemental." I picked my words cautiously.

"So, what is our status, Santi?" she asked, her large amber eyes swirling with hope.

"That if you will have me, Elsie, I am yours. After meeting you, I could never want anyone else," I replied truthfully.

"Then, you are mine and I am yours." She smiled broadly, lighting up her entire face. "We will live happily ever after." She grinned.

"And have lots of children to fill our lives with more love and laughter than we can possibly imagine," I added, never having felt so content.

She didn't respond to that, not the way I thought she would. All the women in the village had dreams of settling down, having children, the whole nine yards. Heck, even I wanted that, although I never thought I would. Yet, instead of looking excited about the prospect, she simply smiled, nodded and kissed me sweetly on the lips before taking my hand and finding the bedroom in her cottage.

Once inside the small but practical room, Elsie looked between the bed and me. She looked nervous, although I could tell she was trying not to. Her large, doe eyes looked up to mine, and I tried to give her a reassuring look. I could see her visibly relax, and she took my mouth with hers once again. Her arms snaked around my neck, and I lifted her up from the base of her ass, making her squeal in delight.

She peppered kisses over my face as she looked down at me from the new position she was in, and I spun her around and gently laid her on the bed. The flimsy dress she wore had ridden up her lithe legs, showing more of her milky soft skin, not a blemish on it. I licked my lips in anticipation, and the heat in her eyes had me crawling up the bed needing to taste her mouth again.

"Let me pleasure you, Elsie. I want to taste you," I growled.

"You are," she said between breaths.

"Down there," I said, keeping my eyes firmly on hers but moving my fingers to the edge of her knickers.

"Uh..." Her eyes widened a fraction before she bit her lip and nodded. "Okay."

Making my way back to the edge of the bed, I pulled her knickers down and dropped them on the floor, exposing her glistening slick folds. I removed my shirt so she wasn't the only one half dressed and licked my lips in anticipation of making Elsie come apart with my tongue. Getting into position, I refused to look away from her mesmerising eyes, not wanting to miss a single moment of her coming undone.

Her soft moans encouraged me to know when she liked the way my tongue moved, flicked and licked her sensitive areas, but when she gripped the sheets and her legs began to shake, I knew I was getting her closer. Concentrating on the bundle of nerves that had her crying out in pleasure, I inserted a finger, which had her bucking her hips. Adding another and moving them slowly in and out of her hole, her involuntary movements became more erratic.

"More. Please." She begged. "Faster." She panted, cheeks flushed, eyes rolling to the back of her head.

I did exactly as she asked, and only a moment later, she was shuddering with her release as she cried out in pleasure. Satisfied and sated, she remained in position, and I crawled up her body and lightly kissed her mouth. My rock-hard dick brushed against her bare belly, her dress having ridden all the way up to just below her breasts. Her cheeks were flushed, and her skin had a soft glow. She kissed me back; I was in heaven with my angel, my Elsie.

Rolling off her, I lay on my side, half sitting up on my elbow, so I could look at her. I could listen to her say my name forever. She wriggled from her position to sit up, resting her back against the headboard, and lightly ruffled my messy black hair. She gently pushed me backwards so I was lying flat on the bed and straddled me, her long hair falling in front of her, so it tickled my chest.

"Santi," she said softly, "I want you to see all of me. I want you to have all of me. I never want this night to end."

She took the hem of her dress in her hands and pulled it over her head, moving her hair so it fell down her back, exposing her naked self and perfect pert breasts. I could feel my heart rate quicken, the sight of her on top of me almost more than I could take. My dick strained against my trousers, and she squirmed on it when she felt it twitch, doing nothing to help my predicament.

"I want that as well, Elsie. I want you. Forever." I had never wanted anything more.

She slid down my legs, reaching down to unbuckle my trousers, and with a little help from me, took them off. My cock sprang to attention. Her eyes widened and looked at it in both awe and trepidation. I laughed a little at her reaction, and she looked at me with a small pout.

"It won't bite you." I chuckled.

"No?" She teased, brows raised in mock shock. "It might hurt though," she said more seriously.

"We can take it slow, beautiful, and if you want to stop–"

"I won't want to stop," she stated firmly.

She moved her body back up mine so she was sitting on me, my dick nestled between her folds. She rubbed herself back and forth gently as we both revelled in the feeling of our naked bodies moving against one another. She slowly increased the pace, and I began to move my hips beneath her, no longer able to keep still.

My hands reached up to cup her breasts; the perfect handful. She gripped onto my hands and encouraged me to knead them, using the leverage of my firm grip to push herself back and forth. It felt so fucking good, and I wasn't even inside her yet. My cock was leaking pre-come, and mixed with Elsie's own juices; we were a slippery mess. She was wet and ready, and I knew I had to take control, or I wouldn't last.

"Lift yourself, beautiful, and then slowly lower yourself onto me. You are in control, take all the time you need," I said gruffly. "Unless you want to switch places?" I offered.

"No. Like this. This is good." She panted.

Elsie did as I had instructed, and I wrapped one of my hands around my dick to keep it steady and in position. As she painstakingly lowered herself onto me, I let go, returning my hand to where it had been. She bit her lip, and a slight glimmer of pain crossed her face as she stilled. Once it had vanished, she sunk the rest of herself down on me, taking me all in.

"Holy fuck, you feel good." I groaned out in satisfaction.

"Oh God, Santi." She looked down at me, the green in her eyes seemingly overtaking the previous amber. "You feel so good," she cried out.

Moving her hips back and forth, she began to ride me like she owned me. She did. I would never belong to anyone else. Gripping onto her hips, my hands moved with the rhythm of her. I moved myself beneath her, matching her pace until she began to slow. The tell-tale sign of her flushed cheeks, eyes rolling and gentle moans told me she was close. I took over from her, moving her hips in the same rhythmic movement she had been.

Quickening the pace just a fraction, I knew I wouldn't be far behind her in my own release, but I wanted her to get there first. After a few more deep thrusts, she let go of her orgasm, and I allowed myself to follow quickly afterwards. She collapsed on top of me, her breathing erratic and shallow, just as mine was. When she had regained her composure, she kissed me lightly on the forehead.

"That was amazing," she whispered. "You are amazing."

"I was just thinking the same about you, princess. You came into my life like a whirlwind, and I can't thank my lucky stars enough that you are here to stay. Tomorrow, we will declare our relationship to the village," I said, exhilarated. "I can't wait to tell everyone how incredible you are."

"Until then,"–she kissed my cheek–"let's clean up and cuddle until you must go. I want as much time with you as possible before tomorrow."

We did exactly that, and I held her in my arms until she fell soundly asleep. As soon as I knew she was out for the count, I slipped myself from the bed, got myself dressed and kissed her softly on her forehead. I knew she couldn't hear me, but I promised to see her in a few hours when she was introduced to the village, and then left her room, making my way back to my own home.

I knew I had to sleep. I had training and duties in the day and my shift in the tower later in the evening. However, it was difficult to settle with the rerun of images giving me a blow-by-blow reconstruction of my night with Elsie. Perfect in every way, I couldn't wait to announce our relationship and be a proper couple. Having Elsie made me want to shout from the rooftops.

Eventually, I drifted off, but all too soon my alarm rang to tell me it was time to get up. I groaned as I dragged myself out of bed. I would be meeting Elsie a few hours after breakfast at the village meeting point. First, I had training, and she had a meeting to discuss which job she would like to take on. Taking myself straight to the training ground, I discovered three of my top men were missing and I knew they weren't on duty.

"Where are Brindley, Harrington and Piper?" I barked.

Silence.

"Fine." I huffed. "For not knowing, you can all do an extra half hour of combat training, and that doesn't give you permission to be late for the village meeting at 9 a.m."

Groans filled the air, but no one outwardly spoke their annoyance.

When the training session had come to an end, we all left to go to our homes to clean up before the meeting. The training grounds were on the other side of the village to where Elsie's place was situated, so I had no good reason to walk past and check in on her, even though I really wanted to. Instead, I forced myself to wait.

Just before nine, the village meeting point brimmed with people, chatter and murmurers of what Elder Johan would say. I smiled to myself knowingly. I couldn't wait for Elsie's introduction to everyone. I manoeuvred myself as close to the front of the stage as possible, knowing Elder Johan would want me to join them on stage. Then I would be able to share our news. My heart pounded with excitement and nerves as he walked onto the stage and began to speak.

"Thank you all for attending the meeting this morning." His booming voice echoed around the open space. "I know you all have work to do, so I won't keep you long."

As he spoke, my eyes darted around to find Elsie, but I couldn't see her anywhere. I didn't understand; she should have been right there for Elder Johan to bring onto the stage to introduce her. Elder Johan continued, but I was barely listening anymore as I continued to search for any sign of where she could be.

"Last night we had a very close call with an intruder who would have put our entire village at risk. This was not simply a near miss of a bandit breaking in, but had the perpetrator not been reprimanded and dealt with, our entire village could have been destroyed and pillaged. We were very lucky to have been able to capture the culprit, and we have our warriors to thank for that. I would like to personally thank Santi, Brindley, Harrington and Piper. Please come to the stage so we can all give you the praise you deserve for keeping us safe once again."

My feet moved of their own accord. People were patting my back, cheering, and clapping as I passed them. I had no idea what Johan was talking about. What intruder? I hadn't been on duty last night, and confusion enveloped me as I tried to understand why, as head warrior, I had no idea what was going on when Brindley, Harrington and Piper seemed to be completely in the loop. Still, despite my perplexity, I couldn't help but continue to scan the crowd and the back of the stage for any sign of Elsie.

Noise continued to fill the air as we were treated like heroes, and while Elder Johan said nothing more about the incident, he kept looking at me, a shifty, unnerving look in his eyes. I waited for the crowd to settle, hoping that he would ask Brindley, Harrington and Piper to leave the stage so that he and I could get on with introducing Elsie to the villagers. However, my stomach dropped as the people went quiet and the introduction never came.

"Thank you all for your time, you may go on with enjoying your day with the knowledge we are safe from threat, and your warriors will always keep you that way," he said, ending the meeting.

He turned his back to me to leave the stage with Brindley, Harrington and Piper following him one by one. Assuming that I too should follow, I did. Yet I knew not for the same reasons as the other three men. They had been prepared for this meeting. I had not. Elder Johan and my men would need to tell me what the hell that had been about, and I certainly intended to find out, but I felt sick with the thought that I had refused to infiltrate my mind only minutes earlier.

Elsie wasn't anywhere to be seen, and Elder Johan had no intention of introducing her to the village, and that only meant one thing. She had to have had something to do with what was going on. It made no sense, and I feared that whatever Elder Johan, Brindley, Harrington and Piper had done wasn't going to sit well with me. My fear turned to anger and panic as I followed them in silence to the secret underground prison block that only the few elite, trusted warriors and senior members of the village knew about.

Chapter 5
Elsie

Being in Santi's arms made me feel safe. I had never felt so complete. Yet, I knew I should have told him about what I really was. Guilt coursed through me as I felt him get out of bed and leave to return to his own home. I should have stopped him, told him the truth, before he announced to the entire village we were together. Give him a chance to back out.

Only, in the heat of the moment, after he had told me he wanted us to be together forever, I had imprinted on him, and I knew if he left me, it would hurt beyond anything I could possibly have imagined. Yet, it hadn't been that that stopped me, as much as the thought of him leaving me crushed my soul, led to me keeping quiet and pretending to be asleep as he kissed me softly on my forehead and whispered in my ear, he would see me soon.

My conflicting feelings stopped me from even trying to go back to sleep. It made my heart flutter with excitement, but the fear of telling him the truth and the guilt for allowing it to go so far without being honest was eating me alive. With my conscience screaming at me and taking me in a thousand directions, I failed to hear the footsteps that inched their way towards my bedroom door.

When the door crashed open and three burly men came rushing towards me, I shrieked out in confusion and panic. Still naked, I grabbed the sheets and pulled them close to my chest, fearful of what they would do to me, not understanding why they were in my room. Elder Johan had agreed to my stay; in only a few hours, I would be officially a member of the village, and yet these men thought they could just enter my home and do what? I was too scared to think that far ahead.

"Please don't..." I began, uncertain of what I was about to beg them not to do.

"Shut up, beast." One of the men growled.

"Behave, and we won't hurt you," another said gruffly.

"Behave?" I looked up in uncertainty. "Beast..." I whispered, suddenly realising they knew my truth.

My body stiffened, and I could feel the colour draining from my face. I felt sick, and panic rose in me, bile threatening its way up my throat. *Had Santi known all along? Had this been a ruse to get me to the village and take my life? I had let him...we had...I had imprinted on him!* I couldn't think straight, as the men manhandled me, taping my mouth shut and binding my wrists and ankles. One of the men threw me over his shoulder, my hair trailing down his back, having not even allowed me the decency to dress.

With my bare ass in the air, one of the men slapped it, and the tears started to slowly roll down my cheeks before they came freely, no longer able to hold them back. One man led with me in the middle flung over another, and the third man kept up the rear, as I was removed from the house that I knew had never been mine. Elder Johan somehow knew who I was all along and had planned this the moment I left his home. The thought of Santi having anything to do with this made my tears flow ever quicker.

The sky, still dark despite the early hour, made for an awkward walk. I could see clearly, night vision being something I had been blessed with, but these men, clearly human, stumbled through the darkness. The cold air of the winter morning, fresher than further down the mountain, whipped and licked around my naked skin and caused goosebumps to appear on my pinkening skin. I felt completely humiliated.

I couldn't see much from my position, but when the man holding me set me down, I could see we had reached a small building on the outskirts of the village, much further away from the rest of the village. I could see it looked run down. It was a small space with nothing in it but some tattered curtains, which were closed, and a dusty old rug on the floor. The man who had walked in front, the one who slapped me on the ass, looked me up and down with a sly grin on his face. Another surge of bile tickled the back of my throat.

"Pack it in, Piper. Elder Johan said not to touch her, and you already did that!" the man who carried me barked at his friend.

"Your hands have been all over her naked body," he scoffed back. "All's fair–"

"Enough. I had to carry her, dipshit. She wasn't going to be able to walk with how tight Brindley tied her ankles together." He sounded increasingly annoyed.

As he spoke, the burn on my wrists and ankles became the focus of my attention. I had hardly noticed earlier with the fear and shock that had seated itself so deeply into my soul. However, knowing they had orders not to touch me had strangely made me a little less nervous in the moment, and the deep stinging pain of the ropes had become the forefront of my discomfort.

It crossed my mind to shift, break free from the bonds and fly away, but the thought of Santi stopped me. The time we spent together felt real and honest. A raw and strangely magnetic connection between us that neither one of us wanted to deny ourselves of. He sounded sincere, and I didn't think someone like him could be that good of an actor. If it had all been a lie, then he was a bloody good liar.

Maybe, if I could prove I wasn't a threat and could be an asset to their village, they would give me a chance to stay. If Santi explained our situation, Elder Johan would know I wouldn't be a threat to the village people and allow us to be together. If not, my life without Santi wouldn't be worth shit anyway, so they may as well just kill me. So many what ifs made my head begin to spin once again.

"Fucking hurry up and open the damn door," Brindley said, unamused.

"I'm doing it!" Piper huffed, moving the rug to one side and unlocking a trap door hidden beneath it.

"You can stay here," the one that had carried me said.

"Why do you get to make the decisions, Harrington?" Piper scowled. "Why don't you stay here!"

"Because, you idiot, you can't be trusted with her, and Santi isn't here to make decisions, so Elder Johan put me in charge. Just do as your fucking told. If Santi doesn't play ball with this, Elder Johan will deal with him, and I will be the lead warrior, so just remember your place." Harrington shot back.

With my mouth still taped shut, unable to communicate how badly my wrists and ankles hurt under the overly tight ropes that had begun taking the skin off my limbs, I remained seated on the dirty floor, trying not to move. It was the only way I could stop from making the injuries worse. I listened to everything they said and tried not to show any sign of the relief I felt, when it dawned on me that Santi knew nothing about my capture.

New hope that he may be able to help me, solidified my stance on allowing the men to take me to wherever that trap door led too. If I had a chance to salvage anything from the situation, I would take it. However, I knew whatever happened, I would never trust the village, its warriors or people again. Should Santi still want to be with me after he found out the truth about me, he would have to accept we couldn't stay in the village.

Harrington unceremoniously picked me up and helped me stand. Brushing the hair that stuck to my face with the dampness of my tears, he took out a pocket knife and brandished it in front of my face. He eyed me curiously before holding the knife to my throat. Eye's widening, I swallowed hard, making the metal of the blade touch my flesh.

"You aren't going to try anything funny if I cut you loose now, are you?" he raised his brow menacingly.

Shaking my head furiously, trying to blink away my fear, he smirked and bent down to cut the rope from my feet. He went to touch the reddened marks and open flesh wound on my ankles, and I flinched, making him fall backwards.

"Bitch," he hissed, slapping the raw skin.

I yelped, but it came out more as a muffled, throaty mumble. Piper and Brindley chuckled, and I couldn't be sure if it was aimed at me or their fearless leader. Either way, I didn't care, and apparently, nor did Harrington. He stood up, brushed himself down and put away his knife. Looked like he wouldn't be cutting my wrists free then.

"I don't know why you're laughing, dumbass. Elder Johan won't be happy about that." He pointed to my wounds.

"He won't care. When told not to touch her, he meant her pussy. He didn't want us to be contaminated by the beast. He is going to get Santi to hurt her when he turns up. Only way to get the truth out of her. She isn't going to volunteer the information." Piper said, looking directly at me with a wicked grin on his face. "And if you, oh leader, were really Elder Johan's top dog, you would have figured that out for yourself." He directed his words to Harrington. "Now who's the dumbass," he mumbled under his breath, much to Brindley's amusement.

Harrington growled under his breath in annoyance and grabbed at the rope on my wrists. He could clearly see they were causing as much pain and damage as the ankle rope had, but it seemed to pleasure him to see me wince in agony as he pulled me forward. He pushed me in front of the open hole in the ground, towards a set of stairs that looked modern and clean, entirely different to the shack in which I was being held.

"Well…" Brindley barked. "Hurry up, beast. We haven't got all day!"

He nudged my back, and I descended the stairs with both men following closely behind me. Lights automatically turned on, and the trap door above slammed shut. Reaching the bottom of the stairs, we were in a modern looking hallway with three solid steel doors on the left and two on the right. The third door on the right, closest to us, was also made of steel but had a window in it with steel bars across it.

"In there," Harrington said in a raspy voice, pointing to the first door on the left.

Unable to open the door or speak, I looked down at my wrists to indicate my predicament. Harrington huffed, pushed me to the side and opened the door. Inside, I wasn't surprised to find steel bars splitting the room in two. A door to the other side of the bars was open, and Harrington pushed me towards it. I went inside with little argument and sat in the corner, bending my knees to my chest and lowering my head to cover as much of my body as I could.

Hearing the internal prison door shut, the lock snap in place and the external door close with a thump, I braved a look into the room. Alone at last, I took in my surroundings and allowed myself to sob, body aching and throbbing with terror and dread. I contemplated what would become of me, with Santi never far from my thoughts as I waited for him to come. I wondered what he would think when he saw me like this, scared to find out if he would fight for me, or if he would torture me for information that I couldn't be certain I had.

Time seemed to stand still while I waited for someone, anyone, to enter the room. I remained unmoving from my spot in the corner. The stark windowless room was dimly lit, but it made no difference to me. I could see every inch of the box I had been put in, and with no way of knowing how long I had been in it, every second seemed like an hour.

Eventually, I heard the click of the door. Part of me desperately wanted to look up and see Santi; the other half didn't have the energy or the nerve to do it. I battled with myself over what to do, but the harsh edge to the voice that barked at me had me snap my head up and look at the man before me.

"Elsie. I am glad to see you were a good girl and came quietly," Elder Johan said with a sickly-sweet undertone to his voice.

Glaring at him, my mouth still taped shut and my hands bound in front of me, I shut my eyes and lowered my head once again. I wanted answers, but I wanted Santi more. He threw something into my side of the prison room, and I gave in, looking to see what he had allowed me to have. An oversized cotton t-shirt lay on the ground not too far from me, and I scrambled to get it. Then collapsed to the ground once again when I realised I couldn't put it on.

Elder Johan laughed bitterly, and I could feel my anger rising. *What was wrong with these people?* They were vile and twisted. I had done nothing to deserve the treatment they were giving me. My parents were right. Nothing good could come from us being involved with humans. All I had done was ignore the one thing they had warned me about.

"*Stay away from them, Elsie; they will never understand us.*" My mother's voice drifted into my head, and I wanted to cry all over again. I had let them down.

"Do you know why you are here, Elsie?" Elder Johan spoke coldly.

Shaking my head to acknowledge that I did not know why, he looked at me sceptically.

"In that case, let me enlighten you." He paused for thought before he began. "Thousands of years ago, your kind came from a distant land and infiltrated our race. You took whatever you wanted, whomever you wanted and almost destroyed our earth. Over time, we were able to find you and take back what was ours. When more of you came, it was my village that alerted the Monarchy, who sent warriors to take you out of the skies before you could even land. For years thereafter, this village has been the single most important place in our kingdom. We see you first. We stop the attacks, albeit it has been some years since we had the displeasure of having to interact with **your** people." He emphasised the 'your', and it made me shudder. "You are nothing but vicious snakes of the sky."

As much as I wanted to turn away from him, I also wanted to know more. There was so much yet to understand. Perhaps it was a blessing that my mouth was taped, as should I have been able to speak, I probably would have said something to implicate myself in something I had no knowledge of or give him reason to hurt me even more. He looked at me, not with sympathy or pity in my unclothed and battered state but with anger and torment.

"Several years ago, two dragons came from the wrong side of the mountain. I knew then they had been living here for some time under the radar. Somehow, they had escaped our warriors on watch. We killed the male instantly. They are far too dangerous when cornered, but the woman—females are protective of their young and will do anything once captured to save their kin-" he smirked, "she vowed she had no children and died under duress to keep you a secret, but I just knew you were out there somewhere. While Santi had no idea what he had stumbled upon, I knew the minute I saw you. I haven't been the Elder of this village for as long as I have without good reason, Elsie. We need some answers from you. Soon. But first, I need to have a conversation with young Santi. See where his loyalties really lie, because he seemed pretty smitten with you, before he knew who you were, and it's about time he found out. Don't you think so?"

Withdrawing back into my corner, clutching the shirt I couldn't put on, I tried to use it to shield myself a little more than I had previously been able to. I watched as Elder Johan left the room, shutting me back into the perpetual silence of the room. He had left me waiting and wondering what he was saying to Santi and how Santi would react about my secret. If everything Elder Johan had said about my ancestors and my kind had any truth in it, then maybe he couldn't see past me being half beast.

It was difficult not to wonder what had really happened in the past. After all, my parents had said a lot about their lives and how they came to meet one another, but they could only tell me what they knew. None of it involved dragons ravaging the human world for their own gain. My heart sank at the thought. No wonder humans hated me and my kind if it was true, but, I had no way of really knowing if it was.

Chapter 6
Santi

We arrived at the familiar shack on the outskirts of the village, and I still had no idea what to expect. However, the silence of the walk did nothing to ease my growing discomfort. Harrington, Piper and Brindley seemed relaxed and almost energetic, which only added to my anxiety. They obviously knew what this was about, having just been praised for saving the village from a threat, and deep down so did I, but I simply didn't want to believe it.

Elsie had disappeared, and I had been pulled on the stage and thanked for my part in bringing the threat down. I had two plus two and was making four. The more I tried to convince myself that the threat wasn't Elsie and I wouldn't find her locked in a prison cell, the more I accepted that was what I would be walking into. I just couldn't imagine how they had come to that conclusion.

I did not have long to find out if my calculations were right or to get the answers to my questions. I followed Elder Johan and the three warriors I had trained, and considered not only my comrades but my friends into the interrogation room. In the plain whitewashed room, I saw the stark room differently for the first time and found it incredibly intimidating.

The only furniture in the room was a table screwed into the floor with one chair facing the wall and two facing the door, which had a small window with bars across it at sight level. All three chairs were also screwed into the ground. I didn't need to wait to find out why we had been brought to this room instead of one of the cells. It wasn't for anyone else's benefit but my own, apparently.

"Sit." Elder Johan commanded.

All of us looked at each other. With only three chairs in the room, and five of us, we were trying to figure out who he wanted to sit where. With Elder Johan not elaborating, I sat in one of the two chairs facing the window. Harrington sat next to me with Brindley and Piper standing behind us. Elder Johan took his position in the remaining chair.

"What do you know about dragons?" he asked sincerely.

Piper started to laugh. Brindley nudged him hard and stiffened, but said nothing. Harrington and I looked at each other equally confused before turning back to Elder Johan.

"As in, flying, fire breathing, gold hoarding dragons? The mythical creatures from story books? The tales of the dragons...you believe they are true?" I finally spoke as no one else did.

"Exactly." He looked utterly serious. "Only, they aren't mythical, and the tales of the dragons are very true"

Stunned by the odd revelation that I couldn't quite take as genuine, I glanced at Harrington, who had the same expression on his face as me. This time Piper couldn't stop his mouth from moving before his brain engaged.

"You're not serious!" He scoffed.

"Deadly." Elder Johan said, pokerfaced.

Piper stopped himself from uttering another word as Elder Johan shot him a death stare.

"I need to know you boys are going to listen to me and accept everything I say. You are my top warriors, and this information is on a need-to-know basis. The terrifying world we live in goes far deeper than the bandits we see up here on the mountain, and I hoped you would never have to hear the truth; it's chilling. However, Elsie changes all of that. Because she is one of the beasts. She is a dragon," Elder Johan said evenly, looking directly at me.

"When you said she was a beast, I thought you meant beastly, like a bad person, a decoy or I don't know, a...a...murderer or something..." Piper trailed off.

"Me too..." Brindley murmured.

"A dragon..." Harrington whispered, visibly paling.

"Wait, you mean to say,"–I turned to look at the three men–"you believe this bullshit?"

"Santi!" Elder Johan exclaimed. "Watch your mouth, or you will find yourself in a very precarious position."

"I'm sorry, it just seems a little far-fetched. I'm listening," I said more evenly.

The idea that he could be telling the truth seemed far beyond my reasoning. I couldn't believe his ridiculous notion, but at least if I heard him out, I would be in a better position to understand where this crazy idea came from.

Elder Johan seemed pleased with my reversal of position and told us a tale of a war years gone by between a clan of dragons that tried to take over our land. While we managed to hold onto our land, we have since had to sporadically keep it safe from their scouts, which they send out from time to time. It's believed that they come from their realm once in a blue moon to see if we have dropped our guard so they can launch another attack on us.

"Elsie is a scout?" I asked, trying not to sound incredulous.

"That she is. Her parents came from the mountain side; they had been watching us for years, gaining intel to pass back to their kind. We intercepted them. We had a fair idea they had a child, and as soon as I saw her, I knew who she was. We believe they raised her to take their place should they fail their mission to return to their realm. She wanted to join our village to gain enough inside knowledge before going to her people. We can't let that happen," Elder Johan said firmly.

Harrington, Brindley and Piper spent the entire time Elder Johan spoke verbalising their shock with noises and gasps, followed by nodding and agreement. As if it all made perfect sense and none of it seemed at all insane. Elder Johan looked at me for acknowledgement and my approval. I did the only thing I thought would let me see Elsie and shook Elder Johan's hand.

"Count us in. What do you need us to do? The village and the village people are our priority, but if our kingdom needs us, then we will do whatever it takes." I stated firmly.

"I knew you wouldn't let me down." Elder Johan looked positively beaming. "We just need to know if she is aware of any more of her kind here. As soon as she gives them up, we can stop the interrogation and put her out of her misery," he said happily.

He spoke as if it were normal to torture young women for information until they give in, say anything to stop the pain or die, only to be killed anyway. Elsie wasn't a dragon. I refused to believe such crap, and somehow, I had to get her out of there, because if I didn't, she would suffer and die. Over my dead body would that happen.

"Let me talk to her on my own. She may just give me the information if she thinks there is a way out of this for her," I suggested.

Hoping Elder Johan would allow it, I watched him carefully for his answer, trying not to give away my desperation. I wanted some time alone with Elsie, time to think of a way to get her out, a way to stop them from harming her and to make sure she was okay. She had become my entire world, and I would kill every single one of them before I allowed them close enough to her to harm her.

After several minutes of silence, Elder Johan nodded his head in agreement.

"Cell one. I'll let you in; knock when you want me to release you."

He opened the steel door, not giving me the key to the inner door. Clearly, he didn't trust me as much as he once had. He locked me in, and I scanned the room to see Elsie tucked into the corner of the cell, her hair a blonde, wavy mess covering her body. She looked to be wearing a white cloth of some kind, and her ankles looked bloody with fresh cuts.

"Oh, Elsie," I cried, running over to the bars. "What have they done to you!" I cried.

She lifted her head, and I saw the tape over her mouth, her bound hands and the T-shirt that had only been placed over her naked body. Tears streamed down her widened eyes, her cheeks already stained with spent tears. Her eyes were dark and puffy, and she looked terrified. I turned to the steel door, so angry I wanted to murder each and everyone of the men behind the door. How could they do this to someone so sweet. So innocent. The door opened only a moment after I pounded on the steel.

"That was quick," Elder Johan stated flatly.

"I won't get much information from her with her mouth gagged," I retorted sharply.

"Ah, I see." Elder Johan looked at the three men standing behind him. "Yes, well, I will remove the tape and then leave you to it," he said, walking into the room with me.

As much as I wanted to kill them, I needed the prison door between us to be open so I could get her out. I had no plan, but with the door locked, I had no chance of escaping with her. He walked over to the inner door, opened it with a key and stepped inside. Elsie looked petrified, and my heart lurched. My poor princess. I wanted to run to her, hold her, clean her wounds and tell her everything would be okay, but if I didn't get her out of that prison cell soon, I knew those words and actions would all be lies.

Elder Johan ripped the tape off with force. Elsie gasped for air before crying out in pain as the skin on her lips split and light ribbons of blood fell from her mouth. Anger bubbled inside me, and before I even had a chance to consider my actions, I ran for the man and threw a punch at him right in the gut. He cried out as he fell to the ground, and the three idiot men that once had been my loyal comrades and friends took me down and began kicking and punching me. I couldn't see any end to the beating.

In the corner of my eye, I could see Elsie, her eyes gleaming golden liquid amber; a sparkle of something I had never seen before. She got to her feet, and I internally begged her to back away and let them hurt me, at least that way she would be free from their torture a little longer. The higher beings were not listening to me, and she somehow pulled her hands apart, ripping the rope binding her hands clean off her wrists. I stared in shock.

How did she do that? And why on earth hadn't she done it sooner? The white cloth covering her had fallen away, and the sight of her bruised and bloodied, naked body made my anger excel even more with wild thoughts of the things they may have done to her. The beating slowed momentary as Harrington followed my gaze to Elsie, and I cursed myself for drawing attention to her.

Piper and Brindley looked her way too, but none of them seemed to notice her hands were free from their restraints. Or if they did, they hadn't realised she had done it herself through brute force. Elsie cocked her head to one side and then the other, wiping her tangled hair from her face, eyeing the three men with a burning anger behind her eyes. She looked slightly deranged but also sexy as fuck. It felt wrong to be thinking like that, but I couldn't help it.

"Hey there, pretty lady." Piper smirked. "Fancy a final fuck before we end yours and your pussy boyfriend's lives?"

"Can she even have sex?" Brindley asked. "I mean, she's a dragon, right?"

"A dragon," Harrington repeated. "Just remember that, you fucking idiots."

They really did believe it. Good. Maybe if they feared her enough, they would let us leave. It would at least give us a fighting chance. Elder Johan remained curled on the floor, but he hadn't been unconscious, and he groaned, reminding the three men he could hear their conversation. Piper stilled, having forgotten Elder Johan was even in the room with us. I inwardly sighed that those three men were the best warriors we had after me, and

I began to reconsider everything I thought about my time in the village. I didn't know them at all.

"A dragon." Elsie smirked, her lip twitching eerily. "You know, this space may be small, but I can still pull on my abilities in human form." She played the part well. "In fact, If I wanted to shift, it would probably kill you all because I would crush you."

The colour drained from Piper's face, as Brindley backed away, and if it wouldn't have hurt so much, I would have laughed. She really played the part of the avenging dragon woman incredibly well. She stepped forward, and I tried to move myself into a sitting position, but it wasn't easy. Every bone in my body ached, and I could feel the warm liquid of my blood trickling down several areas of my body.

"Santi." Elsie's voice had softened as she looked down at me. "Stay still, my love. I will help you when I have dealt with these bastards." She soothed.

She had just said she was going to manhandle three elite warriors and then help me escape. Who was this woman and where had she put Elsie? Piper swiftly ran, and Brindley began to edge his way out of the room, but Harrington didn't back down. He stood his ground as she slowly but with sure feet closed the gap between them. I couldn't help but watch in horror as she inched closer, and Harrington showed no sign of being fooled by her.

"If you were a fucking dragon, you would have shifted and killed us before we even captured you. If everything you say is true, you could have escaped long ago, you stupid bitch," Harrington snarled. "Don't think you fool me. You are nothing but a lying pathetic nobody."

"You are the fool," Elder Johan gasped, much to Harrington's dismay. "You could have been a hero, but instead our entire Kingdom is at risk because of you." He groaned, trying to get himself off the floor.

"I am a dragon. I wanted to live in peace with you in your village. I had no qualm or issue with you, nor did my parents. They were born and raised in this kingdom. You have made an enemy of me for no good reason. I could have helped you, protected you; I wanted nothing more than to fit in and be a part of your world," Elsie hissed, sounding so sincere even I believed it. "But you!" She pointed to Elder Johan. "And YOU!" she snarled at Harrington. "YOU ruined everything!"

The bitter and hollow laugh from Elder Johan shocked me. Harrington looked more uncertain than he had but remained rooted to the spot. Able to stand for the first time since this debacle started, I groaned as I got to my feet. My aching muscles and bleeding open wounds didn't feel remotely less aggravated. In fact, the movement made them feel even worse. I wasn't sure what I had intended to achieve.

"Really?" Harrington scoffed. "If you are a dragon, then prove it!" he said triumphantly.

"Fine. You asked for it," she said as she shrugged her shoulders innocently.

"Noooo..." Elder Johan cried.

It was an odd sound hearing him panic and whimper. He really believed she was a dragon about to shift. Instead, I panicked that her lack of being able to shift into some dragon beast would have Harrington all kinds of feisty and ready to knock her out. I was in no fit state to fight the man. Even if he was a complete twatwaffle. However, what happened next blew my mind and my very centred beliefs in the world into a whirlwind of undeniable turmoil.

The shift in the atmosphere changed so slightly it was almost undetectable, but I felt it. Harrington felt it, as did Elder Johan. I could tell simply from the way they stilled. We all watched Elsie with immense tension, and as her body cracked and changed, everything I thought I knew changed in an instant. It happened in seconds but felt like a lifetime.

In the blink of an eye, she had transformed from the beautiful woman I had come to know and love in such a short space of time; in her new state I realised I didn't know her at all. Her full form took up the entire room. The steel bars on the prison partition collapsed, and the stone walls around us shuddered with her size. Her red and orange scales glistened and shone, even in the dimmest of light.

Somehow, she had managed not to crush me, but Elder Johan hadn't stood a chance. Harrington had been pushed up against the wall of the prison cell, and as the urine leaked from his trouser leg, I knew he wouldn't be putting up a fight. Elsie was a mother fucking dragon! Holy shit! She roared, and the entire underground room shuddered with the force. The walls began to crumble and shake. Shifting back into her human form, as the building began to collapse, she looked at me with worry and fear in her glowing amber eyes.

"You didn't believe it, did you?" she all but whispered.

"No," I admitted softly, not wanting to lie.

"I'm sorry, Santi. I wanted to..." She paused as a piece of the ceiling crashed to the ground. "We must go. We can talk about this when you are safe!"

She grabbed hold of my waist and helped me out of the crumbling building. Pushing past Harrington, who stood frozen on the spot, unmoving. For a moment, I felt a pang of guilt, wanting to get him out as well, but I soon shook myself from my idiocy as I recalled what he had done. It didn't take long for us to escape the prison block.

We reached the shack, climbed out of the trap door and fell out of the door into the open air just before the entire place collapsed in on itself. Elsie held me, her arms wrapped around my body as if it would be the last time she ever got to feel me in her arms. Her quiet sobs were not missed by me when we lay quietly in each other's arms. It was as if nothing and everything had changed between us, and I felt completely at a loss.

Chapter 7
Elsie

S anti let go of me, as I knew he would. My heart hurt from the loss of the connection. I couldn't stop myself from looking at him. Guilt washed over me, and the tension between us was unmistakable. How could I possibly make it up to him? An ancient being, from a world I had no knowledge of. Nothing more than a beast in its rawest form. With large, yellow-gold eyes, fiery orange scales and a tail that could whip men to shreds in an instant. He deserved better than me and anything I could give him.

"I'm sorry, Santi," I said, tears brimming my eyes.

"Elsie, I won't lie and say it wasn't a shock, but nothing has changed. Not for me anyway. What they did to you was unforgivable, and you are still the same beautiful and enigmatic woman I fell in love with. But..." I winced waiting to hear the words that would break my heart, although they never came. "We have to leave! Piper and Darlington will be back with the entire army of warriors, and I don't want you to get hurt any more than you already have been."

"We? You want to come with me?" I said in shock.

"Of course I do, Elsie; home is wherever you are." He smiled softly.

"It would be quicker and safer if I..." I looked worried, as if my shifting would make him change his mind.

"It's okay, Elsie." He soothed. "I agree. Bring out your dragon and I will jump on your back. Take us as far away from here as you can. We will find somewhere to rest and then figure out where we go next. Okay?"

With a sharp nod of my head, I shifted into my dragon and watched carefully as Santi looked at me, not in fear but in awe.

"So beautiful," he said softly, as his hand caressed my scales.

Dipping my head and taking my cumbersome body as low as I could, he climbed on, just as we heard the entire village of people shouting and taunting. The words 'beast', 'vicious', 'die', and 'kill' all carried on the wind. Santi moved a little quicker as the light of fire glowing over the horizon got a little closer and he held onto me for dear life. I spread out my wings, ready to take off when the first fiery arrow narrowly missed my back.

"Go, Elsie, NOW!" Santi roared. "Head out to the water away from this kingdom. Your people come from that direction, somewhere," he said, uncertain of himself. "Maybe they will accept us, if we find them."

Unable to answer him even if I had wanted to, I hoped he was right. I didn't need to be told twice to leave that awful place, and I took to the skies as several more shots came towards us. They failed to hit us as I swerved from left to right trying to make us a more difficult and unpredictable target. I had no idea if my people really were out there somewhere or not, but at that moment, all I cared about was getting as far away from the onslaught from the villagers as possible.

Instead of worrying about where we may end up, I just kept flying. I had been flying for so long I began to struggle to stay awake while in flight. It had been so long, the sun had begun to rise, and a small island came into view. Santi had been quiet for most of our journey, possibly too scared to speak, or perhaps knowing I couldn't respond to him. Too tired to even make a sound to alert him that I could see land, I remained silent as I pushed forward, desperately hoping to make it before I collapsed.

The closer we got, the larger the island became, and behind it, an even bigger land mass almost four times the size of the island came into view. Deciding the smaller piece of land would be a safer bet, and it being much closer, I started to descend. Lush trees, open lands and large mountains covered the ground. Houses could be seen dotted around the place, and one large castle caught my eye as we finally landed, firm ground beneath us instead of the never-ending sea.

No longer having the energy to care if we were about to land in enemy territory, I found some open land near what looked like the outskirts of a small village, not that far from the castle I'd seen. If it happened to be royal quarters, then maybe Santi and I could have an audience and request permission to stay. We didn't want any trouble; we just wanted somewhere safe to stay and be together.

The relief of knowing we were finally safe and able to rest, along with the exhaustion I had refused to give into, suddenly seemed to hit me like a ton of bricks. Landing haphazardly and tumbling to a stop, my body seemed to give up on me. In the corner of my eye, I thought I could see dragons flying overhead, but in my delirious state, I figured I was most likely hallucinating. I wanted to open my eyes. I wanted to hear Santi's soft voice tell me he would get help, and everything would be okay and feel him get off me, but his weight on my back remained unmoving.

"Santi..." I choked out, barely able to speak above a whisper.

I must have been in and out of consciousness; I couldn't be certain. Soft voices drifted through my awareness, and every now and then, I tried to call for Santi. He never replied. Periods of time meant nothing to me, but the feeling of movement startled me back to being in an awakened state before nothing once again. Another realisation that I no longer lay on the meadow grass in a field, but in a soft plush bed made me smile and sink further under the covers; calling out for Santi again, before I must have drifted back out of reality, having not opened my eyes once.

When I eventually did wake up, being able to open my eyes and see where I was, a beautiful young woman sat at the side of my bed. Long, thick, red, wavy hair framed her face, her piercing green eyes soft with affection and worry. She didn't make me feel remotely scared or concerned for my life. I felt well rested, and I believed I had this woman to thank. When she noticed I had awoken, she smiled and held my hand.

"I'm so glad to see you awake." She spoke softly. "My name is Ember, I am the Queen of Artaminis, the realm of the dragons, which is where you are, should you not be aware."

She paused, watching my reaction to her words, as my mouth went even dryer than it was, if that could be at all possible.

"Realm of dragons?" I croaked out. "We made it," I said under my breath in disbelief, and then I burst into tears.

"You did." She smiled, handing me a tissue and a glass of water. I wiped away my tears and guzzled down the drink too quickly, nearly choking.

"Slow down." She chuckled lightly. "There is plenty more. What's your name?" she asked.

"Elsie," I replied. "Your Highness," I added, remembering I was speaking with royalty. "May I ask...why are you caring for me yourself?"

"You landed in my warriors training ground, not far from the palace guards' quarters. Bringing you to the royal hospital was the closest place for you and your companion, and you both needed serious medical attention. I did none of the work; I have just sat with you when I could so you had someone with you when you woke," she explained.

"Santi!" I exclaimed in a panic, having been too disorientated to have asked out right about him. "Where is he? He needed medical care. Is he okay?"

"It's okay, Elsie. He will be okay. However, he had been hit by an arrow at some point in your journey and he had lost a lot of blood. He had a slow puncture, so it took quite some time for him to get to the state he was in. He is going to be just fine. He's resting. With him being human, he required some quite extensive care, but he is on the mend; it will just take a little longer in recovery than you. Where did you come from?" she asked.

"It's a long story." I sighed. "Can I see him?"

"Absolutely, but not today; it's late and he is sleeping. It is better not to wake him. You need to eat and rest a little longer. Tomorrow. In the meantime, why don't you tell me your story," she urged lightly. "I have time to listen; if you want me to, that is."

"Okay," I replied, getting comfortable.

There was something quite magical about the woman before me. She seemed powerful and strong but calming and welcoming. I trusted her immediately, and after what she had done for me and Santi, a human and an unknown dragon in her realm, the least I could do was tell her what had happened to me and how Santi and I became bonded runaways. So, in my hospital bed, I began the tale from the beginning. When I had finished, Ember hugged me so tightly in her arms I thought she may break a rib.

"I am so sorry you went through all that, Elsie. How harrowing. I came from a human realm as well. But I don't think it's the same one." She looked thoughtful.

"There is more than one?" I asked, astounded. "I don't know why I am so shocked," I added. "I didn't even know there was a dragon realm." I sighed. "I just really hoped there was."

"There is so much more about our universe we have yet to learn." She mused. "But you and Santi will be safe here. You will always be welcome in Artaminis."

"Thank you." I tried to hold the tears back.

"There is something else I need to tell you, Elsie," she said, holding my hand.

"Did you know...you are pregnant?" she said happily.

"I can't be!" I choked. "Santi and I only bonded yesterday!"

"Elsie, you have been here for over a week, and dragon pregnancies are easily detectable early on. Our nurses had to test you before they treated you," she explained, her eyes alight with glee.

"Pregnant," I whispered, looking down at my flat stomach. "I can't believe it."

~THE END ~

Hers

by

Blood

by Pamela K. Isley

Blurb

On the night of her birth, her destiny was changed and what was hers by blood was stolen. Now Aella carves a deadly path through the nobility as she tries to save her people from ruin.

Prologue

The lands of Dreavia have long been ruled by three clans of dragon shifters. The ruling family shifted from one clan to another as the Life of the Land passed from one generation to the next. Always inherited by a male, the one with The Gift was crowned king, and his queen was the firstborn female of the same generation. Sometimes The Gift stayed in one clan for several generations, sometimes it changed swiftly. Always, though, the agreement ensured a hostility free succession of the throne, and kept the ruling families long in power.

As had happened for eons, The Gift passed to Prince Aeon of The Sweeping Storm clan. Aeon was a large dragon with a deep, stone grey color, whose lightning was so consuming it danced in his eyes constantly, and rumors abounded that he could call it to his fingers. The first female born to the clans was Nabia. She hailed from The Consuming Ice clan and her scales were a deep royal blue. However, Nabia was angry. Her entire life was planned the moment she was conceived and there was little she could do about it.

Growing up, she'd tried to run away once or twice, only to be put into her father's prison to keep her from fleeing. It was only at her betrothed's word that her father let her again roam the family palace. No one could understand her visceral reaction to being paired off. It was tradition. It'd happened for eons, and it would keep her family in power. It wasn't until she tried to take her own life that the gravity of the situation truly hit.

Fearing for her safety and sanity, Aeon insisted she be handed over to him immediately. Something had to be going on beyond her desire to be free. Her father was only too happy to be rid of his troublesome daughter and the pair were wed in private.

Once Aeon had her safely in his palace, he began to unravel the mystery of what plagued his mate. It seemed the more she craved freedom and shunned her family's position, the tighter the noose became around her neck. Her father clamped down with an iron fist, controlling every aspect of her life, and punishing her harshly, trying to break her. Only she didn't break the way he expected, with her falling in line. She broke, seeking to end her life.

With a gentleness not seen in most male dragons, Aeon came to an agreement with his soon to be Queen and he helped her to find the light in the darkness. In time, he became her light, and the kingdom continued to prosper, none the wiser.

Nabia, while content with her life, and enjoying the love of her husband, always felt like something was coming. A change was on the winds, and it wasn't going to be pleasant. Five years into their reign, an uprising began. One of the smaller dragon clans grew tired of being under the yoke of the royal clans and a rebellion began. Nabia was too close to giving birth to their first daughter to be on the fields of battle with her mate, and Aeon fell to the rebellion's claws the moment she pushed out their daughter.

Aella was born with her father's gift. Everyone could feel it in the air as the newborn's eyes sparked with the storm of her father, and the plants in the room burst into full bloom despite the time of year. The midwives were in shock. Never before had The Gift been seen in a female and when the shock wore off, fear sat heavy in the room.

It was as Nabia was settling Aella into her bassinet that night that her most trusted knight, Kieran, came to her with life-shattering news. King Aeon was dead and worse, the families were gathering to discuss disposing of Aella. They refused to let a woman rule, called her "the mistake that would be the downfall of their kingdom" and were going to put forward King Aeon's young cousin Riordan as the heir.

Nabia was in shock. With tears streaming down her face, Knight Kieran helped her pack some clothes and supplies onto a horse and sped her into the night and away from the danger that was about to crash onto their heads. With little time to grieve, and a child depending on her, the young queen shoved the throbbing pain in her heart and rode hard through the night. By morning the horses were exhausted and Kieran led them to an old inn where he introduced her to the innkeeper, Morgan, a contact for the true rebellion.

And so it was, with the true heir being raised in the shadows of her own kingdom, that the realm began to deteriorate. Crops began to produce less and less, finally failing altogether. Forests withered and died, and violent storms swept the land. King Riordan and the royal families explained it all away as rebels learning dark magic and poisoning the land. In actuality, it was the loss of The Gift from the true ruler having been rejected by those in power.

Chapter 1

Racing through the treetops, jumping from one branch to another, wasn't how this night was supposed to go. Behind me, I could hear the crashing of the trees being felled to the ground as Captain Rainer pursued me and I winced inwardly at the destruction he was bringing to one of the few forests left in our realm. *Asshole.*

I guess if I was being fair; it was a little my fault. I just killed his charge, a one Marques Lucious Martone. That old, greedy bastard had it long coming, though. He was one of the few who refused to let go and let mother live her life in peace. For men as fearsome as they once were, they were absurdly afraid of her. Afraid of what she represented. A symbol of their disgrace.

Rainer's roar of rage shook the trees, and I was aware of just how little space I had left. The forest was starting to thin out and if I didn't think of something, I'd be forced to shift...and that would give my identity away. Taking a leap I wasn't sure I'd make, I heard the crashing behind me stop in a ground shaking thud. There was silence as I leapt and did a tuck and roll to the ground. *He wouldn't... yes he would and he's going to. 3... 2... 1...*

I skid to a stop, turn to face my pursuer and shove my hands to the earth, calling upon what little nature there was. The land answered my call and two rows of beech trees sprang up out of the ground, reaching nearly seventy feet in height. Rainer's fiery breath weapon scorched against the newly formed trees. I winced hearing the whispers of their screams, but quickly turned and kept moving. *Shit, that'll definitely give me away. Fuckity, fuck, fuck. Maybe he won't have noticed?*

It was silent again. No more fire came, nor did I hear the telltale crashing sounds of a dragon bursting through the tree line. Hazarding a glance over my shoulder, I saw the knight standing, staring at me dumbfounded as I kept running. His lips moved and I could swear I heard him say something like, "Your Majesty?"

Making my way back to the village by use of the familiar back roads was easier after my flight from Castle Martone. Our little hamlet is deeply hidden, midway up the Navarre Peaks, with a sort of dummy village called Murcia in the foothills. Walking through our small farming land, I slip off my mask and push back my hood, greeting those working with a smile. I reach down and touch the earth, greeting the land and apologizing for the sacrifice the trees made for me. One of the things mother has impressed upon me is the need to not only respect the land and the energy within, but to not use this Gift frivolously. I'd like to think I've mostly succeeded in that and thus far the land has not rejected me.

As I reach the village proper, I'm met by our leader, Ferdinand. He's a tall, boorish man with dark features; his body littered with scars.

"What took you so long?" he asks gruffly.

"A certain captain decided it was the one time he'd deviate from his routine and came to check on his lord as I was climbing out the window," I answer him with a shrug. "He pursued till we reached the forest border and didn't follow any further." I'm glossing over the fact I used my Gift. I know he knows there is more, but Ferdinand simply grunts.

"Sloppy. Do better," he chastises me.

I give him a mock salute before sidestepping him and continuing on to my own hidden home. Mother and I built it into a cave just behind the homesteads of many of the families living here. The cave's front is sealed with wood panels. A single door and large window take up the rest of its space and above that, another opening is sealed with a window as well.

"Mother, I'm back," I call into our home as I shut the door and strip off my boots, careful to place them in their bin before stepping off the mat. She hates it when I track dirt through the house.

My mother comes from the hall to her bedroom, a pile of folded laundry in her arms that I hurry to take from her, kissing her cheek. Her eyes narrow on me slightly, and I can't quite meet her gaze. Why do I suck so badly at hiding things from her?

"You used your Gift," she states rather than asks. "Aella, you can't keep doing that. Someone is going to see and put it together, and..." She gasps as the pointed tips of my ears redden. "Aella de Asturias!" she all but shouts at me, switching to Catalan. "If I've told you once, I've told you a thousand times! Do NOT use your Gift in sight of others!"

"But Mamá, what choice do I have when I've got fire barreling at me? Shifting would have been far more revealing!" I protest. Her hands are on her hips now and I sigh. "I know, I know, use my head. I'm smarter than them. It's in my blood," I respond for her, more snarkily than I intend.

"My Light..." Mother pauses as she pulls me into a hug. "I'm sorry. I should not jump straight into scolding you after you've just escaped with your life and limbs intact. I know you know. I know you try your best," she tells me softly. "So tell me then, Lucious went down?" she asks and I pull back with a nod.

"Like a stuck pig," I answer with a grin. "How that man remained in power for so long is beyond me. He had no skills to speak of to defend himself with. I don't think he even still had his flame." I scoff. I didn't even have to be especially sneaky, and it was pure rotten luck the Captain saw me leaving through the window. I frown slightly.

"Captain Rainer was entering the room as I left. He wasn't on duty today, so I don't know what he was even doing there. He chased me to the edge of the forest," I explain as I sit down on the sofa. "By all reports, he doesn't even like serving the Martone Brood."

Mother chuckles at the near pout I have going on over being seen. "My Light, you were bound to be seen by someone at some point. As for the captain, well, he may not like whom he serves, but he does serve faithfully. It's a rather annoying trait with most of the knights, really," she notes, pushing a stray lock of blonde hair behind my ear.

"Worked out well with Uncle Kieran," I point out.

She laughs, while the tips of her ears turn pink with her blush. "Yes, well, Kieran was sworn to me."

"Mmm, I know. You know, Mamá, I'm a full, grown ass woman now. You two can stop dancing around this whole thing and just... see where it goes," I point out, refolding one of the towels that fell when I'd placed the laundry down. "I doubt very much that Papá would deny you your happiness in his absence."

She gives me a sad smile. "I know he wouldn't. Your father did everything in his power to see me happy and content. This isn't the time for such things, though," she says, pushing aside her thoughts of my father and Kieran both, as she walks over to the map of the realm. She grabs a black push pin and pushes it into Martone Keep. "Go take a hot bath and I'll get supper ready for us."

I nod, and go kiss her cheek before heading back to my rooms. The cave system here has natural nooks and rooms with small hot springs throughout to bathe in. My own cavern is large enough for me to take my dragon form and stretch my wings from time to time. I strip out of my leathers, folding them and placing them by the bin with my cleaning supplies to take care of them later. I check myself in the mirror, noting the bruising on my shoulders where arrows struck me but didn't pierce the skin. A soak would do me good.

With deliberate steps, I head deeper down a passage on the right and slip into the hot spring with a sigh of relief; letting my eyes droop shut. Three Marques down. Next would be a step up: Duque Ordoño. Ordoño and his brood were particularly loyal to the imposter King. His army comprised of mostly men from that brood, and getting into their keep would be no easy task. The entire main city on their lands is heavily fortified and "justice" is meted out swiftly and violently. Kieran had already been there, feeling out the people and figuring out exit routes for me.

There were a few options on the table for infiltration. I could pose as a maid or some other normal person looking for work. Nobles always ignore or straight out forget that people 'beneath' them exist. They hear and see everything and have access to some of the most vulnerable moments of the ruling class.

Then of course, there was the upcoming royal ball. Ordoño's son Alfonso was said to be searching for a wife. I shudder at the thought of having to get dressed up and pretend to be interested in anything remotely related to high society. I *can* do it, my mother trained me, of course, but I don't like doing it. Don't get me wrong, the dresses and the subtle ways they can be used to express oneself are gorgeous but the ostentatious display of wealth while the people suffer...that I could do without.

I let myself sink under the water for a few moments, trying to let my brain relax instead of getting spun up again, but then the whispers come. I don't hear them often, and I can only ever make out a word or two. It's like a room full of people whisper-shouting at me and it all blends together in a white noise sort of effect. My frustration builds as I try to make the noise stop, but as always, the din just gets louder.

I push myself to the surface, gasping for air. Pain begins at my temples, as if someone was trying to drill into my skull and then through the din I hear someone roar. It's angry and forceful, but it comforts me and the din begins to die down.

What the actual fuck was that! I scramble out of the spring and quickly wrap myself in a fluffy towel. I know it's all connected to The Gift, but there isn't a lot written about it. Mother knows only what she learned from my father before his death but even that isn't a complete knowledge. I was supposed to learn it all from him, not struggle through it on my own.

Squaring my shoulders, I head back into my bedchamber and redress in a loose blouse and leather pants. It was getting late in the day and I wanted to check on the rest of our town, and make sure I wasn't followed.

Entering our living chambers, Mother looks up at me and frowns slightly. "You look pale. Did it happen again?" she asks, setting a plate down in front of my seat as I drop onto it.

I nod in response. "Yeah. Full-blown whispers. I can't make anything they say out though and a loud roar silenced them."

She sighs softly and sets a cup of tea down. "Drink," she orders and I grimace. The stuff tastes horrible. A mix of ground up roots and stems mostly, it's incredibly bitter but it does help me recover from the pain in my head. "I'm sorry this keeps happening, my Light," she tells me as the brew begins to do its job.

"Mamá it's not something you can control. You've got to stop apologizing for my life," I say, gesturing vaguely around us. "Those greedy lizards are the only ones to blame and if the price of me growing up with open eyes is some weirdness and headaches every once in a while then I'll take the weirdness every time," I tell her before gulping down the rest of the tea. I glance at the door and get up, pulling my leathers on as I reach the door. "I'm gonna go patrol before turning in," I tell her as I open the door to find my uncle standing with his hand raised to knock. "Hey Uncle Kieran. She's feeling guilty about things she doesn't own again," I warn him, kissing his cheek and waving at them both as I jog down the entrance of our caves and out into the town proper.

It was a blessedly calm evening. Most folk had already closed up and turned in for the night. The kids all tucked into their beds and the adults relaxing and enjoying their downtime. When I was younger I envied them. The rest of the 'normal' rebel families. I spent nearly all of my time learning about our realm's history and training my skills so I would be as quiet as I was deadly. We knew early on that we could never brute force our way to the throne. It would leave me vulnerable to simply take out the false king and plant me on the throne, surrounded by the vipers who never wanted me there to begin with. There is loneliness growing up as I did. No real friends, no time for play, just learning and honing my skills. In the end it was a simple matter of duty though. My childhood sacrificed so they could have theirs. I'd never change that.

I climb up through our mountains, picking my way through the worn paths to reach Flatiron Rock. The climb feels longer than it actually is, but necessary. It's the only mountain we can launch off of safely.

Once I reach the naturally flat, open ground, I make sure to check the supply stash and note anything that needs to be refilled later, before looking up at the stars. There's a surge of energy I feel building inside me. I hadn't shifted in a while and the beast was getting impatient with my stalling.

"Alright, alright. Calm the fuck down," I grumble at myself before focusing on the magic deep inside of me. I draw in a breath and hold it before exhaling as the magic ripples through every inch of my body, pulling the dragon soul from within and changing my body into the huge dark, silvery dragon I am. I flex my claws, digging them into the rock and earth under me as I spread my wings, stretching out the muscles. My tail whips from side to side as a storm begins to gather on the horizon, bringing a smile to my eyes.

I fight the beast's urge to roar as I gather my muscles and launch into the air. My powerful wings beating the air into submission as we rise into the clouds; the storm in the distance racing to embrace me. There is no better feeling than flying freely through the night sky. I stay high enough up to not be spotted but my sharp eyes can still survey our lands.

I can feel the electricity building in the storm that chases me through our mountains and down into the valley where our dummy village sits. It dances through the clouds, trying desperately to reach my scales as I dive down under the clouds and skim along the trees of what was once known as The Serra de Collserola, but now was called The Forgotten Forest. The storm follows on my tail closely, and I let out a roar of command at it. The clouds open up, releasing the rains they carry and the lightning rushes to follow but I swoop down, catching it with my body. To anyone else, this would knock them from the sky, paralyzing them and causing them to fall. But I am the rightful queen of this world. The storms and the land are mine and the lightning re-energizes me, licking over my scales and horns before being absorbed into my claws.

The trees cried out in relief, I could hear their joyous singing ringing in my ears and couldn't help but smile. *I'm sorry my lovelies. Soon. Soon all will be back in balance.* I promise them as I glide over as much of the woods as I can, not daring to get too close to the Martone hold. As I force myself to turn back towards home I start going over my options again for getting into Ordoño Castle. Going as a maid was my preference but I had a feeling that going as a random well-bred daughter for the ball would end up being my best option.

Sacrifices come in many sizes and forms. The words feel like they're whispered on the winds zipping by me as I make for the mountains again. The voice has a deep timbre and the cadence feels regal. I feel it wrapping around my brain and comforting me at the same time. I come to a skidding landing on Flatiron Mountain, shifting back into my human form, and running out the last of the momentum, thankful as always that our magic keeps our clothing with us. I look back up and out over the lands, watching the storm move on over the land and out to the ocean, before making my way back down the mountains and into our cave.

I feel the echo of the words in my mind as I come through the door, Kieran and my mother waiting for me on the couches. "Alright, let's get into it. I can't sleep yet anyway. Who will I be for the ball?" I ask, much to their shock. *It's just a small sacrifice.*

Chapter 2

Kieran is the first to lose the shocked look and compose himself with a grunt of approval. Mother opens her mouth a few times to speak, but words don't come. I don't think I've ever seen someone dumbstruck before.

"You're right, it is the better way to get close to him. Going as a servant doesn't guarantee I'd be assigned anywhere near him or his quarters and ultimately I need to be close," I say with a resigned sigh. "So I'm assuming then, you have an identity for me to use?" I ask Uncle Kieran.

He nods. "The Hernani Brood is quite extensive. Not just in their heirs, but in their relatives and illegitimate offspring as well. Many of the court take wives and concubines from their number and they too are quite loyal to the crown," he outlines his thoughts. "You will be going as Sofia Storm, illegitimate daughter of a third cousin. Well bred enough to attend, not high enough in the brood hierarchy for anyone to remember or question your presence. The Hernani attend these balls wearing not their own colors, but the crown's. You will show up in the brood colors. We want you to stand out and intrigue Duque Ordoño. In a sea of black and gold dresses, wearing something in red will achieve that goal. Remember, you are a candidate for his son, but Ordoño is just as greedy and lecherous as the others and has a sadistic streak. He'll see the defiance in the dress selection as a challenge and hopefully..." he pauses. He always does at this part, because like any fatherly figure, he hates thinking of anyone looking at me as a sexual object. "...hopefully he'll try to get you alone and to somewhere he can 'break' you in."

Mother finally seems to have rejoined the world of the working brain cells. "I'm sure Lilianna has something suitable in her shop. We can go tomorrow and pick something up," she adds.

"Do we know much about Alfonso? Is he to be a target as well?" I ask them, steering us off the subject of the dress and the very probable fact I'll end up having to let the Duque grope me more than a few times.

"He's been trained by his father for his position since he was a young teen. His older brother was in line for their throne, but he died in a shipwreck years ago, making Alfonso the heir. It's hard to say where he may stand. Use your discretion. If he seems to be too much like his father, kill him. If there is hope for him, then leave him be," Mother replies.

We talked for a bit more before finally deciding to get some sleep. I was exhausted, and they both knew it. I bid goodbye to Uncle Kieran as he and my mother continued speaking of the plans, and made my way to my bed, passing out almost immediately.

If you sat me down and asked me what I thought the most torturous day would be like for me, this would be it. Dress shopping with my mother. She has all these lists of dos and don'ts and I just want to be comfortable. Mother had me try on what felt like an endless sea of huge ball gowns with tight corsets. Many of which looked like basically the same dress, with only minor variations.

I was reaching my limit and about to snap at my mother for the umpteenth time when Lilianna's daughter came out of the back with a red dress in her arms. I couldn't see it very well, but my beast stirred.

"Hey, Arletta, what do you have there?" I asked her. A slight panic hit her features, and she hugged the dress to her body. Lilianna frowned with disapproval.

"Oh, don't concern yourself with that. It's just a dalliance Arletta has," Lilianna says dismissively. "Arletta isn't very good with staying on trend or the shop's brand."

I can see my mother frown at how Lilianna dismisses her youngest daughter so easily, and Arletta looks like a beaten puppy at her mother's biting words.

I hop off the pedestal that I was on while looking at the latest dress, and strip it off right there in the middle of the store. I catch the faintest smirk on my mother's face as Lilianna gasps and sputters at me being in my underthings.

"Arletta, can I try it on?" I ask when I reach her. "Something tells me it's the right one," I whisper to her as she blushes furiously.

"I don't know, Aella. It's really not very good," she replies softly.

"Maybe not for most of these women, but for those of us who want something different, something lighter and more comfortable, I bet this is perfect," I tell her as I lightly finger the material. "What's it made from?"

"Silk tulle. It's very light, but I've layered it so it doesn't show things it shouldn't," she answers.

"That's perfect, please, I'm begging, can I try it?"

She glances from her mother to mine, then back to me before nodding slowly. Arletta helps me into the dress and I look down with a smirk as I notice the appliques she used are hand cut dragon's heads, that morph into vines and leaves as they trail up the dress to the high-necked halter top. The entire bodice is covered with glass beads and crystals alike that fade as they reach the skirt. The ropes of beads flow from my collar, and drape around my arms in gentle sleeves before looping to the back.

Arletta helps me onto the pedestal again and murmurs, "I have a cape for it too. Same applique on a single layer of tulle."

It's the very opposite of the current fashion. Dresses are made of heavy brocade or satin and are topped by tight corsets. The material is light and easy to move in and the dragons just make me smile even more.

"It suits you," Arletta whispers in amazement, and I turn to her.

"This dress is what I never knew I needed. It's like you've plucked from my mind everything I hate about dresses today and given life to a dress I'd not just tolerate, but love. Please Arletta, can we buy this from you for the ball?" I watch as she glances at her own mother again, Lilianna still trying to hide a scowl of disapproval, before looking back at me. I give her my best puppy dog eyes and she cracks a small smile at my over-exaggerated antics before nodding.

"Ok, I'd be thrilled for you to have it," she tells me.

I give a small clap of glee and lift the skirt before hopping down and sweeping her into a hug. "Thank you! You've just made this whole thing a hundred times more bearable."

Mother goes to talk to Lilianna about a gown for herself, no doubt to placate the woman, and Arletta helps me carefully out of her design. She takes my measurements to tailor it properly, and I hand over a pouch of coins for her. It's more than I'm sure she'd ask for, but it's clear her mother is stifling her creativity and confidence, and I won't stand around and let it happen.

"I'll have it ready for you tomorrow, Aella," Arletta tells me, and I nod.

"Again, thank you. And any other future needs I want only from your hands," I tell her, before taking her hands and leaning in to press my forehead with hers; a sign of kinship for us dragons. "I'll see you tomorrow."

Picking up the dress held no further arguments with Lilianna. Whatever my mother had said to the woman seemed to work, or at least kept her away from me as Arletta did some finishing stitches and handed the gown over. I swung by the jeweler's shop and picked up the mask my mother commissioned to match the dress, and made my way back home.

Kieran had a horse-drawn carriage waiting, and I sighed to myself. *Stupid nobles. Like it's so taxing to simply fly to where you need to get to.* Pushing the door open and heading inside I find them whispering to one another, and can't help but smirk as they almost leap away from one another like teenagers caught kissing behind a barn.

"Don't stop on my account," I mention, heading towards my rooms. "I think I've told the both of you often enough my thoughts on the matter." I add in the dig, closing the door to my hall as my mother begins her usual protests.

I get ready as fast as I can, taking my time with my makeup so I don't screw it up, and once I'm in the dress, Mother comes in to do my hair up.

"Remember, no unnecessary risks and keep your beast in check. She's likely to hear things she doesn't agree with and get angry. As talented as you are my daughter, you are not invincible and they have the numbers here," she warns me. I can see the worry in her eyes as she goes over basic protocol, things I've known since I was five, but I know it makes her feel better to ramble like this.

When she finishes I stand and add the mask, before turning to face her. "I promise Mamá, I'll keep the anger in. I already know all they are capable of; their deprivations. I have a goal and I won't let anything, including myself, get in the way of that."

She fusses a bit more, straightening the mask before resting her forehead to mine. "I love you Aella. Come back to me in one piece and with no new holes."

I chuckle and nod. "I promise. One piece, no new holes."

She leads me out to the carriage. Uncle Kieran is dressed in his suit and mask, and one of Ferdinand's brothers is playing our driver for the day. "I'll be back by midday at the latest," I tell her as we set out for Castle Ordoño.

Uncle Kieran timed it out so we'd arrive later than most, allowing the castle to fill with people. While my name wouldn't make even a ripple with those gathered, the choice of dress would. As predicted most show up in Ordoño colors to impress their hosts, or the Crown's colors, incorporating their own house colors into the blacks and golds or whites and silvers.

Exiting the carriage I can hear the murmurs begin. I smile as I take my uncle's arm and he leads me into the castle. We wait in line to be announced as he makes small talk, pointing out various lords.

Entering the ballroom I look over the walls and ceiling at the various painted scenes decorating the panels. Battles between houses throughout history, nearly all wins by

Ordoño or my father's house, the Asturias. The pillars lining the wall every ten feet or so are coated in gold paint and have candle lamps on each. A golden chandelier the size of a dragon takes up the center of the ceiling. Servers maneuver the large, crowded room with trays of food, mostly ignored by the nobility gathered.

It's entertaining to me, watching the ripple happen as we're announced and people take in the dress. Most are disgusted by it; someone daring to slight their host by not wearing the requested colors. I squeeze Kieran's arm and smile at him as we descend the grand staircase, and he leads me to our assigned seating.

I watch as some settle at their tables, most are mingling and sizing one another up, still others dance as the orchestra plays very traditional music. The sheer opulence and vapid displays of wealth make me want to gag. I look around the room noting the exits and watch the servants moving like ghosts. That is until one of them gets knocked over by a woman in a large black ballgown with gold floral embroidery. Her skirt hoops are so large she misjudged the space she needed as she backed away from her conversation, and hit the poor girl carrying a tray of drinks. The glasses go flying, most landing on the ridiculous skirt of the dress, causing the noble woman to screech and berate the poor girl now lying on the floor.

I'm not even consciously thinking as I get up and rush over to help the girl, who's clutching her wrist to her chest as tears stream down her face. I bend down and place a hand on her wrist gently probing it to make sure it's not broken. "Hey, hey, it's ok, you're gonna be ok," I assure her, terror dancing her eyes as she does her best not to look at anyone. "It's not broken, but it's swelling. You need some ice and a wrap," I tell her softly.

I notice now the crowd forming around us, the hysterical noble woman screaming for the girl's head over her ruined gown. I stand, keeping myself close to the girl and glare at the woman, pinning her gaze with my own. "Oh, do please shut up," I grind out at her. "You caused this whole accident and you're only making it worse by acting like an overgrown gecko."

"HOW DARE YOU SPEAK TO ME LIKE THAT!" She turns her rage on me like I'd hoped she would. I can see Uncle Kieran, a resigned look on his face, moving to help the girl up and hopefully slip her away from here.

I smirk at her anger. "Like what? Like you're acting as a spoiled child who has no control over their own actions? My word, you must be exhausting to be around," I note, watching a few of the males snicker softly.

"HOW DARE YOU! I AM A MARQUE'S DAUGHTER AND I COU-" she begins winding up again.

"-ld have my head for such insolence. How dare I insult and demean such a lady of high rank. I'm nothing more than the mud beneath your carriage," I mimic her boredly. "Honestly, you all need to come up with a new script. Now if you'll excuse me, I have better things to do than being in the center of your little tornado of a tantrum. We both know you can't and won't do anything right now, so feel free to come find me after this silly little party is done with," I tell her before turning on my heel, my dress swirling out with flourish, and retreating towards the nearest balcony to rein in my temper.

Well that was just perfect, I grumble internally as I lean on the railing and look out at the night sky. The gardens below were probably very beautiful in my father's time, but now there were only a few bushes managing to sprout flowers at all, and it was clear the plants here didn't have more than a few seasons left in them. It was a stark reminder of why I'm here...and how much my little display in the ballroom might have cost us all.

I sense someone's presence behind me before he even clears his throat. I turn to find a set of bright amber eyes staring at me from behind a black and gold mask. His hair is a mop of dark curls and his lapel pin is House Ordoño's signet with a flame and crown. *Alfonso.*

"I must say, I feel like I should thank you," he starts off, giving me a lopsided grin that I'm sure had most women swooning at the sight of.

I raise an eyebrow at his words. "Thank me? For what?" I ask him.

"For defending my staff from that harpy of a woman," he answers with a casual grin.

My eyes narrow on him suspiciously. "Oh, so we're pretending to be the Lord of the Manor now are we?" I reply sardonically. "'Oh, hello, I'm Lord Ordoño, thank you for saving my servant from the evil noblewoman,'" I mimic.

Alfonso chuckles at me. "That would be a very poor pickup line now wouldn't it?" he asks, his smile never wavering. "I mean, it's a masked ball for a reason and anyone could claim to be anything."

I snort softly. "Except maybe the king. His Gift's aura alone would give him away," I note with a smirk. "Though I suppose one could then claim to have learned to suppress such a Gift. I imagine it's part of his training."

Alfonso nods. "So we've been told," he agrees and I can almost feel his hesitation in the sentence. "However, I am not the king, nor even one of his cousins, and I won't pretend to be. That would most certainly insult your intelligence."

"Oh, so you have me figured out then?" I ask him with a smirk of my own.

He barks out a laugh. "Oh no, I'd never pretend to know that which I don't know. But you most definitely aren't cut from the same cloth as the rest of those inside," he notes. "Literally not one person showed even a hint of upset over the berating my staff was going to receive. Many looked on like hungry jackals."

"Well, you've got me there. I am not cut from the same cloth as the rest of them," I agree. "So tell me then, why are you out here instead of in there placating the Marquesas' daughter?"

The lopsided grin returns. It'd be endearing if I wasn't so on guard around him. "As I said, I wanted to thank you. My staff means a great deal to me, more so than they do to my father."

I hum in acknowledgment of the statement. "So then, do you play along with the expected? Silently watching as those you claim to care for are harmed by those you call family. Or do you do something now to help them?" I can't stop the challenge nor the anger that comes out in my tone.

Alfonso just chuckles and leans in closer to me, whispering in my ear as he slips something into the pocket on my dress. "Consider this my declaration of allegiance to the cause," he tells me before running the back of his hand down my arm and lifting my hand to his lips, kissing it softly. "My Queen."

My blood runs cold and my eyes snap to his. He must feel the tension hit my hand cause he rubs his thumb over the top of it, not yet letting me go. "Shhh. Don't fret. That's a key to my father's rooms and the west walls will be in shift-change in three hours' time," he assures me.

I can't help but continue to eye him suspiciously as he lets go and steps back from me.

"As this may be goodbye for quite a while, I wish you good hunting," he says as his goodbye before heading back into the ball, and leaving me alone with my thoughts and fears.

Two and a half hours later, I'm hidden away in the closet of Lord Ordoño's changing rooms, waiting for the old man to enter with his entertainment of the night. The key Alfonso gave me indeed made this much easier on me, and thus far, there had been no surprises. I'm not naïve enough to believe he's helping out of the pure goodness of his heart. It was well known that his father had no intention of handing down the title until the day he died. Alfonso had to be getting restless waiting for the old man to kick the bucket.

As I'm waiting, going over my exits for the hundredth time, the door to the hallway opens and a guard steps in. He checks the room and balcony before stepping back into the hall, holding the door as Lord Ordoño sweeps into the room. A young male trails behind him, his head down, and through the curtain of ice blond hair that hangs about his face I can see the brand of the whorehouse he's enslaved to. My beast growls in my mind. She had little patience as it was for the idea of servants, slaves she found even more objectionable, and I was in full agreement with her.

"Strip boy," Lord Ordoño demands as he goes to gather his bottle of firewine and settles in the chair near my location. His lust filled gaze watching his toy for the evening.

I can't leave him here. They'll blame him and execute him, I realize as I struggle with the reality of the wrinkle this gives me. He's not a very large male, Lord Ordoño seeming to prefer those he can feel powerful against. I could probably carry him on my back as I scale the walls on the western side, but even with his slight size, it's going to be awkward and slower than I need to be.

I see the tremble in the boy's hands as he undoes his top wrap and look again at the brand. It's not exactly fresh, but it's still an angry shade of red. *He's not done this yet for a client. Fuck.*

Silent as always, I slip from the closet and crawl behind the chair.

Lord Ordoño's anger suddenly explodes. "Hurry the fuck up or I get the whip!" he shouts at the boy who flinches, still not meeting his master-for-the-night's gaze.

I stand from my spot just as the boy dares to raise his gaze and his eyes widen in shock and fear as he spots my hand raised to the side. The single elongated claw of my index finger glinting in the firelight. I give him a reassuring smile, that I'm certain doesn't quite register in his brain, before using my left hand to cover Lord Ordoño's mouth and rip his head back. With my right claw, I slash his throat from one ear to the other. The muffled cries from his gagged mouth mix with the gurgling sound from his neck as he bleeds out.

"You dishonor King Aeon and I am here to take back what was mine," I tell him before he dies.

Normally I'd sit and enjoy the sight for a little before fleeing, but I have a new problem. The boy screams before he passes out and I can hear the metal clang of knights' footsteps as they race down the hallway to find out what has happened.

Dropping my prey, I leap over the chair and scoop up the boy into my arms, running out to the balcony. I study the western wall and see the guards are beginning their shift change, but I don't have time to wait for the perfect moment anymore. With a resigned sigh, I tuck the boy under my left arm and begin to climb up to the rooftop where I know there is a landing pad of sorts.

Shouting below alerts me to the fact I've been spotted; which honestly isn't a shock. I'm scaling the castle in a bright red, flowy dress. I'm hard to miss unless you were blind. Arrows begin to whiz by me as I reach the top and set the boy down. *Sorry Mother,* I silently apologize as I shift into my dragon, gently scooping him in my left claws and cradling him to my chest as I leap into the air and make my escape.

More arrows chase me over the wall and I hear a metallic grinding noise I don't recognize, and can't see where it's coming from; circling back would be a huge mistake. I hear a thud and the air around me whooshes as an arrow that's more like a large javelin goes sailing along my back, missing me by inches. *Holy-fuck-shit-cockballs!*

I push myself harder, picking up speed to get out of its range when I hear two roars behind me. One I vaguely recognize and a quick glance confirms it. *Rainer. Of all the rotten fucking luck...*

As I push myself harder, putting distance between myself and the keep I hear the grinding again followed by the thwang when a voice digs into my head: *ROLL!* it demands and I hesitate before doing so. The hesitation proves to be my undoing as the huge bolt slices into my wing, severing the main blood vein that runs through my patagium. I roar in pain as I begin to fall out of the sky, the wound not healing. *Of course it was laced with sphalerite.*

I use my good wing to try and slow the fall, keeping the boy tucked to my chest, and at the last moment turn to take the hit to the ground on my back. Pain tears through me as I skid through the dead forest, coming to an abrupt stop as I slam into a boulder. Rolling on my side with a groan I set the boy down before shifting back into my human form. He's awake again and seemingly completely dumbstruck as he struggles to form words.

I give him a small smile. "Hi, I'm Aella. You don't need to share your name. I'm sorry about tonight. I wasn't going to leave you to take the fall for me and I won't abandon you now. I can bring you somewhere safe, we will take care of you," I promise him as I look around us. "I can't fly us further and we need to get moving. They're going to be coming," I add, holding out my hand to him.

"You're wrong on that count, *Princess*. I'm here," Rainer's deep voice rings out calmly as he steps out from the trees.

Chapter 3

As soon as Rainer stepped through the trees I put myself between him and the boy, whose name I still didn't know. His face was devoid of emotions making it hard to get a read on him. My beast thrashed within me, urging me to shift and rip his head from his shoulders but something was making me fight against that urge as I let my claws descend from my fingers. If he twitched in our direction I wouldn't hesitate to protect my charge.

Rainer doesn't move from his spot as he studies my face, seeming to try and assure himself that what he thought wasn't true. The problem is, I look very much like my father and his storm rages in my own eyes.

"That's who you are, isn't it. Princess Aella de Asturias," he states calmly as something flickers through his eyes. "What I don't understand is how...how you're standing here? The whole realm mourned you, your whole family, the loss of our King was a catalyst for," he motions vaguely around us. "all this dark magic."

I can't stop the snort at his ridiculous words. Sure I knew the official word was Mother died giving birth to me, a birth I didn't survive. But for the people to really believe the rebels had somehow tapped into an unknown dark magic source and were killing the land...for what end? To rule over ashes?

"You believe this to be the work of dark magic?" I ask, my eyes narrowing on him. "From where would anyone get such power? And why use it to destroy what they supposedly want to rule? For the love of the goddess, *Captain*, use those few brain cells you have in that empty head, and really think about the claims of the false king."

He has the good sense to look slightly ashamed as I voice how dumb that all sounds. "I don't have time to sit here and explain it all to you. You have a choice. One way or the other, I am taking this boy and leaving. You can walk away with all your blood inside your body, or I can claw the life from you so you never trouble me again."

The clouds begin to gather, looming ominously over the castle we're fleeing from and the electricity in the air begins to grow thicker. I didn't call this storm, it's a symptom of the larger problems at play, and in my currently injured state I can't fly up to corral it. A deafening clap of thunder rolls out over the land and the boy behind me crouches down, covering his ears.

"What about a third option? I come with you," Rainer offers, immediately raising my suspiciousness of him. "Look, you're injured and can't heal, and there are more knights coming. Let me help you. I'm not asking you to spill your secrets to me, but I am asking for a chance to prove my loyalty has only ever lain with the crown. Riordan is clearly not the crown," he tells me, his gaze softening for the first time.

The trees begin to whisper urgently to me of the knights entering the mostly dead forest and I sigh, turning to the boy and crouching down in front of him. I pull his hands from his ears and lift his face. "What's your name?" I ask him firmly.

"Manuel," he answers shakily.

"Ok Manuel, here's the deal. I'm taking you home with me, but first we need to find shelter and escape the knights. Rainer here wants to prove he's with us, so we're going to give him that chance. I can feel your dragon is weak, I'm guessing it's been suppressed, so when you feel it stirring, I need you to tell me so we can safely let him out, okay?"

Manuel nods at my words. "Yes Princess," he adds softly and I shake my head at him.

"None of that. For one, I'm not technically one anymore, and two, it's safer not to mention it. You can simply call me Aella." I stand, helping him up and turn to Rainer. "That goes for you too, grumpy pants."

Rainer's grumpy look doesn't change at my teasing, but he nods at my words. "Let's get moving. If we're lucky, the storm will force them back and we can reach Alicante by morning," he says, naming the small town at the base of The Mother's Maw mountains.

Manuel's gaze reflects his distrust for the knight, but I'm following both my gut and my mother's words here. I let Rainer take the lead and keep myself between them as we move with a quickness. I let my hand touch the trees we pass, giving them some of my energy as they tell me of the movements of the Ordoño knights.

As an hour or so goes by, I watch Rainer carefully. He's surprisingly aware of Manuel and when he begins to falter, Rainer slows our pace. "The trees tell me the knights have stopped searching," I tell them both quietly and Rainer nods.

"We should rest then. If you'll let me, I can check your back," he offers.

With a sigh, I nod. Injuries to our wings can show on our backs, giving our healers an idea of what's going on as we heal. I help Manuel settle against a boulder and put my hand to the ground. With great effort, a blackberry bush springs up, full of its fruit. "Eat, Manuel, you need the energy."

He stares at me, his eyes wide and filled with wonder. "You really are the lost Princess," he murmurs softly, and I nod with a warm smile.

"I am. I'm trying very hard to set things right, without a full-blown war breaking out," I promise him, as he scoots over to the bush and begins eating. I grab a handful and walk back to where Rainer stands, looking out at the horizon, his shoulders sagged as he thinks no one notices.

I place my hand on his shoulder, causing him to tense and flinch away from me. "Hey. Here, you should eat," I say, offering him the berries. He takes them from me with a muttered thanks. "I know all of this is hard on you. I'd imagine you've got that whole inner battle thing happening, even if you wish it were as easy as 'I serve the Crown.'"

"It is that simple. Or it's supposed to be," he tells me quietly.

I nod. "If the world were as simple as most of you knights believe it to be I don't think we'd all be in this mess," I note. "My uncle Kieren was like you once," I tell him.

"Major Kieran Hernani? He was Queen Nabia's knight," he says in contemplation.

I smile sadly. "He is, and it's because of him she and I even escaped the night I was born. His duty was to her, not to these evil men who couldn't fathom a female leading our people."

"We were told that night that he had fallen trying to protect you both from the rebellion that killed His Majesty," he tells me, and I simply nod.

"I know. We have people everywhere who kept us in the loop over the years."

"Why? Why would any of them doom us to this...dying world?" he mutters.

"Power. Fear. Greed. Hubris. Take your pick. The Gift has never manifested in a female before, but it was never written anywhere that it couldn't be," I answer as I pluck a berry from his hand. "In the end, the why doesn't matter anymore. It's the what-we-do-next that does. What you do next. My path is clear before me. I will not leave our world to die in the hands of those men."

He's silent for a long time, lost in his own thoughts. "How many?" he asks me.

"How many have I killed or how many do I have left?" He snorts at my question.

"I killed six of the seven Marques. Marques Leon really did die of a heart attack two days before I was going to make my move. There are two targets left," I answer both.

He nods, no doubt having figured out those who may be left in my crosshairs still. Finally he touches my shoulder and nudges me to turn around so he can look at my back. With surprisingly gentle touches, he moves aside my hair and runs his fingers over my shoulder blades, checking for tenderness.

"The poison is still present," he tells me, tracing over the black veins that show the effect. "We can fly the rest of the way there. I'll carry you both," he offers as he drops his hand from my back.

I turn back to face him, practically feeling the emotions roiling inside his mind. "Look, how about when we reach the town, I get word to Kieran to meet with us?" I offer. "I'm sure he can add some perspective to it all that I lack."

Rainer just nods before moving a few yards away from us and shifting. His dragon is a magnificent beast. His scales are a shade of copper that I'm certain gleam in the sunlight. He has two massive horns atop his head that have two rows of decreasing size horns trailing down his neck, stopping just before his wings.

He's just about the same size as my own dragon. I think as I call Manuel over and we walk to Rainer. I run my hand along his neck as he watches us move to his back, and his muscles ripple underneath my touch.

Rainer huffs as I drop my hand and move to help Manuel up onto his back before climbing up behind him. I have to show him where to hold on and quickly lock my arm around the boy's waist to keep him from slipping.

"Hang on tight. Taking off is always turbulent," I warn before nodding at Rainer. He gives a draconic smile before making the massive leap into the air and launching us upward.

Manuel screams in fright, but my hold ensures he is in no danger of falling and I can't help but laugh with joy as we sail through the sky. I love flying. Doesn't matter if it's on my own power or not, flying is the freest sensation in the world.

I feel someone dig into my brain again and this time I nearly fight it before I realize it's Rainer. Telepathy is a very rare power. One thought to have died out with the Galicia brood decades ago.

Sorry for the intrusion, he apologizes. *Is the boy ok?* he asks.

He is. He's just scared, which I get. I've got a tight hold on him, I assure him as my thighs keep us both anchored to Rainer.

It was you...earlier. Wasn't it? I ask him.

There is a mental snort. *You didn't listen in time,* he points out.

Yes well, when you're running for your life and some unknown person pushes into your mind, you tend to not trust it, I retort teasingly. *Speaking of...do you have Galicia blood?*

I don't know for sure but I can only assume so given this ability, he replies. *We're almost there. I will land a mile or so out so as to not alarm the villagers,* he adds before I can feel his presence slip from my mind again.

I reach down and squeeze Manuel's arm to me as Rainer makes his descent. He uses his wings to catch the air currents and slow us before making a running landing to further soften the jarring end of our flight. I leap off his back and catch Manuel's jump before Rainer shifts back.

I look between the two of us once more and sigh. "We both stand out quite a bit," I note. Between his armor and my tattered gown we'll draw a lot of attention.

Manuel pipes up. "I can go and gather some things for you to wear," he offers quietly.

I give him a reassuring smile. "That's a great idea but I don't want you doing anything dangerous either. Here, take my coin and buy something that won't stand out; include yourself too. We could all do with a change of clothing," I add.

The boy looks at me with a surprised expression but nods, taking the purse of coins and heading off towards the town...leaving me alone with the grumpy knight.

I walk us back into the sparse trees and settle down against a dying tree trunk. The tree's sorrow begins ringing in my ears and I sigh.

"What's wrong?" Rainer asks, studying me intently.

"The tree. It's sorrow is filling my mind and begging for aid," I answer.

"So why don't you...do your magic?" he asks.

"The Gift is draining to use and I'm still affected by the poison. That bush I grew took a lot out of me and I don't have much left in me right now," I answer, trying not to get angry at his question. He didn't know how it worked and it was a valid question to ask.

"I see you also have your father's storm," he notes with tenderness in his tone now. "He was a great man."

"So I'm told. Often. It didn't stop what happened though, did it?" I snap, feeling my hold on my emotions begin to fray.

"No it didn't. There will always be those with darker hearts who wait for their chance to strike. It seems your father had inadvertently surrounded himself with many of them," he says, ignoring my slight outburst. "You must take care not to repeat the mistakes of the past. Some who present themselves as friends have ulterior motives. One of the things you learn as a knight is just how two-faced royals can be."

"And you? What are your ulterior motives?" I ask him.

"I'm no royal. I serve the rightful rulers of our land," he recites again and I roll my eyes at him.

"Rainer, everyone, not just those in power, has other motivations for their actions. It's just a part of living life."

"It's my duty and my purpose to..."

"Fuck your duty. Duty has led thousands of men astray. How many knights are out here right now, defending the usurpers and punishing the people all because of blind duty!" I begin to get worked up, shouting at him as I stand and stride into his personal space.

"Duty is a cloak you all wrap yourselves in to tell yourself you have no blame for the actions you take. Duty gives you an excuse to make blatantly bad decisions, because ultimately you can blame your Lord for giving an order." I feel the storm gathering within me as my anger flows through me. "Duty is the biggest load of bullshit and the cause of so much suffering throughout the realm. So I ask again, what are your motives?"

Rainer is taken aback by my outburst. I know I shouldn't push him so hard. Helping me was a first action against his sworn duty. He's rationalized it though since I'm the true heir. Giving himself permission for the act of free will he took.

"You have to start thinking for yourself without 'duty' being the reason for everything. To make your own choices and your own moves on the playing field. Do something for yourself, not in a selfish way but something *you* want to do. Follow your gut or your heart." I urge him, watching his brain begin to turn and the fire he is born to sparks in his eyes as he stalks away from me, pacing as he struggles with himself and I feel disappointment flood me. I shouldn't be surprised. Knights all have the duty stick shoved so far up their asses they can taste wood.

But then, I feel him push into my mind again. *Fuck, you drive me crazy,* comes his voice as he rushes me, grabbing me to him and slamming his lips against mine. Everywhere our skin touches feels like the most pleasant warmth explodes across it. My arms snake around him, reaching for the buckles that secure his armor to him, not liking the barrier that stops me from feeling that warmth dance across all of me. The armor falls to the ground with a clang and he steps out and over it as he pushes me up against a tree.

Rainer works me up into a panting mess, moaning with need as his hands explore my body. One hand begins to slip through a rip in the dress when he suddenly stops and pulls back from our kiss.

"Why'd you.." I begin to ask when he shushes me softly.

"Manuel is returning," he tells me, looking back down into my eyes. "Fuck Aella..."

"Don't. Don't you fucking dare finish that thought. I swear on all the storms, if you dare tell me you regret this or it's a mista-"

Rainer silences me with another kiss, pressing himself against me again.

I don't. Not a single second. His mind touches mine again and the warmth I feel on my skin, seeps into my mind as well.

Rainer steps back this time and turns to go grab his armor. "I'll need to hide this. Bury it. I figure once we get in town we should find a healer to work the poison out of your system. Then we need a plan. We need to get you home, and Manuel to safety," he outlines as I try to regain my equilibrium.

I nod, adjusting the dress as we see Manuel crest the hill, two bundles in his arms and new clothes fitting to himself. I'm sure I'm still quite flushed looking and while Manuel is young, he was also enslaved so I'm sure his eyes miss nothing as he approaches.

"The tailor had a few pieces I felt would work for you both," he tells us, avoiding eye contact with both of us.

"That's great, thank you Manuel. Did you see a healer's hut?" I ask and he nods.

"It's deeper in town, past the inn," he answers. "I'll just...go behind the boulder while you both change," he says before hurrying to do so.

I nod at his retreating back and quickly change once Rainer turns his back to me to do the same. I can't help but pause and catch a flash of his ass as he slips into the new pants. *His ass had to be sculpted by the gods...just wow!*

Rainer chuckles softly as he catches my thought and I blush fiercely having been caught leering at him. He walks over and takes my hand before we find Manuel and head into the town.

Luck is on our side as we find the inn and get a room to rest in. No one seems to recognize Rainer and no one questions either of us much. Folks out in the smaller villages tend to want to keep to themselves and questions can bring trouble. The innkeeper's wife accepts my message scroll and I watch as she ties it to the leg of the dwarf wyvern and sets him off on his journey. It'll take two days to get a response or maybe a day if Kieran comes himself.

The two days pass quickly and quietly and on day three I begin to worry. With no word and no sign of my uncle I'm up earlier than the boys, so slip downstairs to go for a walk and clear my anxieties. The poison still lingers enough in my system to deny my beast her form and I find myself becoming more of a bitch than I'd like.

I feel him before I even see him on the horizon; my uncle's dragon speeding through the open landscape at breakneck speeds. I can't help but smile a little sheepishly as the town suddenly sounds the warning horns with how he's coming in hot. Kieran skids to a halt as he lands, pushing up clouds of dust before he shifts running to me and scooping me into his arms.

"Aella de Asturias how DARE you do something so incredibly reckless and without thought! Your mother and I have been scouring the continent looking for you!" he scolds me as he squeezes me to his chest and I feel a tear hit the top of my head.

"I know, I'm sorry I-" I don't even get to finish the sentence before I hear a roar of challenge coming from behind us. I try to reach out to touch his mind with my own. *"Rainer, it's ok. I'm ok. This is my Uncle Kieran!"*

Rainer's copper dragon lands before us and Kieran tenses on guard, shoving me behind him.

"Uncle, it's fine. Can you both put the testosterone away for a second so I can explain?" I grumble as I step out from behind him. "Uncle Kieran, this is Rainer. Rainer, my Uncle," I tell them both as Rainer shifts back.

"I woke and you weren't there, and the horns sounded..." he tries to explain, and I sigh.

"I know, I'm sorry, I needed to clear my head, when Uncle Kieran showed up. They don't know him here and he was coming in fast."

Kieran and Rainer eye one another still before Kieran turns to me. "We should talk about what happened to have you trusting him so much now."

I nod. "And I need you to meet Manuel. He's coming home with us. The poison still hasn't faded enough for me to shift."

Kieran sighs but nods, watching me as I take a few quick steps and take Rainer's hand in mine, bringing his fingers to my lips and kissing them softly. "I'm sorry I worried you," I whisper before walking with him back into the city with my uncle trailing behind us. Neither saying a word until we reach the inn. Rainer goes to the innkeeper and explains the false alarm before we head up to our room, and I make introductions for Manuel.

With a sigh I drop myself onto the bed and pull my legs up while Kieran takes the chair and the boys settle on the floor; Rainer nearest me always. Carefully I go over our flight from the castle and the events that led us here. Rainer adding a bit from his perspective as well, while Manuel stays silent.

Kieran nods and grunts at times, and his eyes flick to Rainer when he reaches up and pulls my leg down over his shoulder to rub my foot. "Alright so...what is this?" He motions from Rainer to me.

"We haven't really talked about it," I answer. "He knows what lies before me and I did suggest he speak with you as he struggles with his oaths," I point out.

"I won't interfere with what she needs to do. I want to help her where I can, but I understand that ultimately, she needs to do this on her own," Rainer answers.

"That's all well and good, and she wouldn't give you a say in that anyway. You two need to really consider what this is and what it means for you both. If this is something more than a comfortable fling that means you will be a king," Kieran spells it out bluntly.

I flash Kieran a look of warning. "Uncle it's been only a few days and we've been mostly on the run or laying low. I think it's far too early to be having this discussion."

"Is it? Really think about this Aella. You have one duque left before Riordan. Despite this...delay, Martin's appointment is still on track. There isn't much time left before you take your throne; then begins every eligible male vying for the right to be your king. And that's assuming they don't try to force one on you by the laws that saw your mother going to your father in the first place. Those are things we all knew would be happening." He looks over at Rainer, who's eyes flicker briefly with rage, causing my uncle to smirk. "If what's going on between you is something real and something you want to hold onto, well, you'll need to sort out a solution with your mother. She knows the laws inside and out."

"Fine. We'll have the conversation...when we're home. Can we please get out of here?" I ask, trying not to sound as whiny as I feel.

Rainer stands with a nod. "I'll carry you. Ser Kieran, will you take Manuel?" he adds using Kieran's title.

Uncle snorts. "Drop the title, it doesn't apply to me any longer...*Ser Rainer*," he shoots back.

Rainer shrugs. "I don't think that applies to me any longer either," he points out as we all head out of the inn. Kieran pays for the stay and once we are out of town he and Rainer shift, taking Manuel and I on their backs for the flight home.

Chapter 4

When we land in Murcia and Kieran and Rainer shift back again, I can feel my mother's presence hurrying to us. I don't even bother ducking as her sandal comes flying through the air with lightning precision and hits me in the temple. Rainer stands in stunned silence as she then launches herself at me and wraps me in a desperate hug.

"I'm fine, Mamá. Mostly. Just gotta work this little bit of sphalerite out of my system and all will be right as rain," I try to soothe her.

"Don't you ever do something so incredibly reckless again, do you hear me?!" she chastises me as she pulls back to look me over.

"Mamá you're gonna hate this, but...I need you to listen. Manuel needs a home and help. Please get him situated with Margarita, or maybe Isabella. They can help him settle in and start working on his trauma. We can still make the next appointment if I leave tonight."

"Wait, you can't be serious! Aella, we can move that a few days off. Tensions are too high amongst the nob-"

"No. Tonight. They've had a few days to figure out what happened at Ordoño keep. We can't give them even more time to think and prepare," I argue softly. Motioning my head to the path out of Murcia and to our homes.

She looks about to say something again when Uncle Kieran steps up, and takes her gently by the elbow. "Come, let's have this conversation at home. We'll see Manuel to Margarita's home and then we can discuss all that has happened."

Her gaze lands on Rainer and I see her eyes narrow in scrutinization at his proximity to me. I can see her pull that queenly aura she's long kept hidden and Rainer, to his credit, doesn't flinch. "Cause my daughter to shed even a single tear and I will make her kills look like mercy."

Rainer gives her an appeasing smile before looking down at me. His grin softens and morphs into the same one I've seen for days now. "Queen Nabia, if there should come a day I caused Aella to shed a tear, I would tear out my own scales one by one."

Mother still doesn't look pleased, but she does shove her feelings back down on the matter and turns leading up along the path. We stop and bring Manuel to Margarita, who happily takes him in. We give her a brief rundown of what he's been through and promise to deliver anything they need before heading to our home in silence. Rainer takes it all in, looking over the path and then the real town intently, and I feel him brush against my mind again.

You've all just been hiding up here in the mountains the whole time? he asks and I hum my acknowledgement.

It hasn't failed us yet. If you had kept following me, you still wouldn't have found it. I'm always very careful to be sure I have no followers before returning, I assure him with a smirk.

He chuckles and nods, pulling my hand into his and bringing it up to kiss my knuckles again. *Your mother is a clever woman. I don't think many gave her the credit she was due. There were stories of how many of your father's victories were thanks to her strategies, but few believed them. They were told by the maids and servants of the castle,* he explains.

She and Uncle set this up with the, then, head of the rebels. It's been our home since I could walk. That flat mountain to the northeast is where we launch from, I tell him as I brush my hand along the bushes and their flowers immediately open again.

Rainer blinks at the action and I smile. "We are well fed here and our plant life flourishes."

He's quiet as we make our way up the path to our home and Mother lets us all in. I can feel her anxiety and I know she's going to fix a tray of tea and biscuits for us, so I lead Rainer to the couches.

"How about I begin with what happened? I'm sure Kieran told you about the ball, so I'll just pick up from what happened in the pandejo's rooms." I go on to retell again what happened and the escape from the castle. How Rainer found us and helped us make it to Alicante. I tell her about our conversations and Kieran coming to us.

"It's clear you two think you love one another," My mother gets right to the point, barely keeping the scoff from her tone and I shoot her a warning look.

"And I'm aware you probably want to believe it's just a touch of white-knight syndrome. And maybe that is a catalyst in this but I don't have time to properly explore it now do I? I simply have to trust my heart and my gut, and both seem to be in agreement for once. So, I am not asking you when I say this, I'm telling you. Accept this as it is. Accept that Rainer is my choice of partner and that I trust him. Accept that there is the very real possibility that I take him as my king."

It's very rare that I stand up like this to my mother's opinions. Most of the time I do simply agree with her judgment, but for goddess' sake she was the one who told me to give him a chance, and now she's upset that I didn't do it in the way she assumed I would? Tough titties.

Mother brings the tray to the low table and sets it down, without slamming it. *Kudos for that I guess.* She sits and purses her lips in annoyance, as Kieran ignores the battle of wills and hands out the tea like nothing is going on.

"Alright," she finally says, letting out a breath.

I blink at her for a moment. "Alright?" I question, confusion clearly written all over my face.

"Alright," she says again. "You're to be queen, Aella. I cannot keep meddling in things if I ever expect you to be truly leading our people," she acknowledges.

I nod and push aside the stunned feeling I'm still having. "Ok then, you're not gonna like this any better but yes, I intend to leave tonight for Castile la Mancha. I will be keeping Martin's appointment."

Her frown returns. "The poison isn't even fully out of your system. You need to rest and we need to come up with new contingencies since the disaster at Ordoño keep. You can't just go in half co-"

I can't help but growl softly at her as she begins to get worked up. "Mother. I appreciate that this past week has scared you. I am aware I will probably never understand just how much it did until I have fledglings of my own. But I need this to end, *we* all need this to end. The land is nearing its critical mass and I cannot begin to fully describe for you the very real pain that lingers in every muscle of my body, as it dies." I tell her the one thing I've been keeping from them both. We all knew the land was dying. What they didn't know was I was experiencing its death, and I wasn't fully convinced I could survive it.

Three heads whip to stare at me intently and I'm very quickly reminded of why I kept this to myself as all three start talking at once. Rainer's hand tightens on the one of mine he is holding and I sigh softly. "STOP!" I shout just loudly enough to be heard.

"This is why I haven't said anything. This right here. The frantic worry and desperation that's choking this room now," I look directly at my mother. "The Gift is tied to the land. We knew this. It isn't so hard to believe that my own life force is also tied to it. So yes, I've felt the fatigue and the pain as our lands die more and more. There wasn't anything anyone could do about it so I didn't burden you with it."

Everyone sits in silence for a beat before my mother speaks again. "If you had said something sooner..."

"The opportunities wouldn't have changed. These were all still our best windows for the kills. And this is the time to move on Martin."

Rainer clears his throat and gets up to stand in front of me. As I meet his gaze, my heart breaks a little seeing the pain flittering in his heated eyes. "It changes nothing, you're right. You need to take this shot now and I...I will return to my post. I am of no use to anyone here, but I can still be of use in the knighthood. My regiment is slated to be at the seat of the kingdom for the anniversary of Riordan's ascension. I presume you mean to have the confrontation then?" he asks me and I nod, not liking the thought of him putting himself in danger, but my beast purrs within me. "Then, I will be there, and I will find you more allies amongst the knights. And when the time comes, no matter what situation you find yourself in, I will be at your back," he tells me with a stubbornness I recognize.

That's a week apart, and we haven't even discussed if you want to accept that being with me means being a king, I silently point out.

His expression softens. "I accept that being with you brings new responsibilities, chief among them is having your back and protecting this pretty neck of yours from those who would come for it," he declares as his hand slides up my arm and caresses my neck, sending a wave of heat through my body. "I will be your king if it means I am beside you always."

I can feel my eyes watering at his declaration and he tuts at me softly, reaching up to dry them. "Careful. Your mother made a promise," he reminds me teasingly and I can feel my cheeks burn with embarrassment as she chuckles.

"I did indeed," she agrees, with a heavy sigh. "Alright then. Come. Let's get a proper meal going before we send you off again, and Rainer, you're staying a bit more before we send you off too," she tells him firmly. He nods without looking at her, his eyes still locked with mine.

And will we have some time alone before you leave? he asks of me.

I think we can squeeze in a bath in my hot spring, I promise him before we get up to help with the meal.

Rainer's hands explore every inch of my body as we soak in the hot spring that is my bath. I don't bother trying to quiet the moans and gasps that escape my lips as he learns everything about my body; from the spots that turn me on, to the ones that are susceptible to being tickled. Sitting here between his thighs as he gently strokes my pussy has to be one of the most relaxing and hot moments of my life. His cock stirs beneath me but he makes no moves to hurry us into acting on its demands.

"Rainer..." I breathe out, unsure how he'll react to me being more demanding of him.

"Yes, my queen?" he murmurs into my ear, sending a shudder through my body.

I shift around, turning and tucking my legs around his hips as I straddle him and rub my core against him. "I need you...to stop hesitating and take all of me," my beast's growl joining my tone with her own demands.

His eyes flicker again, his beast peering back at mine with pure, unadulterated hunger.

"My queen, I have never..." he begins to explain what is holding him back, and I silence him with my finger.

"Neither have I. We will just follow our hearts," I tell him before he surges forward, his lips commanding mine to let his tongue enter as he lets go of the fear of disappointing me.

I roll my hips against him, his cock seeking my entrance as the water sloshes around us. Rainer's hand slides down to again find my bundle of nerves, rubbing in a small circle before he guides his cock to me and slides inside. My muscles ache and burn as they stretch to accommodate his intrusion, and he waits until he feels the fluttering of my pussy around him.

"I've got you, I will always have you," he whispers to me as he kisses up my neck and nibbles on my ear while slowly thrusting in and out. "My queen, my mate, I will worship at the altar of your body for as long as you will have me." His promises repeat over and over like a fervent prayer, and I answer with promises of my own.

"My mate, my king, my light in the darkness. It will be you and me till the very end," I promise him with a gasp as he begins to increase his tempo. I feel my beast stirring, her mind and mine as one. In Rainer she has found a worthy mate, and as our gazes lock once again I see his beast as well.

We want... comes Rainer's familiar voice, but it's interrupted by what I can only assume is his beast's thoughts. The voice is deeper and I feel the violent edge to it that mimics my own, *...you to bear a mark,* he demands as my dragon purrs in agreement. It's an ancient practice, not done in centuries. The act of biting your mate and licking the wound with your breath's weapon to seal it. A sign to all that you are claimed.

Do it. My own beast's urges surging through every fiber of my being to make her wishes known.

Rainer slams into me again and I begin to feel the building up of an orgasm as my fangs become more pronounced. I pull myself to his shoulder as he thrusts up into me and bites into the spot his shoulder meets his neck. The tangy copperiness of his blood fills my mouth and I gulp it down before exhaling a small breath of lightning against the wound. The sparks dance across it, sealing it with ancient magic before I feel him bite into my own shoulder and the orgasm explodes in both of us. The fire of his breath caresses my skin and seals the wound, as he fucks me harder; it feels like forever before the orgasm ebbs away and he leans back taking me to lay against his chest in the pool of water.

We're both taking in deep breaths of air as we recover and this time when I reach out to his mind I find no resistance at all. In fact I can feel his emotions as easily as I feel my own.

Rainer what...what's happened? I ask him, confused but not afraid.

I think there is more to this than just showing others we are claimed, he muses as our breathing begins to even out and I start to notice our hearts beating at the same rate.

Rainer stands, lifting me with him, and takes us out of the spring. Carefully he sets me down on the bench and grabs a towel, wrapping me in it as he inspects the wound.

"There is ancient magics at play in this," he tells me. "The wound is barely a wound now. It's more like a burn scar in the shape of the flame I kissed it with."

Looking up at his own I can see what he means. Overlapping the bite scars I left on him the skin looks kissed by lightning and shimmers slightly when light hits it.

"I feel you more clearly than when you touch my mind," I tell him and he nods. "And our hearts beat together."

Rainer nods and looks over at the leathers laid out for me. "Come my queen, my mate, if we delay any further you will miss your window and I will not be able to let you go," he tells me, the tone of his voice and the pain I feel in his own heart, echoing in mine.

With gentle touches and kisses over my skin, Rainer helps me into my leathers and laces up my boots tightly. He kisses over the scar from the ballista bolt and grunts softly before spinning me around to face him. He cups my face and stares intently at me. "Come back to me, my beat. I cannot have gained you, gained an us, to lose you so soon."

"I promise. I'm coming back to you, and we're taking down the false king. We will restore our world to balance," I tell him before he gives me one more searing kiss, and we head up to Flatiron Rock for a last goodbye with Mother and Kieran.

The journey north to Castile la Mancha is a long one. Luckily it's one I can fly instead of take on foot, as few travel to the Consuming Ice lands. The frigid temperatures and rocky lands make for an unwelcoming atmosphere. Duque Martin really is at home in his native lands. He is a cold and heartless man who rules over his people through violence and fear. He's also the most fit and fearsome of the lords, training his knights personally and it's said none have landed a hit on him.

The window tonight is slim. His wife is away in hiding, giving birth to what he hopes will be a son. The previous three pregnancies, all girls, curiously did not live to survive their births. His mistresses have given him sons, but he refuses to recognize them as legitimate since it would give those women bargaining chips to use over him. Duque Martin owes no one anything, and his wife was something his father paid handsomely for.

So while she is hidden away, the duque is home in his castle, a rarity these days. He is supposed to be gearing up his knights, putting them through some rigorous training, before the celebration for the king. Kieran gave me a few options for tonight, places I can slip in, hide, and pounce as I have been, but the more I consider it, the more I want to directly challenge him...and I know just when to reveal myself.

After taking down a patrol and slipping into their armor, I find my way into the training grounds and watch as Duque Martin strides into the center. The general has us all circling the space where the duels will take place and I've made my way forward to be in the front rows of knights. The general explained that any who wished to be on the detail for the king, would have to first fight the duque himself.

The general is the first to take a duel and while Duque Martin makes swift work of him, the man puts up a good fight. When Martin nearly takes his arm off, he yields, the duque giving him a pass to lead the squad that will be attending. Five others decide they have the skills to make it, and only two get a pass from his lordship. I can feel the nervousness flittering through the rest of the knights.

I push through with a growl as another knight tries to pull me back. "I want my turn," I declare, dropping my tone a bit.

The Duque's eyes narrow on me. "You seem awfully young to be in my knighthood," he states, trying to place me.

"I am, but I'm skilled," I state.

The general, not wanting to be found incompetent, backs me up. "My lord he did indeed pass all requirements and tests we have for the knighthood. I assure you."

"Fine. Let's see the prodigy then," he says, taking a somewhat lazy stance that I've seen him use a dozen times already. I took a deep steadying breath as I stepped up and raised my sword, taking a basic stance, and getting the reacting snort from Martin I expected.

With two quick strides, Duque Martin comes charging at me in his usual brutally forceful manner. He likes to use his size and strength to dominate the space, but I have always been quick and light on my feet.

With calculated precision, I parry his blows, my own sword darting to intercept his attacks. I sidestep, twist, and dance around his strikes, feeling the wind rush past as his blade narrowly missed me. The duque's frustration grows apparent as my movements seem to mock his raw power.

As the duel continues, I focus on finding openings in his defense, small weaknesses to exploit. My sword darts in, grazing his unguarded flank with swift, calculated thrusts. The other knights' gasps and whispers fill the arena as I make cut after cut to the lord's leathers.

Martin's strength is unwavering, but his energy is finite. With every swing, he seems to slow, while I find myself settling into the rhythm of the fight. My sword is an extension of my will, and my movements become a seamless dance that leave him bewildered.

Then came the moment of truth. Duque Martin, perhaps in desperation, launches a mighty overhead strike that leaves him vulnerable. It is a split-second opportunity, and I seize it. I stepped into his attack, my sword darting upward. It makes contact, slicing into his shoulder and sending his broadsword crashing to the ground. Duque Martin staggers back, clutching his wounded arm and roaring in rage. I feel the air around us drop to a freezing temperature and his beast comes roaring into his gaze, his aura pushing out and demanding submission.

With a roar of my own, my beast pushes her aura out to meet his as I run at him and kick him square in the chest, sending him onto his back and his dragon into retreat. Lightning dances across my arms, calling the storms to me as my anger and power was on full display. Tossing my helmet to the side I grin down at him.

"Hello Martin, I'm afraid your beast won't come to your aid right now. His queen has demanded his submission and he has chosen wisely to accept," I taunt him loud enough to be heard by those around us. Martin moves to try and push me from him when vines burst forth from the earth and bind him to the ground.

"No. You're dead. You're supposed to be dead!" he shouts in disbelief as I roll my eyes at him.

"Those are what you want your last words to be? A boring declaration of how I shouldn't be alive? Do you have any idea how cliché that is? I suppose you wouldn't, it would require you to read."

I turn, still standing on his chest, to address the knights, some of whom seem ready to pounce and save their lord.

"My name is Princess Aella de Asturias. Daughter of King Aeon and Queen Nabia. And it was I who was born with The Gift," I declare, pushing out my aura to try and keep their beasts in check. "On the night of my father's death, my mother delivered me and the men of court decided I should be murdered. That having a queen sit the throne was unconscionable. Due to the Queen's bravery and her loyal knight, we escaped and I lived. The land isn't dying due to some previously unknown dark magics. It's dying because these greedy men decided they knew better than the gods, than the land itself."

I look down and meet Martin's angry, calculating, glare. "You will die here today," I promise him as I look out at his knights. "What you do with his castle, his lands, I do not care. I have promised to save these lands from their death and I shall. But know this. Come at me with violence, become like these men and trample on the people around you to gain power, and I will come back and you will join the former Duque in death."

Martin's body begins to be dragged into the earth by the vines as I stand on his chest. As soon as he understands what's happening he begins to fight and scream at his men to save him but the fight, for now, has left them. They are unsure of what I can do as they watch their lord be dragged into the earth, buried alive.

The general finally finds his voice, "It's been you, these last years. Hasn't it?" he asks me and I nod.

"All that remains is my cousin," I affirm.

"Will you grant him mercy?" he asks.

"Does he deserve it?" I counter before pulling the magic within me and shifting into my dragon again, her magnificent silver scales shimmering even through the storm clouds that begin to release their icy rains, as she spreads her wings, sending the knights clamoring to get out of her way.

Touch their minds. I hear again the deep voice that silenced the whispers before.

Trusting my gut I do as it tells me and try to push into their minds. It doesn't work at first until I think about Rainer and how it felt connecting with him. On a whim I pull at the bond I feel, borrowing some of its strength and then I feel it click. It's not my power, it's borrowing my mate's power and it's not the same as with my mate, more like opening a small space to be heard from.

Do better than those before you.

Chapter 5

The day-long flight to Castilo de Salas was more tedious than anything else. While I always love the freeness that flight gives me, this flight has purpose and, I hope, an end to our hiding. An end to the greed and hubris that is killing our world. An end...and a beginning.

As I approach the keep, I see the streets are decorated with black and gold banners and streamers hung from one lamppost to the next. The streets are largely empty, the populace having gathered at the castle for the re-coronation. My cousin takes a new crown every five years on the anniversary of his crowning. It's ridiculously pompous of him.

I coast silently to a rooftop near the back of the castle proper and shift back, landing with a soft thump on its tiles. Climbing down the trellis that resides at the back of the house, I make my way up the cobblestone road that leads to the castle.

Outside, I find the crowd of commoners clamoring for a glimpse of the nobles who arrive one by one in carriages of gold and ebony. I slip through the crowd, my beast pulsing her aura enough to make people move from my path subconsciously, making space before me like a bow through the sea. I reach the front of the crowd as Alfonso steps from his carriage, the last to arrive, and his head swivels to meet my gaze; feeling my presence. With that lopsided smile sitting on his lips, he whispers to his guard and motions to me. The guard nods, then turns to me and taps his fist to his shoulder in salute.

My beat. Are you here? Rainer's presence fills my mind, making me smile.

I am. Alfonso and his guard have acknowledged me. How have your last few days gone? I have missed you, I tell him. I know I shouldn't waste time, but I need him to know I thought about him constantly.

I feel his chuckle. *Very dull. The upper echelon have been in a panic with no word coming out of The Consuming Ice. Riordan received back his messenger's head today with a note I wasn't privy to, attached. I think you left an impression with them. There is support here for you. When the usurper falls, I think most will fall in line.*

Where are you stationed? I ask, making my way to the side door and taking Alfonso's guard's offered arm.

Hallway duty. Just call for me and I will be at your back.

I reach out to the guard's mind. *I'm sorry for the intrusion, but this is the safest way. It's an honor to make your acquaintance, Ser Gregory.*

I feel the knight stiffen briefly before he looks down at me, and I give him an apologetic smile. *The honor is entirely mine, Your Highness. What is it you need of me?*

Find Ser Rainer for me. He's on hallway duty. I'm afraid I'm going to have to make a scene here in a moment.

He nods at me before going in search of my mate, while I creep back around to the servant's doors that lead into the main hall where the ceremony is being held.

I find the door cracked open, a few maids peering in to see and hear what's going on within. I stay silent as I approach only letting my foot scuff the floor to warn them when I am close enough to whisper to them.

They yelp as I shush them and my dragon again pushes forward, pulsing her aura in a new manner, calming the girls with a purring sort of sound from my chest.

"I'm sorry for scaring you," I tell them softly. "I just wanted to see what's going on."

One of the girls, a young red-haired woman, nods to the door. "The king is giving his speech about how he's going to bring down the rebels. His Lordship will be crowned again shortly. Do you want to peek?" she asks and I shake my head. "Keep your place. I don't want to intrude," I tell them before backing off and going back to the main doors.

Pressing my ear to the door, I hear Riordan's booming voice as he recites the pledge of the king. Hollow empty words that mean nothing to him.

"Today, I stand before you with a profound sense of duty, humility, and gratitude. It is with a heart full of reverence for the traditions and history of our kingdom that I accept the weighty responsibility that has been placed upon my shoulders. I stand here as the chosen steward of this land, ready to accept the crown and all that it symbolizes. With your support and the grace of the divine, I pledge to serve you with all my heart and soul. May our kingdom continue to shine as a beacon of justice, prosperity, and unity for generations to come. With The Gift of the gods..."

I've had enough of this bullshit, I growl to myself as I kick the doors open, their slam against the walls reverberating in a completely satisfying way.

"...which you DO NOT have." I cut my cousin off while unleashing my dragon's aura. Her presence fills the entire grand hall, demanding the submission of all present.

All heads snap to me as I walk down the aisle that leads to the throne. "Tell me cousin, how long did you really think you all could keep up the facade? How did you deal with those demanding proof of your claims? Did you kill them? Is that what happened to the Galicia? Bribe them?" My eyes land on the nobles in the hall, sons of the men I've killed over the last year.

"Please do show us the wonders of The Gift. Can you even grow a small flower?" I taunt as the crowd begins to grumble and the guards begin to move in towards me.

Riordan seems genuinely confused as I approach, which isn't surprising, as he was told I was dead that night.

"Who the hell do you think you are?!" he roars, as he finds his anger. "You dare interrupt a sacred tradition and defile my court with your vile claims!?"

Aella this wasn't the plan, comes my mate's hurried words as I feel his anxiety spike.

A guard makes a lunge for me, and I lash out with a bolt of lightning, wielding it like a whip as I crack it around his ankles and yanking him to the ground.

"My name, *Duque* Riordan, is Princess Aella de Asturias. Daughter of King Aeon and Queen Nabia Asturias, bearer of The Gift, and true heir to the throne you sit upon... and I have come to claim what is rightfully mine, and restore our land," I declare as I feel his beast trying to push mine to submit.

Behind me, I hear fighting in the hall and something thuds at my back before I feel my mate's hand on my shoulder, sending warmth through my body.

Just because I will always have your back, doesn't mean you shouldn't watch it. He tries to be playful but this bond between us ensures I know how scared he just was.

He's going to shift and I am going after him. Get to the ballistas. I don't need their complications... and thank you. I'll try not to get so cocky.

With a frustrated roar, Riordan begins to shift when he can't make me submit. He launches himself into the open air above the hall and hovers, spitting lightning down into it, caring not for the others still in the room. People begin to scatter, so many of them no longer have their dragons to protect them, as Riordan's breath weapon sears through several rows of seating. I don't have time to count the dead nor can I shield them, but I can distract him and pull him away from here.

Feeling my intentions, and with a roar of my own, Rainer cups his hands together and I step into them quickly. With all his strength he helps launch me into the air and I shift in a quick and fluid motion at the apex of his throw. My beast roars her glee at being free again, before turning to find Riordan.

Lightning suddenly crackled from his maw as he unleashed a furious bolt of electricity towards me. I twist my serpentine body gracefully through the air, coiling around the deadly arc of energy as it fizzles out. With a roar I find him following the bolt and slamming straight into me, his jaws snapping onto my neck as he tries to tear a chunk out of me.

A panic tries to creep in before I use my back legs to dig into the flesh of his underbelly, working to kick him off of me as he tries to bring me to the ground. I get in three good slashes before he releases me, my neck burning where he bit me and refusing to heal.

No. How?! I panic realizing his jaws seem to have been coated in sphalerite. I swoop and straighten out my fall as I try to flee the city and get us away from the innocent people below; Riordan blessedly giving chase as his rage consumes his every move.

Rainer? I try to reach my mate's mind, unsure of how far away from him I am now and feeling weaker as the poison begins to get into my bloodstream.

AELLA... His fearful reply comes into my mind but I can already feel the bond being muted by the sphalerite. *...where...coming...my beat...*

My vision begins to blur and all I can do is try to land safely before I lose my form. While the landing isn't as crashing as before, it's certainly not graceful. And this time I'm on my feet as I become human again.

Riordan lands in front of me with a ground shaking slam. He grins as I back away from him. "Where's your bravado now? Your little tantrum proves that weakness like yours was long due to be culled. The gods got it wrong. Women only serve as vessels for the true heirs," he tells me with that imperious attitude I've seen from them all.

Holding the wound on my throat, I cough trying to clear the searing pain that exists. "So...weak...you had to...resort to poison..." I spit back at him.

Riordan shrugs off the insult. "Says the assassin who slinks in hallways and closets. You have no room to talk." He takes his sword off his hip and twirls it in the air. "I think I'm going to cut you into a thousand pieces and scatter you through the city as a warning to the rest of your rebels," he tells me before grinning and rushing me, his arm swinging out for a first hit. I drop to the ground as he swings at where my chest was and I call upon the earth.

Come to my aid, one more push. Let me end this, I beg and for a brief moment there is nothing. *Did I lose it too?* I wonder before suddenly roots erupt from the ground and lash themselves to Riordan's legs. I nearly cry in relief as he roars and curses, using his sword to try and free himself. *You are never alone, daughter.* I hear the voice again, whispering through my mind.

"I have...The Gift," I remind him. "The land...knows who...belongs on the...throne, and it answers to my...call."

In the distance I see dragons flying to where we are, one of them surely my mate. I smile and look back at Riordan as I hear his sword hit the dirt and the roots continue to engulf his body.

Rainer lands, shifting and running to me, his eyes widening in horror as he sees my throat.

"It's...not that...bad..." I try to say, but his look of shock and concern stops me before he even tells me to shut it.

"It's worse. Stop speaking," he scolds me softly as he lifts my chin and pulls out a cloth to clean and check the wound.

Several other dragons land and shift, among them Ser Gregory, and they take in the scene before them. Ser Gregory turns to the knights who came with him and begins barking orders. "You two fly back to the castle and inform the infirmary Her Majesty has been injured with sphalerite poisoning and to prepare for her arrival. Ser Jovan and Ser Hector, gather the lords that remain and bring them to court." His eyes find mine and I nod seeing where he is taking this. "Prepare them for the arrival of our Queen, the true heir and," he again looks at me for confirmation, which I give with a small smile. "and her king consort, Ser Rainer."

Rainer finally finishes bandaging the wound and kisses my lips softly before turning to Ser Gregory. "I will bring her back and dispose of the usurper. Please gather the knights and see to hunting those who fled." Ser Gregory nods in acknowledgement and leaps into the sky with another knight leaving two with us for protection.

"There are those who like the status quo," Rainer tells me. "They fled into the foothills. How would you like to deal with the usurper?" he asks me, as my cousin's muffled screams still come from his root coffin.

I can see his eyes peeking between the roots as I consider what to do with him. *Will you incinerate him, my king? As much as I'd love to draw out his torture, I just want this to be done.*

Rainer nods and kisses me again. "Incinerate him," I croak out and steady myself against a tree as Rainer shifts back into his dragon and launches into the air. He hovers over the bound and helpless Riordan before opening his mouth and unleashing a torrent of white hot flame onto him. His screams pierce through in the brief moment the roots withdraw from him so they don't get burned, and are snuffed out just as quickly as he succumbs to the fiery tornado pouring from Rainer's maw.

Rainer lands and shifts, coming to me and sweeping me up into his arms. "Come my queen, let's get you healed so we can crown that beautiful head of yours," he murmurs as he walks us back to the keep.

Rainer walks with me in his arms until we reach the fields that once surrounded my family's home. They've sat barren for years now turning the plains into a sort of dust bowl. I wiggle from his grasp despite his protestations and kneel in the dirt at the foot of the old plots. I can sense dozens of eyes watching from the small homes that dot the area, as I bury my hands in the earth and pull some of my own magic to breathe life back into them.

It's a far more draining thing for me than asking the plants to aid me, but the land here was already dead and there is nothing to pull from...so instead, I give. I give until I feel myself getting dizzy and Rainer scoops me up again.

"Enough. You can't do it all in one day," he growls softly, causing me to chuckle painfully.

"Don't go...bringing back...the grump now," I scold him with a smile. "And look," I urge him, pointing to where I kneeled.

Sure enough the soil has taken on a richer, darker color now ready for planting.

Did you set people to opening up the food stores and getting what's been hoarded out to the people? I ask him.

Yes. Kieran and your mother have arrived. He is seeing to the food, and she is waiting in the infirmary for you. This, he gestures at my work, *is going to upset her...more,* he warns.

The people of Castilo de Salas and its surrounding village watch cautiously from their windows as knights go door to door handing out baskets of food and instructions, for how things will go moving forward along with the announcement of the false king's death. Messengers have been dispatched to all the villages to spread the word, as the now former rebels work to secure the towns and assure everyone that change is coming. It's harder for them without my presence to show them the world will not die, but I have every ounce of faith in my people.

Mother of course frets and fusses over me when we enter the healer's rooms, driving the poor man near to snapping with her hovering. To his credit he doesn't yell at her, though he does have to gently push her away from time to time. He recleans and dresses the wound, warning it will scar as there isn't much he can do, but let the antidote take its course.

Over the next several days we find a rhythm, working to both assure the people of the truth of things and make sure everyone is fed and clothed. The surviving nobles grouse and complain every step of the way, with the exception of Alfonso who had already been making changes in his own lands once I'd killed his father. His support goes a long way as he reminds them that their titles are in my hands.

They of course push for a lavish coronation, but Rainer and I quickly put an end to such talk. Instead we have a smaller ceremony held outside the castle walls, with any who wish to attend present. To my utmost surprise, nearly all the townsfolk gather to celebrate with us.

And so I stand in the center of the fields that now flourish with fresh sprouts. I call upon the earth once more, and form the new Tree of Life. It shoots up almost forty-five meters tall, sending ripples of excitement through the gathered crowds. Its trunk is a twisting of ebony, redwood, and birch trees forming a beautiful kaleidoscope of color.

My mother steps forward looking proudly upon me, and begins her speech. "The suffering of our lands, of our people is no more. Today we gather to crown the true ruler of Dreavia. Princess Aella de Asturias, do you solemnly swear to uphold the traditions of your forefathers, of the bearers before you? To tend the lands and tame the storms? To protect and serve the people who place their faith in you?"

"With my life, so I swear," I answer firmly as I kneel before her and she takes from Kieran a crown I've never seen before. It's made from ebony and birch branches, twisted together with a single pearlescent opal in the center.

"With this crown, the crown of King Aeon de Asturias, and with the grace of the earth, I so enthrone Queen Aella de Asturias, bearer of The Gift and steward of the lands of Dreavia. LONG MAY SHE REIGN!"

The End

A Vow of Protection and Devotion

by Allie Carstens

Blurb

For as long as anyone in Ansterra can remember, the protectors of the fae monarchs of Evania have been chosen from the dragons of Tidirath. Lorcan and the fae princess Corinna's protector bond formed just after her sixteenth birthday, and the two have been almost inseparable since, each harboring secret feelings for the other, even though a relationship between them is forbidden. But will the summer solstice change everything?

Chapter 1
Corinna

I was being hunted. Chased. Followed.

The forest was dark and cool as I worked my way around the tall, ancient trees, my footsteps muffled by the damp earth and moss beneath my bare feet.

I crouched down behind a wide trunk, peering through the leaves of the royal fae ivy climbing and winding its way up and up until it could no longer be seen, the leaves a perfect match to the mark that wound around my wrist and forearm.

The racing heart in my chest beat a rhythm matched only by the solstice drums we would dance to the next evening just before sunset. I breathed in and out once, and then again, to abate the pounding muscle.

My eyes and brain flitted about as I assessed and calculated the size of the clearing, glancing between the ground and the gap in the trees above. The dark oranges, reds, and pinks of the sunset streaked across the sky, unhindered by the opening in the forest canopy.

Perfect, I thought to myself with a smirk.

I closed my eyes and inhaled through my nose, my palm resting against the trunk of the tree. The magic of the earth hummed and buzzed under my touch. I focused my connection to it towards the vines and branches in the surrounding trees, willing them to do my bidding, weaving them together to create the image in my mind.

The beat of heavy, leathery wings against the cool evening air had me snapping my eyes open and darting further behind the tree, further into the undergrowth of the forest floor. The dark greens and browns of my tunic and breeches helped me to hide among the greenery, dirt, and tree trunks.

The rays of the setting sun glinted off the hide of the silvery beast in the sky above me as he circled the clearing and let out a bellowing roar. With one last push of my magic, I finished my task just as he landed.

Right where I wanted him.

From my hiding spot, I waved my hand, causing dirt, leaves, and twigs on the other side of the clearing to scatter and skitter across the forest floor, pulling the magnificent beast's focus. His colossal head whipped around fast—fast for a monster of his size, at least—and before he could muster two steps in that direction, he found himself in the air again.

Only this time, he wasn't flying of his own volition. Oh no. He was suspended in the air, caught in a web of vines, branches, flowers, and leaves—a magical net made to hold any beast of his size and caliber.

With another bellowing roar, he let loose a pillar of fire. But of course, I thought he would try that and imbued my trap with magic to prevent it from burning.

Still, I let loose a stream of water from my hands, pulling it from the moist ground and the surrounding air. I directed it towards his flames, and the two opposites met with a steaming hiss in the air, the fire evaporating before it hit the ground or the other trees.

I sauntered out from my hiding spot and looked up at my pursuer. The great silver dragon who was now my captive.

"That's what…138 times now?" I said to him.

He huffed and rolled his eyes, smoke emitting from his nostrils. I'm sure he would have crossed his arms or put his hands on his hips, too, had he not been in his dragon form.

'I let you win,' he said to me in my mind, using our protector bond to speak to me.

"All 138 times?" I countered, looking at my fingernails. "I don't know, Lorcan, if it was one or five I'd maybe—"

My words were cut short by the snapping of bones reshaping, the whoosh of air from a portal forming, and the thump of a large, solid, muscular body slamming into my own, taking me to the ground with it.

Powerful arms wrapped around my waist and shoulders as he rotated our bodies so he would take the brunt of the fall. Then he rolled us over to slow our momentum until we came to a stop. He pressed my back against the forest floor, his body hovering over mine, his chest a breath away from touching me, and his dark curls framing my face.

"That's what...138 times now?" he echoed back to me, mimicking my words and my voice. He bent his arms, and his body lowered so it brushed against mine. "Maybe if you weren't so cocky about catching me, I wouldn't pin you every time you did, *banphrionsa*," he added, his voice returning to its normal baritone.

The deep timbre of his voice combined with the vibrations from his low laugh sent a thrill through my body. I was once again grateful that, as my protector, the magic of Evania gifted him with the ability to keep his clothing intact when he shifted.

It wasn't an issue when he was first revealed as my protector—when I was sixteen and he had just turned twenty. But almost three solstices passed since that day. And with them, my youthful innocence.

No longer did I view him as just a friend, just my protector. My heart and body yearned for something more.

He stayed hovering over me for a moment more, and it took every power within me to not run my hands over his broad chest and shoulders or close the minute distance between us and kiss his plush, full lips. I didn't, of course, because that would have been improper for a female fae of my status. And because he rose to his knees and sat back on his heels before I could even summon the courage to do so.

He held his hand out to me, and I took it, letting him help me into a seated position. His eyes raised to the sky as I straightened out my tunic and vest, readjusting the fabric so I was covered.

"We should return to the palace," he murmured, his brown eyes lowering back to mine. "The hour is growing late, and I will be departing soon."

"Departing?" I asked, my movements stilling. "To where?"

"To Tidirath. To visit Bran," he told me. "The same as I have every year on the solstice."

"But it's my birthday," I whispered.

His eyes stayed locked on mine, unblinking. No trace of emotion lingered there, no hint of regret, want, or desire. Just as always, I could never read him to know if he returned my secret longing.

Not that I'd ever given him a hint of how I felt. I kept those desires locked up tight, never allowing even a glimmer of attraction to show on my face or in my actions.

He was my protector. He had a job to do, and that didn't include bedding me. And beyond that, I would meet my mate soon. Most likely the next evening, at sunset on the solstice, the one day a year all fairy-kind could recognize their mate given to them by Gaia.

"It's your birthday every year on the solstice," he said with a glint in his eyes.

"Yes, but—" I sighed and looked down, my fingers fidgeting with a hole in the knee of my breeches.

He leaned forward, entering my space again, his fingers brushing through the waves of my long, brown hair. I closed my eyes and let his scent fill my lungs—his rich scent that made my stomach tighten and my heart flutter and stutter in my chest.

I kept my breathing steady, even though anticipation raced through me. I opened my eyes, and he still leaned close to me, his gaze focused on my hair while his fingers continued to stroke through the locks.

I mustered up my courage. I could do this. I didn't care if it was improper. I didn't care what they expected of me as the heir of Evania. For once in my life, I was going to choose for myself.

But just as I was about to close the distance and press my lips to his, he pulled away, a twig and several leaves in his hand, and he chuckled.

"I know you are a princess of the fae, a being of Gaia, but you really need to keep the earth out of your hair," he teased.

I huffed out an annoyed laugh and slapped his hand away. Then I stood, turning my head side to side as I brushed through my wild waves, trying to rid them of any remnants of the forest and to hide the pain and embarrassment in my eyes.

It was stupid of me to even consider kissing him. To even think he'd been considering the same. And yet, it still hurt more than I dared to admit.

He stood as well and gestured to me as he used his protector magic to open a gateway back to the palace.

"After you, Princess Corinna," he said, switching back to formalities and court protocol.

I walked by him and through the gateway into the courtyard without a word to him, for there was nothing I could say. Not without pouring my heart out to him.

"Corinna Drakos!"

My mother's shrill voice rang out, bouncing off the stones of the courtyard, not even muffled by the heavy ivy adorning every wall of the palace.

"Where have you been? And what are you wearing?" she demanded to know, her ice-blue eyes scanning over me with distaste as she entered the courtyard, her own protector, Sir Cillian, trailing behind her.

"I've been training with Lorcan, and I'm wearing breeches," I retorted.

She tutted, her hawk-like eyes landing on the hole in the knee. I grimaced but didn't flinch or hide the offending rip.

She switched her assessing gaze to Lorcan behind me, but I didn't dare turn around. I knew what I would see if I did. Lorcan, his eyes lowered to the ground with his head bowed, his hands behind his back.

Her eyes moved back to me slowly. "I thought we decided no more training? That it's unneeded. You have your protector. His job is to keep you safe. Your job is to rule the kingdom."

"You decided," I told her. "I did not agree. What kind of queen would I be if I did not fight alongside my people? If I expect them all to defend me while I sit safe inside the palace?"

"If you die in a fight, then the Drakos line ends, and there will be no one to rule over Evania," she reminded me.

"If I die, it will be because I cannot fight. Because you would not allow me to learn to defend myself and my people," I insisted, my volume rising with my words, my hand on my chest.

"And who would you be fighting? What battles do you see ahead for us?" Her eyes moved behind me again. "Sir Lorcan? You have something to say?" she asked, one dark eyebrow raised.

I did turn around at that. Lorcan no longer had his eyes cast down, but stared straight at my mother.

"Your Majesty. Queen Eirene," he began. "While I understand your concerns and see the validity of your arguments, Her Highness also makes an excellent point. While there hasn't been war in decades, and while you may not be at war now, peace is not everlasting.

Should war come to Evania's borders, it would behoove Cor...Princess Corinna to be capable of defending herself."

My mother's lips pursed at his slip-up, but she waited for him to continue, her sharp gaze and features emphasized by her raised brows and the tight bun in her black hair.

"Might I suggest a compromise?" Lorcan proposed.

"And what do you have in mind?"

"Princess Corinna be allowed to train, so long as the training does not impede her duties as the crown princess," Lorcan explained.

Her face remained pinched as she considered his words and his proposal. Lorcan returned to his dutiful protector position, and I kept my eyes forward, watching my mother, not daring to show even a splinter of hope on my face.

"Very well," she gritted out between her teeth as if the words were bitter medicinal herbs in her mouth. "You are dismissed, Sir Lorcan. Sir Cillian," she said, nodding to both of them. "We will see you at sunrise after the solstice."

"Come, my lady," Myrrhine, my handmaiden, said, touching my shoulder. "We must begin our preparations for tomorrow night."

I gave her a smile that did not quite reach my eyes, and followed her through the arches of the courtyard. I turned to look at Lorcan one last time, to bid him farewell, but he was already gone.

Chapter 2
Corinna

"Are you excited for the solstice, Your Highness?" Myrrhine asked, combing through my clean, damp waves as I sat in a tub of water warmed by my magic.

"I have seen many a solstice, Myrrhine," I sighed, leaning forward against my raised knees. "They are all the same."

"But this solstice you will be nineteen. You may very well find your mate."

My heart clenched. My mate. My mate, who wouldn't be Lorcan. My mate, who would likely be a high-ranking, powerful member of the fae royal court.

"I am not ready to be mated," I told her, shaking my head. "I am still young."

"It is unlikely your mate is not of age yet," she reminded me. "Your father, King Kallias, was nearing his thirtieth year when he and your mother mated."

I frowned. Yet another reason to not want to be mated. I did not want someone who was almost ten years older than me. Someone who'd enjoyed many women through their adult years while awaiting the appearance of their mate every summer solstice. I wanted to experience life, too.

"Maybe I will not attend this year," I said. "Maybe I will instead visit Tidirath with Lorcan. It has been an age since I have seen our allies in the dragon kingdom."

She chuckled, then tapped my shoulders, signaling me to stand. "Lorcan is probably halfway to Tidirath at this hour," she informed me as she wrapped a blanket around my body. "And your mother would not approve."

"My mother never approves of anything I do," I said with a dry laugh, stepping out of the tub and walking to my wardrobe.

"Queen Eirene only wants what's best for you," she said, pulling out my white night-gown.

"What's best for me, or what's best for her?" I muttered, then I shook my head. "Thank you, Myrrhine. You may take your leave. I can dress and put myself to bed," I commanded, holding my hand out for the garment.

She pressed her lips together but didn't argue with me and left my room with hurried steps. I pulled the nightgown on roughly, my cheeks and body heated with anger and indignation. I held in my growl of frustration and sprinted to the window, flinging the curtains wide to let in the fresh air and the starlight.

I hated this place. Hated the rules, protocols, and expectations. It was a cage, and I was a bird. An ornamental bird whose purpose was to sing when asked and to look pretty at all other times.

I longed to open a gateway to Tidirath, or spread my wings and fly to meet Lorcan there. But gateways couldn't be made between kingdoms, and leaving the palace grounds without Lorcan or my parents was one of many things they forbade me from doing.

So instead, I curled up on the cushioned window seat, closing my eyes against the tears pooling there, praying to Gaia and Eos for Lorcan's safe return.

Chapter 3
Lorcan

I lied. To my princess. I lied about where I would be during the solstice. Just as I did the last two solstices.

I wasn't visiting Tidirath. Queen Eirene and King Kallias never allowed me to leave Evania. Not while Corinna remained.

The truth was, I hadn't been to Tidirath in almost three years. The last time I was there was just weeks after her sixteenth birthday, when her family visited the kingdom and her fae magic chose me as her protector. The last time I was there, I was the second prince of Tidirath, one of the dragon kin. Now, I was just the protector of the only fae heir to the throne of Evania.

Such was the life of a dragon protector. Such was our duty. Our sacrifice.

Each dragon protector that came before me, and each dragon protector that would come after me, made the same sacrifices—their position and title within the kingdom, their citizenship, and their chance at having a mate.

I did not regret any of it. Not in the slightest. It was a great honor to be chosen as the dragon protector, to be the one to protect the next king or queen of Evania. I made my sacrifices with pride, honor, and dignity. I took my vows seriously, and I would follow them until the day I died.

But having pride and honor in my position, and having no regrets, didn't mean it was easy. Far from it, in fact.

I hated lying to my princess, but I couldn't bring myself to tell her the truth. To tell her they did not invite me to the solstice celebration. To tell her I wasn't allowed to visit my homeland. That I hid in the forest and watched the celebration instead.

I didn't tell her these things because I didn't want to influence her view of the fae kingdom. Even though I knew she could see the cracks in the facade Evania presented to the rest of Ansterra, I couldn't be the one to break her, to ruin her optimism and her pure heart.

I didn't tell her I watched her. That I noticed her. Noticed her kindness and her determination. That I noticed her smile and the sparkle in her eyes when she laughed. That all those things brought a joy into my life that was incomparable to anything I'd felt before.

I sighed as I rubbed argan oil into the damp, dark skin of my chest and arms before dressing. I'd hoped a bath would help ease the tension in my body, would relax and calm my troubled mind.

Instead, all I could think of was how Corinna would look as she danced around the bonfires tonight, as the drums beat and her body worked to keep pace with them. All I could picture was the way she'd danced last year, swaying and twirling, her brown waves flying and the soft purple fabric of her dress floating around her. All I could remember was the complete rapture on her face, her eyes closing, and a gentle smile on her lips. I remembered wanting to join her, to wrap my arms around her, or place my hands on her hips and hold her body against mine as she moved to the music.

But I wasn't allowed. They did not welcome me at the Evanian celebrations, and my secret feelings for Corinna would have to remain just that—secret. I could never act on them, as position, duty, and circumstance made that impossible. Position, because I was her protector, the one who should be ever on his guard to ensure the Drakos line continued. Duty, because I gave up the idea of having a mate the day I became her protector, the day the fae ivy mark appeared on my arm and linked us together. Circumstance, because we were of two different species. Her, a fae, and me, a dragon. And even if my dragon imprinted on her, even if the great silver beast held within me chose her as his mate, she would never reciprocate the bond from her end.

So, I held myself back. It hadn't been a problem at first. The first two years, I saw her as nothing more than what I should—a friend, and the girl I was chosen to protect. But as she grew closer to eighteen, I saw her in a new light. She was no longer a girl, but a woman. A beautiful woman, who drew me in with even the tiniest of gestures or the smallest of smiles. That was why I'd spent the previous solstice hiding within the trees instead of holed up in my small cabin. So I could watch her.

Over the past year, the desires became harder to control. Especially when we spent every day together. Especially when her spirited attitude and sharp tongue made me want to grab her by the chin and kiss her smart remarks into oblivion, or pin her against a tree and use my hands on her body to show her which of us was truly in charge.

Instead, I used our proximity during training to get closer to her. Tackling her to the ground or pulling leaves and sticks out of her soft hair both eased the ache and provoked my need to claim her body, a cruel delusion that something was better than nothing.

Once my deep green tunic was on my body, I pulled my dark curls out of the leather strap holding them together at the base of my neck. I walked to the small round table in the center of my one-room cabin and poured myself a glass of red wine from the jug resting on the top. I took a long sip, not savoring the rich flavor but swallowing as much as I could in one gulp.

The distant beating of drums signaled the beginning of the fae's solstice celebration, and the beating on my door, followed by raucous laughter, signaled Cillian and Cahir, the former King Isaak's protector's arrival at my cabin.

"Open up, Lorcan!" Cillian crowed.

I grimaced and downed the rest of my wine, already regretting agreeing to drink with them tonight. I'd evaded their invitation for the last two years, but this year, I accepted.

I accepted because watching my princess find her fated mate would rip a hole through every fiber of my being. Not that seeing her with him day in and day out would be any easier. But that initial meeting between mates—that moment when both recognized each other, and they touched for the first time—was always regarded as the most important, intimate, and marvelous moment for fated mates, aside from when they marked each other.

I could not stand by and watch her experience that moment with someone who wasn't me. Watch her find the man she was destined to be with, while I would never have that. Not with her. Not with anyone.

My duty. My sacrifice.

"Lorcan, you lazy ass, let us in, or at least come and join us by the fire!" Cahir's raspy voice yelled.

"I'm coming, I'm coming," I grunted, slamming the wine goblet on the table and stalking to the door in two long strides.

I yanked it open, and there on my threshold were the two dragon protectors who came before me. Their muscular arms laden with wine and ale jugs, and the fire in the clearing between our homes blazed with a crackling heat that grazed my cheek even from the interior of my cabin.

"Don't tell me you're backing out on us?" Cillian asked, his red eyebrows raising up to his hairline.

"It's been a long day," I grumbled, crossing my arms.

"All the more reason to have a drink!" Cahir exclaimed, laughing and making his braided blond beard shake. "The wine will help your beast relax. And you need to remember we're just a thought away. If they need us, we will feel it and they will call for us. So for now, just put aside your duty and join us for a drink or two."

The drums continued to echo around the protector dwellings, and I contemplated his words. The great silver beast inside me was restless because of our princess's distance. And though we knew she could protect herself, knew the fae were beings of great and terrible magic, the protector bond caused us to worry no matter how powerful our charge was.

Cahir was right, though. A drink would settle me. And Corinna was safe. I could give myself this small moment of peace, this imbibing of spirits to maybe forget what might occur.

"Fine," I grunted, stepping out between the two other protectors and shutting my door behind me.

"That's the spirit," Cillian said, slapping me on the back as best he could with his hands full of wine. "Why should the fairies be the only beings to enjoy this solstice night? We may not be invited to their festivities, but we can create our own and continue the tradition of the protectors drinking away their worries while the Evanians dance and fornicate under the solstice moon."

"Hmm," I replied, sitting on a log near the fire and accepting a jug of wine from Cahir. "Only the mated pairs will fuck, though," I reminded Cillian.

"Not true," Cahir said as he plopped down beside me. "All the fairies of mating age are expected to find a partner tonight. To spread their fairy magic throughout the kingdom by coupling with another after the sun has set, whether or not they find their mate this eve."

"I myself am hoping to find a sprite or perhaps a nymph to keep me company for the night," Cillian grinned, running his hand through his hair. "A nymph. Definitely a nymph," he murmured, nodding to himself.

I almost choked on my wine. I froze, keeping the jug to my lips and pretending I was taking a long swig, but I was processing the words I just heard.

I lowered the jug. "You mean...you're going to—"

"They don't invite us to celebrate with them, but they are more than willing to use us for pleasure." Cillian shrugged. "I see no reason not to enjoy myself. I gave up a fated mate to be a protector, but I didn't give up sex completely."

"Of course, but don't female fae usually find their mates during the first solstice after they turn nineteen?"

"Only if their mate is nearby," Cahir explained. "Evania is a large kingdom, and not every fairy in the land is able to travel the distance to the palace for the solstice celebrations every year."

"And I accept males and females into my bed equally," Cillian added.

"So? Do you think you'll find yourself your own fairy to dally with tonight? Eos knows it's been long enough since you've found pleasure with another," Cahir teased.

I gave him a half smile but otherwise didn't respond to his taunting. He wasn't wrong. It had been over a year since I'd been with a female. I'd experienced a few encounters in the months I'd scoured the human realm for a mate before becoming Corinna's protector, and I'd been with an unmated dryad a few times during my first year in Evania. But there was only one fairy I wanted to bring into my bed this eve, and there were many reasons that was a terrible idea.

Now that my companions planted the seed, however, now that I knew what the Evanians would expect of her tonight and what my current drinking companions would leave to do once the sun set, I could think of little else. Thoughts of her lips on mine, of my hands on her body, of her moaning and sighing into my ear consumed my mind.

As painful as it would be to let her go at sunrise, I did not want her to be with anyone other than me if she did not find her mate. I wished to be the one to bring her pleasure, to show her how a man should bed a woman, to be the male she would compare all others to. To have her for one night and then never again was better than to never have her at all.

And deep within me, the silver dragon prowling in circles agreed, pushing me to go to her, to take her in my arms and pour my love for her into her soul.

I took a gulp of my wine, and then another, not at all listening to Cahir and Cillian as they continued their drunken banter. My eyes flicked to the sky, gauging the hour with my practiced eye. There was still a bit of time before it would be close to sunset.

"Thank you for the wine," I said, interrupting their laughter by slamming the jug into the dirt. "But I must retire. The stress of the separation from Princess Corinna has taken a greater toll on me than I expected. If you will excuse me."

I gave each of them a curt nod as I stood, then turned and strode back into my cabin to wait out the time until just before sunset.

Chapter 4
Lorcan

The rhythm of the drums continued, speeding up as the sunset drew closer. Each beat was a stone dropping into my heart, weighing down my soul. Each strike was a twist of my stomach, turning it inside out and tying it into knots.

I'd already resigned myself to my plan, and I intended to see it through. I would watch Corinna from the same spot I stood in the year before, catch a glimpse of her just before sunset, and then wait. Wait and see if she found her fated mate, her soulmate, the one destined for her. And if she did not, I would reach out to her and make my presence known and...

Well, I hadn't thought that far. I didn't know how she would react to my proposition. To my confession of my desire for her. I didn't know if I should tell her the depths of it or if I should present it as just lust. I wasn't sure which would hurt me more once the night ended.

Cahir and Cillian's voices faded. I peeked out the small window of my cabin and caught their retreating bodies, splitting from each other at the fork in the path, one heading north and one heading northwest.

Urged by my beast, I decided to let instinct guide me. I would know what to do when I saw her.

I exited my home once Cahir and Cillian were out of sight, and I opened a gateway in the clearing, straight into the small copse of trees on the edge of the Evanian royal forest. My dark green tunic and dark brown breeches, in addition to my dark skin and hair, helped to hide me in the shadows and the brush.

It didn't take me long to find her. I was always drawn to her, connected to her. Not just by our bond as protector and fae heir but by the friendship and camaraderie we'd cultivated over the last three years.

My eyes landed on her dancing form, swaying wildly to the beat of the summer drums, her eyes closed, her light brown hair flying around her, her arms waving and swirling, and her silvery blue dress twirling with each of her spins and movements.

She entranced me with her dancing, her body moving in perfect time with the music and the drums. Unlike the other fae and fairies around her, she had her white wings hidden because she didn't like them being touched.

My dragon stirred beneath the surface, giving Corinna his undivided attention. A soft smile graced her lips and her gray eyes opened. A low, rumbling growl started in my chest, vibrating through every bit of my body, my dragon pushing forward to stake his claim.

His claim on her. On Corinna.

"No," I muttered, stumbling backwards, losing my footing on the loose sticks and leaves on the forest floor.

The air left my lungs, and my heart constricted in my chest, my hands tensing and grappling for purchase against the bark of the tree behind me. Longing and dismay filled my soul in equal measure, the reality of the situation ruining what should have been the most joy-filled moment of my life. The day my dragon chose our mate, now forever marred because I could never have the female he chose.

I couldn't breathe, couldn't move, couldn't think of anything beyond holding my beast back from taking over and forcing me out into the clearing to claim her publicly. My fist clenched, and I slammed it back against the tree trunk, welcoming the pain and the blood trickling from the split skin of my knuckles.

In the clearing, Corinna froze mid-step, and I realized too late I'd left my walls down, and she would feel my pain and my despair through our protector bond.

"Fuck," I whispered to myself, throwing that mental barrier up and blocking my negative emotions from her, but it didn't matter.

She'd felt it.

She excused herself, meandering through the crowd. Her dress flowed and swirled behind her as she walked, giving me glimpses of her soft, pale legs through the slits on either side of the skirt. Her brow furrowed as she approached the table laden with food and wine. Her eyes scanned the crowd, back and forth, before coming to examine the edge of the forest.

'Lorcan?'

I swallowed and shut my eyes, but my beast forced them back open, forced me to stare at her, to watch my mate.

My mate. The setting sun bathed her light brown hair with gold, her whole body glowing with ethereal splendor. Her gray-blue dress sparkled. The beadwork and embroidery on the fitted bodice caught each ray of diminishing light and reflected it back to the world in shimmering beams.

'Lorcan, I know you're out there,' she pressed, moving around the edge of the celebration. *'I felt you. I felt your pain. What is going on?'*

I gritted my teeth and didn't answer her. I couldn't answer her. If she came to where I hid, there was no telling what my dragon might do. Or what I might do.

I needed to get away, get back to my cabin to wrangle control of my beast and myself. I needed some time to think about how I would handle this situation, how I would keep myself from claiming her, from revealing the truth to her.

I couldn't reject her. That was the whole reason I stopped going to the human realm—because I would have to reject any mate I found, and the pain of a rejection would put my dragon and me into a deep, hibernating sleep for at least two years, making it impossible for me to fulfill my duties as Corinna's protector.

I would have to hide it, hide my claim on her, hide that I'm her mate. I'd have to endure seeing her be with and feeling her bed another for the rest of our lives.

If it didn't kill me first.

'I'm fine, Princess Corinna,' I forced out, pushing off from the tree and searching for the path back to my cabin.

Usually, my keen eyes would find the path with ease. But between the pain in my hand and the effort to keep my dragon in check, I could focus on little else. The world spun, and I placed my palm back on the tree to support myself, to keep myself from collapsing to the ground and blacking out. My eyes closed as I focused on my breathing, on relieving the tension in my body and the nausea and anxiety in my gut. In and out, in and out, my lungs expanding and collapsing with each breath.

"You're not fine, Lorcan," she said tenderly, her voice carrying on the breeze from the trees nearest the clearing.

Every hair on my body stood on end as a shiver ran from my head to my toes. The softness of her voice had me leaning even more on the tree for support as the sound washed over me, my knees buckling under my body weight.

"Why are you here? Why are you not in Tidirath?" she asked. My eyes shot open, and I found her with her brows furrowed, a tiny line forming between them. "Did you return early?"

"I never left," I confessed, my gaze locked on her face, the words out before I could stop them. "I haven't been to Tidirath in years," I continued.

Her forehead wrinkled even more at my words. "But—"

"Do you really think your mother would allow me to leave? Do you really think she would let me be that far away from you for even one night? Are you really so naïve to not notice the treatment of myself and the other dragon protectors? Do you really not see the inequality, the blatant dehumanization of us?"

I spat each word, my temper flaring, my anger from her being my mate turning into hostility against her, making me speak to her in a way I never would have under normal circumstances. But nothing about this situation was normal.

I pushed off from the tree and stalked towards her, my feet moving my body with each word and with the rhythm of the drums as they increased their pace. "I have a duty. I made a vow, and I sacrificed the idea of having my own life to protect yours. This is the way of the dragon protectors, the way it has always been. Our life for yours."

I stopped a few steps from her, gaining control of myself before I got too close. Her scent had yet to reach me, but I knew if I moved any closer, it would ensnare my senses, and I would lose my grip on the reins of my restraint.

She tiptoed back a step at my advance, her frown of confusion turning into a glare. A fire burned in her eyes, and it took everything in me to not grab her and pull her tiny body against mine. To relish in the feel of her pressed to me, to hold my mate in my arms, even if only for a moment.

"My mother may handle me with kid gloves," she murmured, pulling me out of my spiraling thoughts, "but I am not blind, Lorcan. I am not so naïve to not notice you are considered less than by her and many others. And I hate it," she declared, taking back the ground she lost when she'd retreated from my vitriol. "I despise her for it. I see what it does to you; I see the hollowness in your eyes where there once was light and joy, and I want nothing more than to—"

I held my breath as she moved in closer, avoiding her scent and waiting to hear what she wanted to do to bring the light back into my eyes, but her words were cut off by a sharp intake of breath as the sun set in the distance. An unnatural wind swirled through the palace grounds, formed by the air magic of the elder fae who already had their mates, formed to guide the scents of any newly mated pair towards each other so they could find each other easier.

Corinna's scent at last entered my lungs, a mix of sweet basil and bergamot and sunshine, bright and clean and uniquely her. Her eyes shone like silver stars in the fading light, moving from my face to the space between us. I inhaled as much of her scent as I could, using it to calm my dragon, hoping it would be enough to keep him happy for the time being. Her chest rose and fell in the same rhythm, every inhale through her nose audible. Her eyes followed a path between her chest and mine, and when she looked at me again, her eyes sparkling and wide, the last word I ever expected to hear fell from her lips.

"Mate?" she whispered.

Chapter 5
Corinna

"Mate?" I whispered, staring up into Lorcan's brown eyes.

His face hid in the shadows, his mahogany skin blending into the dim light of the forest. His entire body tensed, his hands in fists at his sides, blood running down the knuckles of one and dripping onto the forest floor in an alternating rhythm to the drums still beating in the distance and the pounding of my heart in my chest.

I glanced back down between us, down at the golden tether connecting my heart to his heart. The golden tether only I could see. The tether that connected a fairy to their fated mate, that appeared once a year at sunset on the summer solstice.

I couldn't believe it. I hadn't even entertained the delusion that Lorcan might end up being my mate. The rarity of interspecies mates combined with the complexities of dragon bonds made the idea impossible.

But it happened. The proof lay between us, in the cord tying my soul to his. He was mine. I just needed to know if I was his.

I looked up at him again, and where I usually found a blank, stoic face or a teasing, goading gleam in his eyes, I found a mirror of my heart staring back at me. The same longing, the same desire, the same need I'd held back for over a year was reflected to me and mixed with pain. There was still a small gap between our bodies, a gap I could close by taking one step forward.

I waited, though. I waited for him to claim me. He hadn't said a word since the bond appeared for me. He just stood there, a dark statue in the forest, frozen in pain and fear. His jaw ticked, and he swallowed, his hands unclenching and clenching again. The wind created by the elder fae still blew, and Lorcan's scent of lemon, mint, and cedarwood wrapped around me and filled my lungs, sending a zing of pleasure through my body and awakening butterflies in my stomach.

The silence and space between us gnawed at me. I needed him to claim me, needed him to say something. Anything.

"Lorcan—"

My voice ignited something in him. A spark glinted in his eyes, and he stepped forward, stopping when our bodies almost touched. His hand lifted to my face, reaching for my cheek, but the touch I longed for never came. His hand hovered there, hesitating. His eyes scanned my face, his brows furrowing as he debated his next move. But I knew what I wanted.

"You can touch me, Lorcan," I muttered.

He shook his head and formed a fist in the air, then lowered his hand to his side again.

"I can't," he said, but he didn't move away.

"Why not?"

"If I do, I'll never want to let you go. I'll never want to stop touching you."

He stayed right where he was, stayed as close to me as possible without touching me. The golden thread between us vanished, but the emotional and spiritual connection from the mate bond was still there, still tying us together, as it would until we completed or severed the bond.

"I wouldn't want you to stop," I admitted.

My confession snapped the last thread on his restraint, and he closed the distance between us. He took my hands into his, his thumbs running over my knuckles as his nose brushed against mine, his mouth a breath away from kissing me. His hands traveled up my arms, to the edge of my pointed cap sleeves, and then back down, leaving tingles of pleasure in their wake, a shiver pulsing through my body from the sensation.

"Corinna..." he whispered, his lips brushing mine with the lightness of a feather.

"Say it, Lorcan," I demanded, pulling back so our lips no longer touched. "Out loud. Tell me what I am to you."

A growl vibrated in his chest, his pupils darkening his eyes more than usual. He moved his hands to my waist, pressing his palm into my lower back to push my body closer to his. The noise and vibrations from his body rippled through me, weakening my knees. The primal sound had a dizzying effect on me, and I grabbed onto his shoulders, clinging to him to keep from collapsing, my fingers gripping the dark green fabric of his tunic. He dipped his head to my shoulder and slid his nose along my neck until he reached my ear.

"Mine," he purred into my ear, holding me to him with his muscular arm, his fingers splayed against my back. "My mate, my heart—*mo chroí.*"

His other hand cupped my cheek, his thumb tilting my chin up as he placed light kisses along my jaw, stopping when his mouth was back over mine, his warm breath tickling my lips. The moment stretched between us, and I savored it. As much as I wished for his kiss, I didn't want to rush this moment. It was a moment to be enjoyed, to be etched into my memories so I could relive it time and time again.

"Please tell me this isn't a dream," he breathed, his thumb padding over my bottom lip, my heart stuttering in my chest. "Please tell me this isn't some cruel fantasy my mind has conjured in an attempt to satiate my desires."

"It's not a dream, Lorcan," I replied, my hands stroking his chest. "It is very much real."

"I didn't dare to allow myself even the slightest hope that you would be mine."

I blinked. "You wanted me?"

He huffed out a laugh and kissed the corner of my mouth. "For so long, I have craved you, Corinna. You do not know how difficult it has been to hold myself back from the thing I wanted most but could not have."

His lips brushed mine as he spoke, moving his mouth from one side of mine to the other and kissing the corner of my lips again. A tremor ran through me as goosebumps rose on my skin, my nipples tightening and straining against the bodice of my gown. His kisses that weren't quite kisses added to the anticipation and the need growing within me, and I wasn't sure how much more I could take.

My eyes watered at his confession, at the realization he wanted me as much as I wanted him.

"You don't have to hold back anymore. I am yours," I whispered.

"Mine," he repeated with a growl.

His hand slid from my cheek to the back of my neck, holding me in place as his mouth met mine in a full kiss. His dark curls fell forward, curtaining my face, and his plush lips took mine in slow movements, each kiss lasting longer than the previous.

I sighed into our kiss and leaned my body into his, letting him hold me up with his powerful arms. My mouth opened for him, and his tongue brushed against mine, deepening our kiss as his arms wrapped around me. He tasted of robust red wine, and between that taste, his smell, and the feel of his body as I pressed mine against his, I was drowning in a heady storm of lust and longing.

I draped my arms around his neck, moaning, and he growled again, lifting me and spinning us so my back lay against the tree, his hand bracing himself next to my face. My legs slipped through the slits of my skirt, encircling him.

Our kisses grew more intense, more needy, both of us putting everything we'd held back for so long into each one. I couldn't get close enough to him. I couldn't get enough of his touch and his kisses. He was everything, and I was nothing without him.

His hand moved from the tree to my body, exploring the spots he could reach, his touches and caresses gentle compared to his frantic kisses. He cupped the back of my knee, sliding his palm along my thigh, his fingertips coming dangerously close to the hem of my smallclothes. I gasped, breaking our kiss as he brushed over my center through the fabric, then rolled his hips against me, letting me feel the proof of his desire for me between his legs.

He wanted me. He wanted me in the way I wanted him, had held himself back the way I held myself back all this time. His hardened cock pressing against my core sent a wave of heat through me, my cheeks turning pink. This was uncharted territory for me, but the thought of joining with another no longer terrified me, as it did that morning. Because this wasn't just a random encounter to spread magic throughout the land. This was Lorcan. My mate.

His mouth traveled along my neck, exposed to him by my sharp inhale when he'd brushed his fingers against my lower lips. I panted, my chest heaving and my body writhing under his touch, seeking more, seeking friction and release. His fingers stroked the back of my thigh, and he smiled against my skin, enjoying my reactions to his attentions.

The celebratory music and echoing drums bounced around the trees, reminding me of where we were and what was happening around us. All over the royal lands, fae and fairies would find their mates, or find a partner to share the evening with, spreading fairy magic to renew the land as they found euphoria together.

I swallowed, and Lorcan stilled his movements, pulling back to look at me, his eyes clouding. The world stopped, and my heart sank as he lowered me to my feet and stepped away from me, his jaw set.

"What's wrong?" I asked him, my palms pressed against the bark of the tree to keep myself from collapsing, to hold myself back from closing the distance between us again to have him consume me with his embrace.

"I can't do this," he choked out, his hands gripping the strands of his hair at the roots.

I frowned, my heart cracking down the center at his words. "I thought you wanted me?"

"I do," he said. "But your mother will never allow this union. The fae will not approve."

"How could they not?" I asked. "It's not just your dragon that chose me. Gaia has blessed our bond. You are my mate, too."

"Because any children you give me will be male dragons," he reminded me, dropping his hands to his sides and meeting my eyes. "The fairies will not accept a dragon as their heir. As their future king."

I opened my mouth to argue but could not discredit his claim. He was right. Dragons were always male, and dragons only ever produced dragon children, no matter what race or species their mate was. But surely Gaia had a plan. She would not choose Lorcan as my mate if it meant the end of the royal line.

"You should return to the palace," Lorcan murmured, turning from me. "I will create a gateway, and... and leave you for the evening."

"I can't," I whispered, looking down at the forest floor. "I cannot return...intact." His nostrils flared and his back stiffened. "They expect this of me, as the princess. They expect me to...to partake in the ritual...and my mother will know if I have not," I confessed, my voice trembling.

The strained roar he released vibrated through the ground, rattling my knees. I stumbled, but he caught me, his arm around my waist and his hand wrapping around my throat, tilting my face to look in his eyes.

"I cannot take you, Corinna, *mo chroí*," he told me, his voice still a raspy, low growl. "My dragon will want to mark you, and I do not think I can hold him back. And if I lie with you, our scents will mix like that of a mated pair, and your mother will know the truth of our bond."

My lip trembled and my stomach lurched, the butterflies turning into a roiling sea storm. My fluttering hands pressed against it, attempting to staunch the nausea and the dread pooling there.

"I will have to tell her about us, Lorcan," I whispered, shaking my head. "I cannot lie to her."

His hand gripped me tighter, his face stern and his voice insistent. "You must. For now, you must. Until we can learn more, until we can find some answers about our bond, you will not tell her we are mates."

"But the ritual—"

"Tell her you were too heartbroken that you didn't find your mate, and too shy to find a partner for the evening. Play it up as much as you have to. Save the tears forming in your eyes right now and use them in the morning to convince her you speak the truth."

My throat tightened, and I squeezed my eyes shut, pressing my lips together to keep my cries from erupting. "I do not wish to be parted from you," I rasped out. "Not even for one night."

"Corinna—"

"Let me stay with you," I insisted, gripping his tunic and pulling myself to him. "Let me stay in your cabin. I will leave at first light and bathe your scent off my body, but please do not force me away from you. Let me sleep in your arms; let me lie next to you in your bed. Let me breathe in your scent and savor your closeness. Please do not deny us any of this, any of our first night together as mates."

He wrapped his arms around me again, crushing me to his chest, cradling the back of my head with his hand. His body was warm, solid, and safe, and I never wanted to leave the circle of his arms. "Please, Lorcan."

"It is very difficult to say no to you, *mo chroí*," he muttered.

"Then don't," I replied.

His full lips pressed a kiss to the top of my head, a smile forming against my hair. Around us, his protector magic crackled, the energy from the gateway he created rustling the leaves, my dress, and my hair. He stepped through the portal without relinquishing his hold on me, closing the portal behind us as soon as we were in his small cabin.

He let go of me once we were ensconced in the safety of his home. He moved to his bed, perching on the edge to take off his boots.

I'd only been inside his home once when he'd first moved here after he became my protector, and not much changed since then. There was the same small round table near the fireplace, the same bed just big enough to fit his massive frame, and the same drafty window and door pointing towards the communal area in the center of the other protector's cabins. The only changes were the additions of his personal touches—his clothing in the armoire, his sword and armor stationed near the door, and his journal on the table by his bed.

It was small, but it was his. His scent lingered in the air, calling out to me, begging me to stay there with him for all time.

"Come here," his gruff voice ordered, his hands resting on his thighs as he stared at me.

He'd removed his tunic, and his dark skin was smooth and rich, shining in the moon and starlight streaming in through the singular window. How my hands longed to touch him, itched to trace over the ridges and valleys of his muscles, to feel them tense and relax under my touch. I wanted to know the feel of his skin, to memorize it so I would never forget any bit of him. I wanted my fingers to be the stars in the universe of his body.

I walked towards him, as tentative as a fawn taking their first steps, stopping just in front of where he sat. His heartbeat echoed in my ears, loud enough to be my own, his chest rising and falling in a rapid rhythm. I reached my hand out to touch him, but he snatched it in midair, his lips twitching briefly before spinning me to face away from him.

He let go of my wrist and moved his fingers to the laces on the back of my dress, untying and loosening them. My hands came up to my chest to hold the dress up.

"Here," he said, holding his tunic out for me. "Put this on." I turned towards him again, keeping my dress against my body with one arm as I took the tunic from him. "I'll close my eyes," he muttered, looking down at his knees.

"You don't have to," I told him.

"Corinna," he groaned. "If I am going to keep from bedding you, then yes, I have to close my eyes."

"But—"

"Don't test me on this," he growled, his eyes flashing in warning, his hands in fists on his thighs. "Holding back from you is difficult enough as it is."

I nodded, and he sighed and closed his eyes, covering them with his hand, giving me privacy to remove my dress and put on his tunic. The forest green fabric swallowed me, the hem reaching my knees and the sleeves hanging past my fingertips. But his intoxicating scent engulfed me, and I hugged the material to my body, lifting the collar to my nose to breathe in even more.

I stepped closer to him, leaving my dress in a pile on the floor, and took his face in my hands, lifting his gaze to mine. His eyes scanned my face, then my body, his mouth twitching and his eyes glinting at the sight of me in his clothing.

"Lie down," he rumbled out, jerking his chin at the bed behind him.

I perched on the edge of the bed and scooted back, keeping myself covered as best I could until I was under the dark brown blanket. Not because of modesty, but because he was struggling enough as it was. I didn't need to add to his temptation.

He slid in next to me, and I stayed in my spot, my eyes staring up at the ceiling, as stiff and tense as a soldier after their first full day of training. I wasn't sure if I should curl myself into him or keep my body away from his. His touch and his embrace were addictive and sweet, and if I let him hold me, I might insist on him doing more than just that.

My mind spun as I lay there, spiraling down into deeper and darker depths as I thought of what was to come, of what we would face in the light of day.

"Lorcan, I—"

But he cut me off, leaning over my body and lowering his mouth to mine, giving me a tender kiss.

"Let us sleep. Let us leave our problems for tomorrow, and for tonight, let us just be mates," he said, holding my face and thumbing over my cheekbone.

He laid back down, his arm circling around me, warm and strong, and he pulled me into him, holding me just as I'd asked him to. He rubbed my back in long strokes, taking his time to spread warmth and pleasure to me from his touch. I melted into him, relaxing my body and my mind by focusing on his touch, his scent, and his presence. My breathing deepened, and I closed my eyes, letting my worries and fears drift away towards the solstice moon, forgetting them until I awoke in the morning.

Chapter 6
Corinna

Too soon, Lorcan's hands caressed my face, his lips and breath brushing the shell of my ear. "It will be light soon," he whispered. "You need to return to your quarters in the palace."

I blinked my eyes open and found him gazing at me, his eyes soft but bloodshot, black circles darkening the skin of his lower lids.

"You didn't sleep at all, did you?" I asked, my voice dry.

His head shook, his shoulder-length brown curls swaying with the movement. "I was thinking."

"About?"

"Our next steps."

"And?"

He sighed and rolled away from me, sitting up on the edge of the bed. His hand rubbed over his face, and he stood, crossing to the small table near the fireplace. I sat up, staying under the blanket but hugging my knees to my chest. I'd only spent one night in his arms, and already I felt the aching emptiness that was his absence in the bed, and from my side.

My gaze lingered on the muscles of his back as they tensed and shifted with his movements, his hands unwrapping a loaf of bread from a towel and tearing off a piece. He reached for the small dish of butter, taking a small lump of it with his knife and spreading it over the piece in his hand.

He held the bread out to me. "I baked the bread and churned the butter myself," he said. "I know it isn't much, but..." He trailed off, his eyes downcast.

I stood from the bed, my bare feet padding on the dirt floor as I crossed the minimal distance to him. My heart fluttered in my chest as I stopped in front of him, taking the bread from his hand and stroking his face so he would look at me.

"It is enough," I reassured him. "You are enough."

I reached up on my toes to give him a light kiss on the lips. His arm came around my waist, holding me to him. His eyes focused on the bread in my hand, and I sensed his dragon at the forefront of his mind, focusing on me as well, waiting for me to eat the food they'd provided for me.

I kept eye contact with him as I took the first bite, as we partook in this sacred, age-old custom between dragons and their mates. A quiet growl sounded in his chest as I chewed, and he sat in the singular chair at the table, pulling me into his lap as he did.

"Lorcan!" I declared, blushing. "This is hardly proper," I reminded him, pulling away so I could stand.

"This is the custom," he argued, anchoring my waist with his arm. "You are my mate, and I will hold you how I want when we are in the privacy of our...of my home." I looked over my shoulder at him and stopped my struggling. "You did not care so much when you begged me to let you into my bed last night," he added, his eyes glinting.

I narrowed my eyes at him but said nothing, instead taking another bite of the bread he'd given me. He stroked my hair and kissed my shoulder blade, breathing in and out in slow inhales and exhales through his nose, taking in my scent.

"The dragon sages may have information about our bond," he murmured into my back. "About what it might mean for our children."

"But you said my mother won't allow you to visit Tidirath," I said.

"You will have to ask her," he sighed. "Tell her you wish to visit to reinforce the alliance between our kingdoms, to meet with Prince Bran before he takes over the throne from his father."

"Your father," I corrected him.

"His father," he repeated. "I am no longer a prince of Tidirath, Corinna. You know this."

I clicked my tongue. "I will change this," I said. "The old ways need to stay in the past. They should not force you to give up everything you are just because of this," I spat, lifting my arm with the fae ivy etched into the skin.

He chuckled. "You will be an excellent queen, *mo chroí*," he told me. "With or without me by your side."

I finished the last bit of bread, then turned towards him and wove my fingers into his brown curls, resting my forehead against his. "With you, Lorcan. Only with you."

He didn't respond to my declaration. He just closed his eyes and held me to him, his heart beating in time with my own.

"You need to return," he said. "I will not be far behind you, and I will wait for you in the courtyard."

I nodded but didn't move. Facing my mother would be a challenge, and I would need all the strength my mate could give me.

The whooshing crackle of a portal opening sounded behind me, and I swallowed, pressing myself further into Lorcan's body, hoping to meld with him so we would never have to part. The rise and fall of his chest matched mine, and even though the gateway was open, he didn't move me from his lap, didn't attempt to send me on my way.

There was no other choice, though. I could only find solace in knowing we would not be parted for long, that it was only so I could wash off his scent and speak with my mother about traveling to Tidirath. Then I would be back at his side, back in his arms.

"Just one more kiss," I breathed.

Immediately, his lips were on mine, his arms winding around my waist, pinning me to him. His kiss was demanding, both a promise and a goodbye, and a declaration of the unspoken fear in his heart.

Before I could deepen the kiss, though, before I could enjoy it and melt further into him, he lifted me off his lap, setting me on my feet just in front of the portal.

"Go," he ordered, pointing at my room through the gateway, stepping backwards and away from me.

My lip trembled, but I held it in, saving it for my performance as he'd said last night. I bent to the floor and picked up my dress, then stepped through the portal into my room before my feet could decide to run into his arms again.

The portal closed behind me with a snap, and my knees buckled, sending me to the floor. My hands clutched my stomach and covered my mouth to staunch the choked sob threatening to escape.

One minute. I gave myself one minute on the floor of my room, and then I stood. I prepared my bath with heavier perfumes and oils than normal, mixing sage in to neutralize Lorcan's scent. I removed his tunic and threw it and my dress into the fire, ridding any trace of his scent from my belongings. I scrubbed my skin until it was as pink as a newborn fae and washed my long tresses, until the only aroma left was sage and frankincense.

Once clean and dressed in a simple day dress, my bare feet carried me through the palace to the throne room. Just on the other side of the doors was the courtyard, and a tug on my heart reminded me Lorcan was out there, waiting for me. I caught a whiff of his scent through the arched windows, and I breathed in, closing my eyes, letting it carry me through my next task.

'*I am here, mo chroí,*' he said, his voice a soft caress on my frayed nerves. '*I will wait for you.*'

"Good morrow, Mother," I said, dipping into a shallow curtsy, clasping my hands in front of my green skirt as I lifted my eyes to meet hers.

Her sharp, icy eyes scrutinized me, and she stood from her golden throne engraved with the royal fae ivy, the same ivy circling my wrist and Lorcan's; circling her wrist and Cillian's. She stepped up to the edge of the dais, her long, dark blue dress trailing behind her, Cillian only a sword's length away.

"Did you enjoy your solstice evening?" she asked me.

"Yes."

"You seem well rested?"

I examined her face, taking in the shadows under her eyes and winced. The last thing I wanted was to think of her and my father—who was noticeably absent—in the throes of passion, taking part in the annual ritual of love and magic.

"I-I was too shy to find a partner for the evening," I confessed, lowering my eyes.

I remembered Lorcan's cock rubbing against the lips of my entrance through my smallclothes. The heat of desire from that memory spread over my face, imitating a blush of embarrassment.

"I take it this means you did not find your mate, then?"

"No, Mother, I did not," I lied.

"Hmm," she hummed, descending the steps of the dais to where I stood in the center of the room, her train rustling against the marble floor. "I wonder, Corinna, would you be open to...a proposition?" she asked as she reached me, taking my hands in hers and lifting my chin to look up at her.

"What kind of proposition?"

"A betrothal, really," she clarified.

I blinked at her. "A betrothal?"

"The Antoniou family has long desired to see our lines united. Their son Viktor is twenty-eight and has yet to find his mate. He is...very interested in a union between yourself and him."

The blood drained from my face, and I lost control of my hands, my fingers trembling within her clutches. "Mother, I am just nineteen. I have only seen one solstice sunset since reaching mateable age."

"The Antoniou line is strong, just as the Drakos line is. A union between our two families would produce powerful heirs. A line of heirs that would rule Evania for generations to come," she continued, ignoring my protestations.

"Please, Mother. Do not ask this of me. I do not wish to give up the idea of finding my mate given to me by Gaia," I whispered, my throat tight.

"Just meet him. Get acquainted with him. I think you will find him to your liking," she told me with a wink.

Footsteps sounded behind me, and I whipped around to find a tall, pale, dark-haired male fae with midnight blue wings striding towards me. He wore fine clothes, all rich, dark colors and fabrics, and his hair was shorter with a soft curl. His facial features were sharp, and, in his own way, he was a handsome male.

But he wasn't my mate. He wasn't my Lorcan.

"Princess Corinna," he crooned, bowing, with one leg extended in front of him. "You are even lovelier in the full light of day," he said as he rose. "I thought surely you could not look more splendid than you did dancing under the setting solstice sun, but I see now I was mistaken."

I stepped backwards, colliding with my mother's body, her hands gripping my shoulders with a fierce insistence. She walked forward, taking me with her, until Viktor was only a step away.

"You will make a lovely mate," he murmured, running his gloved knuckles over my cheek.

I gagged and flinched back. Wrong. His touch was so wrong, even with the gloves, sending prickles of disgust through my body, making me shiver.

I yanked back and pulled myself out of my mother's grip, using the strength and speed Lorcan instilled in me during our prohibited training sessions.

"No!" I yelled, glaring at my mother. "I will not let you use me as a pawn for more power. I will not take Viktor as a chosen mate. I can not take him as a mate."

"And why not? Why is it you can not do this duty for your kingdom? Countless other female heirs before you have done the same, myself included. What makes you better than us?"

I gaped at her, sure I'd misheard her words. Misunderstood. "What?"

"You heard me, girl. I was happy to forsake the idea of finding my fated mate and forge a bond with a potent male, with your father, knowing it meant our heir would be powerful and beautiful. And you will do the same."

I shook my head, creeping backwards, step by subtle step, my hand pressing against my chest. "You may have been willing to do that, but I am not," I said. "Not when I've already met my mate. Not when I'm already in love with him."

It was her turn to gape. "But...who—?"

"Lorcan," I said, standing up straighter, lowering my arms to my sides.

"Then where is he?" she asked, marching up to me and gripping my chin. "Why would he let you come to me alone if you were truly his?"

"He's in the courtyard, waiting. I spent the night with him in his cabin, in his bed, and in his arms."

"Don't lie to me, Corinna," she snapped, yanking me closer, her eyes searching mine for the truth. "I am not so easily fooled."

"It is not a lie. His dragon chose me, and Gaia has blessed our bond."

Her nostrils flared, her gaze still locked with mine, still searching and waiting for me to falter. Then she glanced behind me. Before I could turn, someone placed iron cuffs on my wrists, my skin hissing and stinging from the contact. I screamed, crying from the pain in my wrists and my magic being stifled.

"Kiss her," she snarled. "Then we'll know if she speaks the truth."

Gloved hands replaced my mother's on my face, turning my head to the side. Viktor forced his lips onto mine, swallowing my cries.

A roar of fury and pain ripped through the courtyard, echoing through the windows of the throne room.

"Restrain him!" my father yelled, his voice carrying through the windows, alongside Lorcan's roars and growls.

I froze when Viktor first kissed me, too stunned and in too much pain from the iron to do anything. But Lorcan's roaring and fighting woke me up, calling me to action. I pulled Viktor's lip into my mouth and bit down hard, drawing blood.

"Bitch!" he exclaimed, flinching back.

"Lorcan!" I shouted, fighting against Viktor and my mother's hold on me. "Let him go! Please!" I cried.

Alone, they would have been no match for me, but together and with me cuffed in iron, there was no chance for me. I pulled and strained and reached out for the door to the courtyard, but they yanked me back, Viktor's hands wrapping around my upper arms with unrestrained strength.

"Take her to your room," my mother commanded Viktor, the whoosh of a portal opening behind us. "You will lie with Viktor," she ordered me, ignoring my sobs and my fighting. "You will mate with him, and once you have provided the kingdom with enough full-blooded fae heirs, then you may...play with your dragon as you see fit."

Tears streamed down my face, and I continued to struggle against Viktor's hold, spurred on by the noises from the courtyard, the sounds of Lorcan fighting against the palace soldiers.

"Come with me to the courtyard," she ordered, turning to Cillian. "King Kallias will need all the magic we can muster to restrain the beast."

Viktor pulled me backwards with him through the portal. Just before it closed, my eyes met Cillian's as he turned to leave the throne room, his gaze apologetic but resigned.

"Cillian!" I cried. "Cillian, please!"

But it was too late. The portal closed, and I was trapped, trapped in the spiderweb that was Viktor's arms, in his quarters, powerless and without allies.

My eyes darted around the room, searching for the door, a window, for any way out of this unfamiliar space. The window lay in front of me, the bars on it indicating the room's location on an upper floor of the palace. The door was not within my range of sight, meaning it was most likely behind me, behind Viktor.

He gripped my hip bone, fingers digging in, his other arm wrapping around my shoulders and tilting my head to expose my neck to him.

"Let's see how much we can make your lizard scream," he taunted.

His tongue slid along my throat, and I jerked, pulling away from him, but his hold on me was firm, powered by his magic. He pressed a kiss to my ear, thrusting his hips against my ass, and chuckled.

"We're too far away to hear him, it seems," he sighed. "But that won't stop me from having my way with you."

He spun me to him, his fingers grabbing my hair and pulling hard as he smashed his lips to mine again. I fought and flailed, hitting his chest and scratching his neck, but my futile movements only hardened him, only aroused him more.

"Arms down, by your sides," he ordered, his eyes spiraling and locking on mine as he spoke. "Hold still."

My body moved without my permission, my eyes widening at his wielding of hypnotism, one of the rarest forms of fae magic. And because of the iron cuffs he'd placed on me, I had no choice but to obey.

"Your mother said you had some fight in you," he sneered, snaking his arm around my waist and pinning me to his body. "But I'll tame you yet."

He pulled on the shoulders of my gown, ripping the bodice and exposing my white chemise. My chest heaved from the exertion of fighting him, drawing his eyes down to the swell of my breasts just above the lace-trimmed neckline of my undergarment.

"Do you think your reptile will still want you after I've taken my fill?" he asked, his fingertips trailing along the top of my chemise. "Do you think he'll want a sullied female, an impure mate?"

"He will love me anyway," I snapped. "He will know you took me against my will."

"We shall see," he chuckled. "On the bed. Remove your dress and lie on your back," he commanded, using his hypnotic stare and voice on me again.

My feet carried me to the bed, my mind fighting against the command but unable to break the spell. The tears continued to fall, my lip quivering and my throat sore from holding in my sobs. My trembling fingers fumbled with the belt around my waist, loosening it and letting it fall to the floor, my torn dress falling with it, leaving me in my thin, white chemise. I reached for the hem, but Viktor stopped me.

"Leave that on. I like the illusion of innocence and modesty it gives," he smirked. "Now on the bed, like I said," he added, pointing.

I crawled onto the mattress, even though I didn't want to, rolling and laying on my back, my whole body shaking with my withheld cries as I stared up at the ceiling. He lifted the skirt of my chemise, his hands trailing along my thighs as he did, exposing my bare legs and spreading them apart as he knelt between them.

"Please," I begged, closing my eyes. "Please don't do this."

"Open those eyes, little princess," he ordered, his hands loosening his belt. "I want—"

The crackle of a portal and an echoing roar cut off his words. His body was lifted off mine by a large, dark hand gripping the nape of his neck and yanking him backwards. Viktor flew across the room, thrown by Lorcan, hitting the wall near the door with a loud crack.

Lorcan stormed towards him, rage emanating from him in potent waves, his wrath locked onto Viktor as Viktor scrambled to get to his feet. Lorcan's foot met Viktor's stomach, making him double over as he grunted in pain. Lorcan leapt onto him, pinning his front to the floor, his legs straddling Viktor's hips and his already blood-stained hands gripping Viktor's right wing.

A singular claw extended from Lorcan's index finger, and he slid it down Viktor's wing, slicing the delicate membranous wing with a slow, deliberate drag of his hand. When he reached the bottom edge of the wing, he lifted his hand back to the top, repeating the motion. Over and over, from the tip to where his wings protruded from his back until the entire wing was in tatters. Then he moved to the left wing, giving it the same treatment.

Viktor screamed and whimpered, begging Lorcan to stop, but my mate was unrelenting in his ministrations. With his focus on the torture he endured at Lorcan's hands, Viktor's spell on me finally broke.

But I was now hypnotized by the power and dominance on display by my dragon. I stood from the bed, my arms wrapping around the post, still weak from the assault on my magic and my body, and watched him torment my tormenter as I regained my strength and composure.

His brow furrowed in anger and concentration, his pupils blown wide. Even with the iron cuffs on my wrists, I could sense his dragon close to the surface, sense the strength of the magic he wielded from both his protector abilities and his dragon prince powers.

He gripped Viktor's shredded right wing again, and Viktor yelped. Lorcan's foot pressed into the small of Viktor's back as he stood, using it to leverage Viktor's body weight against him as he pulled, ripping the wing off Viktor's body.

Blood spurted from Viktor's shoulder blade, pulsing with each frantic beat of his heart. Lorcan tossed the wing behind him, discarding it as though it was only a soiled rag, ignoring the blood splattering his body, his hands already gripping Viktor's left wing, preparing to remove it in the same fashion as the other.

The scream Viktor released was unlike any I'd heard before. Shrill and strained and drawn out, and I reveled in it. Reveled in the sound of his pain, in the ferocity of my mate and his brutality.

But I wanted Viktor to feel more. I wanted a turn. I wanted to strike him while he was already down, to add to the agony he was already in.

I tore my eyes away from Lorcan, searching the room for something—anything I could use against Viktor. I still couldn't access my magic, but I was resourceful. Lorcan worked with me, trained me to use what I could find in case of this exact situation. In case I was captured and cuffed in iron and my magic suppressed.

My eyes landed on the fireplace, on the fire poker nestled into the embers. I lunged forward, snatching it up and moving to Viktor, stalking in front of his face. Lorcan froze, his hands still gripping the remaining wing, his eyes locked on me as I knelt in front of Viktor.

"Look at me," I growled. "Open those eyes, little lordling," I taunted, twisting his derogatory phrase and spitting it back at him.

He whimpered and flinched away from me, but my hand darted out and forced his eyelids apart, forcing them to remain open as I pressed the scalding hot metal against his eye.

His screams smothered the sizzling and searing of his flesh and his organ, and, in tandem with me, Lorcan ripped the other wing from Viktor's back as I moved the poker to his other eye, scarring him for life, preventing him from using his hypnotism on anyone ever again.

If he lived.

His body trembled even harder than mine did when I was in his thrall. Blood pooled under him and sprayed the walls and furnishings of the room around us. I dropped the poker with a clatter, standing and stumbling backwards and falling to the floor in a heap, my adrenaline fading and leaving me weak-kneed and breathless.

Heavy footsteps crossed the room in a heartbeat, nimble fingers unlocking the cuffs around my arms and tossing them aside. Lorcan stroked my wrists, his fingers that just inflicted such pain on Viktor now caressing me with tender care and concern. He cupped my cheeks with his bloodied hands, staring into my eyes with an intensity and a ferocity that matched what I felt in my soul.

"Cillian gave me the key," he muttered, answering my unspoken question, his fingers weaving into my hair.

"I had to tell her about us," I whispered, pressing my forehead to his, my hands clutching his blood-soaked shirt. "I'm sorry."

"No, *mo chroí*." He shook his head, cupping the back of mine and pulling me closer. "You have done no wrong. The fairies should have known better than to stand between a dragon and his mate."

A sob escaped me, loud and full, unable to be withheld. My arms wrapped around his neck, my upper body pressed against his. He clung to me, enveloping me in his embrace, holding me tighter than ever, as if he was afraid I would disappear if he let me go.

"Take me away, Lorcan," I choked out through my tears. "I can't live as a caged bird any longer. I wish to be free."

"Where would you have me take you?" he asked.

"I don't care, but I can't stay here," I insisted. "They will break me."

He stood and pulled me to my feet, keeping me close and opening a portal for us to leave through.

"They will hunt you down," Viktor rasped from behind us, his breaths shallow, wet, and shaky. "They will see you killed for what you've done."

Lorcan's lip curled in a snarl, his hold on me tightening. "I'd like to see them try," he growled.

"Ignore him," I said, pushing Lorcan towards the portal. "He's not long for this world in his state."

Lorcan growled again but took me through the portal, closing it behind him.

"Where are we?" I asked as he released his hold on me and removed his cloak.

"The border between Evania and Tidirath. I'm taking you to my cave. They won't be able to reach us there."

"But your family can," I reminded him as he wrapped his cloak around me, fastening it at my neck.

His jaw tightened, and he placed his hands on my shoulders, pressing a kiss to my forehead.

"Let us hope they see reason, then." His hands cupped my face again, and he lowered his lips to mine for a brief kiss, a tentative kiss. "Are you...did he—"

"I am fine," I assured him, stepping closer and holding his wrists. "A bit shaken, but otherwise fine."

He nodded but didn't kiss me again or pull me closer. So I took the initiative and gave him a full kiss, a deep kiss.

"I promise you, I'm fine," I repeated as I pulled away.

"I believe you," he said, stroking my cheekbones then stepping away from me. "We need to leave. I hope you're ready."

"Ready for what?"

"To fly on the back of your mate's dragon," he replied, shifting his form before I could respond.

His beautiful silver dragon took over, stretching his wings and neck while still staring straight at me. My stomach fluttered and my heart raced. I could easily fly with him, spread my own wings and soar through the sky at his side. But flying on his back was another important element of the dragon mating customs—the way they bonded with their mate after providing them with food and before marking them.

I rushed to his side, stroking his scales without a thought, marveling at the warmth and how I could still feel the ripples of the mate bond even when he was in this form. His eyes closed at my touch, a warm huff of air releasing from his nostrils, and if he was able, I knew he would be purring.

I longed to extend this moment, but time was not on our side. I hopped onto his back, situating myself between his wings and wrapping the cloak tighter around my body to protect against the chilly air we'd find as we traveled into the mountains. Then I leaned forward, holding onto him with all my strength as he pushed off from the forest floor, not even bothering to glance back at the kingdom I once called home as Lorcan soared away with me on his back.

Chapter 7
Lorcan

I flew through the sky as fast as my dragon could go, my mate on my back bolstering my strength and stamina. Her delicate fingers occasionally stroked my scales, and her cheek rested against the back of my neck, her arms wrapped around me tightly.

We made our journey to my family's cave in silence. I could have spoken with her through our protector bond, but that wasn't what either of us needed. What we needed was something no words could provide for us. What we needed was the strength of our bond to soothe the pain and fear remaining from the events in the Evanian palace.

The entrance to my cave came into view, and not a moment too soon. I would have loved to fly around with Corinna on my back for longer than the journey it took to get here, but we were both covered in Viktor's blood and in desperate need of a bath and some rest.

I landed on the smooth granite stone of the mountain cave, pleased to find the candles and firepits already alight with flames. I wasn't sure if the magic of my family's cave would still work for me. If my mere intention to return there would trigger the spells to prepare the cave for my arrival.

It seemed, in this at least, luck was on our side.

Corinna slid off my back as soon as I landed, and I shifted back to my human form, scooping her up into my arms and moving into the depths of the cave where my personal bedroom lay. She didn't protest as I cradled her body to my chest but leaned her head against me, her eyes closing as she held onto me. Her exhaustion seeped into me—not a physical exhaustion, but an emotional one, wrought from the torment of her family's betrayal, of their willingness to ask her to do something as unspeakable as bedding another while still bonded with her fated mate.

I carried her into my room, where a bathing tub was already filled with steaming water. I halted in the doorway, the surety I felt upon arriving fading. After all that happened, all she'd been through, I was unsure whether she'd be comfortable bathing with me. With being naked with me. I reached out with my mind, asking the cave to fill another tub in a separate room as I sat her on the edge of the basin.

"I will bathe in Bran's room and return as soon as I am finished," I said, unfastening my cloak from her shoulders. "You can wear any of my tunics you find in the wardrobe," I added, jerking my chin towards the attached room where I kept my fine clothes, the clothing from when I was still a dragon prince.

"Don't take too long," she breathed, stroking my cheek.

"I will be quick," I assured her, turning and kissing her palm.

I left, not wanting to waste any time, not wanting to be away from her side for longer than needed. My dragon strained and fought me the entire time I bathed and dressed, unhappy with me for letting our mate out of our sight.

When I returned to my room, dressed only in loose pants, I paused and knocked.

"You don't need to knock," she said, and I rushed into the room before she even finished speaking.

She sat in the center of my colossal bed, wearing a navy blue tunic, her fingers combing through her long, damp waves. Our eyes met, locking onto each other as I circled the bed and climbed onto it with her, sitting behind her and pulling her to me.

Her head fell back against my shoulder, and I hugged her, her hands rubbing my arms and my bare torso as her eyes met mine.

"I love you," she whispered, gazing up at me.

Warmth washed over me and through me at her words. I'd heard her tell her mother she loved me, heard her through the window before all hell broke loose around us. But having the words directed to me, hearing them straight from her lips, and knowing she meant them, affected me in a way I could not voice or describe.

"I love you too," I replied, closing my eyes and leaning down to kiss her forehead. "With all my heart," I added in a whisper.

She placed kisses along my chest and up my throat, turning to face me, her legs settling on either side of my hips. She scratched her nails up my neck and brought her mouth to mine, kissing me with a passion that burned hotter than my dragon's fire.

I returned her kisses with hesitance, caught between my own desires for her and the memory of the ordeal she endured before we came here.

Her hips rolled against mine, and I realized she wore no smallclothes, leaving her completely bare under my tunic.

"Corinna..." I groaned, pulling away and clenching my teeth.

"I need you, Lorcan," she sighed.

"But—"

"I need your love. I need your touch to erase the memory of his. I want you to mate with me."

Her hips rolled again and the scent of her arousal wafted through the air, awakening me and calling to me. My nostrils flared, and I snatched her wrists in my hands, flipping us so she lay under me, her arms pinned up by her head and my weight pressing her down and preventing her from moving.

"I'm not going to mate with you, *mo chroí.*"

Hurt flashed on her face, and she shut her eyes, turning away from me. But I gripped her chin, holding both her tiny hands with just one of mine, making her eyes snap open to meet mine again.

"Mating with you doesn't even begin to cover what I'm going to do to you," I said with a growl. "Mating implies something speedy and meaningless. And I'm going to worship every inch of you. I'm going to take my time to discover the secrets of your beautiful body. I'm going to learn exactly where to kiss and touch to make you beg me for more. By the time I'm done with you, the only word you'll remember is my name, and you'll be moaning it so loudly even the departed spirits in the Ancestral Forest will be able to hear you."

She whimpered and writhed underneath me, her eyes filled with need. I sat back on my heels, pulling her into my lap again, straddling me, my hands already on the hem of the tunic and lifting it up and over her head. She didn't give me time to look at her naked body because she dove forward and pressed herself to me, kissing me. Her round breasts pushed up against my chest, their softness a delicious contrast to my muscularity.

I caressed her smooth skin, my calloused hands trailing up her sides and leaving goose-bumps behind them. I brought my fingertips to the underside of her breast, and she inhaled, releasing my mouth, her head tilting back and her body arching away from me, letting me gaze down at her naked chest.

I groaned at the sight, at her hardened pink nipples and her taut stomach stretching with the movements of her hips. I kissed her breastbone, smiling against her skin and the heated flush spreading up her neck, circling her breast with my fingers, spiraling closer to her nipple with each pass.

Just before my fingers reached that hardened point, I covered it with my mouth instead, nipping it with my teeth and then pulling away. She cried out and then moaned as I gave the other nipple the same treatment, her fingers clutching my hair.

I shifted our bodies, still lavishing hers with attention with my mouth. My arm wrapped around her waist to hold her while I removed my pants, shimmying them down my waist and hips until they were no longer in the way, no longer on my body.

She settled back into my lap, her entrance lined up with the length of my erection, and she gasped and clung to me. My hands held her hips, held her still, held her so we could just feel one another, feel where our bodies touched, and the tingles of pleasure from our bond formed.

She was wet, but not wet enough. Not wet enough for me to enter her. Not if I didn't want to hurt her. The stretch of my initial penetration would still sting a bit, even with proper lubrication, but I planned to lessen that hurt as much as I could so her focus would be on the enjoyment of our coupling.

There were so many ways I could accomplish that feat, but only one that was fitting for our situation, only one that would appease my dragon after the day's events.

When we discovered our bond the night before, I wasn't sure how things would work out for us, whether I'd be able to give her my mark. But now, that was the only thing on my mind, the only solution I could think of to ensure our bond remained intact.

I reached between us, fingers trailing over her breasts and stomach until I landed on her entrance, on her clit. I circled it and kissed her, swallowing her whimpers and moans of delight. My other hand traced up the length of her ear to the delicately pointed tip. She broke away from me, panting and gasping for air, her chest heaving and her body flushing with her desire.

She was exquisite—breathtaking—as she let herself go, let herself be in the moment as I caressed and teased her, as I showed her just how much pleasure I could give her, how much pleasure her body could take.

I explored her body again with my mouth, kissing and sucking her skin, searching for the perfect spot, for the reaction from her that told me I'd found where I would place my first mark. I kissed the soft spot where her neck met her shoulder, the traditional marking spot, and her whole body shuddered. A long groan pulled from her lips, and her fingers dug into my back as she clutched at me. I smiled and kissed it again, inserting my finger inside her tight, wet heat, and she pulsed around my digit and groaned again.

Her reactions to my attentions were music to my ears, her body responding just how I wanted it to, just how I'd imagined it would. I slipped a second finger inside her, my thumb working her clit as my fingers carefully pumped in and out of her, and I covered her marking spot with my lips, bringing my dragon fire forward, the heat of which would never hurt my mate and which would leave my first mark on her.

"Ooh!" she cried, the sound drawn out and breathy, her body tensing as I brought her closer to her release.

'Mine...' I growled into her mind. 'Say it for me,' I commanded her.

"Yours!" she exclaimed, her pussy squeezing around my fingers as I moved them faster, moved them to the rhythm of her squirming and rolling hips. "I'm yours, Lorcan."

Her body arched, pressing into me, her walls clenching one final time before they pulsed around my fingers. Her moaning and mewling filled the room, her body quivering and clinging to mine as she came for me, my mouth still attached to her neck as I finished placing my mark there.

Mine. So beautiful, so perfect, and so very much mine.

I released her neck and kissed the still-healing skin, already wondering how the mark would look when we woke up the next day.

She slumped against me, still breathing hard, but I wasn't done with her yet. I needed our bond to be completed. I needed to be inside her before I combusted. I needed to sink my teeth into her neck and feel her coming around my cock.

I pulled my fingers from her dripping center, and she twitched at the loss of my touch, but I was already gripping my cock, lining the tip up with her entrance, biting back a groan, and clenching my abs to prevent myself from slamming up into her. I needed to take this slow, and I wanted to take it slow. I wanted to worship her like I'd promised.

But my princess had a different idea. She slid herself down my length, taking me inside her in a slow drop of her hips. Her body tensed as I filled her, and my hands gripped her hips, my teeth still clenched, so I could focus on keeping my body still, on letting her take the lead.

She rose and fell along the length of my dick, taking in more of me each time until I was fully seated in her, and I could go no further. Our eyes met, and her arms wrapped around my neck, bringing our bodies somehow closer together.

"Are you all right?" I asked her, smoothing her hair back and cupping her cheek.

She answered me with a kiss and a roll of her hips, lifting and lowering herself on me again and moaning into my mouth as she did. I kissed her back with equal fervor and let go of my restraint, letting my body react to hers and move with hers.

"Mark me again, Lorcan," she whimpered, her mouth still connected with mine. "I don't want to wait. I want to be yours in all ways."

Her smooth body rubbed against mine, skin stroking skin. No space to fit even a piece of parchment between us. Pleasure erupted from every point of contact, sending lines of fire into my soul.

I pushed her chin up with my thumb, my hand cupping her neck, my lips working their way back to her marking spot, to the already healing fire mark I'd placed there. Corinna held nothing back from me, her body and voice unashamed in response to every caress, every kiss, and every movement of mine.

I brushed my lips over my fire mark, then blew on it at the same time my fingers found her breast and pinched her nipple, eliciting a sharp cry from Corinna. Her walls clenched around me, making me groan and pull her closer, my arm winding around her waist in a fierce embrace. I scraped my teeth over that spot, over the sensitive skin my canines would pierce and embed into, marking her as mine for all time, for all to see. With both of my marks there—both my fire mark and my bite mark—there would be no denying she was mine.

I waited, kissing, licking, and nipping at that spot, waiting until her body was ready, until she was right on the edge of her climax. Her nails scored the skin of my back, her body tensing as she climbed higher, and just as she was close to falling, I sank my teeth into her neck.

I cradled the back of her head as my jaw locked around her marking spot, my tongue swiping over the blood spilling from the bite marks. Her moans filled the room, filled my ears and my heart, a melody for me and only me.

Only ever me.

'Only you,' she confirmed, her hand moving to my chest, her body still trembling and writhing through her orgasm. *'You will always be mine. My protector, my best friend, my lover, my mate,'* she continued. *'My mark is yours and will only ever be yours. Now and forever, in this life and the next, in this realm and when we pass into the Ancestral Forest, my heart and my soul will always be yours.'*

A tide of warmth and gold light washed over me and through me, touching every piece of my body and my soul as she gave me her fae mark. I released her neck and cried out as I released into her, clutching her to me so all of her connected to all of me, so I didn't know where I ended and she began. We were light and love personified; her pleasure was mine, and mine was hers.

The waves of our pleasure ebbed and our movements with them until our bodies stilled, except for the rise and fall of our chests as we breathed. We still clung to each other, still kept our bodies connected in as many spots as we could, and our lips found each other again, meeting in a slow, deep kiss that said more than any words or declarations of love could.

"Corinna..." I sighed, laying back against the pillows, cradling her spent body in my arms, and savoring our completed bond. "Corinna, I love you," I whispered, cupping her cheek.

"I love you more than life itself," she replied, kissing me again and trailing her fingers across my shoulder and down my arm, tracing the fae mating mark I knew would now be there.

Her head rested against my chest, right over my heart, her breathing slowing until she drifted off to sleep in my arms the same way she did the night before, the night we'd learned we were mates. Nothing went the way either of us wanted, the way any newly mated couple would wish their first days together would be. But even with the knowledge of how everything would play out, I wouldn't change this moment, wouldn't change the way we'd claimed each other.

She was mine, and only death would break our bond.

Chapter 8
Lorcan

A week passed since those two fateful days in Evania. A blissful week with Corinna by my side, morning and night.

Of course, we'd spent the last almost three years in much the same fashion, albeit as friends, as protector and protected instead of as mates. As lovers. Before, I did not know the secrets of her body, had not lain with her naked in my arms, whispering pretty words into her ear as she fell asleep, or waking her up with my large hands on her soft, petite body. Before, I had not shown her true devotion, had not spent the long hours of the night wringing every last drop of pleasure from her body, showing her just how much I loved her.

I could feel her in a way I hadn't before. The protector bond connected us, gave us an awareness of the other in situations where we may be in danger. But this was different. She was not just connected with me, but combined with me. She was an unwavering presence within my soul, embedded into the fiber of my being. Her peace was my peace; her joy, my joy; her pleasure, my pleasure, and her pain and sadness, my pain and sadness. Even more so now that I'd marked her soul—marked her the way the fae marked their mates. I may have been a dragon, but because I was her mate—and technically the next fae king—there was fae magic given to me when she marked me, which enabled me to mark her like a fae.

As she slept in the safe circle of my arms in the early hours of the morning, I trailed my lips over her bare shoulder, over the fae soul mark that now lay there. A large sun and its rays spread across her chest to her shoulder, with a vine of fae ivy wrapped around it that wound around her upper arm all the way to her wrist, entwining with the mark that appeared when our protector bond formed three years ago. A matching mark covered my chest, shoulder, and arm in the same spot, signifying me as her mate, the other piece of her soul.

Her head rolled back and to the side, exposing her neck to me, her body responding to my possessive touch and claim on her even in her sleep, my beast preening in my mind over how we affected her body. My fingertips played across her chest to the other side of her neck, to my dragon marks, one right on top of the other. I circled it, feeling the raised skin of the bite mark scar and imagining the triangle surrounding it, the alchemical symbol for fire left behind after my fire mark on her healed.

She whimpered in her sleep, pushing her body back against mine, rubbing herself on my already hardening dick. Goosebumps rose on her skin, her nipples tightened, and the scent of her arousal wafted through the air.

But a voice cut my lazy morning exploration of her body short, a voice reaching out to me in my mind.

'Lorcan.'

I closed my eyes with a sigh. I should have known the sanctuary we'd found here was only an illusion, that our peace would only last for so long. At least it was Bran and not his father. My father. The king of Tidirath.

I tore myself away from my sleeping mate after giving her a kiss on her cheek, pulling on light brown breeches before exiting my bedroom in my family's cave.

I paused in the archway, locking eyes with Bran where he stood in the entrance to the cave. I fought the urge ingrained in me to bow to him because we were now equals in rank—he, the future king of Tidirath, and me, the future king of Evania. The only difference was, with his fine clothing and well-groomed hair, he actually looked the part, while everything about me screamed hardened warrior, not regal future king.

We both stood still, proud, and tall, neither budging. His face gave nothing away, no hint of his purpose in visiting us here. My stomach wrapped itself in knots. He might have shown nothing on his face, but if he was here, it couldn't be for just a friendly visit between brothers. He wouldn't seek me out after three years of no contact just to say hello.

His gaze wandered down from my face to my shoulder and my arm, examining my mark from Corinna.

"She's yours, then?" he asked, meeting my eyes again.

"The cave wouldn't allow her in if she wasn't," I reminded him.

"I wasn't sure if the protector bond would override that part of the magic," he said.

"Why are you here?" I asked, crossing my arms, skipping pleasantries.

He swallowed and moved from the entrance, walking to one of the large chairs in the center of the cavern. I mimicked his movements, sitting after he'd sat, waiting for him to talk.

"I came to warn you," he said. "The fae are threatening war if we don't hand you over to them. They think we are harboring you. They claim you went on a violent rampage and kidnapped their crown princess." He paused, his lips pressing together as he prepared himself to tell me the rest. "They're saying you killed the queen," he murmured.

I sat up straighter, my breath catching in my throat. My mind wandered back to that day, to the courtyard.

"They tried to chain me up and shackle me to the whipping posts in the courtyard," I rasped out, emotion swelling my throat. "They were going to let another male bed my Corinna and force me to endure the pain of her being with another, force me to sit there and do nothing while I felt her terror and her despair."

"Lorcan—"

"I couldn't just let them do that to us. To her. I'd resigned myself to feeling her mate with another when my dragon claimed her, before I knew I was hers too, but as soon as I knew the bond was two-sided, that all went out the window. She is mine—mine to protect and mine to love." I scrubbed my hands over my face and pushed my hair away from my forehead. "So yes, I went on a rampage. I did what any sane dragon would do if they felt their mate suffering and panicking. I lashed out at every fae and fairy that dared to get between Corinna and me. I even fought against Cillian and Cahir, as their duty dictated they fight me to protect Queen Eirene and former King Isaak. But Queen Eirene was not—she was breathing when Cillian surrendered and gave me the key to the iron cuffs they'd placed on Corinna."

"I understand why you did what you did, Lorcan," Bran said. "I'm sure I would have done the same if I was in your situation. But while you may not have intended to kill her, the unfortunate truth is Queen Eirene is dead."

"My mother is dead?"

Bran and I both stood at the sound of Corinna's voice, and I turned to face her as she entered the room. Her hand rested on the archway frame, her eyes darting between Bran and me, her expression unreadable. Her hair was in a long, thick braid down her back, and even dressed in only my tunic belted at her waist, she exuded a regality I could only hope to match one day as her partner on the throne.

If the fae even allowed me that honor.

"Yes," Bran answered. "Queen Eirene died from the injuries she sustained in the fight against Lorcan. So did Lord Viktor Antoniou and various other fae soldiers who fought in the courtyard and tried to keep my brother from you."

"And my father?" Corinna asked, still not showing any emotion on her face or through our bond.

"He is acting as regent until your safe return," he told her. "That is why I am here. Our father, King Oscar, plans to hand you over to the fae so we can avoid a war. He and my mother are coming tomorrow evening to take you and Lorcan back to Evania. I came to warn you, to help you."

Corinna swallowed, and her hand tightened on the wall, the only outward sign of the turmoil within her. Her jaw ticked as she clenched it, and her eyes glistened as they moved to me instead of my brother.

I stayed frozen where I stood, even though everything in me screamed at me to go to her, to take her in my arms and be the eye of the storm for her. But it was my fault. I was the reason her mother was dead. I was the reason Evania declared war on Tidirath. It was my actions that brought this all down upon us.

She turned towards the wall, her forehead pressing against the smooth interior of the cave, her hand coming to cover her mouth as a choked sob worked its way up from her chest.

I couldn't restrain myself after that. I couldn't let her just stand there and endure her conflicted pain on her own. I was her mate, and though I caused all of this, I was still the only one who could provide her with the comfort she needed and with the strength to endure this situation.

I stood in front of her, blocking her from Bran's view, giving her some semblance of privacy as she broke. But I still didn't touch her. I waited, waited for her to make that move, to show me I was wanted and needed.

My hand rested on the wall near hers, and I leaned into her while still not touching her. "For-forgive me, *mo chroí*," I whispered, closing my eyes and inhaling her scent.

Her fingers laced with mine, and she pulled my arm around her, wrapping herself in my embrace and burrowing into my chest with her body. The skin-to-skin contact of her cheek against my bare chest and her soft hands on my hardened muscles sent a jolt of pleasure and love through me, amplified by the reassurance she sent me through the bond.

"There is nothing to forgive, Lorcan," she murmured. "How can I be upset with you for doing what you needed to do in order to protect me? If you hadn't...if you'd just stood idly by, then...then..."

A growl rumbled through my body at her unfinished thought, at the idea of what would have been if I hadn't fought back against the fae who'd tried to keep me from her. Her grip on me tightened, and I clutched her to me, fully embracing her. Her quiet tears continued to fall, her body shaking with her withheld sobs, hiding the noise from Bran and possibly even from me.

"You are allowed to mourn her," I said. "She was your mother, no matter what she did at the end."

"It's not that," she replied. "It's everything. All of it. We will never be free of it. We will always live with this fear, with the threat of my kingdom finding us and forcing us apart. There will never be peace for us."

"I have something that may help," Bran said.

I glanced at him over my shoulder, and Corinna peeked around my body to look at him.

"I have a cave. I was planning to use it as my own, to have a place for myself and my mate once I found her. But for you—for my brother and his mate—I would relinquish my claim on the cave so you can claim it as your own. So you can live in safety and not have to worry about anyone finding you since you would no longer be tied to this cave."

"But what about you?" Corinna asked, her eyes narrowed.

"Once Lorcan sets the enchantments, my knowledge of the cave will disappear, as it will belong only to him and you as his mate, and any offspring you may have until they choose their own caves if they wish to."

Our eyes met, and I gave him a nod, my throat too tight to properly convey my gratitude. The act of him giving us his cave, the cave he'd chosen for his mate and family, was more than I would have ever asked or expected from him. For him to sacrifice that for us said more than any words ever could.

Corinna's thoughts raced too fast for me to keep up with, although I caught snippets here and there. We looked at each other, locking eyes and communicating without words, communicating with a single glance in the way only mates could. I cupped her face in my hands, pressing my forehead to hers and sending all my love for her through our bond as her resolve settled within her.

'It's the only way,' she told me. 'The only way we can have our happiness, our life together.'

'Then it must be done,' I said, brushing her cheekbones with my thumbs as her eyes closed and a single tear fell.

I ducked to kiss it, my lips replacing my thumb and caressing her skin, tasting the salt of her pain and feeling the softness of her skin.

"We will leave in the morning," I said to Bran, my eyes never leaving my mate's as I, too, resolved myself to our new future.

Chapter 9
Corinna

We spent the rest of the day planning our move to the new cave with Bran, and we spent our night in our bed, wrapped in each other's arms, with Lorcan worshiping my body, following through on his promise from the night we marked each other.

We'd agreed to meet Bran in a small valley between this cave and the new cave so he could lead us there. He returned to Tidirath so he wouldn't raise suspicion, and he couldn't transfer the claim on the cave to Lorcan without first showing us the exact location.

Which was why Lorcan and I waited in this small valley; Lorcan near a small stream, still in his dragon form, drinking from the clear, cool waters and sunning his wings; me near the trees, picking ripened and plump berries off of a bush. I popped one into my mouth, my eyes closing, savoring the tart juices as they danced across my tongue, and as I did, something zipped past my ear, rustling my hair and breaking the tranquility of the small valley we'd found respite in.

I turned to follow the noise, to find whatever flew near me, when a wave of pain hit me, followed by a roar and the stomping and splashing of Lorcan's dragon as he writhed in agony.

I clutched at my stomach as I fell to my knees, my vision blurring as more pain hit me from Lorcan's end of the bond. Through my watery and unfocused eyes, I saw two arrows sticking out from his wings, black lines traveling through the veins of his silvery, leathery wings, indicating only one thing—liquid gold poisoning. Someone shot him with an arrow dipped in liquid gold.

His dragon writhed and thrashed around, roaring and growling. I pushed myself up from the ground, ignoring the pain, ready to run to my mate to help him pull out the arrows and use the power of our bond to jumpstart his healing.

But my steps were halted by two iron chains thrown over my head and wrapping around my body, tightening and trapping my arms against my sides and stopping me in my tracks. I screamed through my teeth and strained against the chains holding me in place, but just like in the palace, there was no use.

"Lorcan!" I cried, calling out to him as he shifted back into his human form, unable to maintain his shift because of the liquid gold inching towards his heart with every panicked, pained beat.

He grunted and gritted his teeth together, curled onto his side with the two arrows still protruding from his back, his eyes unfocused and blinking with each breath he took. They yanked the chains around my body backwards, pulling me further away from him, and I whipped my head around, snarling and baring my teeth at those who'd captured me and injured my mate in such a grave manner.

Two warriors from Tidirath flanked me, each gripping one chain, each winding their chain around their wrists to pull me further towards them. And just beyond them was Bran—longbow in hand with a third gold-tipped arrow already nocked and ready to fly—and my father, with a small contingent of fae warriors.

"Bran?" I muttered.

His eyes wouldn't meet mine as he walked by me, towards where his brother lay, curled in agony, struggling to even breathe.

"How could you!?" I exclaimed. "He is your brother!"

I pulled and strained against their hold on me again, tears falling from my eyes and my breath coming in heaving sobs. Lorcan's body twitched, his eyes clenching shut as a long groan escaped him. Bran approached him, ignoring my screams and curses against him, his focus solely on Lorcan.

He raised his bow, pulling on the string and readying his arrow, eyes locked on his brother's body. I turned to the fae warriors behind me and glared at them.

"Stop him!" I commanded, my voice hoarse but steady. "I am your queen, and Lorcan is your king! You cannot allow this to continue!"

But they stayed still, stayed in their ranks behind my father, who gave me a patronizing look.

"They do not answer to you yet," he said. "I am regent, and I will wear the crown until after your...mate...has been disposed of."

I glanced at his head, and sure enough, the olive branch crown rested on his brow, designating him as the highest power in the kingdom until he passed the crown to the rightful ruler—to me.

"Please!" I cried, turning my attention back to Bran, to where he stood, still locked in a staring contest with Lorcan, standing over him, ready to fire his last arrow. "Please don't do this!" I sobbed.

Bran set his jaw, his muscles tensing as he prepared to release the arrow, and I fought even harder against my restraints, ignoring the chains rubbing against my skin and tightening around my waist. The grass beneath my feet came loose in divots from my scrambling and straining, and I slipped in the mud, falling to my knees and lying prone on the ground, dirt and grass staining my dress and my skin.

"In this life, and the next," Lorcan promised, his head turned, his eyes locking with mine, the black poison in his veins showing even in the whites of his eyes.

The twang of the bowstring echoed across the valley floor, bouncing off the surrounding mountains as Bran loosed the arrow straight into Lorcan's heart.

"No!" I yelled.

Lorcan's entire body quivered and jerked at the impact of the arrow, the tendons in his neck sticking out as he strained to keep eye contact with me, to tell me of his love for me with only his eyes. The impact on his heart reverberated through me, too, hitting my heart like a woodcutter's ax against a tree. The pain ripped through my body and my soul in pulses, each one slower than the last as Lorcan's life force drained from his body until the shuddering was mine and mine alone. I sobbed and winced as the bond between us ripped from my body. The marks he gave me would fade into oblivion, leaving no trace of their existence behind, save for the mark he'd left on my heart that could never be erased.

I writhed on the grass, sobbing in silence, my voice raw from all my screaming and shouting. My body curled in on itself, my hands clutching at the skirt of my dress.

It felt like they'd ripped my soul from my body, like a million splinters pierced through my heart. I felt empty, hollow, like I would never be whole again.

And I wouldn't. There would be a Lorcan-shaped pit in my soul for the rest of my life. Until I joined him again in the afterlife, in the Ancestral Forest.

Bran strolled back across the valley, slinging his longbow over his back. He stopped before my father, not even sparing me a glance as he held his hand out, and my father deposited a large sack of gold into it.

"I added a little extra as a thank you for your cooperation," he said.

Bran nodded, then looked at his two warriors who held my chains. "Release her," he commanded.

I let out a gasp of relief as the chains loosened, and I curled my knees to my chest, my arms circling them. With the chains no longer binding me, the pain of losing Lorcan was even greater, more profound than before. An ache, a rip in the fabric of my soul, a wound that would never fully heal.

The two dragons came forward and removed the chains from my body, my limp form giving them no resistance as they jostled me to retrieve it. I had nothing left, no fight to give.

"Get her off the ground," my father ordered the fae soldiers with him.

"Yes, Your Highness," one replied.

Silent tears still streamed down my face as he lifted me, holding me against his chest, my cheek rubbing against the hard, cold metal of his armor. He held me the way Lorcan held me, but where Lorcan's touch and embrace brought me peace, strength, and warmth, this fae warrior's touch only pushed me further into my despair, reminding me of what I'd lost.

My lip quivered as more sobs worked their way through my body, my chest heaving and my body shivering from both the physical and emotional pain. I didn't even notice we'd left the clearing, that we'd taken a portal back to the border near Evania and another to the palace, until my father said, "Take her to her room and bring her back to me when she has ceased her incessant wailing. Then we will hold her coronation, so she can take her rightful place on the throne." The soldier holding me nodded and turned to leave. "And do not let her out of your sight," he added. "Without her, the Drakos line ends."

He nodded again and left without a word to my father, carrying me through the palace to my quarters.

"You don't have to watch me," I mumbled to him as he sat me on my bed. "I will not kill myself. I know my duty to the kingdom. I know I am the only one who can bring about change and lead us into the future."

"You shouldn't mourn your mate in solitude," he said. "I will stay as a friend, so you don't have to be alone."

I rolled to look at him and noticed the faded fae mark on his neck, showing he too had felt the pain of his bond breaking with his mate. "Does it ever go away?" I whispered.

"Not really," he replied. "But you learn to live with it."

I nodded and laid back down, closing my eyes and letting my exhaustion pull me under into a deep and dreamless sleep.

Epilogue
Corinna

TWENTY-FIVE YEARS LATER

I stood in the shadow of the trees, hiding from everyone, watching as my daughter, Aikaterini, and her mate, Vissarion, danced in the middle of the crowd of fae and fairies. Her emerald eyes and golden hair shimmered in the sunlight, and the olive branch crown of Evania graced her head more beautifully than it ever did mine.

She was the spitting image of her father, Gus, the soldier who kept me company the day Lorcan died. The soldier who became my chosen mate. And she had his heart, too. She was exactly what Evania needed, and I knew she would continue on the path her father and I laid the foundation for, building Evania into a strong, forward-thinking kingdom.

He and I worked hard together, invoking a change in the ways of the Evanian people and their treatment of outsiders. My new protector, Alexander Edwards, a werewolf from Volkor, kept his full citizenship in the werewolf kingdom, and he lived a long and happy life with his mate and their three children. And Aikaterini's protector, Gerald, a panther shifter, was given the same liberties.

We'd cut all ties with Tidirath, and it seemed the fairy magic understood that there were to be no more dragon protectors for the heirs, instead choosing other shifter species to protect us.

A few of the older generation resisted the changes, but most of the younger fairies and fae embraced the future we described for them; they hungered for it. They worked side by side with Gus and me, finding compromises that eased the transition for everyone.

And through it all, I always remembered my Lorcan, remembered that he would have been by my side had it not been for the prejudices I worked so hard to eliminate.

Less than a day after Lorcan's death, Gus brought me in front of my father, and he passed the crown to me. As soon as the crown touched my head, as soon as the full power of the title as monarch of Evania flowed through my veins, I named Gus as my regent, imprisoned my father, and then hid myself away, mourning my mate in the way a dragon would—by seeking solitude for at least two years. But while dragons would fall into a deep, restorative slumber during that time, I remained awake—awake and alone—for the entirety of those two years.

When those two years ended, I returned to Evania and began my reign as queen. Gus became my closest advisor and friend, and when he asked me to be his chosen mate, to be his partner and companion, so neither of us would have to be alone, I accepted without hesitation. While the love I felt for him would never match the love I'd held for Lorcan, I knew Lorcan would not want me to be alone and unhappy forever, that he would understand when I met him again that Gus was not his replacement, but someone who loved me and helped me in his own way.

I smiled as Aikaterini smiled, my heart warming at her happiness and her pure soul. I gave her the life my parents should have given me: a life of love, respect, and trust. Both of us—Gus and I—until Gus passed into the Ancestral Forest two years ago. His loss hurt because he was my best friend, but it couldn't compare to the pain I felt when Lorcan was ripped from me before he was ever truly mine.

I slipped further into the shadows of the trees until the celebration was no longer within my line of sight, and then I opened a portal to take me to the edge of the kingdom, to the border between Evania and Tidirath. From there, I released my white wings from my back, stretching and fluttering them before taking off into the sky and soaring towards my destination.

I found it easily, the valley where Lorcan died. It was a place I would always remember, a place etched too deeply in my memories for me to ever forget.

I'd marked the spot where he'd said goodbye to me with a small circle of white and gray stones. The grass had grown around them, hiding them from view, but I knew exactly where they were. I would always be able to find them.

I laid myself down on that spot, and closed my eyes, letting the sadness I'd held at bay for twenty-five years consume me and drag me down. My breaths slowed, and my heart with them until all was still and silent.

Soon, warm hands cupped my face, sending delicious magic dancing across my skin and through my veins.

"I've been waiting for you, *mo chroí.*"

His voice made my heart skip a beat, the voice I hadn't heard since he'd promised to find me in our next life. I held my breath and opened my eyes to find Lorcan kneeling before me, bathed in golden light, exuding warmth, strength, and love.

I rose and threw myself into his arms, holding him tighter than ever. He pulled me to him, rising to his feet, his lips brushing mine as his hands wove into the strands of my hair, gripping me as if he was afraid I would slip through his fingers.

"We promised each other, Lorcan—in this life, and the next," I reminded him as our mouths parted, our eyes meeting again.

He smiled at me and dipped his head to kiss me a second time, this one longer and lingering. As he pulled away, he took my hands in his and turned towards the light, taking me with him to the world that lay beyond it.

THE END

THE GIRL OF THE FLAMES

Stephanie Light

Blurb

Kaleia was just a house slave when the Flame soldier's arrived at her village to demand all the women be turned over to them. Now in the custody of Yusan's most feared knight, Kaleia must do what it takes to survive.

Chapter One:
Dancing Flames
Kaleia

T he smell of burning wood drifts into the village, awakening me as it fills the house with thick smoke.

The Flame Soldiers must be here, I think to myself, scrambling out of bed and tripping over Briar in our pitch black room.

"Hey!" she snaps, a small gasp leaving her lips when she too smells the smoke. The ceiling trembles as the masters race across their rooms, dust particles showering over us. The door to our rooms suddenly slams open, the youngest of our masters, Master Vince, holding a lantern in one hand and our shackles in the other.

"Get up!" he snaps, Briar and I holding out our hands obediently to be chained up. Screams fill the night air outside in the village, my heart thumping so loudly in my chest that I'm sure Master Vince hears it too as he places the shackles on me.

"Are the Flame Soldiers here?" Briar asks, a sob in her throat. "Please Master Vince. Don't let them take us away."

"If the Flame Soldiers want you, they can have you," Master Vince snarls. "I'm not about to risk my life for two cows anyways."

"But I thought we were-"

"We were what?" Master Vince growls. "Did you honestly think I loved you?" he scoffs. "Me? Love a slave? Gods, you're even stupider than you look. You're my slave. I could fuck you if I wanted to, but claim you in front of the Flame Soldiers? Don't be stupid."

Briar bursts into tears instantly at his harsh words and there is nothing I could say to ease her pain as we are dragged outside the house by the dirt road. Master Lorne is already there waiting for us, and we're forced to kneel beside him.

I avoid making eye contact with Master Lorne, but steal a glance up and down the road; other Masters bringing out their youngest maidens, be them slaves, maids, or their own daughters, and forcing them to kneel on the side of the road. Screams break out in the center of the village, likely from families who refuse to give up their younger maidens, and before long, several homes go up in flames.

"We're going to die," Briar whimpers.

The Flames Soldiers are the knights from the Kingdom of Yusan, a distant land rumored to still have dragon-shifters, though no one here in our small village of Devensy has ever seen a dragon in the flesh. They died out hundreds of years ago in Iris, our kingdom.

For the last seven years, the Flame Soldiers have been invading many lands, rounding up all the young maidens between the ages of 12 and 25, and burning them alive. No one knows why they do it and it seems I'll never live to find out.

The sounds of hooves thunder down the first road and a group of knights pulling a large cart full of women stop in front of the house. The leader of the group dismounts his horse and without a word, takes our chains from Master Lorne's hands and drags us towards the carts.

"Please Sir," I beg, Briar too frightened to speak as he opens the door to the cart, several girls cowering back in fear. "We can offer our services to you or your King," I weep, the knight remaining silent. "We are very skilled...I-I can even read." Still he says nothing, lifting Briar up and tossing her into the cart like a rag doll. When he turns to me, my instincts kick and I scream, turning on my heel to run away. A pair of cold hands wrap around my waist and lift me in the air, a shriek escaping my throat.

"NO!" I scream, the knight tightening his grip on me.

A second knight climbs off his horse, a torch in his hand. Panic sinks into my bones as the first knight slams me on the ground and winds up my chain around his hands. He yanks the chain back when I scramble onto my feet to try and run, and I fall with a grunt, the scent of the earth and ash filling my nostrils as the second knight stands over me.

"For running, you'll be the first to burn," he snarls at me, bringing the torch down over my nightgown. The fabric is instantly engulfed in flames, the other girls screaming from the cart as the fire washes over me.

I scream in fear, expecting the excruciating pain to overpower my senses, but the pain never comes. My skin tingles as the fire dances across my bare flesh, my nightgown nothing more than a pile of ashes by the time the flames die out.

The knights, the girls, and my masters stare at me in shock as I lay nude on the dirt road, not a burn mark on my flesh.

"She's the one," the first knight mutters, the second knight remaining silent.

I stare at them in disbelief, sitting up on my knees with my hands across my chest to hide my breasts from the onlooking men. The second knight forces me to my feet, gripping my arm tightly in his hand as he leads me to the cart.

"Return the others back to the owners," the first knight orders the two knights leading the cart. "We found the one we've been looking for." "Kaleia is my slave!" Master Lorne snarls. "Do I not get any compensation for the loss of my property?"

"She belongs to King Arathorn of Yusan now," the knight seethes, climbing onto his horse. "We owe you nothing."

He remains on his horse as the other knights unload the cart, the women sighing with relief to have been spared.

"Kaleia!" Briar calls out as she's handed back to Master Vince, the second knight forcing me into the cart and slamming the iron door shut.

I grab onto the bars and cry as the cart starts to move forward, Briar fighting against her chains in an attempt to chase after us, but it's no use. We're both still slaves.

Chapter Two: One Bed

Kaleia

For several days, we travel, stopping in small villages to rest along the way. I am always given my own room to sleep in at whatever tavern we happen to find, but the knights take turns watching me every night while I sleep. I learn the names of my captors while watching them during our travels. There is Sir Arys who is the captain of the group, and although he is fairly young, he commands his men with an iron fist. His second in command, and the one who set me on fire, is Sir Magnus. He has a temper on him and the word '*quiet*' doesn't seem to exist in his vocabulary. He is the first one up every morning, barking orders at everyone to get dressed for travel and the only one, besides Sir Arys, who dares to go near me. Everyone seems to be afraid of me and I cannot even begin to fathom why. It's unsettling, but at least no one tries to touch me.

Between towns, my cart is kept covered so I hardly ever know where we are, but at least the cover keeps me out of the hot sun.

After a particularly long day of travel, we stop at a tiny village near the sea for the night, the ocean breeze filling my nostrils. I have never seen the ocean.

Sir Arys comes out of our inn with a deep frown on his face, Sir Magnus equally annoyed as he opens the cart doors for Sir Arys to grab my chains.

"Let's go," Sir Arys growls under his breath, tugging on my chains for me to climb out.

He pulls me inside the small inn, my eyes wandering as I watch the other knights settle into their rooms. There appears to only be one exit from this hall out to the lobby of the tavern, my heart sinking when I realize I would easily be seen by anyone working at the counter. Sir Arys stops at the last room, yanking on my chains as he steps inside and pulls me in with him. He closes the door behind us, panic bubbling in my chest when I hear the latch click shut.

Sir Arys removes his gauntlets and his gloves, before pulling off his armor piece by piece.

"There are not enough rooms here for you to have your own," Sir Arys mutters, continuing to undress himself. "You'll stay with me tonight."

The blood drains from my face as I look at the single bed sitting in the corner of the room.

"Believe me, I'm not at all amused," Sir Arys continues, removing his tunic over his head. "But this appears to be only inn here for miles and my men are tired."

I try not to let my eyes wander as a sea of rippling muscles flex with every movement Sir Arys makes. His skin is sunkissed, almost glowing from the beads of sweat dripping down his sculpted abs.

There's a knock at the door and two young men bring in two large tubs of water, washcloths, clean tunics and towels for us; Sir Arys thanking them under his breath.

A small gasp leaves my lips as the knight removes his boots and begins to unbuckle his pants.

"Turn around if you're so frightened," Sir Arys growls in annoyance, pulling off his pants and dipping a washcloth in the water.

Embarrassed, I turn around and face the wall, listening to the sound of water splashing as he cleans himself. I only turn around when the knight goes quiet and I find Sir Arys drying himself with a towel. His back is equally very toned but I don't dare look any lower, turning around and facing the wall again.

After a few minutes, I feel a tug on my chains, the Knight staring at me as he points to the second tub of water.

He can't possibly want me to take a bath in front of him!

His serious expression, however, doesn't falter and I realize very quickly that he really does. When I remain frozen, he turns around to face the wall.

"You have ten minutes to wash and change or you will sleep outside in your cage," he snaps.

Not wanting to spend another night in the cart, I undress, covering my nudeness with my hands over my breasts as I reach for a washcloth. The water is cool to the touch and feels amazing after the long journey, but I waste no time savoring the sensation, eager to get back into some clothes again. My eyes scan the room for a possible escape, and I realize the windows have no bars or steel frames. There are just two little wooden shutters standing in the way of my freedom. The door is locked, but I see the key tucked away in Sir Arys' utility belt.

Either way, I have two modes of escape, I think to myself, growing giddy at the possibility of escaping.

I finish washing and change into the tunic Sir Arys left on the bed. It's massive, but better than being naked.

Once changed, the knight turns around, grunting under his breath as he looks me up and down. He takes the end of the chain and wraps it around his wrist, locking it in place with a small lock and stuffing the key in his pants pocket.

Without a word, he drags me down to the mess hall where I am fed stew and stale bread. The other knights make no attempt to speak to me and sit at other tables.

The only one who dares eat with us is Sir Magnus, yet he never speaks to me either, ignoring me entirely as he exchanges a few words with Sir Arys. It seems we will arrive at Yusan's capital, Foryn, tomorrow evening so I'll have to escape tonight.

After dinner, Sir Arys takes me back to the room and locks the door, informing me that there will be two guards at the door throughout the night.

"You've sat in a cage the entire trip," Sir Arys, says as he pulls back the covers to the bed. "But I've had to ride and walk for almost two weeks now. You may choose to lay in bed with me or on the floor, either way, I'm sleeping on the bed," he says, clearly annoyed by the situation.

He kicks off his shoes and climbs into bed, turning his back to me. The chain is long enough that I can sleep on the floor, but despite the warmth earlier in the day, nighttime is almost freezing here. With trembling hands I pull back the covers and climb into bed beside Sir Arys, keeping my back to him and facing the door.

I can feel the heat of his body and despite the comfort, I refuse to let myself inch any closer to him, reminding myself that I have to escape tonight. Hours tick by as I listen to Sir Arys breathe while he sleeps. When I'm sure he's fast asleep, I slowly inch towards the edge of the bed, stopping every few seconds to listen to the knight. It's a slow process but I manage to slip out of bed without pulling on the chain too hard and waking him. The belt with the key is on my side of the room, hanging on a hook along with all of Sir Arys' armor.

I tiptoe towards the hook but it is just out of arm's reach. Still not ready to give up, I stand on one leg, and use the nightstand to help me stay balanced as I reach for the belt with my toes. Beads of sweat gather on my forehead as I try to pull the belt, only to realize the buckle is wrapped around the hook with a knot. I give the belt a shake, freezing when the buckle makes noises.

"Need some help with that?" Sir Arys says, a gasp leaving my lips as I jump and fall to the ground.

When I gather my bearings, I look up to find Sir Arys sitting on the edge of the bed with his arms crossed across his chest. I gulp as he rises to his feet and walks over to the belt, grabbing the key to my freedom and tossing it at my feet.

"It's yours," he says, laying back in bed without so much as a second glance.

I stare at his back in disbelief. "You're not going to stop me?" I ask.

He groans, pulling the covers over his shoulder.

"The nearest town is 20 miles away, back towards the mountain. It's freezing. You have no food, no water, and no idea where you are. You'd also have to cross through a forest with ogres, who would likely make a light broth out of your bones, as there's not much meat on you anyways," he says with a tired sigh. "You'll be dead by morning."

"If you don't think I'd survive, why am I still in chains and why are there guards at the door?" I ask, the knight throwing off the covers and rising to his feet as he storms up to me.

He takes the key from my hand and unshackles me, throwing the chains on the floor at my feet.

"Are you satisfied?" he snarls, walking to the door and unlocking it. "By all means, go."

Knowing I may never again have this opportunity, I scramble to the door and run out, no one stopping me as I step out of the inn. I look down the road in either direction and realize I have no idea where I am. Still, I'm not about to go back to the tavern, so I walk down the empty road, searching for anyone who could possibly point me in the right direction. Rounding a small flower shop near an alley, I hear two men chattering amongst themselves in the dark.

Mustering up a little courage, I walk towards them. "E-Excuse me, gentlemen, but could you help me? I'm a bit lost. Could you point me in the right direction to the nearest town?"

The two men look me up and down, exchanging glances as sinister smiles appear on their lips. Something in my gut tells me to run, so I back away slowly, apologizing for disturbing them.

"Where are you going?" one to them asks as he reaches out and grabs me.

"Well, aren't you just the sweetest little thing?" the other says, sniffing my hair. "What will you do in exchange for this information?"

"Oh-I...I don't have any money," I smile nervously, attempting to pull my arm out of his grip.

"That's alright, dearie," the older of the two men whispers in my ear. "We take other forms of payment."

My skin crawls as the scent of liquor fills my nostrils, the man tightening his grip on my arm when I try to pull away.

"Where do you think you're going, miss?" the other says, slapping my asscheek and standing behind me so I have no means of escape. "You wanted our attention. Now you've got—"

The man behind me stops mid sentence, collapsing on the floor with a thud. From the corner of my eye, I see the man on the floor, a large dagger sticking out of the back of his skull. The other man stares at something behind me, his eyes wide with fear.

"I believe the girl is mine," Arys says calmly, the man nodding in return.

"Yes sire," the man says, letting go of my arm. "Apologies—"

Sir Arys throws another dagger just above the man's head, the blade burying itself in the wall of the flower shop.

"The next one goes to your head if you speak out of turn again," He bellows, wrapping his arm around my waist and pulling me to his chest. "Now go, before I change my mind."

The man wastes no time scurrying away, leaving just the knight and I in the dark alley.

"Let's go," Sir Arys' snarls in my ear, pulling me along in the direction of the tavern again.

I don't dare contradict him, walking alongside him in silence. Back at the tavern, two knights greet Sir Arys as he pushes me inside, Sir Arys ignoring both of them. He takes me back to the room and says nothing as he opens the door for me. I walk in willingly and stand by the nightstand, ready to receive my punishment.

To my shock, the knight only sits on the edge of the bed and kicks off his shoes, placing his belt on the nightstand in front of me.

"Are you hurt?" The knight asks and I shake my head silently. "The next time you wake me from my sleep, I'll let them have their way with you," he threatens. "Am I understood?"

"Yes, sir," I whimper, tears pricking my eyes at the thought of what could have happened to me. "T-Thank you—"

"Do not thank me," he replies curtly, settling into bed. "My only job is to turn you over to the king, in whatever condition I please."

"Why does the King want me?" I ask, but the knight only turns off the lamp and rolls over on his side away from me.

Getting no answers, I reluctantly climb into bed again, wrapping my arms around myself as I try hard not to burst into tears.

I don't know when I fall asleep, but I find myself curled up at Sir Arys' side when I wake up, his arm draped around my waist. It's the first time I've seen him so relaxed, tufts of his long black hair framing his cheeks. I hadn't noticed how handsome he is.

What am I thinking? I scold myself.

I scramble out of bed, waking up the knight as I trip over his boots at the foot of the bed.

"You were crying in your sleep," he mutters, sitting up as he yawns.

I stare at him in silence from the floor, watching as he stretches and takes a deep breath. He ignores me as he starts to dress for another day of travel, putting on his pants and lacing up his boots. Having been a slave all my life, I carry pieces of his armor to him, the knight raising an eyebrow as I place the pieces on the bed beside him.

"Do you need any help, sir?" I ask, feeling anxious just watching him dress.

He says nothing as he fastens his breastplate, Sir Magnus shouting wake up call from the hall. As he finishes suiting up, he grabs the shackles again and demands for me to hold out my hands. The thought of me wearing those things again makes my eyes water. With trembling lips, I hold out my wrists, the skin raw and bruised from the harshness of the chains

"Your crocodile tears won't work on me," he says curtly, opening the shackles. "So you can stop that nonsense."

I bite down my lower lip to keep it from quivering, watching as the shackles lock mercilessly on my wrists.

I'm tired of being traded and carted off like a mule.

I've had three masters since childhood...I don't even remember what my mother looks like anymore. She could walk past me and I'd never know.

But I will remember Sir Arys, I tell myself. *And he will be my last master.*

"Are you finished?" Sir Arys asks coldly. "Then move it," he snarls when I nod.

He walks me out of the inn and into my cage, Sir Magnus locking the door behind me.

"Alright men, let's move quickly!" Sir Arys commands his men as he climbs on his horse. "I want to reach the capital by sunset."

I curl up in a ball in the corner of the cart as he utters those words, trying my best to remain calm knowing that in just a few hours, I'll be facing the most malevolent being to ever walk this earth.

Chapter Three: The King
Kaleia

Minutes turn into hours as the cart sways from side to side on the bumpy road. We make a stop for lunch and after yet another failed escape attempt, Sir Arys has my cage uncovered as punishment, the scorching sun searing my face and my arms.

Finally, we arrive at the outskirts of a large city, a deep blue ocean stretching out for miles just beyond its shores. Colorful houses sit atop rocky cliffs overlooking the sea, with cobblestone pathways carved along the ridges. The weather is pleasant, a gentle warmth kissing my cheeks as I press my face against the bars of my caged cart, and a light sea breeze blows through my unkempt hair. From the entrance of the city, I can make out a beautiful palace on the peninsula, several large black birds flying over it. As we approach the city, however, I realize those are not birds at all, but large beastly dragons.

"Cover the girl," Sir Arys snaps at Sir Magnus. "The King will be the first to see her when we arrive at the palace."

Large black cloaks are thrown over the cart, and I am left to cower in the dark, feeling the cart sway once more from side to side over the cobblestone. The sounds of crowds gathering around me grow louder the further we go, the knights working diligently to shield me from the prying eyes of the people. I lose my sense of time as the cart drags on, and by the time the cart stops, I've nearly fallen asleep, the sudden movement of the cloaks startling me. The light burns my eyes as Sir Magnus pulls open the door and grabs onto my chains, tugging me toward him.

Knowing my punishment will only worsen if I try to resist, I follow his instructions willingly as he helps me out of the cart. My eyes widen in shock as I find myself standing before the entrance of a grand palace, white marble pillars positioned on either side of the door.

"What are you gawking at?" Sir Magnus snarls, draping a large black cloak over my shoulders and shoving me forward so I nearly trip over my feet. He hands over my chain to Sir Arys who, with one silent glare, orders me to walk.

I know better than to look any nobility in the eye without permission, so I keep my head low, staring at the glimmering marble beneath my dirt covered feet.

Sir Arys pulls on my chain, guiding me down several corridors as servants step out of the way. When we finally arrive at a door, Sir Arys orders me to wait outside as he slips in, his hands still gripping my chain. I take advantage to look around and realize I'm in an area reserved for lower ranking members of the household; the floors made of wood that creaks beneath my feet and the walls bare. Sir Arys steps out moments later with several older looking maids who look at me with deep worry and concern.

"These women will help you wash and dress into something more appropriate to meet the king this evening—"

"The king?" I interrupt, Sir Arys clenching his jaw in annoyance.

"You will do exactly as these women say and if you try to run, there's not a place in this city I won't find you, and when I do, you'll have wished you'd burned instead," he snarls, handing the chains to one of the maids. "She's all yours. We'll be outside if you need anything."

Sir Arys steps aside to let me through as the old maid pulls me inside and he slams the door shut behind me; the sound of the lock clicking letting me know that there is no escaping.

The room is small with stone walls and no windows, but there is a large wooden tub in the center of the room with steps built into the side. A tin pitcher and bowl sit on a wooden dresser next to the tub along with an even smaller tub containing water.

"This way, m'lady," the maid says, her voice kind and gentle as she helps me undress. "We'll get you washed and dressed for His Majesty."

She guides me into the tub, the other maids quickly pouring in buckets of cool water. I gasp at the coldness and the elder maid apologizes as I shiver. Not long into the bath, they all begin asking me questions.

"What is your name, dearie?" one asks, pouring a bottle of white liquid over my head and lathering it up into a foam.

"Where are you from?"

"How was your journey?"

"Did you really survive the flames?"

"ENOUGH!!" The elder maid shouts, the others quieting down. "I'm sure the girl is frightened enough without us overwhelming her." "Kaleia," I answer, the eldest of the women looking at me in confusion. "My name...It's Kaleia."

"Oh, that's a beautiful name!" one of them exclaims. "You'll make a darling pair with his High—"

"Elise!" the elder maid snaps, Elise falling silent. "Don't mind these old bats," she sighs. "They speak nonsense. The King would like an audience with you. That is all. Whatever happens after is at the mercy of the gods."

Realizing the older maid will not allow them to answer truthfully, I give up on trying to figure out what I'm here for and instead let them do their jobs without fussing.

After I'm rinsed and dried, the maids escort me to a room adjacent to the bathroom and dress me in a long white gown with long lace sleeves. The skirt has a long train with embroidered dragons and if I didn't know any better, I'd say it resembles a wedding dress. My long brown hair is combed and neatly pinned up, the maids adorning my hair with flowers and jewels. As a finishing touch, a long veil is placed over me, my heart racing as I look back at the bride in the mirror.

What am I doing here? I wonder.

To my bewilderment, as I'm led to the door, the maids each kiss the palm of my hands, murmuring 'your grace' under their breaths.

Never in my life have I been treated as someone of any importance, but as I look down at my shackled wrists, I remind myself that I am still not.

The maids open the door, the knights already waiting for me outside. Sir Magnus takes the chain from the elder maid and walks me down the corridor, speaking to me through gritted teeth.

"You will not speak unless spoken to — not a single word," he warns me. "And you will not look His Majesty in the eyes. You will bow when you stand before him and then you will get on your knees and touch your forehead to the ground. Do not lift your head unless told otherwise by his Majesty. Am I understood?" I decide it's best to keep my mouth shut and simply nod at the knight who grunts in satisfaction. Lowering my head, I watch as the wooden floors turn to white marble again. We come to a halt at a double door in a grand hallway, two harolds standing on either side of it. They bow before Sir Magnus and I, the knight turning to me.

"Now I'm going to remove the shackles. DO NOT RUN," he snarls. "Or you will pay with your life."

I glance up and down the hall, but there are knights stationed at every pillar. Even if I wanted to, I'd be caught within seconds. I hold out my wrists to the knight, and he slowly removes the shackles, my flesh raw from the metal rubbing against them.

The doors open, revealing a great church adorned in white and gold furnishings, with two thrones at the head of the room. At the altar, stands a priest dressed in red and gold robes, and another man facing him. Though his face is hidden from me, he has long black hair and wears a brilliant white cape with gold trimmings and a small gold crown on his head.

In the pews stands another man, dressed in a black tunic with gold embellishments and a black belt wrapped around his waist. The crown on his head is much larger than the man's at the altar, meaning he must be the king. He rises to his feet and walks towards the altar, turning to face me as Sir Magnus walks me down the aisle.

Sir Magnus kneels when he reaches the foot of the altar and I follow his lead, never looking the King in the eyes as I bow, and drop to my knees.

A pair of black boots nearly step on my fingers as I touch my forehead to the floor, but I don't dare move, too afraid as I wait to hear of my fate.

"So this is the girl of the flames?" King Arathorn scoffs. "She looks like a common peasant."

"She was a slave from the Kingdom of Isaris," Sir Magnus explains.

"A slave?!" King Arathorn cries out in shock. "My daughter in law, a slave?"

Daughter in law? I gasp, a sickening feeling filling the pit of my stomach.

"I'm afraid so, your Majesty," Sir Magnus replies.

"And you confirmed she can survive the flames?"

"I watched her burn myself, sir," the knight offers.

The king hums to himself under his breath, circling me like a vulture. "Rise," he commands, when he comes to a halt behind me.

Not wanting to test his patience, I jump to my feet, my knees shaking as the king scrutinizes every inch of me, his eyes practically boring holes across my body. I steal a glance at the man beside me, my eyes widening in shock when I recognize him instantly.

"What do you think of her, son?" the king sighs.

"I think it matters very little what I think," Sir Arys says. "I don't even have a choice."

"That's enough, Arys! I've heard enough of your tantrums," the King roars, Arys unfazed by his father's temper. "The prophecy indicates that you must marry the girl of the flames to unlock your beast, and you *will* earn your dragon. The next great King of Yusan will not be some mere mortal without its wings. Eight generations of dragons have sat on that throne," he snarls, pointing to the large golden thrones. "And you will be the ninth."

My mind can hardly keep up with all the revelations. Prophecies? Dragons? Marriage? Heirs?

I turn to Arys, hoping for some sort of explanation or even words of reassurance, but he offers nothing as he glares at his father.

"Your grace," the king calls out, settling into his seat. "You may begin the cerem—"

"No, wait!" I cry out, looking around at the men in bewilderment.

This can't be happening...

"We wait for no one, child," the king snarls back. "Proceed, your grace."

"But—"

"One more interruption from you and I shall have your tongue removed," the king warns, gesturing to the priest to continue.

Beside me, Arys remains ever silent and annoyed as he looks at the priest and I realize I have no choice in this matter. I'm marrying a prince, one who I thought was nothing more than a common knight. I suppose there are worse things that could be happening to me right now, but the thought brings me no comfort as Arys slides a ring down my finger and the priest asks me if I accept Arys as my husband.

I look to the king who glares violently at me and then at Sir Magnus, his hand on his sword ready to strike me down if I try to run. Unable to bring myself to look at Arys, I nod silently.

"You must say 'I do', my dear," the priest insists, my lips trembling as I hold back a sob.

"I-I do," I whimper, the priest giving me a sympathetic look.

"Then I now pronounce you husband and wife," he declares, Arys turning to his father.

"Are you pleased now?" he seethes, the King sitting back in his chair with a sinister grin on his lips.

"Shall we feast?" the king replies curtly, rising to his feet.

Chapter Four: One Bed

Kaleia

I hardly touch my food as I sit at a grand table with the King, his daughter, Elara, and my new husband, along with a few nobles I know nothing about.

"Are you not hungry?" Elara asks, looking at my full plate of food. "Or do you not like the food?"

Afraid she or the others might take offense that I'm not eating, I stuff a spoonful of soup in my mouth, trying my best to not let my hands shake.

"I'm sorry," I say, lowering my gaze and forcing myself to swallow the mouthful of food whilst holding back tears. "It's delicious."

"I think my wife and I shall retire to our room now," Arys mumbles. "It's been a long day."

"Eager to consummate the marriage, are we?" A noble teases, the king roaring with laughter. "We'll have a palace full of hatchlings soon enough!"

A shiver runs through my spine at the thought, Arys ignoring the comment as he takes my hand and leads me away from the table. We hear more chatter and laughter erupt from the table as we leave, but all I can focus on is the sound of my heart pounding in my chest, desperately trying to escape its prison.

Arys doesn't let go of my hand as he leads me through the several corridors and flights of stairs, until we arrive in a dimly lit bed chamber with a grand canopy bed in the center of the room. Though dark, I can still make out the details of the plastered ceiling art, and the many gold trinkets sitting on dressers. I stare at the single empty bed, rose petals spread on the sheets, gripping the skirt of my dress to comfort myself and dreading what's to come.

The door slams shut behind me, a gasp escaping my lips as I hear heavy footsteps walk towards me. Still, I remain frozen in place, holding my breath as I feel Arys stand just behind me. He raises a hand to my shoulder, running his fingers down the length of my arm to my fingertips.

"Are you afraid?" he asks, his voice low but commanding.

"N-No," I whisper, unable to make my voice sound strong.

"Then why," he replies, leaning in close enough that I feel his breath on my ears, "do you tremble?"

He spins me around, forcing me to face him as he glares down at me with a deep frown on his face. His eyes travel to my lips, down the length of my dress, and then back up to my face. He takes a few steps back, wordlessly removing his coat and unbuttoning his shirt to reveal those beautifully sculpted muscles of his.

"I have every right to claim you..." he sighs, kicking his shoes off and removing his pants so that he stands only in his underwear. "If I wanted to..."

He pushes past me, wiping off the rose petals from the bed and blowing out the candles across the room. A sweet aroma fills my nostrils as he pulls back the sheets, and he closes the blinds, the room almost pitch black so that only our silhouettes are still visible.

I start unbuttoning my dress, but struggle with the corset, unable to reach the ribbons currently constricting me. I feel a pair of hands grab me by the waist and pull me backward, my back colliding with his bare chest.

"Hold still," he mumbles, untying the ribbons.

A sigh of relief leaves my lips as the corset drops to my ankles, my hands instinctively flying up to cover my breasts. One by one, Arys pulls the pins and jewels from my hair, releasing my curls and running his fingers through each ringlet. Minutes seem to trickle by until finally, I can take his silence no longer.

"I-I've never been with a man, your Highness," I whisper, my heart caught in my throat as I force back a whimper. "P-Please, I beg you. Be gentle."

There is a long pause of silence before he sighs heavily, the floor creaking as he steps away from me.

"I have no desire to bed you, Kaleia," he replies as I watch his silhouette move toward the bed. "I wish to sleep. Good night."

He climbs into bed and rolls over so his back is to me, while I remain standing, staring at his back. I look to the window and then to the balcony, neither one locked or out of reach.

If I could just wait until he falls asleep, I could maybe find a way to escape this prison...But then what? I don't know my way around this kingdom. I don't even know my way around the palace! Where would I go? How would I get around? With what money? I don't even know the currency! Oh gods, what am I doing? I can't be this close to my freedom and so useless! Think. Think. What did I see when we entered the capital?

"If you are planning your escape, I'd give it up," Arys snarls. "There's not a place in this kingdom I wouldn't find you."

"I wasn't planning anything," I lie, staring longingly at the window as I climb into bed.

"Of course not," he scoffs, moving to the furthest corner of the bed.

With my body facing the balcony, I imagine myself climbing down along the wall with rope and running through the streets for the first time without a chain around my neck or ankles. I try my best to stay awake, but my eyelids grow heavier the longer I stare at the balcony, until finally, I drift off into the darkness, free at last in my dreams.

The sound of the bed creaking and shifting as Arys moves in his sleep awakens me and I freeze in place, listening to him open a drawer on the nightstand and rummage for something. The sun is just barely rising, casting a yellowish gold hue over the room through the window. A metal clink rings in my ears, my heart racing as I try to think of what it could be he's searching for. Still I dare not open my eyes, afraid of what I may see.

He gently pushes his hand against my shoulder, rolling me over on my back so that I'm facing the ceiling. I lay there motionless for what feels like an eternity before the bed creaks again, my eyes opening to tiny slits so I can peer out into the dimly lit room. To my horror, Arys stands over me, a dagger raised above his head aiming for my heart.

Chapter Five: Awakening
Kaleia

I don't move, I don't even breathe as I wait for my fate, when suddenly, he lowers the dagger to his side and sighs tiredly.

"I can't do it," he mutters under his breath, walking around to his side of the bed and sitting down to look at the moon outside the window.

Finally, he sets the dagger down on the nightstand and gets up, grabbing a robe and walking out of the room. I let out a deep breath and sit up, my hands shaking as I come to terms with what just happened.

"He wants to kill me," I whimper to myself, hugging my knees to my chest. "I need to get out of here," I say, scrambling out of bed.

I grab the dagger from the night stand and search the room for supplies, finding a small burlap satchel in the wardrobe that I can use to store my things. I stuff it with two pairs of underwear I find in my dresser, some matches and candlesticks, and several pieces of jewelry that I can hopefully barter for cash.

With my things prepared, I put on the single dress I find in my wardrobe and toss my hair up in a ponytail. Locking the bedroom door, I peer over the balcony, my heart sinking when I realize our room is in the tallest tower of the palace, and no amount of bedsheets would make an adequate rope long enough to get me down.

I'll have to go through the palace itself, I sigh, tying the satchel underneath my dress to conceal it.

Peering out into the hallway, I breathe a sigh of relief to see no guards standing outside my door, and I quietly tiptoe out into the corridor, careful not to make too much noise with my heels. I stay close to the walls, stopping and listening for the guards and staff every few paces, but it's so early in the morning, there's hardly anyone awake in the palace.

I don't exactly know where I'm going but I manage to find the stairs to the first floor and make my way through the grand hall. As I near the temple from earlier, I notice the door is slightly ajar, two pairs of voices arguing within.

Inching closer to the door, I dare to peek inside, my eyes widening when I see both Arys and his father arguing at the altar.

"What do you mean you couldn't kill her?" the King roars, Arys glaring defiantly back at him.

"She's an innocent girl who hasn't even loved or felt love before," Arys protests.

"All the more reason to kill her quickly," the King snarls. "She has no idea what she's missing." He grabs his sons by his shoulders and shakes him. "Listen to me, Arys. She has no family, no one to come looking for her. The prophecy says you must kill her while you mate to unleash your beast. You cannot be king without awakening your dragon!"

I cover my mouth to stop myself from screaming while they discuss my fate, terror filling my veins to know the truth of what brought me here.

"There must be another way," Arys pleads, his father shaking his head.

"This is the only way, son," the king says solemnly. "You are almost thirty years old. Your time is running out, and there are plenty of others in line just waiting for the perfect opportunity to strike and take your crown, one way or another. For the good of your kingdom, for the good of *this* family, you must kill her."

I slowly back away from the door, still holding my hand to my mouth to silence myself as I tiptoe out towards the courtyard. Once outside, I let myself breathe, desperately trying to swallow back the sobs caught in my throat.

Oh dear gods, what do I do? I whimper as I stumble towards the stables, several massive black horses looking back at me.

I've never ridden a horse before, but I don't have time to be frightened, so I pull out my dagger from my satchel to cut one loose from its restraints.

"Trying to escape your fate, are you?" an unfamiliar voice calls out behind me, the hairs on the back of my neck standing on end as I freeze in place.

Slowly turning on my heel, I find a little old woman in a dark, hooded cloak staring back at me, her beady blue eyes gazing into my soul. Her face is a sea of wrinkles and sunspots, and her hair looks like white straw sticking out from under her hood, but it's her blue eyes that send shivers down my spine.

"W-Who are you?" I ask, the woman smiling back at me.

"That's not the question you should be asking," she chuckles, pulling out a small crystal orb from within her cloak and holding it out for me to see. "You should be asking 'how do I get out this predicament?'"

I gaze into the orb as flashes of green light swirl inside of it, until the light subsides to reveal a story within.

"There once was a greedy prince, second in line for the throne," the old woman begins. "As the second son, he was not meant to rule, but as his father aged, he grew hungry for power. On his father's death bed, his older brother was named King and ruler of the dragons. The young prince was furious, for he felt he was much better suited for the throne than his brother, and he challenged him to a duel by dragon. The two brothers fought, but ultimately, the older brother came out victorious, and banished his younger brother from the kingdom.

Filled with rage, the young prince traveled to the furthest lands just beyond the sea, where he met a powerful sorceress. He demanded she give him the strength of two beasts so he could defeat his brother in battle and take the throne. The sorceress agreed, but only if he swore to bring his first born son to her. Thinking he would never see her again, the young prince agreed and she conjured up a potion for him to drink, warning him to return on the night of his son's first birthday.

Disregarding her warning, the prince drank the spell and his dragon grew to the size of two. Now bearing the strength of two beasts, the prince returned to his kingdom in time for the coronation and once again challenged his brother to a duel by dragon.

The future king accepted and the two brothers fought once more. But the future king was no match for the young prince, and he fell from power that very night. Now king and ruler of the dragons, all the king had to do was bring his first born son to the sorceress as he promised.

The king soon married and had a son not long after, but on the night of his first birthday, the king forgot to bring his son to the sorceress, for he had been too blinded by greed to remember such minor details. Days melted into years, but the king never returned to deliver his son to the sorceress.

On the night of the child's twentieth birthday, his dragon was meant to awaken...but it never did."

Within the orb I see a young Arys at his awakening ceremony, attempting to call his beast forward, but remaining in his human form to the dismay of his father.

"Never dismiss a sorceress's warnings," the woman chuckles. "The king returned to the land beyond the sea to rectify his mistake, but it was too late, the sorceress would not return the boy's dragon.

Still, the sorceress pitied the child, for he had done nothing wrong to lose his beast. And so she gave the king a choice: Sacrifice. To be selfless for once, and sacrifice his own dragon to give to his son, or sacrifice a pure dragon soul, from the old dragon bloodline, during a mating."

My eyes widen in shock when the orbs reveal an image of me the day of my burning.

"Can you guess what he chose?" the woman laughs.

"But I'm not a dragon," I reply, shaking my head. "I'm just a slave girl from another kingdom. It can't be me!" I protest.

"Pure dragon souls cannot die by flame," the woman explains. "Dragons don't burn."

"I'm sorry," I whimper, stepping away from the stables and the woman, "but you've got the wrong woman."

I pull out my satchel from under my skirt, and run as fast as my legs can carry me across the courtyard, desperately trying to get away from the crazy old woman. As I round the corner, however, I run face first into a hard chest, a surge of pain pulsating from my abdomen. I look up into the cold dark eyes of the king, a sinister grin on his lips as he pulls out a dagger from my belly.

I stumble back against a wall, holding my bleeding wound as I stare at the king in bewilderment. Footsteps thunder behind him, until Arys appears, his eyes widening when he sees the blood on my dress.

"Finish her," the king commands, handing the dagger to the Prince. "Fulfill the prophecy and earn back your dragon."

Arys looks down at the dagger and then at me as I slide down the wall, a metallic taste filling my mouth. My eyes struggle to stay open, but I manage to see both father and son fight over the dagger as my vision darkens and blurs.

"Kaleia!" Arys shouts, but his voice sounds so distant as he calls out to me. He is nothing more than a blur as he screams my name. "Kaleia, wake up!"

"KALEIA! Wake up!"

My eyes burst open as the smell of burning wood hits my nose, my hand still clinging to my belly. I look around and recognize the room as my old one back at Master Lorne's house, chains still wrapped around my ankles.

"Hey, wake up!" Briar snaps as she helps me up.

The ceiling trembles as the masters race across their rooms, dust particles showering over us. The door to our rooms suddenly slams open, the youngest of our masters, Master Vince, holding a lantern in one hand and our shackles in the other.

Oh my gods, I gape, looking around in confusion. *What is happening? Why am I here again?*

"Didn't we already do this?" I hiss, Briar looking at me as if I've grown a second head.

"What in the world are you talking about?" she asks, holding out her hands to Master Vince.

Screams fill the night air outside in the village, just as they had before.

Had it all been a dream? I wonder.

"Is it the Flame Soldiers?" Briar asks. "Have they come to take us away Master Vince? Please don't let them take us away."

"If the Flame Soldiers want you, they can have you," Master Vince snarls. "I'm not about to risk my life for two cows anyways."

"But I thought we were-"

Just like before, Briar bursts into tears instantly at his harsh words as we are dragged outside the house by the dirt road to kneel by Master Lorne.

As in my dream, screams break out in the center of the village, several homes go up in flames.

"We're going to die," Briar whimpers, the panic in my body disappearing as the sounds of hooves thunder down the main road.

The Flame Soldiers pull up with a large cart full of women and stop in front of the house, Arys dismounting his horse and taking our chains from Master Lorne's hands. Briar begs for mercy, but this time I do not join her.

No, this time will be different.

VERA FOXX

THE HUMAN PRIZE

A Fated Mate Story

Blurb

In the not too distant future, the world basked in the serenity of peace. Humans reveled in the symphony of coexistence, their lives harmoniously entwined. However, an ominous force abruptly tore open the fragile veil separating realms, unleashing a torrent of races upon the Earth.

Humans were captured and enslaved, their existence slowly fading away as these monstrous creatures ravaged them. With each passing day, human numbers dwindled, leaving only Alice, the final, prized human. She relies on her cunning and intellect to outsmart the malevolent High Dark Lord Fae Amurath, who reigned over the once vibrant southern lands of the United States.

Alice was decorated in gold chains, they were unforgiving, encircling her delicate neck, their presence a constant reminder of her captivity. She realizes there is no salvation, no reprieve from becoming nothing more than a mere plaything in the Lord's sadistic game.

Tsar Hindrik, a formidable dragon shifter, descended upon the earthly realm alongside his brethren. Yet, unlike the others, he possessed an aura that defied darkness and evil. His mission has diverged from the power-hungry dark fae; instead, his kind discovered that humans in this realm are their mates. Now they hunt not just for justice, but their life long partners.

Chapter 1

L ord Amurath tangled his extended fingers into Alice's long ebony hair. His knuckles were boney and skin unnaturally pale, as his fingers twisted and twirled her perfected straight locks.

She sat beside his opulent throne, as she always did on a day such as this. The Battle of the Lords.

Alice shivered, but not in a good way, as some of his sharp nails grazed her scalp. One false move, and he could easily slice the skin right open and reveal her skull.

Those fingers resembled something of a demonic nature. They were the type of fingers that would grab your foot if you left it hanging over the side of your bed in the night. They would pull you off, drag you under and eat you, or take you into another world while they played with you until you died a merciless death.

Alice always had an overactive imagination.

However, that was the only unattractive thing about him. Those fingers. He was a dark fae, and he practiced his trade so diligently that when he wielded his evil magic, his hands became twisted and curled into monstrous tools. But his face remained that of etheric beauty, just like in the fairy tales she used to read as a child.

It was a small price to pay to be powerful.

And Lord Amurath, though with a face that was the epitome of beauty, his behavior and temperament were far from what one would expect from the heavens. His actions were driven by his selfishness, cruelty, and brutality in such a way that it was almost unbearable.

"One would think with being a dark fae, he would want to prove his title wrong and use his magic for good," Alice often thought. *"But no, he had to go with the crowd on that one."*

Alice felt three tugs of her hair, signaling her to rise.

She slowly rose from her pillow made of luxurious purple satin fabric. The iron clasps securely attached to her ankles clinked together as the chain connecting them moved away from the soft material. It dragged across the marble floor as she walked slowly, sensually, with her head bowed to stand before her dark lord and master.

Alice had to be primed.

By the way he pulled at her hair, she knew exactly what he wanted her to do. The gentle tug he gave her warned her to get up and stand before him. He had a task for her, and if she did not obey, who knows what would happen.

No food, water, sleep, or worse yet, help perform tasks in his bedroom, such as handing him sexual toy props and listening to him ravage one of his concubines.

Gross.

Alice knelt on the warm marble, having been exposed to the late afternoon sun for some time, and bowed before Lord Amurath. The heat of the marble stung, but not enough for her to make a wince. She was too terrified to do so.

Her hair clouded her vision, keeping her face obstructed. Amurath chuckled deeply, leaning forward from his throne and crooked his finger under her chin. Her head tilted, and she stared into those blood-red eyes.

"Oh, Pet, I've told you time and time again you could look upon me," he crooned.

Yes, he had told her she didn't need to bow, but gods, the eyes felt like they were ripping into her soul. His eyes had a brilliant scarlet color that seemed at their most intense directly after he had eaten.

"He's more like a vampire than a fae," she thought to herself.

The sparkle in his eyes reassured her she was safe from the possibility of being made to feed him at that moment.

He didn't need to drink blood. No fae did. Alice figured he did it because he believed he was drinking their life force.

That was what she figured anyway.

"That's a good pet. Now, I need you to go to the dungeons to check on the new merchandise." Alice tried to hold back a shudder from the power he radiated, but it rolled through her in waves.

She hated to feel so powerless, so weak, so vulnerable. But what was she to do? She was at his mercy and to all the creatures that stumbled into Earth's realm fifteen years ago. The only reason she was here now was her strong will to survive.

Alice could stand up for herself and hold her own against many of these creatures. Her mother said she had a strong backbone, but Amurath's power was stifling. Any level of magic for a human was overly powerful, but his? It was downright despicable.

Alice didn't show weakness, helplessness, and fear like most. She gave him submissiveness, however. There was such a fine line, and she had mastered it well. Alice knew it intrigued him, and it was why he kept her around.

It kept her alive.

Fear fed Amurath's lust for blood, and excited him to watch life fade from the weak's eyes. Alice knew all this, so she did her best to shield her fears with a mask of indifference.

The last few slaves didn't last long. Amurath sucked them dry before her eyes to show her what happened when there wasn't submission. She was so afraid she had almost wet herself, and after that day, she promised she would show a submissive demeanor, but every day, she planned for his demise; however, it never came.

She knew she wasn't strong enough. But something in her gut told her to hold out, that she would get her chance for freedom one day.

"Ah, no need to be afraid." Amurath twirled his finger around her jaw, popping his finger on her nose like a dog. "He will be in a cage, chained by magic. No harm will come to you."

With a nod, Alice replied, "Yes, Lord Amurath, I am here to do your bidding."

"That you do, and what a wonderful pet you have been," he crooned. "The last four years, you have served me well, and with that, I hope to give you a present on your upcoming anniversary serving me."

Oh hell.

"It would be an honor coming from you, my lord. I do not deserve such kindness." She tried to keep her voice from trembling.

Keeping her fear from oozing from her body was getting harder and harder each day. The longer she stayed here, the harder it became.

The lord's gifts were not nice. In fact, they could be downright deadly.

"That you don't." He chuckled. "But, with a pretty face such as yours, it is a shame to waste it."

As the crowd of the arena erupted in a loud cheer, the lord gracefully stood in response. His clothing, long dark robes, was swaying back and forth from the strength of the wind. The open-air gladiator field, once a giant football stadium, roared with applause. The dragons fighting in the ring continued to wrestle with each other until one dragon had the other pinned by his neck.

The pinned, green dragon huffed out a large puff of smoke, slowly choking from the lack of air. high dark fae lord Amurath Ravafiel raised his arm for silence to sweep across the cheers and applause.

Alice continued to stay on her knees, knowing that he had not yet released her from her submission stance. Her body remained rigid, head bowed, ready for the next order.

"Release the loser, Ukan the Brave. All praise goes to my own dragon, Daildran the Insane." Amurath smiled wickedly, his dragon blowing fire into the stands as more people cheered.

The dragon's red scales shimmered in the sun as he reared back and blew out more fire across the arena. Alice knew that the fire was almost blinding, and the heat of the fire could be felt on Alice's back. These dragons, although large, could not withstand the fae's power. Their magic consumed everything, turning the earth into a dark, void place.

Once a planet oozing with humans and technology and almost on the verge of world-wide peace, Earth was now reduced to a time it had never seen, with fae and magic.

But there were different races other than the fae. Elves, dwarves, orcs, every one of them evil. They rattled their metal cups, clubs, and swords, screaming praise to Daildran and his owner, His Lordship. Despite these races looking like primitive beings, with their prehistoric concoctions of metal and stone, they also carried something more that helped ruin the earth.

Magic.

"Now, my pet, I need you to check on my new dragon." Amurath rubbed his hands wantonly as he sat back on his throne. Another fae female plucked a grape from a large food tray and placed it in his mouth.

Alice stood, her head still bowed, the chains clinking together. "Yes, my lord, I will return shortly."

Her bare feet touched the marble that now coated the private box once meant for humans and football viewing. The walls were now adorned in tapestries and paintings of fighting fae in a world she had never known.

She traveled to the stairs, all the guards watched her with lingering eyes. It wasn't often they were allowed to watch the little human walk around alone. The high lord didn't want anyone looking at what was his, and that meant that no other slave, no guard, or anyone in the court would dare look at the last human, Alice.

Which, to her, she felt like it was a blessing.

The lord was too powerful, and no one wanted to face his wrath, especially regarding his *things*.

As Alice descended the curving staircase, she noticed that the number of guards had grown with each step. As she moved down the steps, the chains that bound her clinked and rattled against each stair. It was a constant reminder of what she was.

There was no running. These races were all faster than humans. His lordship only kept the chains on Alice's ankles to remind her that she was his property, his exotic slave pet. The cuffs that clung tight to her ankles were enough.

Carefully, she ran her fingers along the golden collar with its bejeweled surface. Sure, it was nicer than many slaves used to have when there were other humans. It didn't rub up against her neck like the iron ones. But it was there because the lord wanted to flaunt his wealth. By putting gold around Alice's neck, he saw it as he had so much wealth that he didn't know what to do with it.

So, he put it on his pet.

Once Alice's feet hit the ground floor, she listened to the dragging chains and walked outside the stadium. Horses, beasts of all kinds that Alice still didn't know the names of, all tied to posts ready for their masters to return. Some were beautiful, while others were monstrous, but they all stayed like good little slaves and waited.

She shook her head, and made her way to the dungeon's entrance, located away from the main stadium. Amurath built his palace just next to the stadium. He was damn proud of it, too. When other lords visited, they oohed and awed over how amazing his stadium and palace were, because they made him look much richer.

The intimidating, large wooden door was situated right in front of her. She knocked in a sequence pattern, and the door unlocked. The rumbling of the gears and the chains as they worked together to pull the immense door open reverberated through the air, followed by the sound of the door rising upwards. Alice stepped inside before the door completely opened, giving the mixture of race slaves on the other side a break.

She gave a slight nod in acknowledgment, but they did not respond. They had the same signs of exhaustion and fatigue as the other slaves.

None of them were human. In fact, Alice hadn't seen another human in nearly three years. She wondered if they had all been worked to death, sent off to quarries, or made into sex slaves. It was becoming downright lonely not having another person of your kind around.

"Am I truly the only one left?" she often thought to herself.

Alice kept going further into the darkened dungeon until she eventually came across the cage at the far side of the prison. The magical iron bars served as a barrier, keeping the large black dragon with silver scales around its face at bay. The magnificent dragon's head lay lifeless on the floor, its eyes closed. Magical chains were on all four ankles, one around its neck and tail.

Alice had seen dragons many times chained to these walls. She often felt sorry and took pity on them because they were just like her. Chained and unable to be free. But what of dragons? They are meant for the sky, but around here, they shred their wings and dose them with magic, so they cannot heal or fly away.

Alice's hands clutched the iron bars as she watched the steady rise and fall of the chest of the gigantic creature. Her heart beat faster, her lungs filling with the scent of burnt marshmallows and graham crackers. It was a nostalgic smell, one that reminded her of a time before the earth had been taken over.

"Are you here to check the product?" A large ogre entered the room. He was easily five times taller than her petite size, his skin a pale blue-grey and warts on every crevice of his body.

Alice stood up straight, her hand reaching out for the giant clipboard in his hand. He grunted, his hot breath almost blowing her over.

Once the clipboard was in her hand, she read over the details quickly. This dragon has never fought in the arena but already concluded he was a class five dragon. Meaning he was an alpha dragon and would likely not be tame enough to fight.

"Are you sure this is the right dragon?" Alice asked, staring at the ogre.

He huffed in annoyance and leaned down. He took a large sniff, and Alice's hair nearly flew right up his nose. "You may be treated like a pet because of His Lordship, but down here, you are nothing but dirt between my toes."

Alice glanced down at his feet. They were bare with only three toes, the toenails bitten off almost to the quick. He wiggled them, and Alice had the urge to throw up. "At least dirt is better looking than those toes," she muttered.

"What?" He snapped. His hand reached out to grab her, but she was faster and squeezed through the bars of the dragon's cage. "Nah, ah, don't want to touch His Lordship's things." She waved her finger, backing away.

The ogre growled and stomped off while Alice took the clipboard and did the rest of her duties. She had to check for any scars for identification purposes and ensure the dragon was healthy, viable, and would wake from the magic alright. If this dragon died after being given too much magic, the gifter would be put to death, and it wouldn't be quick, either.

These baffling creatures like to torture people.

After looking over the dragon's body, all seemed right. She had to wait until the dragon woke to confirm that it would shake off the magic. For the first time in an extended period, Alice took a seat and situated herself against the far wall.

The dragon wouldn't be able to reach her from here. The chain leads were too short, but despite sitting and resting, her body was unreasonably unsettled.

Alice has touched none of the dragons that came in and out of these gladiator chambers. Not one, because she didn't need to. But this one, the shiny silver scales peppered along its jaw, mesmerized her.

Alice adjusted her grip on the chain so it wouldn't touch the ground and walked closer to the dragon. She paused, watching the rise and fall of the beast's chest.

"One touch won't hurt," she muttered. Then she lowered herself to her knees in front of the giant beast. Alice's hands reached out, ready to pet the giant's head.

Instead of pushing outward to be used as a fighting device, his horns were curled under like a ram's. Her finger trailed just beneath its eyes, and it responded with a contented purr.

"Like a cat," she whispered.

She wondered what he looked like under all those scales. You wouldn't see a dragon shifter in their human form. These beasts were constantly pelted with magic to keep them stuck in their animal form, to keep them from talking or escaping the giant cages with wide bars that guards could easily come in and out of.

Alice let out a frustrated frown as her fingers slowly ran through the creature's scales. It was not a fair situation by any means. Almost all shifters were compelled by the magic the fae had brought to this land. Wolves, tigers, and lions were the ones she had seen, but she never saw them shift; only heard they were just like the dragons. *Shifters.*

Alice's hand ran under the dragon's eye. It was only a matter of time before the creature awoke, but her curiosity still compelled her to reach out and touch it.

His scales sparkled beneath her fingertips, and the black dragon's scales shimmered gold and brought warmth to her fingers.

It had been a long while since she felt genuine warmth, the kind you usually find within family and friends. All her family was gone or taken, now she was the only one left. This warmth felt familiar and safe to her.

She shouldn't feel safe, not with these magnificent beasts. Even though she felt sorry for them being captured, used, and abused by His Lordship, she knew the dangers these beasts could bring. The dragon could easily stomp on her and rip her to shreds without barely lifting a claw.

Yet she was drawn to it like no other dragon she had helped bring into his Lordship's fold.

Alice knew she was being careless and stupid, she knew. But she was tired, her body, her mind, the constant banter with herself trying to find an escape. She wanted to rest, a full rest where there was no worry, and with this dragon, she felt she could get a moment's peace.

The guards wouldn't dare go near this black dragon. Wouldn't attempt to come into the cage if they tried to pry her body from it. She was safer there than with the lord and all the guards.

So Alice decided. With a dragon of this size, he was obviously doused with large portions of magic and would be asleep for quite a while, and she wasn't about to leave until he was awake. This was her chance to rest.

Alice became comfortable, sitting on her knees, moving the chains away from her body to absorb some of the dragon's heat. A comforting sigh left her lips as she snuggled closer to its eye. But then, when she went to touch the eyelid, it opened, and a large red pupil gleamed back at her.

Chapter 2

Hindrik took in her scent, and it was a wave of warmth washing over him. As soon as she entered the chamber, the sweet smell of her natural fragrance filled the room. It fluttered around his nostrils; all he could do was pretend he was in a deep, coma-like state and not tear down the bars and rip the chains from the walls to get to her.

Her aroma grew as she approached. Invading his lungs, his senses. The hint of strawberries and wine twisted with her natural smell made his lip curl into distaste. He knew she was bathed in the finest oils to fit Amurath's taste, but it was no matter. He would soon bathe her in *his* scent.

Hindrik had to control his dragon just a little longer. It was all he could do to keep his eyes closed, to sneak just tiny glimpses at her while his mate looked at every inch of him.

She was looking at his scars, every scale, his tail, his thick, sturdy legs, his wings, his horns, for intake of course, but in his dragon's mind, this was a test.

This was similar to the ways his clan once was. Back in his realm, the females would circle the males, scrutinizing each body part to see if they were a worthy mating partner. That was then, however. This is now. This female was destined to be his.

She was gifted to him.

This female, his mate, had now seen his dragon. She had noticed he was sturdy, robust, and immense. A most healthy male that would protect her and any hatchlings that may come from their mating.

Hindrik was aware that he was a highly desirable male. He was the sovereign of his realm, and in his world, he was a tsar. The best warrior, and most experienced fighter, he fought thousands of dragons to continue his family's reign and title. However, this little human could bring him down in an instant.

Hindrik wanted to flap his ripped wings and heal them in an instant to show her his healing abilities. He wanted to shake his head and let his fire scorch the top of the dungeon to show his strength and power. To show his worth would be much better, than for her to imagine his supposed value to the lord she served.

But no, he had to lay here, like an injured fool, and wait. He had too much at stake. A plan, if you will.

He had to follow the plan he designed himself. To save his female and destroy an empire.

Another problem presented itself. His mate has only seen him in his dragon form. She had yet to see his human self. She could still change her mind. She could flat-out reject him, no matter how much he showed off his reptilian form.

He wasn't the youngest of the clan anymore. He was older, much older, in fact. He was nearing four hundred years old, while this human looked to be in her mid-twenties.

With age, Hindrik was well versed in battle and also in nesting. He could hunt, forage, and build her a proper home and nest. Not to mention he would take care of his mate sexually. And with the way his cock was already pressed against the seam of his dragon's body, he would have no problem keeping up with her, either.

His clan would hold her in the highest regard, not just them but all dragon shifters, because she would soon be his tsarina. Many would bring her gifts and tokens for good luck so that she could enjoy a life of ease. The calluses on her hands would fade away with time, and her feet remain unscathed.

Because he would carry her everywhere.

Yes, it was decided. In the beginning, he thought about giving her an option. Offer her freedom once he rescued her and let her walk away if she wished. But no more.

She would have no choice because he would not give up. He would win her heart. For a tsar would never give up on his prize.

His dragon had chosen her five years ago, and he wasn't about to give up now.

Hindrik's dragon purred loudly, as she came closer, and released a calming pheromone to attract her to his body. With this being Hindrik's first time using it, he stiffened his body with trepidation as he heard the small patter of her footsteps come closer.

As he used his sense of smell and hearing to sense her presence, his claws scratched into the stone floor, accompanied by pieces of straw pressing against his paws. The scales on his back felt like they were crawling, and he could feel the spines rising with every breath he took.

"Come closer," he pleaded with her silently. *"Come sit by your nest-mate."*

When her hand touched the hardened scales of his body, the shimmer of his scales activated the bond he knew they shared even further. A dragon smelling their mate was the first step, then the touch. When he had sensed her nearly five years ago, it drove him into a frenzy to find her, and he had hunted her since.

When Hindrik heard the dragon's call, telling him that a single human remained in the southwest lands, he desperately hoped and prayed that it was her.

The gods answered his prayers.

And now his heart soared because his pheromones had eased his mate's fear. She was laying her head against his body, relishing in the warmth and comfort that *he* was providing her. His excitement was palpable, and he could no longer contain it. He must gaze upon her with his own eyes.

He needed to *see* her.

His female's dark ebony locks were a beautiful contrast against his shimmering scales. Her big blue sapphire eyes that reminded him of the blue skies of his home realm stared back, not in fear, but wonder.

His pheromones relaxed her further, his eyes trained on her neck.

Hindrik was ready to mark her as his. After waiting five long years searching the foreign land, he didn't want her to escape now that he had just found her. To wait much longer would undoubtedly test his resolve.

He flicked his tail. Patience was not his strongest attribute.

But here she was, so curious, so accepting of him. Well, his dragon form, at least.

His female blinked. No fear shone in her eyes, at least not on the outside. But deep within, through the tethered bond of a tiny string that attached their souls for the time being, he could feel it.

The hopelessness. The despair.

He heard the fire crackle in his belly and smoke filling his lungs.

He would eradicate those fears soon enough.

He gazed at his mate, and the sound of her steady breathing was enough to slow his racing heart. To even look at her this close was a blessing before him.

Hindrik was well aware of her beauty, which was likely a big part of the reason Amurath chose to keep her around; however, she must have also possessed an impressive level of intelligence in order to stay by his side for so long.

She was the longest-standing favored slave to kneel beside Amurath in both realms. An impressive feat.

His partner was most definitely the ideal complement for him.

Unfortunately, this also implies it will be even harder to take her away from the repugnant demon's grasp.

Since coming through one of the many portals that opened onto Earth, many shifters were finding their mates. Shifters thought mates were nothing but myths their forefathers spoke of. But now, it was all coming to fruition.

Humans were the missing pieces that the shifters were looking for, and he was the last of the dragons to find what was his.

His forked tongue slithered in his mouth, trying to contain the saliva that nearly escaped the corner of his lips.

"What is your name, little human?" Hindrik spoke with such softness as not to alert any guards in the vicinity.

It was vital that they didn't know that dragon shifters could speak in their beastly forms. Otherwise, it would cause a crutch for the plan he had in place.

His female stared up at him with an expression of surprise, her perfect red lips slightly apart. They covered her in fae paints to enhance her features. Hindrik was ready to lick away the filth to see her true and natural beauty.

"My name?" She breathed, her breath coming in short pants. "You want to know my name?"

Hindrik tilted his head, nostrils opening and closing to find a scent of what emotion she could be unfurling.

"Why wouldn't I?" he grumbled. "What else would I call you?"

He watched his mate's face blush, tinging the already pink skin from sitting in the intense sun for far too long.

Now he was angry, not understanding why she would hide.

Her body tried to scoot away from him, her chains inhibiting her from moving quickly. That his little mate was bound and chained angered Hindrik, so he pulled her closer with his tail to keep her with him, close to his body.

"No one has called me by my name since I've come here," she muttered, pushing on his tail. "I'm called, *pet*, by my Master or, *slave*, by any other creature." She panicked, her heart racing.

Hindrik hummed, his pheromones releasing to calm the beating of his mate's heart. He had no desire to upset her, nor did he want her to feel obligated to return his affections, but to provide her with a sense of ease and assurance for once in her life. She needed to feel secure so she could find solace in him.

"Alice." She turned away with a blush on her cheeks.

"Beautiful name for a beautiful female," Hindrik purred. "And that is what I will call you, your true name. Alice."

She gave a grateful, shaky smile.

"How can you talk?" His mate whispered, her heart now steadying.

As she rose to her knees, she was met with the intensity of his single glowing red eye. His pheromones had an instant effect on her, quickly washing away the fear she felt and allowing her bravery to grow with each moment.

"Most dragon shifters speak in their beast forms, sweet Alice. The fae are unaware of this."

Alice tilted her lips to a smile and traced her finger around the dragon's eye. Hindrik saw curiosity flicker in her eyes. And the beautiful blush in her cheeks that accompanied it when he said her name.

He would say it more often, especially when he cried out his release.

"Why do you and the rest of the dragons hide their voice, then? Why talk to me?" She cautiously moved backward, settling onto her knees and gazing into his eye.

Hindrik found her curiosity amusing and gave out a soft, contented purr of laughter. "We do not speak to species we deem lower than us. They do not deserve our intelligence. We only speak to those who are worthy to be spoken to."

Alice frowned, her hands now clasping in her lap. Hindrik cocked his head to the side, attempting to decipher the strange emotion.

"Then why talk to me? I'm a human; I'm not strong nor worthy. I'm stuck in chains and a slave. I don't remember the last time I saw my kind, and I'm just waiting for my death. I'm weak." She turned her head, looking everywhere but him.

Hindrik's stomach growled, signaling that his inner fire had been ignited.

He heard her gasp as his belly swelled, seeing the furnace light within his body despite his dark scales. He tried to calm the beast inside him, but to no avail. It angered him that his mate felt this way, but it was no surprise after being kept in slavery after all these years.

"You are not unworthy. Your heart is pure, and you are strong." Hindrik rumbled and settled the fire that burned his belly, his tail wrapped around her waist once more.

This time, she didn't move away. She even placed her hands on his snout.

He took his nose and nuzzled it into Alice's stomach. He could feel the swell of emotion coming from her, his dragon's purr growing louder by the second.

As impure as his thoughts were, he grew excited as he nestled his nose on her stomach. Soon he would bury his cock inside her, mating her, rutting her until her soul accepted and latched onto him. They would become one, and soon bear a fledgling that would carry on their line.

Humans and dragons would come together as one nation, bringing back both species to their rightful population of growing numbers.

When he felt the tiniest of tears fall on his snout, he huffed. "'Tis true. You have survived. One of the last humans on earth, the strongest human I have come in contact with thus far."

A perfect tsarina amongst all dragon shifters.

"I only survived. And for what? This glamorous life?" She licked her lips. "I learned how to play the dangerous game."

Hindrik, the most haughty of all dragons, did not take kindly to seeing his future mate with such a despondent face. He raised his tail, moving so the tip lifted her delicate chin to stare into his eye.

"But you are strong, sweet Alice. You have survived in a world where these creatures should not exist, and here you stand."

His little mate smiled at that, wiping away the tears, before the black paint smudged around her eyes. "If I had known you all could talk, that you could understand me, I would have tried harder to free the dragons. I feel bad about it now."

Hindrik purred, his nose nuzzling into her stomach again. "You have no need to save us, for it is us that will do the saving."

Alice opened her mouth to speak, and Hindrik's cocked stiffened at the sight. But the fantastical boom in the dungeon, and the hushed whispers that accompanied it, made Alice wiggle out of their loose hold on her body.

She tripped, falling forward and squeezing herself through the bars of the cage.

Hindrik bared his teeth in a threatening growl, and his tail whipped through the bars trying to bring her back through. The chain clanked against the magical iron, echoing through the dungeon.

He had to show vulnerability and fragility for this plan to work, which was difficult for him to do.

He wanted nothing more than to order his mate to come back through the bars so he could keep her safe from harm, but they both had a role to play.

His pointed fangs quickly ground together, and he made a loud, rasping sound that could be heard throughout the dungeon. He didn't like Alice being out of reach.

"Alice," he hissed. "I will protect you. Come back to me."

By the gods, he meant it too. If Alice would just cross the bars, he would show Amurath his true strength and maybe more.

Images flashed in his head of him and Alice in erotic and beautiful scenes. One with Alice, laying down on her back in the cage with him, her slave skirt pushed above her waist and his tongue delving into the sweetness of her cunt.

Hindrik did his best to hold his cock inside his dragon's body. They could not find out that he had grown too fond of Alice. Not now.

Dark High Lord Amurath's arrival was heralded by his heavy steps echoing through the chamber. His dark robes brushed the dirt as he moved, leaving behind a trail of deep, dark grooves like a snake slithering through the sand. He walked past all the other dragons that growled in his lordship's direction, hissing and banging against the bars.

"Soon, my brothers, soon," he sent them through their dragon bond.

Hindrik held his head high as the dark fae approached. He bowed to no one.

Alice, who stood just outside of the iron bars, was already on her knees, head bowed, and her beautiful hair hung into the dirt as her master came and petted her on the head like she was an unworthy animal.

Hindrik did not like this.

Not in the slightest.

"Pet, is the intake complete? We have a celebration party to attend." Amurath took a clipboard from an ogre, signing off on a paper, and pulled on Alice's hair.

That was the last ounce of patience that Hindrik had. His nostrils flared, the smoke escaped his lungs, and fire escaped his throat. The snarl echoed through the cave, shaking the iron bars and chains that kept his feet secured to the floor. They rattled to where the spokes that kept the chains pinned to the stones shook free.

The chains groaned and tightened around his ankles until they snapped. Hindrik took his ram-like horns and butted against the bars, over and over. Anger filled his vision because no one would treat his mate in that manner.

Absolutely no one.

Amurath bellowed, demanding that the ogres bring him cattle-like prods with electrical and magical properties to jab the dragon.

Her dragon.

Wait a second. Did she just claim that dragon as hers?

This dragon had been the only soul that had shown her any ounce of kindness since she had been separated from her family. Actually said her name, and used it more than once and on purpose, no doubt.

Like he *knew* it would make her happy.

The few minutes she had with the lizard beast was the closest thing she ever had to a friend, someone to fight for other than herself.

Alice stood from her submissive pose, watching the bars shake. The magic of the bars was nothing compared to the power of her dragon. She could feel it. Somewhere deep inside her, she could feel his anger, the power inside.

Her dragon continued to ram against the bars. They were crumbling, the magic that held them together falling away faster by the second. If they completely fell, the entire dungeon may also fall in, since they were all interconnected.

Alice pressed her lips together, unsure of what to do.

Lord Amurath's anger flared, his hands wielding the dark magic of black smoke from his hands. Alice had seen it before. It sucked the life out of countless people. She wasn't sure whether it could do it to a dragon, but she didn't want to find out.

She scrambled from her frozen position. Screaming for her master to stop. Damning the consequences at that moment.

Instead of crawling on her knees and begging him to stop, she ran towards the furious dragon with fire in his belly.

A ticking time bomb, that was what he was.

Alice ran through the red-hot bars, ensuring her delicate skin didn't touch the bending metal, heated from the friction.

She couldn't understand why she was running toward an angry dragon, but knew she needed to put a hand on his body, at least. To calm him. To tell him that she was okay. Once she entered the cage, she looked up and down his muscular body. His scales rippled with each hit of the bars. His grunts and growls grew louder, and there, at the other end of his body, she found the perfect spot to grab.

His tail.

She heard her heart pounding in her ears as she took a deep breath and tried to think of a way to make him stop. And so she leaped, straddling the large black-scaled tail.

"Stop, please, he'll kill you!" she screamed at the dragon, hugging his tail.

Because those fingers do terrible things!

Her dragon stopped immediately like she had said some magical words.

That's right, her dragon. Again, she had claimed him.

And her dragon turned his head and cocked it to the side like a cute little puppy. Alice smiled, shaking her head, and put her forehead to his tail.

Oh, thank heavens, he stopped.

She tapped her forehead several times on his tail until the dragon laid back on the floor. He took his tail, brought it to the front of his body and had her sit right in front of his large red eye.

"We are in trouble now," she whispered to herself, but she knew her dragon could hear.

Lord Amurath stood there dumbfounded, his fingers still weaving the black smoke around his fingers until he dropped his hands. He shook his head and rubbed his temples, swearing under his breath.

The ogres had been dismissed, and Amurath put the iron bars back in place while muttering to himself.

Alice gazed warily at Lord Amurath, her expression reflecting her unease. She braced herself, expecting him to be angry and scold her, or even yell at her and bring her back from the edge of the bars. Not knowing what he would do was the hardest part for her.

The unknown.

But her dragon? He was purring. His tail curled around her waist, waiting for her lordship to give her orders or, worse yet, delve out punishment.

Chapter 3

Hindrik made the wrong move. He knew he did. He had a terrible temper, but gods be damned, he didn't want to see his mate in such a submissive state.

She was worth more than that. Witnessing her head bowed in the dirt, her beautiful ebony tresses extending into the sand, was a blasphemous sight.

He needed her by his side where he could protect her, and needed Amurath to see she was his. The knocking of the bars was just for show. He only meant to show a minuscule amount of strength to get a rattle out of the dark fae. If he showed his true power, the entire dungeon would crumble and surely crush his mate's body along with it.

He couldn't have that.

Amurath's robes puffed out from the exertion of his magic. Hindrik rolled his eyes. Stupid, dumb-ass fae. Amurath wasn't that powerful, not compared to *him*.

So overdramatic.

Henrik watched Amurath's amusing glare reach his mate, now as frozen as stone wrapped around his tail.

Hindrik's subtlety was gone in an instant. There was no way he would let her go now. He would have to bring this dungeon down, curl up into a defensive ball and shield her from the tumbling rocks from above if he had to protect her.

Amurath flicked his fingers at his side, his black nails clicking together.

What a disgusting creature he was, those long, slender, bony things. Such a terrible comparison to his face.

"Ah, I see what is going on here," he said so smoothly it tested Hindrik's patience.

Did he know?

Of course, he couldn't know. Mates were sacred. No fae, ogre, or fairy could know of a shifter's strong bond they wielded. It was all but a legend amongst their kind.

"You want to rut, dragon shifter, don't you? Or do you just want a companion?"

Ah, so there it was. He thought Hindrik wanted to rut?

Which wasn't completely a lie. He wanted to rut her, his mate. But he also wanted to bond with her. He wanted to come full circle, to bond their souls, and have her fall in love with him. His heart fluttered at that thought.

He stood on all four of his his powerful legs, testing the thick trunks and blowing smoke through his nostrils through the iron bars.

Amurath narrowed his eyes at his challenge and waved for the giant ogre in charge with two fingers, who brought the clipboard over.

"Level five-class, alpha dragon. Almost unheard of to be captured, let alone dosed with enough magic to keep in animalistic form. You must be growing old and tired for fae magic to penetrate you."

Hindrik hissed, letting hot steam blow through Amurath's long, blackened, straightened hair.

Amurath only chuckled, handing back the clipboard.

"I know you are still powerful." Amurath put his hands behind his back and paced the iron bars. "You could break these bars, break down the whole dungeon. But if I keep you sated enough, I believe we could come to an agreement." He paused, staring at Hindrik's mate.

Alice didn't cower in fear, but bowed her head when Amurath stared at her. "She is my pet, my slave. She may tend to you as a gift from me. You cannot shift to touch her in any intimate way. If you so much as damage these walls, hurt my guards, or lose a fight in the ring"—he dramatically paused and turned his back to them—"then, she is mine once again, and she will fulfill her purpose to me that she was originally intended to do tonight." He licked his lips.

"And, I'm sorry to tell you this here, Pet, in this place." Amurath looked around the dungeon with a distasteful curl of his lip. "But you were to be promoted to the lord's head concubine during tonight's celebration. But we will postpone, so that we can see how long this dragon can have a permanent hard-on before he's castrated. You know how much of a sadist I am. It will be like a gift for me."

What in god's name?

Alice audibly gulped, her heart nearly stopping in her chest. Hindrik darted his head to her, seeing she was not giving Amurath the satisfaction of a reaction. But, he felt her hands tremble around his tail, and his tongue slithered from his mouth and licked her cheek. Hindrik would let nothing happen to her.

Not now, not ever.

Amurath chuckled, his shoulders rising and falling. "Ah, I knew you would be excited." He clasped his hands together. "In fact, as a reminder, I'll remove the collar. Come here, Pet. I'll still call you that, because I am rather fond of it."

Amurath strode to the bars, his finger crooking in a beckoning manner to Alice. She immediately complied, pushing Hindrik's tail away.

It was hard for Hindrik to let her go, but he had pushed his limits enough today. So, he watched his mate take quick steps to the bars. Her head lowered, and she waited for Amurath to remove her collar.

Amurath's long fingers reached through the bars and grabbed hold of Alice's neck, fiddling with the lock. He pulled a long gold chain from around his neck, took the key, and twisted it in the lock until it clicked. The collar fell to the ground, but his hold around her neck did not loosen.

Hindrik's tail twitched, his eyes narrowing, watching the muscles in Amurath's fingers, wrist, and arm for any ill intent of a twitch to harm his mate. Hindrik was much faster, stronger. He would kill him in an instant.

"He will not harm you, Pet," Amurath whispered to her. "Keep him happy. I need him to win the next fight, and then it will all be smooth sailing, then..." Amurath leaned forward, his cold lips brushing against her ear.

At least, Hindrik imagined they would be cold, as cold as his vicious heart.

He leaned ever so slightly closer to ensure he could hear every word left Amurath's lips. "I will have our celebration chambers prepared for afterward."

Hindrik heard Alice's heart rate quicken and saw the sheen of sweat coating her body. This wasn't good. His mate was in obvious distress.

Amurath stepped away, and as soon as he did, Hindrik took his tail and pulled Alice from the bars, pulling her to his body. His warmth would comfort her, and his pheromones would soothe her stress, bring her peace; even if it was just for a while.

Attending to his mate was all he could do for the moment.

"Now, win my fights, black dragon," Amurath ordered, "and she is your little pet, on loan. For as long as I deem necessary."

Amurath snapped his fingers, and Hindrik watched him intently. Servants from the dark corners of the dungeons appeared as if from nowhere and approached him, bowing, not looking at him above his knees. "Bring my pet all her things. While she stays in this hovel, I want her at least comfortable."

The other dragons hissed and pulled at their chains, as Amurath and his entourage walked by them to leave. Several snarled, but the prods of electrical sticks thrust into their cages quieted them.

It didn't hurt any of them, just a pinprick, but they were doing what Hindrik trained them to do. To cower back and stay away from the electrical, magical blue charge.

Time, just a little longer.

Alice continued to watch the back of her fleeting master. It wasn't of longing; it was another emotion Hindrik could not decipher. The bond was not yet strong enough for him to understand it.

Hindrik knew to bide his time. However, the emotions circling his mate were powerful, that much he knew. Females of any species that held potent emotions were dangerous and one wrong move...well, he knew dire consequences would follow.

The ogres picked up the rubble he created, grumbling along the way. Then went along with their chores, throwing hay for his bedding and setting out meat carcasses for the dragons that fought in the arena. Hindrik scoffed at the pigs next to his cage, but to keep up his strength, he ate them anyway.

After a time, three slaves entered the dungeon, two females chatted amongst themselves, giggling and laughing while one lone male whose scent he recognized carried the food. They all were more carefree than his mate ever made out to be. They were fae, the same race as Lord Amurath.

Hindrik scooped up one enormous pig, dislocated his jaw, and swallowed it in one. His mate didn't watch while he ate. She just sat, with a distant look in her eye, as she watched the slaves come closer, holding only one large bag of her belongings and the other fae with a plate of food.

This bothered Hindrik. Wouldn't his mate be curious about how a dragon ate? His mannerisms? How would they get along? Instead, her expression was emotionless; her body slumped with such defeat.

Surely she did not want to go with Amurath, did she?

Females could be complicated creatures. He had witnessed this in other human females.

"*Patience,*" he muttered to himself.

He would do this right.

Once the slaves approached, she stood, her chains clinking together.

He side-eyed the slaves, who stood on the other side of the bars. They waited for Alice to approach, and when she did, a fae with bright pink hair threw her belongings through the bars instead of handing them to her.

Hindrik watched as Alice turned and saw her blankets, pillows, brushes, and scraps of clothing fall to the floor. The two female slaves giggled and watched Alice bend down to pick up her belongings.

Hindrik growled, slowly rising from his lying position.

"I don't know why our high dark lord gives a pet such precious things," one fae said to the other without addressing his female. "Especially now that she lays with a dragon. She obviously has fallen in favor of having to sleep with the lord's combative dragons."

The other fae female kicked the plate the male had meticulously placed on the floor. His angry gaze turned to the female who had done so. He had been more gentle, giving Alice a warm smile when he had approached.

Hindrik didn't like it, but he appreciated the gesture that one fae was kind.

The male slave stood, disgusted with the female slaves. His skirt was made of blue silk, and three golden tassels were on the right side of his hip. He was a favored slave, maybe more so than the other females.

"You are all fools," he hissed. "After so many years favored by Lord Amurath, you think she would fall so quickly, even with the bedding he brings her?" He pushed his long hair behind his back and reached through the bars to put his mate's food back on her plate. His mate gave a grateful smile, and it was all Hindrik could from snapping at the male slave that smelled far too familiar to him.

But it was a muted aroma he could not place.

Hindrik stomped forward, wrapping his tail around his female, pulling her backward, and glaring at the slave, but he continued to place her food on her plate.

The slave smirked and winked at him.

He winked.

And realization dawned on him.

"She is chosen." He stared at Alice for a long moment. "Soon, you could be washing her feet." The male slave pushed the plate forward, gave a warm smile, bowed, then led the dumb-struck females away from the cage.

[Spacer]

Alice hugged her dragon's tail, frozen in thought, as she watched the other slaves leave the dungeon. Too many emotions swirled in her head for her to process.

Her master left her in the dungeon with a dragon. She was both grateful not to worry about Lord Amurath and the dreadful surprise he had in store for her tonight, but now she had another worry.

A concubine? He kept her for five years and toyed with her that long to now have her as his concubine?

Gross.

And now, she was on loan to the dragon she would stay in the dungeon with, as his *pet*, his *toy*.

She wasn't sure what had come over her, coming to the rescue of this beast. But she knew for the first time in a long time she felt safe with him.

It wasn't right. This wasn't a feeling she should embrace, considering these creatures had taken over Earth, her home. Ripped humans of their mundane lives and forced into slavery and possibly extinction.

Alice felt safe with this dragon, despite knowing him for just a few hours. It was wrong, and she should fight that feeling with all her might. Being fearful was the right feeling to have. He could use her all up, just like Amurath had planned to do.

Lord Amurath traded her to the dragon.

She was now the dragon's pet.

The dragon wanted her in this cage with him. For what, she wasn't completely sure. He couldn't have sex with her. At least, she didn't think so. But the dragon said he was way more powerful than Amurath knew.

He could shift into a human if he wanted. Have his way with her and *rut* with her? *Was that the word?*

Panic filled her.

He wouldn't really do that, would he?

She mentally shook her head. The dragon wouldn't go to all that trouble, not for her. There were many other females prettier than her.

Besides, this dragon seemed to have an ulterior motive. With such power, why be captured? His comrades seem to hold similar power. Why were they doing the same? Taking this torture?

Alice's teeth sunk into her lip as she mulled over her options. She heard the quiet, slick sound of her fingers running across his scales. Was he trying to save her? Was he trying to free her? Why her of all the slaves in the palace?

Maybe he wasn't trying to save her at all.

Her dragon could be spiteful to piss off Lord Amurath. It wouldn't be the first time a species tried to do something like this. Her dragon was just trying to steal a piece of Amurath's prized pet and knock him to his knees, before her dragon delivered a devastating blow to his empire.

She was just a pawn, a chess piece in a war.

And that devastated her.

She thought the dragon might have cared.

How foolish to get her hopes up.

Alice wasn't free or even close to becoming free like she really wanted.

The dragon, yes, she was back now, calling it *the* dragon because it wasn't hers. She was *his* human.

He wrapped his neck around her body. A lulling purr calmed her. Even a musky scent of smoke and burning marshmallows dared to lull her to a calmer state.

Damn him.

"I'll keep you safe from them," her dragon told her. "He won't hurt you any longer."

"But what will keep me safe from you?" she snapped, looking up at the quickly saddening dragon.

Her heart almost ached. Almost.

"I traded a fae for a dragon. I'm no closer to being free."

Despite her best efforts, Alice's feeble arms and legs could not free her from the grip of the scaly tail that had wrapped itself around her body. Her annoyance heightened as she felt the tail tightening around her. The years of pent-up emotion surfaced. The anger, the frustration, the fear, the sadness of losing her family, her species, her life, her freedom. Years of effort to construct her emotional wall were proving futile as it slowly fell apart.

What was this? All this emotion? She was so good at hiding it all. But with this dragon, she felt she could let it all out; let the tears fall onto his scales and let him soak up whatever emotion she could give him.

But that wasn't fair. Not to him. She didn't know him. But with each passing second of him holding her with his tail, she trusted it was for no other reason than to hold her. To comfort and to help her feel safe.

Her dragon's nose cradled into her stomach, his eyes closed, purring like an enormous cat. Its soothing melody beckoned her to continue letting out the feelings she didn't know she had anymore.

Could she? Could she let out the torrential emotions that had filled her for so long?

"Let me feel your pain, Alice. Let me take your burdens so you do not have to be alone?" His voice was soothing, cooing, and damn, it felt so good.

And with those words and a large breath, she let out a sob that echoed into the dungeon, causing the ogres to perk up their heads and stomp towards the iron bars.

Chapter 4

"*Do something about that, will you?*" Hindrik snarled through the shared mind-link with his brothers. Their iron bar cells ran parallel to the ogres that traveled between them. They held long electrical prods, clanking them together, as if that would deter Hindrik from holding on to his mate.

Emotion overcame her, and her body shook with sobs. Years of emotion came in waves and were being released onto him. Hindrik welcomed it. Her soul was accepting the bond; it felt safe next to his.

Her heart would soon follow.

Hindrik let out a deep, rumbling purr, helping her body, with her shivers and tremors. Her cheek rubbed against his scales, his heart breaking in half for the emotional pain coursing through her body.

Hindrik gently held her in his arms in the corner of their dungeon cell, his tail wrapping around them both, providing a sense of security.

His brothers, who he trusted with his life, exhaled a smoky haze, making the ogres gasp for air and cough uncontrollably.

The dragon brothers whipped their tails through the bars with such ferocity that the ogres fell to the floor after their heads collided.

Hindrik shook his head while deep rumbles of laughter continued and turned his back to keep his mate from their prying eyes. They, too, wanted to see their future tsarina. They knew this mission was important, and they worried for her.

But this was his time. They had theirs; they had their mates.

It was his turn, his turn to win his female.

Hindrik watched her tears continue to flow, and his heart ached to see her in such distress.

He could not speak, not knowing what words would console her, to keep her from crying, so he let her be. He let all the emotions that tormented her come out through her tears. She cried for what felt like hours; halfway through the night. And when she finally finished, her cheeks and eyes were stained red, and she stared back up at him.

Hindrik knew she had unanswered questions. He could feel it, but he also knew she was completely and utterly exhausted.

"You do not know me, dear Alice. I know questions plague you." The smoke from his nostrils released, and Alice sighed, a hiccup released from her uncontrolled crying. "I will answer all you seek, but for now, you are tired, and I wish to give you rest. Know you are safe with me. It is a lot to ask. You will rest with me, and I will keep you safe. I give you my word and honor as a dragon. Your life comes before mine."

Hindrik watched as Alice's lips parted, her warm breath caressing the top of his nostrils where he kept his nose firmly planted near her stomach.

His mate's shoulders softened, and her head bobbed in a solemn nod.

It was the start of an understanding. Whatever it may be.

He pulled his head away, rolling to his side, and wrapped his arms, tail, and neck around her, laying his head on her shoulder. She was perfectly covered, with no skin showing except for her head.

"Are you warm enough?" His deep voice rumbled enough that he felt the rock below him vibrate.

Could she feel it between her legs?

Damn it, focus, you old dragon. She just spent the last few hours crying.

But she was still beautiful despite all that.

Hindrik, although prideful knowing he was keeping her warm, wanted to know that his mate would permit him to continue to keep her warm. He wanted the affirmation that he was good enough to touch her, warm her, and keep her safe.

Her sniffles and her tears were still ripping out his heart. He wanted to mend it, fix it all over again.

"Yes, I'm warm," she said weakly.

Then he felt the slightest vibration in her stomach. "You are hungry," he said, disappointed with himself. "How foolish of me. Let me feed you."

His tail, with much dexterity, pulled the forgotten plate closer. He rolled onto his back so his mate could sit on his stomach and wrapped his tail around her again so she did not fall.

Alice smiled, and Hindrik's heart leaped, hoping that this was a good sign.

"I wish to feed you," Hindrik said. He could feel the black scales on his face filling with heat. "But unfortunately, my claws are too large."

Alice stared back at him in wonder. She could see her reflection in his eyes and was completely dumbfounded.

Feed her?

"You want to feed me?" she whispered.

The dragon nodded, smoke rising from his nostrils.

"W-why? Would you want to do that?"

"Because I want to provide for you. I told you I would keep you safe. It is my word I have given to you."

Alice's throat tightened as she looked away from him. The last time anyone wanted to take care of her was when she was a child, before the takeover of all the not-so-awesome fairy tale creatures.

And why would he want to take care of her now? She had cried all over his tail and wailed like a baby for hours on end. She knew she looked like a mess.

Oh, if Lord Amurath could see her now!

His tail was firmly planted around her bare stomach from her scantily clad pet outfit. He was keeping her from falling over, which was really thoughtful. His large stomach, mostly flat, was firm and toned. Falling didn't seem likely, but it was the thought that counted.

"I can feed myself, but thank you for the thought." Alice reached for the plate.

It was fruit, a few pieces of bread, and vegetables. Enough to keep her sated, nothing that will keep her full. Lord Amurath liked her skinny, like most of the fae. Before they captured her, Alice was curvy and had a soft stomach and full breasts. She liked how she looked, but now she was nothing but skin and bones.

"You need more food. I will get you more when we leave this place," the dragon murmured, urging her to eat more.

The dragon reached behind him, and when he pulled his claw forward, a thick piece of charred meat sat on it. Hindrik plopped it on her plate, and his sharp claw cut it in half.

It was cooked pork.

When was the last time she had meat?

"I saved this for you. I do not have spices to make it taste better, but soon I will make you the finest feast, and feed you whatever you wish." He nuzzled her cheek, and her lip trembled.

Alice grabbed the meat and took a large bite into the pork, forgetting the manners her captors taught her through switches, beatings, and whips. It was the best thing she ever tasted. She savored each bite, and she swore she felt her strength returning.

A tear that she thought she had long cried out slipped down her cheek. "Thank you." She wiped away a tear. "But why? Why are you being so nice to me? I just don't understand. No one is ever nice and does not want something in return." She looked up at him. "What do you want from me?"

Thoughts of him forcing himself on her flashed through her mind. But with this beast being so gentle to her, caring for her so thoughtfully, those terrible thoughts fluttered away.

He couldn't...wouldn't do such a thing.

She watched the dragon frown. His large, clawed finger petted the back of her head. He didn't tangle his claw in her hair. Instead, he cupped the back of her head and looked down at her with one eye.

"In time, I will tell you, Alice. Just know you are safe. It is a lot to ask. Especially from creatures that took over your realm."

Alice nodded, clutching the meat to her chest.

"But I hope you can give me the little trust you have, and I will keep it sacred."

Alice didn't have to think twice. He had easily bought her over with the piece of meat in her hand, the warmth of his scales, and a peaceful place to stay away from Lord Amurath.

She trusted him. Only time would tell if it was a good or bad decision.

"Can I at least know your name?" She took another bite of the meat and hummed contentedly.

He chuckled, letting out a thick puff of smoke through his nostrils.

"Hindrik. My clan calls me Hindrik."

Chapter 5

Alice sat on her silk pillow in the viewing box at the top of the arena. There was a strange emptiness in her chest that made her throat ache. She sat in the far too familiar viewing box overlooking the sandy field below. It once held a green thatch of grass for football players, but now it held tumbling dragons slithering in the sand wrestling, and ogres prodding them to fight.

Usually, she felt nothing. She had taught herself to feel nothing while she sat beside Lord Amurath, and as he wrapped his fingers in her hair, petting her head. He wasn't there with her at the moment, thank god. But while he was there, she had learned to push all feelings deep inside; any loneliness, depression, sadness, but now, her emotions were so raw.

It was because of last night. Everything was so fresh and at the surface. She needed comfort, a warm body to wrap around her, a deep masculine voice to tell her everything would be all right.

She had never needed that before. Never required a lulling voice to tell her that all her fears would soon be gone because she knew it would never come. She accepted who she was. She had lost hope.

Alice had learned to cope. She never needed a male or a female's confirmation that things would be okay. Because she knew things would not be okay. A human's world was a mess now. Humans were meant to die, or be captured and put as slaves.

But now, it wasn't just a human world that was a mess. *Her* world was a mess.

A hot emotional *mess*.

Because now, a spark of hope had ignited because of this dragon. She believed him. Believing in hope.

Hindrik raised his head from the sand pits, his face covered in a fine layer of dust as he looked up at her. His black horns shimmered in the golden sun that rained down on him. That was the only part of him that resisted the dirt and grime. A puff of black smoke rose above his head, and when he moved forward, it curled around his horns.

He was a magnificent dragon. She could spot him from any of the others. He was taller and darker. His scales shimmered in the sun, but most of all, the scars he wore were definitely deeper and darker. Not to mention the aura he radiated. He stood proudly, his chest puffed out with authority, pride, and those deep red eyes that looked like they reached into her soul.

Her thighs tightened together. She couldn't have such deep feelings for an animal. But Hindrik wasn't just an animal; he was a shifter. He was a man underneath that animal, but she didn't know what he looked like.

He could be hideous; he could look just like Amurath and be evil all the same.

But, did it matter what he looked like underneath the scales? It was how he acted, and in just the thirty-six hours that she had known him, he was the kindest she had ever known.

Hindrik entranced her, confused, intrigued nevertheless, but entranced. She couldn't figure out why. The magical beast should scare her, just like all the creatures that came out of the portal some years ago that took over the earth. But Hindrik seemed like the gentlest of creatures to her.

Maybe it was the way he woke her this morning...

The soft touch of his tail lightly grazing her arm stirred her from her sleep. How he brushed back her dark hair and nuzzled his nose right next to her cheek like she was a delicate flower.

She tenderly touched her cheek, her heart alive with the warmth of the thought.

Lord Amurath wouldn't have done such a thing. He would have poured water on her head or thrown a pillow at her sleeping body that was curled next to his bed on the floor.

No, Hindrik, despite his size, scales, teeth and claws, was soft.

Hindrik's mouth curled back, showing his large fangs, and let out a deafening roar. The ogres on the field of sand prodded him with the electrical charges of their sticks.

Alice gripped the silk pillow and leaned forward to see what the commotion was about.

A dark shadow hovered over her, and immediately brought her back to her senses. Her back returned to ramrod straight, and her head bowed.

"Interesting how he is so keen on you." Amurath took his seat next to her, draping his robe over the chair. His dark robes were a dull contrast to the bright gold throne.

The male slave, Xavier, who had been kind to her from afar, kneeled before her, giving her yet another plate of food, then stood beside Lord Amurath. "Maybe I should have you as my next pet, Xavier?" Amurath reached between Xavier's blue loin cloth and wrapped his hand around his cock.

Alice tried not to gasp. She had seen Lord Amurath defile many males and females in the times spent in his chambers. It always bothered her, and Amurath knew it, too.

He was trying to rile her up.

"But, I think I would miss this cock far too much." Amurath let go, and Xavier let out a relieved grunt.

"My Pet, come here." He beckoned her with his finger.

As always, Alice didn't hesitate, pulled herself together and stood in front of her lord and master. She knelt on the hot marble, feeling the sting in her knees from the heated surface and the grit of the sand. She listened to the clink of her chains once she settled.

She looked downward, giving her a submissive pose. The wind blew in her hair, and she could feel the sensation of her hair brushing against the gritty sand that had yet been swept away from the private box.

"It is essential you keep my dragon satisfied." Lord Amurath rolled a black grape between his long boney fingers. "But I don't want him touching you in any intimate places," he hissed. "I've waited a long time to complete our game."

Alice swallowed. She didn't realize he planned to take her to bed with him. Did he really play her for all these years? Lord Amurath never once touched her in that way. Sure, she wore some skimpier clothes than the rest of his slaves, but she thought it was because he saw her as a dog.

At least he didn't let her go naked.

Lord Amurath's long claw tilted Alice's chin upward. "Am I clear? You may speak."

"He's a dragon. He cannot shift with your power laying upon him, right?" Alice said with confidence.

Amurath smirked back at her. "Absolutely, he cannot."

"Then, you shouldn't worry, Master. He shouldn't touch me intimately."

Amurath hummed, leaning back in his chair, and waved her away, dismissing her. "In three days' time, this arena will see three times the number of viewers and three times as many dragons."

Alice stared forward, watching Hindrik, who was concentrating on her. The other dragons weren't bothering him, just mingling with each other, staying away.

Amurath's fist tightened. His hand reached over the armrest, grabbed a fist full of Alice's hair, and pulled her head back. Alice screamed at the sudden pain, her hand reaching back and trying to tear away Amurath's grip.

It wasn't the first time Amurath had snapped at her. Maybe for spilling a cup of water, or taking a piece of bread without asking. But this, without warning?

Alice's tears spilled over as his nails pricked her scalp, his hold so strong she could barely breathe. Her tears should have been long dried up, but somehow, they were wetting her lashes far quicker than she would have liked.

Hindrik's ferocious roar echoed in the stadium. The sounds of chairs knocking over, and claws raking down marble and cement, screeched, but it wasn't enough to shake the hold of Amurath's nails on the back of her head.

Amurath had snapped, truly snapped, and she wasn't sure why.

She could feel the blood running down the back of her neck. She could smell the copper, the metallic hint of scent creeping down the mint-colored wrap she wore.

"Please," she begged.

Another roar. This time, Alice felt the heat from the dragon's breath on her skin. It calmed her enough for the tears to dry, and her body relaxed enough to know she was safe.

She didn't know why she felt that way, but welcomed it. She understood little, but one thing she knew for certain, she believed Hindrik's words; he would keep her safe.

What other choice did she have? She had nothing else to believe in.

"She isn't yours, you know?" Lord Amurath tilted his head back, taking in the sight of the Hindrik looming above him. "You shouldn't stare at my things like you own them!"

Alice stood frozen, her head tilted so far back that her mouth hung open in shock. She could see her master's hand swirling with the black shadows of smoke, and her heart leaped with fear.

She struggled to break free, but his hand only tightened around her scalp. She uttered a strangled cry, and Hindrik moved his clawed hand closer to Amurath.

"Don't even think about it," Amurath sneered. "I don't know why you hold my pet in such regard, but I'll keep her now. If you so much as breathe wrong, I will make her suffer and forget what I had her planned for. This competition is far too important."

Hindrik growled, and Alice saw her dragon's belly expand, glowing with fire.

The ogres grew closer, the electrical fire sticks prodding him to back down, but her dragon showed no signs of pain.

It seemed Hindrik was done playing games now, but whatever he had planned, he had yet to divulge to her.

Alice swallowed.

"Don't hurt him," she pleaded. "I'll do what you want, just don't hurt him."

Because the one night of kindness she received from Hindrik was enough to last her a lifetime.

He let her cry on his scales. He fed her, kept her warm, purred loud enough to keep the horrible echos of the dungeon away, so she could sleep. Sure, he was one of those fairytale creatures that took over Earth and she still didn't know his motives, but, for once, she felt cared for.

And that was enough.

Amurath turned his head, fire in his eyes.

She could hear the prodding of electricity trying to push Hindrik away from her and Lord Amurath. "Pet, since when do you think you get what you want? I give you what you deserve."

Amurath's smoke dissipated, and his hand reached for around her throat. Alice looked past his head to look at Hindrik one more time, who shook his broken wings with holes violently. As he did, the holes filled with leathery skin. Once they filled, he puffed with smoke.

Alice watched in awe, her body shaking at the overwhelming power of Amurath and her dragon. The heat alone was enough to want to pull away from the combined magic in her presence.

"Let her go!" Hindrik's belly quivered, and a rush of hot orange flames spewed from his mouth.

The tapestries that hung to shield Lord Amurath's pale skin from the sun, lit afire. The servants that accompanied the lord ran away in fear, grabbing all the belongings they could carry. All of them ran screaming, all except Xavier.

She watched him crawl closer to her while Amurath spouted orders at the ogres. Xavier reached for her hand, but she was too afraid to let go of Amurath's, who was slowly choking her.

"Come," he beckoned her. "Do not be afraid. Not now."

Hindrik was still spouting fire, knocking over the various gold bowls, chessboards, and pillows. He was creating a scene. Hindrik wasn't coming for her.

"Damn it!" Lord Amurath let go of her suddenly, causing her to fall right into Xavier's arms. He cradled her, pulling her away from the torrential fire that continued to spread.

Alice saw the dragons in the arena also causing havoc. Their wings were no longer filled with holes. The ogres had lost control. There was complete chaos.

"We must get you to safety," Xavier yelled over the raging inferno. "This was all premature, so we will have to improvise."

Another roar overtook the balcony. Pieces fell into the stands, and Xavier pulled her into the corridor. He pulled a key from his hip and unlocked the shackles from her ankles.

Confusion must have laced her face, because the fae smiled at her and tugged at her wrist. "All your questions will be answered. Now come."

Xavier pulled on her wrist and led her down an old stairway with a blinking exit light.

Chapter 6

Hindrik was smitten, his eyes glued to her every gesture.

His lack of sleep weighed on him, and he could feel his patience slipping away.

He stayed by her side all night, mesmerized by the soft rhythm of her breathing, her chest rising and falling beneath his scales. He drank her in like a fine cup of mead. His obsession with her had already been ignited before the sun had come up, and he was certain he wouldn't be able to contain his feelings.

What made it worse was when the ogres separated them, made him go down into the pit and spar with his brothers. His blood brothers occupied another part of the dungeons. That put him in a foul mood. They could be insufferable to be around at times.

They tried to lighten his spirits when they entered the arena. They wanted to know about his mate and how she took to him. If she cowered in fear. But he wanted to be left alone to wallow in his pity.

All he wanted was to gaze at his mate. Watch her from afar. The bond had proven strong and tight in his soul in just a few short hours. He was fucking love-struck, and he had never felt such powerful emotions in all of his life.

His brothers had already gone through the love-struck phase; they still were going through it. He was one of the last dragons to find a human mate.

And he would be damned if he took his eyes off the sweet human, unaware of what was happening to her soul. She was so lost; it was breaking him.

He had to tell her what she was feeling soon because she was breaking all over again, and he didn't like it. His mate, his Alice, was a strong female to deal with what she had these years. And now, she was feeling helpless.

And, that cursed fae had to come out of bloody, fucking nowhere. It seems his undercover warlock couldn't keep himself away, which was a huge fucking problem.

The sight of Amurath near his mate made Hindrik uneasy. His scales rippled down his back, and once he saw the dark fae's black claws prick his mate's delicate skin. That's when he lost it. He could smell her blood from here. He could almost see how her blood curved down her spine, stopping at the tightness of the gold chain that wrapped around her middle.

He was absolutely livid and could barely contain his wrath.

He blacked out from rage, and the next time he woke, he saw nothing but flames. The private box was destroyed. Amurath was ordering his ogres and guards of faes throwing spears and balls of light, but even his black shadows of smoke-like death that could take life in seconds did nothing to Hindrik's hardened scales.

Amurath panicked. His magic could do nothing to the dragons, not a damn thing.

"I was going to prolong this game, but you have tried my patience, little pixie." Hindrik loomed over Lord Amurath, his saliva dripping from his long fangs.

The roar of the fire had long scared away the servants and the pretty species of the harem Amurath collected. Even Hindrik's mate was scarce. He pricked up his head, seeing that his spy was also gone.

Good, he must have taken her because he knew his mate wouldn't have left on her own. She was too keen on living, and running would have ensured her death if she left Amurath's side.

His two dragon brothers landed below the private box. They blew out more fire, toasting the ogres that continued to climb. Hindrik gave a shake of his head in disbelief. He knew it was a useless affair to get to their master, not with three dragons feeling no effects of their spears.

Fleeing to the hills would be the wisest course of action for them.

His blue-scaled brother, Hector, blew fire up the concrete steps, scorching several in his path. The rancid smell burning off the rest of their hair burned his nose. The yowls of pain ceased when his brother chomped down; slung one in the air and ate him down whole. He licked his lips, smacking them a few times only to make a terrible face, and gagged. Hector then regurgitated the body back up into the stands, leaving a pile of slimy, half-dissolved mess of an ogre.

His twin brother, Harold, hissed in laughter, fire spitting out his nostrils, burning more of the army who were retreating back down the stands.

Hindrik voiced his displeasure with a deep groan. He didn't know why he was cursed with such insolent brothers.

The sky darkened, ceasing his brother's laughter and the constant gagging noise. Hindrik looked to the sky, not to see clouds from a storm but wings of the rest of his clan. His brothers, luckily, must have linked the rest of his clan that he had moved up the timeline of his plan.

Thank fuck, because he was done playing around.

Hindrik felt a warmth spread through his neck and then a prick of his scales. He lowered his head to see that Amurath had pushed a dark orb to his scales. It had stalled, unable to penetrate his body. Amurath continued to pulse the orb around his neck, trying to find a weakness.

Hindrik snarled, his claws curling around the orb, and flicked it away from his body.

"Impossible!" Amurath shouted in anger. "This is not happening!"

"It is happening. We were just waiting for the right moment. You honestly think dragons had lost their magic when they entered this realm?" Hindrik leaned forward, his nose close to Amurath, who stood his ground. "We have thrived. And we are here to restore the balance. And you will pay for your transgressions. Your death will not be quick."

Hindrik watched as the dragons overhead fell to the platform in their human forms. Once the smoke cleared from their transformation, they stepped forward in their loincloths. They cuffed Amurath in a special dragon-fire welded iron. Amurath screamed in pain as the fire burned his wrists, the heat so intense that it scorched his skin right to the bone.

Hindrik smiled wickedly as he watched the fae contort in agony. If only Amurath knew the searing pain he would feel in the days ahead, the sheer humiliation he would endure.

Amurath would have had more if Hindrik hadn't lost his temper.

Hindrik rubbed a claw down his face.

"Yeah, I know what you are thinking." Harold nudged him, the fire slowly dissipating from the mostly destroyed private box. "You fucked up. You were trying to win the girl over and show her how exceptional you are, but now you have to do it backward."

Hindrik pressed his scaled lips together tightly.

If Harold wasn't his brother, he would have torched him by now.

"But that's okay. Now we can get things cleaned up, and you can shower her with gifts. A nice bed to sleep in, bathe her in pretty tubs. I heard human females like to be pampered. I bet my mate might like to sleep in a bed rather than in our cave."

Hector nodded in agreement.

Hindrik shook his head, using his massive feet to stomp out the rest of the fire. He could still hear the screams of Amurath being dragged down further into the still-burning stadium.

Eventually, it would be destroyed. However, he wasn't sure what would become of the palace. That was for his mate to decide.

"My mate wouldn't find comfort here." His chest rumbled at the thought. "She wants more than gold and jewels."

His brothers gasped.

Hector was trying to pull golden saucers, holding large pools of water, that were becoming dangerously too close to the leftover embers. "Why wouldn't she like gold? It is the shiniest." Hector snapped the gold bowl and showed it to Harold.

Harold preened, looking at his reflection.

Hindrik rolled his eyes and climbed to the top of the stadium, where he gazed outwards. The mostly abandoned suburbs that once housed humans were falling apart. Now the area was crawling with other magical creatures: witches, fae, pixies, orcs, ogres, and various others.

Not all of them were inheritably evil. They were just caught up in trying to keep themselves alive. But it was the shifters that had stayed true. They knew it was wrong to enslave the weakened species.

Using his trained eyes and following his bond, it was then he spotted them. His dear friend, Xavier, the one he owed the most to, with his wild blond hair bustling in the wind, was carrying his mate through the winding streets.

Creatures had long gone into their houses, most likely because of his clan flying into the cities. They were too frightened at the oncoming dragons that continued to pour in front of the West.

"Get the palace cleaned up," Hindrik ordered. "Release the slaves. Get everything prepared. The show must go on in three days." He smiled wickedly.

"And what of you?" Harold slipped, when he landed next to his brother. "Are you bringing her back here?"

Hindrik preened, spreading his mighty wings. "No, I will take her to my nest."

"He's gonna bed her!" Hector landed on top of Harold and gyrated his hips. "Oh, he is going to get laid. He's finally going to be mated!"

Hindrik roared, and his fire spilled from his mouth until his brothers tumbled and fell from the stadium. They laughed in jest, but Hindrik did not take the joke well.

He snarled, taking to the sky, and zeroed in on the raven-colored hair and bloodied tunic she wore.

Hindrik wasn't going to bed her; he would not rut with her. He was going to win her heart and show her what it was like to be loved.

And if she wanted to be taken, he would surely show her what it was like to be loved by a dragon.

Chapter 7

Alice continued to bounce in Xavier's arms. She was overwhelmed, her vision blurred, and her ears rang from her dragon's roars.

What the hell was happening?

She was running from her master, something she would have never done on her own unless she had a death wish. But she did. She ran with another servant who was dead set on getting her out of there.

Xavier wanted to live, and hell, for the first time in a long time, she wanted to live too, but do so freely.

So, she joined him.

Blood dripped down her back. She wasn't sure if she should bleed this much or maybe her wounds were deeper than she thought. None of it could be good.

Amurath never struck her enough for her to bleed. He was not one for leaving any long-term damage to his pet, such as marks or scars. He wanted perfection. He didn't want tainted property.

She reached back behind her head, moving away her dark locks. When her fingers appeared before her, she saw the bright red blood and her vision blurred once again.

"Ah, now let's not look at that," Xavier said, slowing down.

His voice was calm, but with more confidence than usual. Especially, when he was serving Lord Amurath.

He had picked her up after taking off the chains around her ankles. She couldn't run. Her body just wasn't used to that much physical activity. So Xavier insisted that he carry her.

Taking a glance in both directions, she noticed the street was completely deserted.

Clouds rushed by faster than normal, but it was all Alice could do to keep her head up; to look around for any other people.

Her head wobbled, and her fingers tried grasping the robe draped across Xavier's chest. She let out a grunt, her head flopping onto his shoulder.

"Let's check out your head." He softly sat her on the ground.

When Alice laid her head back on the wall, she winced slightly because of the discomfort, but it was still far easier than keeping her head upright by herself.

Alice felt Xavier lift her long hair and brushed it to the side. When she took a glimpse at the side of his face, she no longer saw the pointed ears faes usually had. His ears were curved, looking like hers.

"Xavier?" she hummed while his finger traced her neck. "Your ears? They're not..."

He touched his ears and huffed. "Oh right, yeah. I'm not a fae." He looked at her like it was no big deal. He shrugged his shoulders and brushed her hair away from the blood.

Taking the top part of his outfit, he ripped the cloth and stood, walking over to a rain barrel filled with water. He dunked it several times, and Alice just sat and watched him.

Her head was falling lower. Even the wall was proving to be of no use to keep her head steady.

Xavier wasn't as slim as she first saw. In fact, he was more muscular now. His clothes didn't fit anymore. They were tighter around his body.

"W-what is going on? Who are you? I need to leave." Alice tried to gain footing, only to find her body had weakened further. Between being fed measly meals for years, confined to chains, blood loss, lack of sleep, and the emotional mess she was in, she was just done for.

Weak. Alice felt weak and hopeless.

She hated it.

"Wait, don't get up. Everything is fine." Xavier approached with his hands waving in a downward motion. One held the wet cloth and, once closer, brushed her face with it.

"Hindrik is coming for you. He is ensuring Amurath is subdued before coming. My job is to keep you safe until then." He pursed his lips, checking the wound behind her head. "I've been at the palace as a spy. I'm a warlock that specializes in illusions, a friend of Hindrik. As soon as he found out where you were, I came here to monitor and protect you until he could arrive."

"W-what?" Alice's mind was foggy. Her eyes grew heavy with exhaustion. "He knew who I was? He came looking for me?"

Darkness came over the alley, but Alice didn't feel the looming night or fear in her heart. Instead, she felt safe, wrapped in an envelope of safety as her body slipped further and further into blackness.

The wind blew in her hair as her arms fell at her side. She felt so tired, and questions stirred, but she could get answers later, right? She was promised them, and she believed it down into the depths of her soul.

Just two days ago, she was a slave to Lord Amurath. She did his bidding, slept on the floor by his bed, and did what he wanted. It was all so routine. She had her days planned by guessing Lord Amurath's moods and desires. She kept her emotions locked away, and that kept her alive.

Until *her* dragon showed up, and now everything was spiraling out of control.

A deep part of her had awoken. And she didn't know what it was.

"Embrace it." She felt her soul whisper.

And that was all it took to succumb, because she was tired of it all. She let her life be in the hands of someone else. Because she was tired of looking after herself, she was tired of being alone.

As her eyes closed, she felt her head gently lulling to the side.

"Tsar Hindrik." Alice heard Xavier whisper, but she couldn't open her eyes.

Her jaw tilted in recognition, but she was fading too fast.

Two large, warm hands engulfed her jaw, tilting her head up. Her lips parted, but her eyes still would not open to who held her face.

A deep voice spoke, but it sounded so far away that there was nothing to hear but the same darkness she saw behind her eyes.

Alice felt the soft fur against her cheek. She was warm, her fingers exploring the plush texture of the surrounding fabric. It felt better than the silk, which could feel cold against her skin at night.

This felt so much better. She often froze in the night, especially with the barely-there clothing she wore, and the thin silk and blankets. Amurath liked to see her form at all times, not that he ever touched her.

But apparently, he wanted to.

Now she felt safe, covered in thick furs and darkness. She also didn't feel alone, either. She felt the warmth of a body next to her, a large one. The same one that held her the night before.

When she opened her eyes, she saw her dragon had curled around her but let her lay alone on a bed of furs. The side of his head was tilted down at her, her hair a big mess over her shoulders. His one eye gazed down at her and closed halfway before it opened again.

His large, forked tongue slipped from his mouth and licked her back. She could feel the dried blood clinging to the fabric. She cringed.

It wasn't comfortable.

"We have tended to your head. Let me clean your back. Lower your clothing." His deep voice vibrated through his chest, to the floor, and between her thighs.

She shouldn't have such terrible thoughts, such sexual, beastly thoughts about a dragon, should she? But she did, because that deep voice was damn intoxicating. Plus, he wasn't really a dragon; he was a shifter. He had a body; he had a human body somewhere inside.

But, why was she thinking about any of this being sexual? He was trying to clean her, not trying to do anything else. He was helping her.

And since when had she gotten help from anyone?

Alice shakily reached up around her neck. The claw marks on her skin made her wince when her fingers brushed against them.

Hindrik made a menacing growl.

Instead of flinching, Alice giggled.

"I do not see how that is funny, Alice."

Alice smiled, loving how he said her name. "I just like it that you care." She unclasped the tie around her neck and held the front of her top close to her, not to expose herself. As she looked over her shoulder, he saw the look in his eye that didn't hold only desire but understanding.

"I will always care about your well-being, my Alice."

Alice tilted her head, ready to ask why she was *his* Alice, but his tongue seeped from his mouth and began licking from her lower back to between her shoulders.

His warm tongue shocked her. She rose from sitting on her knees and made a squealing noise, and he chuckled behind her.

Once she got used to the sensation, the warmth of his tongue, the heat of his breath, the closeness of his head, her mind drifted. She really enjoyed the proximity of his body, how erotic it felt.

Her arms loosened, her body relaxed, and her mind floated with the gentle licks that were no longer cleaning her body. They were slower, deliberate, and now she wanted more than just his tongue on her back.

Her breasts felt heavy, her nipples hardened, and her back curved, trying to gain more of his touch.

She was riding a high. The tingles in her back circled her hips and invaded her core. With her pussy fluttering, a moan slipped from her lips, but she wasn't shy with her sounds because she was too caught up in the euphoria.

Alice never had the opportunity to explore her body. She was always on the run, trying not to get captured, but now...

The clothing she held so close to her breasts slipped away. She steadied herself with both arms on either side of her body. Hindrik's tongue pressed her harder and harder, pushing her further and further into the furs.

"Hindrik?" She panted as she rolled onto her back, staring at those deep red orbs full of lust.

His chest rumbled, and the fire in his belly ignited, lighting the room. Alice found this oddly funny because the fire in her own body had exploded, and she was eager to explore what this dragon was going to do to her.

Chapter 8

Hindrik couldn't help but admire the curves of her full breasts. Her nipples were hard, which made them appear more rounded and fuller. It was enough for him to want to take a bite of the rare fruit.

This was going far better than he expected, but he was in his dragon form, and that wouldn't do. He was fully aware of the connection between them that was causing her to experience a range of emotions, and he could feel her soul yearning to be more open with him. That was what the bond did. He'd experienced it watching his brothers take their own females. Their connections were quick, their hearts and souls ready to connect to one another despite their species' differences.

But Alice had been through much, and he wanted her full consent.

By the gods, her arousal was sweet, accompanied by the tantalizing mixture of her musk and his own scent. It was the perfect concoction for disaster to strike. Taking her too soon would be wrong. Not telling her who he really was would destroy any trust that she had given him thus far.

Hindrik lowered his head. His mate's face grew rosier with each passing moment, and he slowly leaned his forehead against hers. "As much as I want to lay my dragon's tongue over the most intimate parts of your body, we have much to say to each other."

When he saw her face fall, Hindrik chuckled. It gave him hope that when he told her the truth, she would want to continue this intimacy later.

"I suppose you are right." She went to reach for the cloth, but he stopped her with his claw.

"You can keep the clothing away. After all, I will be bare-chested when I shift into my human body."

A smile broke out on her face, and his heart soared when she quickly covered it with her hand to suppress it. Hindrik backed away, and her hand reached out toward him.

"Where are you going?" she asked breathlessly.

"I do not wish to frighten you. Shifting can be overwhelming." Hindrik looked her over, to assess her, and when he did, he was surprised.

Her stance was defiant, her hands on her hips and her eyes fixed on him with a narrowed gaze. His cock stirred beneath the seam that kept it hidden inside his body. He stepped back once more, fearing he would let out another beast to grace her presence.

"You don't frighten me, dragon. You would have eaten me whole if you wanted to by now."

Oh, the fire she has.

Little did she know he would eat her later.

He let out a rumble of laughter and shook his hips to make sure his cock did not dislodge from his body. Then he wrapped his body around Alice, curling his tail and resting his body.

If she wanted a show, he would give her one.

"As you wish, Alice." His mate beamed, showing off her pearly white teeth.

Hindrik bowed his head. He let the magical black smoke engulf his tail first. He watched his mate trail her gaze over his body. The smoke rose from his tail first, then to his hips, the spine, across his back, and his shoulders until his entire body was nothing but a black cloud.

His vision went black, and he envisioned himself in his human body once again. He hoped he would meet his mate's expectations. She spent a long time with the fae.

Would she prefer the taller, slim, muscular build of the fae she had grown accustomed to? Or would she like his? He was still taller than the average human, but he had a much darker skin tone than her. Are humans alright with that? And he was also littered with scars, including his face, his long, dark hair now sprouted with white, including his short, stubbled beard.

Maybe she noticed that with his white scales?

Fuck, he was nervous.

Hopefully, she wouldn't sense that. He wanted her to see him as a proud creature, someone she could depend on, to look up to. Someone that would protect her with every fiber of their being.

As the smoke cleared, Hindrik moved his body so he was hovering over his mate. He was so close to Alice that he could feel the warmth of her breath, the heat of her body on his chest. He wanted to be close to her, so close she couldn't see the fullness of his body because he was too damn nervous for her to take him in all at once.

His mate opened her eyes, and that was when he could look at her. *Really* look at her. It was hard to see into those tiny eyes, but now he could see the gold flecks in those blue sapphires.

"Alice," he finally said after a moment of silence.

She blinked several times and said nothing as he lowered and pinned there on the furs. He felt his throat constricting as he held his breath, desperately hoping she would break the silence with her words.

Then, she saw her finger rise and traced his scar from the left side of his face to the right. It was deep. He earned that scar when he was a young adolescent of one hundred and twenty-five and was defending his father's territory against some unruly fae.

Would she find it hideous?

"You're so beautiful," she whispered.

Not what he was going for, but he would take it.

"I think it is you that is beautiful, Alice." His forearms trapped her head, so she could not escape. He was nearly nose-to-nose with her.

With one of his hands, he gently ran his fingers along the freckles scattered across her cheek.

As he traced the apple of her face, her jaw, and then her lips. Hindrik looked into her eyes, begging for permission. He knew he needed to talk to her, but one taste wouldn't hurt, right?

His mate wet her lips with her tongue, and Hindrik tried to hold back the growl, but his resolve fell apart when her hips rose, rubbing his throbbing erection.

"Fuck, Alice."

His lips crashed into hers. It wasn't sweet and gentle as he wanted it to be for their first, but her fingers threaded into his hair, nails scraping against his scalp.

Shit, she tasted just as she smelled. Sweet. A hint of salt from her terrifying run yesterday. But damn, he loved it.

He nipped at her bottom lip. She squeaked in surprise, and her eyes flew open. He paused, waiting to see if he had taken it too far, but she smiled back at him, pulling his head back down and capturing his lips again.

Fire.

She held more fire than he ever thought she had.

When he first saw her, he thought she was a timid, submissive little thing, but it was all a ruse to stay alive. She was so much more since pulling down these walls.

He felt her roll her hips, putting much-needed friction on his cock. He was leaking like a damn fledgling, but he didn't give a fuck. This was his mate, his bond mate, and he was going to spill his seed until it was fully planted into her womb.

Fuck, he had to stop this. Before it went too far.

Hindrik was older and much more experienced. His mate was still young, her hormones still running wild. He wasn't sure if she was still a virgin, wasn't sure if she had time to explore her sexuality. Humans were raised differently than dragon shifters, but either way, they had too many things to discuss before they fully formed the bond they shared.

Hindrik tried to pull away, using the furs as leverage, but her legs wrapped around his waist, her fingers still wrapped around his neck.

His cock was at attention, her slit rubbing his shaft in just the right places because they both were feeling the heat of each other.

So wet, she was so wet.

His nostrils flared, and he swore to himself that he was trying to stop this coupling.

But she was making it so damn hard.

"Mmm, Alice," he said in a strained, muffled voice.

She continued to rub him up and down like a cat in heat.

Damn, his mate was insatiable.

He rose to his knees, leaning backward, but his mate hung onto him like one of those primates he had seen in those prisons, humans kept innocent animals in.

Hindrik pulled away the satin robe covering her ass. He copped a feel because he was male, but his true intention was to get her attention.

But damn, she was so soft. He squeezed, feeling the smooth curve of her ass. He used both hands, squeezing and kneading those globes.

What he wouldn't give to hold them while he fucked her from behind. To see the curve of her back, have his hands on her hips, and watch his cock disappear inside her.

Gods!

Her skirt rose, baring her slit, now rubbing against his loin cloth. Only one piece of fabric was between his cock and her mound. If those two intimate parts touched, there was no way he could pry them apart.

His large hand reared back and landed on her bare ass with a smack. The crack echoed down the walls of the cave.

His mate didn't pause. Her back curved, her head leaned back and pushed her bare breasts against his skin. Hindrik's mate moaned, her nipples rubbing against his hairy chest, and if he wasn't tempted before to place those nipples into his mouth, he certainly was now.

Holy fuck, she's beautiful.

He placed both hands on her shoulders and ripped her away. A beautiful shade of pink tinted her face, and his beard had bruised her lips. And hell, he couldn't wait to do more damage to her skin.

"I must talk to you before I complete our bond, my Alice."

She blinked, the fog of lust in her eyes barely leaving.

"Talk about what? I rather liked this. I've never felt so free?" She laid her head on his shoulder, and he wrapped his arms around her.

The sensation of having her in his arms was pleasant, and he appreciated the chance to provide her with comfort. Part of it was the bond, and he was grateful for it, but he also wanted her to know the truth. All of it.

"I want to answer your questions. Do you remember just a few days ago, you wanted to ask me many things?"

Straight to the point, that was what he needed to do, especially in this state of near undress. Then they could get to more important things.

Like mating.

A lot of mating.

He felt her nodding, her fingers playing with his hair. "I don't understand why I feel so safe with you. It's rather scary. I haven't felt safe since the day those portals opened on Earth when I was younger."

Hindrik lowered himself onto the furs. At the front of the cave, the fire crackled and blazed steadily. It would continue to burn for a long while without fueling the fire with wood or coal. He had stockpiles of food, fruits, and vegetables far deep within this cave to keep them hidden for weeks if he had to. Not that he would take long to convince Alice to be his.

On the contrary, she seemed quite willing to be his, which was a miracle.

But, he was ready to keep her here as long as needed. For her to understand what he was and her new role, if she was willing to accept it. If she wanted to learn more about her position along his side, they would remain here for as long as required. He had enough of a hoard and prepared enough for his mate.

"In my realm, a legend was passed down from generation to generation. That a shifter would one day be gifted a soul mate. A soul mate was a perfect match. They would bring our souls to life, and give life meaning and joy once again. A gift from the gods." Hindrik smiled down at Alice, who was cradled in his arms.

He liked how she was so engrossed in the story. She laid still, hanging onto his every word as he spoke, and never took her eyes away from him.

"We were told that we would know in an instant if a male or female would be ours by sight or by smell. Once the mates are found, a bond is created to seal the souls together. The bond breaks down barriers of emotions to even the most heartless or depressed of beasts and, I suppose, humans, too." Hindrik chuckled. "Souls that once gave up on life, souls that didn't want to feel. The bond brings back the flicker of hope." He placed a kiss on Alice's forehead.

Hindrik watched as a tiny tear welled up in his mate's eye. But that did not stop him from telling his story.

"We noticed that our world's population was dwindling. The fae had suddenly left, and we didn't know why. Around five years ago, we found portals in the fae palaces and entered through to find that your world, Earth, had been overrun with the fae and other species. We decided to help your kind, take them back to our realm, and in the process, the once legend became real. Our souls were awakened."

Hindrik chuckled when Alice's eyes grew wide with wonder.

"My brothers, my clan, found their own mates amongst the humans." Hindrik grew excited. "We found hordes of humans. We took them in droves to the other side of the portal. Our land is prospering now that the fae have left; we plan on keeping the wicked here and bring humans to our realm, so we may live in peace."

Hindrik felt his mate's heart rate quicken as he held her wrist, his thumb rubbing excited circles around her pulse.

"And, I smelled you." Hindrik's voice softened. "We were rescuing a caravan of human slaves, and the wind from the south blew north, and I knew you were near." Hindrik lowered his head. "Sadly, I couldn't go to you, not right then."

Hindrik squeezed her wrist, and when he gazed into her eyes, confusion spread across her face. "I had to help get the rest of the caravan to safety. They were being attacked and—"

Alice ripped her hand from his and cupped his face. She shook her head.

"You had to help those people!"

Hindrik gritted his teeth, unable to look her in the eye.

"You helped my species, my people!"

Chapter 9

A lice did her best to exercise patience as this handsome man shared his words.

But surely, Earth stood still when Hindrik graced the soil in his human form.

His skin was dark, his eyes a deep crimson that spoke to her soul. He looked at her in such a way that made her feel she was the only thing that mattered. It was a gaze so deep that she felt both vulnerable and exposed, but so utterly wanted, despite every flaw she knew she had.

It was exhilarating and downright frightening. But, as he explained why she felt the way she did, about this bond, and how it ripped down her walls in an instant, it made it all so clear.

If an ordinary human tried to explain this to her, she would have never believed it. But after living with these fantasy creatures for years, watching witches and fae take over the land she had once known as boring and magicless, she would have laughed and pushed them away.

But it was all true.

The legend he was telling her mesmerized her. Each word that left his mouth she believed to be true. She felt it deeper than her bones, deeper than a molecular level. She felt it in her spirit.

She felt the connection they shared. And the emotions he was displaying right now, she could even feel.

His face was solemn. She could feel the overwhelming guilt radiating into her heart. It brought tears to her eyes, and she couldn't have that, not when he was trying to rescue her species. Especially the tiny children that were being sold as slaves.

She remembered an attack from dragons on a caravan where the fae had purchased her. There were women and children, all dressed in rags, just like her. She didn't understand if they were friendly dragons or not, but she remembered pressing her face against the bars from a distance. She watched them being carried into the sky and wondered what would happen to the poor souls that were flying further and further away.

And now she knew. It was her dragon saving those helpless slaves.

They were being freed.

"You saved them? Where did they go?" She rubbed Hindrik's face with her cheek. He still did not look her in the eye, but she wanted to comfort him where she could, and that was to give him the touch she knew he desired.

"We took them back to our realm in Aecithra. They are thriving, along with the other humans."

Alice smiled and wrapped her arms around his neck. "I'm so glad they are okay."

Alice remembered the children and how terrified they looked when they took her away from the group. She had a soft spot for the kids because they were born at a time when they could not have a carefree life. They were always on the run, looking out for danger.

"But I left you. I left my mate all alone to suffer for so many years." Alice felt Hindrik bury his nose into her shoulder, his hands running up and down her back.

Alice chuckled, not an angry bone in her body.

"I am happy those children didn't have to suffer. That they didn't have to live the life I did growing up. I would much rather them saved, and me suffer, so they didn't have to."

Alice felt Hindrik's grip on her tighten. A sobbing purr radiated from her big, beastly male. "They blessed me with a selfless warrior." He smiled into her shoulder.

She felt an overwhelming sensation of a variety of his emotions surging through her. Mostly relief.

She loved how his calloused hands cupped her cheek and the way he gazed into her eyes. The way he studied her, like he was memorizing every line, every imperfection on her face. It made her heart leap with anticipation.

Her gaze dropped to his lips, and he leaned forward and pressed his mouth against hers. It was a sweet and gentle kiss. It would have been much more appropriate for a first kiss, but she liked it all the same. Her hands pressed up against his face. She wanted to feel all of him. Every scar on his face, his neck, his chest. He was riddled with them, but somehow that made him all that more beautiful to her.

He had been through much, that much she knew. And the strange overwhelming power he held told her he was much more than just an ordinary dragon shifter. He was much more powerful than any other dragon in that dungeon or arena.

She felt him pull away, and instead of leaning forward, keeping her lips pressed to his like she wanted to, she let him back away.

"How do you feel about all of this?" he muttered. "About the bond? About you being my mate?"

Alice blushed, looking away from him, but the pinch of her chin pulled her back to his gaze.

"I think you already know that. You are just teasing me." She blushed, now trying to hide her breasts.

"That I do, but I want to hear your consent." His faint smile made her squeeze her thighs together, her pussy clenched with desire, and his nostrils flared.

"Can he smell me?" The thought alone was kind of exciting.

Alice took in a breath. It was heavy because she knew with every logical human reason she shouldn't want this. But she wasn't in a human world anymore where logic mattered. She was in a fairytale world where logic didn't exist anymore.

And whatever she was experiencing made little sense, but she knew he came searching for her. He saved her. Hindrik was extremely attractive and was head over heels for her.

"I want this. What this is between us," Alice finally answered, pointing between the two of them. "But, what all does it entail?"

Hindrik held her close, his hands roaming her body with sweet caresses. Alice's body was lit by a fire, turning on more and more by the second.

"We will mate. I will plant my seed into your body. We will not have fledglings or young until you wish. I can control my fertility until you are ready."

Alice giggled. "Oh, that's handy." Her finger traced his Adonis belt. She tugged at the leather tie that held onto his loin cloth.

If only she could pull it just right to get a look at his growing problem. She always looked away when Amurath took his concubines, but with Hindrik, she was insanely curious about what his looked like.

Was it large? Would it fill her?

She knew it would hurt, but would it eventually fill her with pleasure?

Alice bit her lip, the anticipation growing with each panting breath.

"Then I will bite you here." Hindrik playfully bit the nape of her neck. Chills ran down Alice's body, running straight between her legs.

She let out a breathy moan, and her dragon pressed the heel of his palm on the outside of her mound. It was a shame she had covered herself below her waist earlier when he pushed her away. She was ready to feel his skin on hers. She was feeling needy. She had yet to feel anyone's skin against her most intimate parts.

She was so ready, and she was glad that her dragon would be the first.

Alice felt his tongue wiggle on her neck, and when she pulled away, she saw it was still forked. He smiled and pressed his lips against hers.

"One last thing, my beautiful mate," he growled hungrily.

Alice's heart skipped a beat. Her fingers were already intertwined with his loincloth. Her nipples were pressed hard against his body, and her leg was inching further and further up his leg.

"I am a tsar amongst the dragons. Their king, as humans may call it. You will become my tsarina. Are you willing to take on this role with me? To help any other humans or any other species that need help to return to our realm?"

Alice paused, her hand dropping from his loincloth. It was like cold water washing over her in an instant.

A tsar? A king? Like what Lord Amurath was? He was so cold and brutal. Had concubines and treated his slaves horribly.

Oh my god, what if Hindrik had slaves as well?

Alice swallowed heavily, wiggling in Hindrik's hold. He didn't let go, and she saw the panic swell in his eyes.

"Please, Alice, speak to me. Do not leave me," he pleaded.

His soothing voice rushed at her like a wave of calm, and she both loved and hated it at the moment. She needed to run, but she also trusted the dragon.

Everything she knew about kings and lords of the magical types had been evil. The other lords that watched dragons spar were evil. The slaves were beaten and treated poorly. Hindrik was a tsar, but she had yet to see any slave with him.

So, does that mean he didn't have any?

She rolled her eyes at herself. Communication, she should just ask.

"Do you have slaves?" she blurted.

Hindrik sighed, his shoulders slumped, and gathered her back into their once intimate position. Alice took this as a good sign.

"Absolutely not. My title is nothing like those of the fae. I make major decisions and protect the clans. We do not live in palaces or castles. We live in clans or communities, as many of your humans like to call them. The tsars make decisions for the species, such as rescuing humans, helping to provide food, and where to hunt. We all take care of ourselves. I have my cave, my own things. We trade, we hunt, we barter. I do not collect taxes from my fellow brethren. We help each other when we are in need."

Alice felt the truth in his words.

"And is the bond like a lie detector?" Her voice rose as she asked.

Hindrik smirked. "Yes, very much so."

And that was all it took for Alice to pull on his loincloth to get to his goods, but with her weak arms, it wouldn't budge.

She huffed, tugging on it again.

Hindrik barked out in laughter, pushing her into the furs. "Are you accepting me as your mate and your calling as the tsarina of the dragons?" He said, as he stood.

Alice nodded her head quickly, staring up at him.

"Then my Alice, my mate. Let our bonding begin." A snarl ripped through the cave, and Alice's bottom half of her satin robes were ripped from her body.

Chapter 10

H indrik smiled wickedly, his claws holding the shreds of material that had once covered her sex.

Knowing that she was his, the self-consciousness he had previously felt because of his scars was gone. She had accepted him for who he was. His wounded body, his inability to save her sooner were all presented to her, and she accepted.

She was his tsarina, his mate, his lover.

And thank the ancestors who passed down the legends of old; he was blessed with not just a beautiful mate, but such a strong and forgiving soul.

He watched her intently, happiness filling his heart. He was about to claim her, and it was about damn time.

Hindrik took one side of his cloth, barely pulling at the side his mate struggled with so much earlier. He let it fall to the floor, and she gasped.

Yes, he knew he was large. There was no doubt about that. He was a dragon. Who ever heard of a dragon shifter with such a small appendage?

Hindrik grazed his body with his hand, tracing down his abdomen until he reached for his cock. He wrapped his hand around his girth and pulled at the base.

His mate watched eagerly. She sat up in the furs on her knees and licked her lips. Her hands ran over his thighs, and her mouth grew closer to the head.

"Alice, lay back," Hindrik growled, lowering himself to his knees.

He saw his mate's eyes lingered on his cock, her eyes dilated and fixated with hunger. "You will get your chance, but first, I must have my taste of you."

He watched his mate blink in surprise, her head tilting and eyebrow rising in confusion. Hindrik chuckled, pressing his lips against hers and tracing down her cheek and neck, until she laid back on the furs and placed his mouth on her nipple.

His mate let out a delightful sigh, and his hand reached for the other breast and kneaded it until it begged for more attention. He played with and teased her until he could smell her arousal pooling between her thighs.

"More," she pleaded with him. "I want you to touch me more."

Hindrik let go of her nipple with a pop, his fangs elongating when he heard his mate's begging.

"Where does my mate want to be touched?" He lowered his head and nipped her hip.

Alice's face flooded with color as she moved her hands to cover her face.

Hindrik, not being a sadist, nor a patient dragon, trailed his lips to the neatly trimmed patch of hair that hid the bundle of nerves between her thighs. Her scent was sweet, and his cock twitched in jealousy that his tongue would get a taste first.

He buried himself face-first into her pussy, not taking the time to tease her inner thighs. His tongue snaked inside her deep, wet cavern and sucked the arousal from her body. Hindrik pushed her legs wide, giving him ample room to do what he wanted with his mate.

Alice cried out his name. Her fingers dove into his hair, pulling him closer to her body. He damn loved it, loved that she wasn't afraid to pull him closer to her.

He slid two fingers inside. She was tight. Imagining his cock inside, so tight, perfectly nestled inside her tight cunt, was going to be like damn heaven.

His hips pushed against the furs, trying to gain friction against something. It ached, it hurt, and he continued spilling seed all over the nest.

So close, soon he would be inside her. But this was about preparing her. She was obviously a virgin. She had to be. The way she looked so curiously at his cock, how she wanted to touch him, how she was confused when he saw her going down on her. There was just no other explanation.

And he loved it. He loved that he was going to be the first.

"Hindrik! I-I, wait, I might need to stop!" His mate cried out and tried to scoot away.

But Hindrik knew better. He understood exactly what was happening.

"Relax," he paused his ministrations. "Let it happen. I promise this feeling will lead you to great pleasure." He gave her a smile of encouragement, despite the fear in her eyes.

He continued to hear his mate's breath come in short, rapid pants.

This was going to be the best experience of both of their lives, well, besides the bonding they would both share.

Using his slitted tongue, he wrapped both sides around her clit and moved meticulously on either side. Her clit was swollen. He swore he could feel her heartbeat pulsing between his tongue. He groaned as her back arched and her legs clamped around his head.

"Hindrik!" she screamed into the vastness of the cave as she came.

Hindrik forced his fingers to thrust in deeper and harder. His mouth opened wide as she squirted her essence into his mouth and dripped onto the furs.

Hindrik watched in awe as she plucked her nipples while continuing to ride her orgasm. He sucked her lips and thighs, and licked each part of her clean until her pants became small shallow breaths.

Taking one hand, he wiped his beard and smiled devilishly downward at her.

Oh, she was definitely ready for him now.

He crawled up her body, kissing her along the way, and once he approached her lips, he planted one lingering kiss that ignited her fire once more.

"W-what just happened?" Alice panted, when he pulled away.

She was on cloud nine. Never in her life had she experienced something so euphoric. It was like she peed herself. She had never grown so wet in all her life.

Sure, she's had dreams where she was damp. She knew the basic anatomy; knew women had that sort of thing happen.

But full-blown wet themselves?

"You squirted. You must have been so deprived, my tsarina. I will relieve you of all your sexual deprivations over the years."

Alice bit her lips. What could she say to that? She sure as hell would not say no, and if he could do that at least once a day, she would die a fortunate woman.

Hindrik descended on her, his wide hips pushing her much smaller ones out of the way. She got a brilliant look at his undercarriage earlier, and he was much larger than any fae dick she had ever seen.

They looked like skinny, limp noodles compared to her dragon.

She swallowed and gripped his big, meaty biceps. This was going to hurt. It had to.

Hindrik, as if sensing her worry, took her hand and led it to his shaft. He had her feel all of him. Every square inch of the thing. He let her feel the heavy weight of his balls, the full man of him. He wasn't hairless, not in the slightest. He was one hundred percent man.

Once she reached the tip of his cock and felt the wetness leaking from the head, she gasped, her body nearly trembling.

"Are you afraid? You need not be," he promised her.

Alice was holding a dragon king's dick.

She didn't know if she should laugh or be utterly nervous.

So instead, she smiled and shook her head.

"I will be gentle. I will never hurt you, only bring you the most pleasure."

Alice found herself nodding and pulling her soon-to-be mate by the arm back onto the furs. He hovered over her, pressing his lips to her neck, and she soon forgot about his cock; which he would impale her with soon.

He was making her feel good by kissing her, whispering how much he cared for her, wanted her, and had searched for centuries for a soulmate he never knew he could have.

And that was more euphoric than any physical pleasure. He made her feel *loved*.

But that was when she felt the tip of his head entering her body. It was large and thick, and he slowly entered her. She gripped his shoulders, wrapped her legs around his hips, and dug her heels into his back.

Oh, she wanted this. She wanted it so bad now.

Hindrik could feel her urgency. Her youthful impatience made him chuckle.

However, he wanted to savor her like the fine wine she was.

He sunk deep into her pussy. Memorizing the deepness of her cavern. When she arched her back as he stretched her, his mouth descended and sucked her breast into her mouth. His hips gained a steady rhythm, letting her cunt squeeze him tighter with each thrust.

But by the ancestors, he couldn't hold on.

The suction of her breast let go with a pop, and the slapping of their skin became nothing but background noise. Right now, all he could hear was the beating of her heart, the rushing of blood coming from her neck.

He wasn't into drinking blood, but could hear it rushing through her neck, right where he was supposed to bite into the skin. To connect them not only physically but spiritually.

A sweet rush of arousal flooded his cock, his mate screaming. Her heels dug into his back. The lower part of his back tingled, signaling his own release was near.

Soon, soon, they would complete their bond.

Fuck, her pussy was like a damn vice, sucking him inside his body as if she would never let go.

His balls tensed, pulling tight against him. He leaned over her body once more, gripping her tightly, and roared before sinking his fangs into the soft muscle between her neck and shoulder...

Again she screamed, not out of pain but because another orgasm ripped through her body. They both tensed, letting wave after wave of pleasure roll over them.

His seed coated her womb so much that it flooded over his cock, spilling out of her body and soaking the furs beneath them.

Hindrik could feel his fangs ache with relief. It was like his soul had hunted for her for many generations, and now he had found her; it could finally rest. They were complete, and now they could spend eternity with each other.

Epilogue

Hindrik had a bundle of wood tucked neatly underneath his arm as he walked. His brothers, Harold and Hector, flanked his sides. They were to bring in more logs for humans that wished to build more cabins in their clans.

Dragons loved their caves in the mountains to house their mates and hoard, but humans liked the idea of *storage buildings* for their crafts or items to barter.

It was much easier than bringing out their items for trade from higher in the mountains, each time they wanted to meet with fellow shifters.

And the dragons wanted to please their mates. So, they agreed that these cabins would be built.

Dragons and shifters worked on the honor system, and they had hoped that no one would want to steal any of the precious things they wished to trade. Xavier still made locks to ensure no one could steal another's horde.

Hindrik dropped the logs into a pile. All the male humans looked up in thanks and waved their hammers. Hindrik still didn't like the idea of most of their things locked up in the wooden *cabin*. But a dragon would do anything for their mate.

Female dragons also got in on the act. They loved their male humans and would help hand them tools and logs, but after a while they would drag their males off to the forest, and rut them until sunset. This made the progress of producing the cabins long and slow because, let's face it, Hindrik and the rest of the dragons did not know how to build a cabin.

"That's it for the day," Hindrik called when he saw the females pulling their males back into the forest. The humans didn't even blush anymore.

Hindrik shook his head. It was time to find his female, who was supposed to be by the lake with his brother's mates.

They all trudged through the thick, verdant forests, the leaves rustling softly with every step. The air was purer here than on Earth. He took in a large breath, appreciating the crisp mountain air. Aceithra was mostly mountains and large lakes and not a single ocean like that on Earth.

Hector and Harold looked at Hindrik. They were all donned in only their loincloths and leather satchels that hung over their chests.

Their females, their mates, were gathering water in their water skins for the flight back home to their caves. The leather dresses they wore were short for the mild summer.

Hindrik gazed at his mate; she rose ever so slightly that he saw the curve of her ass and the retreating bruise from the bite mark he left on her inner thigh the night before. He let out a low growl of approval, his cock stiffening by the second.

His brothers were staring at their own mates, all three having their own ideas of a hunter-to-prey sort of game.

Hindrik winked at the both of them, each of their throats opening, letting their dragon vocal cords take over. Each one with their own distinctive snarl blasted through their mouths, and their mates stood from their hunched-over form in the water.

Their hair was wet from just being washed, and their bags filled with water, but once Alice saw Hindrik, she knew it was time to put her chores away for the day.

She smiled at him, her cheeks still turning pink after all these years.

Ten years had passed since he had rescued her from the earth realm.

Lord Amurath had been long dead. The overly dramatic death Hindrik had prepared, for all four corners of the North American hemisphere to witness, did not happen.

Hindrik was too enthralled with his mate and was ready to be over and done with the entire ordeal. So he asked his new tsarina what she wanted.

Alice wanted to give Amurath the same courtesy that was given upon her and the rest of the slaves.

A different approach than he wanted to give, but he made it to be so.

They put Amurath to work for all to see inside the gladiator stadium. For three months, he was publicly humiliated. Fae, orc, fairy, witch, warlock, dragon, and other shifters went to watch the spectacle. Hindrik was given frequent reports about how he washed clothes and cooked food for the poor. Amurath was also subjected to public beatings, and floggings and there was a bed in the middle of the stadium for anyone that wished to rape the bastard.

There were few, and the welded dragon chains kept his powers at bay to let it happen.

Amurath's autopsy was ruled a humiliation death, because a fae of his caliber should have survived the workload provided.

Hindrik chuckled, strutting towards his mate. It was a perfect death for the bastard.

His brothers and their mates had long since run off into the forest, but his mate would not. That was because a surprise was waiting just on the other side of her. A sapphire-blue-eyed boy poked his head around his mate. The boy's eyes squinted at him and he giggled, grabbing his mother's bare legs.

"You're done early," Alice said, holding up a water skin for him to drink. "I'm guessing the female dragons are going into heat?"

Hindrik pulled the skin to his lips, taking a long, steady gulp. He felt his mate wrap her arms around his waist and his son jumping at his side, wanting to be picked up.

"Yes, a little early for the season. The question is, are you going to start your heat and want another, so soon?"

Alice chuckled, running her fingers over his sweaty chest. "I never understood that. How do I go into heat, yet I don't get to turn into a dragon? It really isn't fair." She pouted while Hindrik picked up the little boy.

"Because, then, who will ride my back and tell me where to fly? Isn't that right, Kontar?"

"Fly!" He threw his hands up into the sky, right when a thunder of dragons flew in formation back up the mountain.

Hindrik threw his son up on his shoulders and shook his head. "Not this time. I believe we will walk on two legs and enjoy the view."

As they walked, he carried Alice's water skins. She had much preferred the simple life since she had moved to his realm. He was happy about that, for when they returned to the palace where she stayed with Lord Amurath, a thought occurred to him that she might be used to that life.

His first impression of her proved right, however. Alice wanted nothing to do with the palace life. She wanted to be away from the politics, the shows, the fakeness of it all. And lucky for her, she was paired with him.

Here, life was simple. More so than before, when the portals opened and creatures took over the human world.

Humans now roamed this world freely, simply, and waited for those living in this realm to claim them as mates. And it was a propitious time for them all.

Now, Earth roamed with fae, orcs, ogres, and other creatures. Each portal was guarded. Hindrik made sure of that. No evil was allowed back through the portal.

As they walked up the steep path to their cave, Hindrik saw Alice wipe her brow from sweat. He eyed her suspiciously. Since taking on their bond, her body temperature had regulated differently. It worked more like his; she shouldn't be sweating like she is.

"Go wash up," Alice patted Kontar on the butt, and he laughed, running inside the cave with a hot spring deep inside.

Hindrik continued to watch his mate, his lungs taking in deep, heavy breaths—searching.

It was then he smelled it, the faintness of her heat.

He nearly fist-pumped the air. This night was just getting better and better. The next thing he needed to do was to get a fledgling squatter, and he knew just the male.

Hindrik darted out of the cave, the landing in which his cave sat was large, and when he showed it to Alice, she demanded that Xavier live next door.

He would never say no to his mate, but it was a tall order to ask for. Xavier went through a lot to protect Alice, but not as much as he let on. Poor Alice believed that Xavier was subject to endless sexual torture from Lord Amurath, such as getting his cock pulled and being brought into his bed. But actually, Xavier created illusions to make it seem Amurath was doing those things, but it was too real for Alice to fully understand it wasn't.

Alice felt like we owed him a great deal of debt.

Hindrik knocked on his door in great succession, and Xavier opened the door. His mate stood on the other side.

Apparently, warlocks, good warlocks, could have mates too.

"I need a favor," Hindrik blurted.

Xavier crossed his arms and smirked. "Really, black dragon, and what could that be? Hmm." He scratched his bare cheek and looked up to the sky. "My, my, is it mating season for the dragons?"

"Avier!" Kontar came barreling out of the cave, his wobbling legs going as fast as they could take him.

Hindrik watched in amazement as his son wobbled past him and into Xavier's arms.

"Come on, Armenia is in here waiting for you. Why don't you two go play?"

Hindrik groaned. He forgot that he also sat for another couple's fledgling. Hindrik didn't like his son spending time around other female dragons. He wanted his son all to himself for the first eighty years. He was a selfish dragon and wanted to teach him all the manly dragon things.

But he also wanted to rut his mate.

This was a damn hard decision.

"Hindrik!" Alice's plea from the cave was urgent. "I need you now!"

Well, that made his decision for him. He could smell her arousal from here, meaning she was in full-blown heat.

Shit, that was fast.

He sprinted to the cave, hearing Xavier's laughter trailing behind him, and once he arrived, he saw his mate wearing one of her old slave outfits.

Hindrik's cock stiffened at the sight of her bare leg enticing him from a distance. It was all he could see in a barely lit cavern, near the back of the cave where their nest laid. The rest of her body was hidden by a giant boulder.

He pressed his hand to his chest as he walked toward their chambers. He had seen her naked millions of times. Taken her to their nest and rutted her millions more. Because, hell, he learned how to make love to her with her clothes on just to feel his cock wrapped around her cunt whenever he felt like it.

He pulled his cloth away from his body, his heart thundered in his chest as he approached. When he did, he could see a small gold chain glinting in the fire torches that donned the cave.

As she stepped out, thin silk wrapped around the chain from her ankles, her wrists, and neck. Her breasts and pussy were bare, but the scantily clad chains brushed her skin, giving her chills.

He wanted to be those chains that roamed over her white skin. He wanted to be the one to touch her.

Hindrik drew closer, his nostrils flaring, taking in her sweet arousal. This never got old and never would. They had decades to go before either of them would wither away, and even then, they would still be madly in love.

With lightning speed, he wrapped his hand around her waist, his other cupping her neck. The light-colored markings from the gold collar that sat on her neck for years were still there, but they were only reminders that she'd waited. She waited for something better, even if she didn't know it was for him.

"What are you playing at, Alice?" Hindrik nipped her lip.

He felt her nip his lip right back and saw her sly smile. "I want to be *your* little sex slave." Her hand ran up this thick, muscular thigh and grabbed his cock.

He rolled his tongue over his lips and grabbed her wrist. This wasn't the first time they played this game. He rather enjoyed it, and she did too. It was more playful, never harmful, and she was the one to suggest it.

Because he would have never suggested it in the first place, not after what she had witnessed, but again, their dynamic was certainly different from what she had seen. This was wanted, playful, and talked about beforehand.

He took her wrist and spun her around, pinning it to her back. He grabbed the other arm and pinned it to her side. Alice squealed in laughter, snorted even, and Hindrik buried his nose into her neck.

She was completely immobile, just the way Hindrik liked it. He was in complete control, kissing, nipping, and biting every part of her. Her laughs and giggles slowly turned to moans, her body trembling. He took his magical hands and unclasped each gold chain until she was completely naked.

He pushed her to her knees, having her landing on the furs. It didn't take him long to pull her up by her hips and shove two fingers into her cunt.

"You are already wet for me, aren't you?" he growled.

She nodded.

He slapped her on the ass, hard, and she cried out.

"I need words. You speak to me when I talk to you, Alice."

"Yes, I'm wet for you!"

"Good, this pleases me. I'm going to use your cunt for my pleasure. Do you understand?"

"Y-yes!"

Hindrik felt more of her arousal coat his fingers. He never knew words could turn on a woman so much, but now he was happy he knew that with his mate.

"Yes, I can't wait to dip my cock into this pussy. I think this is my favorite pussy." Hindrik withdrew his fingers, rubbing her ass once more before he swatted it again.

"Tell me again, Alice. Whom does this pussy belong to?" Hindrik cupped it, rubbing it with his palm.

Alice moved her hips back and forth, arching her back so she could gain more friction.

"It's your pussy. It's all yours."

Hindrik hummed in approval, lining up his cock and sinking in deep. They both moaned while he gripped her hips and began his fast, heady thrusts.

His fingers dug into her skin, his balls slapping against her inner thighs. He could see the tears streaming down her cheeks after orgasm after orgasm hit her. He knew every part of her. He knew her inside and out. Where her pleasure spots were, what made her tick, and no sex slave would get any of those sorts of pleasure.

Because she would never be his slave, only his lover, his mate.

Hindrik gritted his teeth, his balls tightening. His mate fell from her forearms, and her face hit the pillow. It was just him and her ass, holding it together until the last thrust.

He came with a shout, pouring his seed inside her. He massaged her hips as he continued to spurt inside.

Once finished, he fell to the side, holding her tightly as their bodies cooled until they were ready for the next round.

"Are you ready for another baby?" she asked, still catching her breath.

"I'll take whatever you give me, my mate." He closed his eyes and felt her shake her head.

"That is not what I asked, and you know it." She raised her voice, and he chuckled.

"I would be happy with more. But I know raising one is difficult, too. We can wait as long as you wish," Hindrik said.

They paused for a long while until Alice spoke again. "Well, I want one more. I like the idea of them being close in age. Like you and your brothers."

Hindrik groaned. "I just hope the next one isn't as stupid—ouch!"

"I barely hit you!" Alice snapped. "And don't talk about your brothers like that. They helped rip down the gladiator field and destroyed that palace. We owe them a lot. The rest of the fae on earth learned their lesson because of you three."

Hindrik hugged her tighter, appreciative of her defending his brothers, even though they were stupid at times. "Even if they brought all that gold back here."

Oh.

"Yes," Hindrik cleared his throat. "That was bad of them to take all that shiny stuff."

"Yeah, it's useless. We don't even use gold in this realm," Alice yawned.

Hindrik swallowed. He hoped his mate never got the strength to roll the boulder at the very, very back of the cave, to find all that shiny gold he took from Lord Amurath's palace so long ago.

Dragons just couldn't help themselves. They liked gold. They liked to hoard it, not necessarily do anything with it.

Just to have. You know, just in case.

The

Dragon Queen's

Gambit

Emm E. Goshald

Blurb

In the Dragon Kingdom of Exury, only the woman with the mark can rule.

Queen Maeve's life hasn't been easy. Having had to take the throne, her birthright, by force, was exhausting, but she finally managed to create peace within her kingdom. Years after the bloody fight to the throne, she and her mate, Duncan, finally agreed to start their family.

But just as her hatchling begins to grow in her womb, old enemies surface. Unable to shift for the rest of her pregnancy, she and Duncan have the insurmountable task of protecting her kingdom and her little family from those who threaten her... if they can figure out who's behind it before it's too late.

Prologue

I n the shifter realm of Exury, the birthmark of the divine has always dictated the line of succession of dragon shifters. While Exury was filled with more than just dragon shifters, the dragons stayed away from the rest. Focused on hoarding their collective treasures and traditions, they secluded themselves to the furthest edge of their realm and created their own kingdom.

Few dragons ventured out, and fewer visitors were allowed in. Their political system was a caste system ruled only by she who carried the sacred dragon birthmark on their body. Given a dragon's natural greed and territorial nature, their gods only bestowed this mark on one girl per generation. It imbued them with power over all dragons, much like the power an Alpha wolf had over their pack. The mark often passed from mother to daughter, but if the gods deemed their family unworthy, only sons would be born in the next generation, ensuring the mark would pass onto another family.

Many times, when a reigning family was not blessed with a female, they would hunt down the newborn hatchling in an attempt to claim the daughter as their own and retain power. A few thousand years ago, the mark was passed down through the Torric bloodline for over ten generations, leading the kingdom with fairness and prosperity. Generation after generation of firstborn daughters born with the mark kept the kingdom in peace, but when the marked queen's mate became obsessed with greed and corrupted by power, the mark passed on to another family. The gods vowed it would never remain in the same family for more than two generations after that, often resulting in a bloody transition of power until the dragons realized no family remained in power long enough to be worth the bloodshed.

A few hundred years ago, one family, desperate to retain the power they were granted, went so far as to demand a royal guard be present at any birth in the kingdom after the first queen of their bloodline gave birth to a son. They hunted for the real mark bearer to eliminate them, under the guise of wanting to protect and teach the child the ways of the kingdom from an early age, but the gods weren't easily thwarted, and their disciples were quick to act. The deceit was revealed, and the real hatchling was hidden away until they came of age.

The years between the birth and adulthood of the hidden queen plunged the kingdom into chaos, and it taught those living in those times that only those chosen by the gods should be allowed to rule, lest the gods abandon them and their beasts succumb to their violent natures. The power struggle that ensued during this time consumed their riches and decimated much of their lands. The rivers ran red, and their crops burned or withered. The air became toxic with ash and the stink of the dead and entire bloodlines were erased from the world.

When the true mark bearer appeared, the kingdom cheered and welcomed their new queen. The violence quieted, the lands were allowed to heal and the rivers once again ran clear.

They called this violent period in their history The Gods' Condemnation.

It is said that those who ignore history are doomed to repeat it. So, for the longest time, the dragon shifters ensured every hatchling was taught the history of succession, so brutally learned by their forebears. However, the more generations stood between the hatchling and these events, the more the consequences of those lessons became lost. History became myth, and myth became an old wives' tale meant to frighten those who struggled with the status quo. The truth behind the lesson became blurred by those who wanted to hold onto it too tightly, interpreting the wrong ideals from history to fit their narrative.

Eventually, the greed of dragons became more powerful, and the ramifications forgotten. A sense of entitlement grew from the family who thought they led their people with fairness and success. When the first of the next generation was born without daughters. The king, desperate to retain the power their family had enjoyed, killed the firstborn sons in secret, claiming tragedy. He raped and abused his mate to conceive as many hatchlings as they could between them. He did the same to many other women, in the hopes of birthing a daughter who would carry the mark, convinced that the issue was with the queen, not him, being worthy to bear the heir.

It wasn't until a woman appeared one day, surrounded by the gods' disciples, and bearing the sacred dragon birthmark, that the king roared at his failure. He questioned the right for her to rule, when she had been brought up without the delicate knowledge that was politics.

When the mark bearer presented herself in front of the current queen, her presence allowed the women to come forward; revealing the depraved acts of the king, and forcing the queen to admit her own weakness to stop him. Unwilling to relinquish his position, the king killed the queen and declared the mark bearer an impostor, unfit to lead. The transition of power became a massacre that lasted almost five years. At the end of the war, the young queen stood at the throne. A fire dragon of twenty-five years now, brought half a decade of death to an uneasy peace. Her enemies went into hiding, biding their time and causing dissent amongst the dragon shifters, dividing the kingdom that had long forgotten why the gods assigned the ruler.

Her name was Maeve Hayes, and despite the river of blood that followed her path to the throne, she was kind and forgiving. She had a grace that had not been seen for many years. A breath of fire that ignited fierce loyalties and even more jealousy. She had raven black hair that fell to her knees, cunning hazel eyes, and a smile that brought the sun into a darkened room. Dragons came from all over the kingdom to see if they were chosen by the gods to be her mate, or if they could find a way to win her heart and rule by her side as her chosen mate, not realizing that Maeve would give her heart and the crown to no one, but her fated mate.

The aftermath of the war rippled through the kingdom for years. The queen's soldiers were a long way from retirement. Among them, one soldier rose through the ranks quickly for the manner and fervor with which he completed the queen's orders.

Duncan Taron lost his entire family before the war even began. He watched helplessly while his sister and mother were raped, and then killed when both failed to produce the next ruler. After he joined the queen's army, he became a devoted soldier. A ruthless killer under the service of the queen.

There was no such thing as an innocent insurgent or one worthy of redemption. In his head, if they believed the people who raped and killed his family had a right to remain in power, they were not deserving of the life they lived, while his family had been deprived of it. He wanted them all dead. It was the only way he could ensure no family suffered as he had. Initially, his superiors were impressed with his dedication, but became concerned as the years went on and his tactics became more rage fueled than what was requested by the queen.

After an incident that resulted in the injuries of a few of his fellow soldiers, the stories of her general reached the queen. She called for the dragon to come present himself before her. She wanted to see if there was a man worth saving beneath the rage, or if his and his beast's thirst for blood were too far gone for her to save. As grateful as the queen was to have such a man and beast fighting on her behalf, the queen believed the insurgents were still her subjects, and a fair trial needed to be given to determine those whose actions merited a pardon.

Duncan arrived at the queen's palace, ready to defend his actions to his queen. He was in full officer regalia. His short, cropped red hair and blue eyes viewed the castle gates with trepidation. His chiseled jaw was tense, belying his otherwise calm appearance.

He was determined to explain the dangers the insurgents still held to the kingdom. The dangers that they still represented to the queen's subjects. Every excuse dried up on his lips as he made eye contact with the queen, and his beast roared inside his head at the sight of his mate. He walked quickly toward the platform. Every bone and instinct in his body was calling for him to grab her and mark her, but his mother had raised him better, and this was no ordinary woman. This was not just the queen of all the dragons anymore; this was his mate, his most precious gift. He stopped at the foot of the dais and knelt, bowing before her.

"Who do you kneel before, General Taron?" she asked softly, walking down the dais toward him. Duncan could only see the delicate flats and soft blue fabric of her dress when she stopped before him.

"I kneel before my queen," he said. Duncan then lifted his face up to the woman he had fought for since he'd been able to hold a sword. "And my mate."

"The queen would have you kneel before her, but your mate would prefer you only kneel in private." Her face gave away nothing, but the tone of her voice and the twinkle in her eyes made Duncan stop breathing while he processed the implications of her words. His entire body responded to her words and he stood quickly, pulling her body toward him until she was flush against him. The fire in her eyes was answered by the lightning in his.

Those present talked about this day as many would a fairy tale. The happily ever after for a tortured soldier and a warrior queen. In reality, it was a struggle of give and take on both ends. Maeve wanted peace, but Duncan was certain the only way to get it was through more bloodshed. It took them a year before they were able to compromise, and finally allowed their beasts to claim each other.

It was a day that would not be forgotten in the minds of anyone that witnessed it. Their dragons proudly took to the sky. A vibrant red dragon, majestic and imposing rose into the air first. The queen's beast was enhanced with the gods' blessing. Power emanated from her, and her roar could bring her people to their knees to submit. It twined its body around her mate's dark gray beast when he joined her, and they danced in the air to a tune written in their souls.

Their roars filled the air, and the bodies of both dragons were engulfed in the flames and lightning of their beast's love for the other. A conflagration of passion that painted the entire sky in hues of red and orange, and lit up the darkest corners of the kingdom at the lightning flowing through the skies. If the kingdom wanted to see the crowning of their new king, all they had to do was to look up.

Once the fire was consumed, the beasts continued flying around each other before they began chasing each other through their kingdom, celebrating their union. Young hatchlings watched the mighty beasts in awe when they flew above their heads, giving them hope of a peaceful kingdom. The savior and her warrior.

But, in a tiny corner of the kingdom, more than just hatchlings watched, and it wasn't in awe. The insurgents watched their worst persecutor and the queen's display with disgust. Their plans would need to be altered. Duncan Taron had claimed many of their lives. If they wished to get close to the throne, they would have to play it carefully.

Years passed, and the kingdom appeared to settle into a quiet peace. Rumors of discontent and the insurgency died down and the kingdom knew peace for the first time in more than a decade.

Chapter One

Duncan stood in front of the window of Maeve's office waiting for his mate to finish her meeting. It'd been four years since they finally mated, yet he still couldn't be apart from his mate for too long before he searched for her.

Three years ago, Duncan finally retired from the queen's army and took up his official duties at her side as king. It was a hard decision for him, as he still believed the insurgents were plotting something against the kingdom and his mate. Maeve knew how much his fears plagued him, and they struck a bargain. Maeve gave him a small yet impressive unit, comprising ten soldiers of his choosing, and for two years Duncan worked to dismantle what remained of the insurgent organization.

A year ago, when his time was up, Duncan gave up his crusade and fully settled into life at the palace. He was ready to start a family, and he knew Maeve would never agree to it while he could rush off at any time to follow a lead. He'd worked hard for those two years to ensure his mate would be safe, but he didn't want to waste his life without actually making one.

Two months ago, Maeve gave him the news they'd both hoped for; she was pregnant. Their hatchling would arrive in three short months, and they were ready. They wanted nothing more than to grow their family.

Maeve's delicate chuckles reached Duncan's ears, and he smiled before he even saw her. Everything about her made his heart sing and his beast swoon. She was talking to a young detective wolf shifter, who came to thank her for the assistance Maeve provided in a missing fae child case.

She suspected a dragon was involved, but required the queen's help when he proved difficult to crack. The dragon world was mostly secluded, but it was inevitable to have dealings with other shifters and other magical creatures, no matter how much they wished to be left alone. Education, trade, friendship and the occasional rare mating between species, meant walking a delicate line sometimes between the jurisdiction of crime, politics and realms.

While dragons were less involved than most species, because they had chosen to live so far away from the portals that separated the shifter realm from the rest, they were not exempt from the council's request for assistance. When it came to punishing and questioning one of the queen's subjects, they knew better than to do it without her consent.

Dragons were a patriarchal society in every other aspect of life but the throne. No matter how much power men thought they had, at the end of the day, the queen's word was absolute. No matter how much freedom any given queen afforded to her people, her word was law. Maeve was chosen by the gods to lead them, and she could make them bend to her will. It worked very similarly to a wolf's Alpha command, but the consequences of her command were dire. Maeve avoided using it when there were other ways to achieve her purpose. Her dragon's command was painful, and any that fought it was in danger of losing their sanity and in many cases, their very beast.

Maeve assisted the detective in questioning the dragon, hoping the threat of the command alone would persuade the man to give up what he knew. When that didn't work, Maeve used her command, not only getting the location of the young fae child, but three others that he had kidnapped over the last few weeks. Each child was of a different species, using the species' reticence to deal with each other to get away with it.

"Any time, Detective Sullivan," Maeve was still talking, though of what, Duncan didn't know. He was too mesmerized with his mate to listen to anything else.

"Please call me Berta, Your Majesty. It's been a pleasure working with you. There are a lot of families in your debt. If you ever need anything, don't hesitate to reach out." Detective Sullivan bowed respectfully to Duncan before she made her way out the door. Seeing her mate was waiting for her, Maeve walked over to Duncan, who was still standing near the window.

"Have you been waiting long, my king?" she asked.

"Two minutes feels like forever without you." Duncan sighed, happily wrapping his arms around his mate.

"You're so cheesy." Maeve giggled, but lay her head against his chest. Listening to his heartbeat was her favorite sound. Listening to her laugh was Duncan's second favorite sound; the first being hearing Maeve moaning out his name at the crest of her pleasure.

"Lord Frederick has arrived," Maeve said, having a view of the window from his embrace.

"More whining." Duncan sighed. He was tired of these entitled lords that expected them to clean up whatever mess they should be able to clean up on their own.

"This one sounded urgent. Why would he demand something so soon?" Maeve wondered out loud.

"I guess let's go find out, my queen." Duncan wrapped his arm around her waist and they walked together to greet the lord in the first-floor offices of the palace.

"Lord Frederick, thank you for waiting. What can we do for you?" Maeve asked as she and Duncan settled on the opposite side of the conference table. Lord Frederick was an older gentleman in his early seventies, though to humans, he might look more around his mid-thirties. He was the lord over half the east quadrant of the kingdom. The very same area Duncan hailed from, which was already a bad point against the lord.

Anyone that looked at his face knew that Lord Frederick didn't want to be at the castle, requesting help from the king and queen. He was a storm dragon, much like Duncan, who still harbored a deep hatred for the man, for all he went through under the dragon's watch. Lord Frederick had been old friends with the previous royal family and originally supported their attempt to remain in power. He was also one of the first to flipflop when he saw the war was lost.

"My Queen, I require help. For some time now, I've been receiving threats to my family. I've done all I can think of to find those responsible, but the gods have not been with me, and my attempts have failed. At first, the notes were posted to the door of my estate, but over the past few months, they have gotten bolder." He slid a folded note over toward the king and queen. "I found this tacked to the door to my bedroom, along with a ponytail of blonde hair and the bloody head of my best guard."

Duncan grabbed and opened the folded parchment paper, then he and Maeve read the message.

The time has come to pay old debts. Surrender your lands, or face the decimation of your line. You betrayed us first, so you must be the first to pay. Hand over your weapons and oil before the next new moon.

The king and queen were silent for a few minutes, and Lord Frederick became more anxious as the silence stretched. He knew there was a chance they would turn him away if they figured out the threat was coming from the people he had supported, against them.

"Who does the hair belong to?" the queen asked.

"My youngest daughter, Your Majesty." If it had been any other child or person, the man would probably not be here, but everyone knew his baby girl was his weakness. He would make a deal with the devil himself if it kept his daughter safe.

"How old is your daughter, Lord Frederick?" The king asked this time.

"She's six, Your Majesty."

Three months ago, Duncan would have told the man to deal with the threat himself. He and Maeve would have discussed and fought until he gave in to her logic and empathy, but now Duncan was going to be a father. He knew what he was already willing to do for his unborn hatchling and mate, and for once, put aside his own hatred, thinking of Lord Frederick's young ones.

Maeve waited for her mate to tell Lord Frederick that he would have an answer for him in a week's time, as it often happened when he wanted to say no. Duncan respected his mate too much to begin an argument in front of her people. Lord Frederick was not the only person in that room surprised, when Duncan took Maeve's hand and squeezed it before he spoke again.

"I know a few soldiers active in the queen's army that are expert trackers. I will send them and a few additional guards to ensure your family is safe. If the threats continue and our people are unable to discover the culprits, we can talk about setting you up someplace safe until we have results."

Lord Frederick stuttered for a few minutes. Duncan never made it a secret how much he disliked the man, and the man had prepared to grovel before them to gain their assistance.

"Thank you, Your Majesty. Thank you."

"I want to be clear, Lord Frederick. If we have to move you and your family to a safe place, your hoard will remain behind. I am not putting my people in danger to protect your treasure."

"Of course," Lord Frederick vowed before the king. His hoard was not within his estate. He wasn't dumb. He knew someone would take it the moment it was left unguarded.

"Expect our people in less than a week's time," Duncan said before Lord Frederick left.

Maeve and Duncan remained in the conference room for a few minutes after, both lost in their own thoughts. Maeve snapped out of her reverie first, and she stood and sat on her mate's lap when she did.

"What are you thinking?" she asked.

"That this is just the beginning. Have we gotten more meeting requests from other lords?" he asked, one arm going around her waist, his other hand resting on her tiny stomach.

"One or two. Do you think others are being threatened as well?"

"I would be very surprised if they weren't," he answered, laying his head on her chest.

"What do you want to do?"

"Keep you safe. That's all I want. If that means saving those ungrateful assholes in order to do it, so be it."

Maeve chuckled at his choice of words but felt her dragon beast warming at his words.

"I'll have them pull up the meeting with the other lords. Let's find out what we're up against," Maeve answered. She moved to get up, but Duncan held her in place.

"Later," he said, his voice becoming low and husky. He picked her up and began to ascend the stairs toward their chambers. "I need you."

Maeve grabbed his head between her hands and kissed him while he continued his way to their chambers. Duncan wasn't lying. He needed his mate; needed to reassure himself that she was safe. He had a bad feeling about all of this.

He set her on her feet by their bed and pulled her dress down, latching himself onto one of her nipples. He cherished her sweet moan and her hurried hands as she worked on the strings of his pants, but she was working them too slowly. Pulling back with an impatient snarl, he cut the strings on the back of her loose corset and tugged her dress until it fell down to her legs. He did the same to the string holding his pants, before he let them drop, and he pulled his shirt over his head, while his mate panted with need as she watched him; her lovely breasts heaving invitingly to resume his examination of them from before.

"Duncan," she exhaled his name like a prayer as he did just that and took the rosy nipple into his mouth again. Duncan laid her in bed, taking a moment to look at the beautiful body of his mate, but patience wasn't with him today, and his body was soon covering hers, one hand going south while the other held his weight off her stomach.

Duncan groaned when his hand reached paradise and found it hot and wet; ready for him. His teeth wrapped around her throat, his beast shining through with the need to possess her and reassure himself that she was his was there.

Maeve could feel his worry, and submitted to her mate willingly, moaning as he plunged into her cavern to the hilt in one thrust. Duncan pulled back, releasing her throat and soothing it with kisses, while he plunged back into her. Their bodies moved in instinctive synchronicity together, while he whispered loving words of happiness and heaven that made Maeve feel cherished and desired. As their orgasms began to coil deep inside them, Maeve wrapped her legs around Duncan's waist and met him thrust for thrust, changing the angle so that he could fuck her deeper; faster as their love for each other crescendoed in a roar of completion from him and a wordless cry of euphoria from her; their orgasms crashed over their bodies, leaving them covered in sweat and happy in each other's arms.

"We've got the three lords coming today. Are you ready?" Maeve asked her mate as they prepared to leave their bed a week later. Duncan groaned and cuddled into her bosom, not looking forward to the day.

"I'll have the cook start me off with some alcohol," he grumbled, making Maeve laugh.

"It's not so bad."

"Just pompous assholes that didn't support, you trying to get help. I wish I could have met them on the battlefield."

"You can't kill the entire nobility, my love. There would be a vacuum of power. It would throw the whole kingdom into chaos."

He peeked at her from where his face was nestled in the valley of her breasts.

"Maybe just one or two?" he asked hopefully. Maeve laughed again, and Duncan's heart sang. Some days, he only said ridiculous things in order to hear her laughter. Seeing his mate happy and unburdened, even for a little while, was the only accomplishment he would ever need to feel his life was worth something. He pulled up and kissed her lips. "I love hearing you laugh."

Her eyes softened as they looked up at her mate's face, happiness flowing through her. This was her favorite time of day when the both of them could just be themselves before the doors of the chambers opened and placed responsibilities back on their shoulders.

"I love you," she told him, as she did every morning, and as she planned on doing until the day she died.

Duncan leaned down to kiss her again before he sighed, and looked at the sun in an offended manner.

"Time for work?" he asked.

"Unfortunately," she answered, watching Duncan roll off the bed before helping her up.

"We should run away and live in the country. No more idiot lords and whiny representatives. No more worrying if our little one will be in danger or not." Duncan pouted, his hand going to her tummy. It was still only a small bump, but he loved putting his large palm over her stomach and feeling the curve of it, knowing that it was because her body was growing their hatchling.

"In another life, my love. In this one, the gods chose us to protect their charges." Maeve sighed, a big part of her also wishing the same. Duncan and Maeve helped each other dress for the day. Neither of their beasts allowed any of the staff to help the other.

They grabbed breakfast before they went into the great hall. They had a few meetings that morning before the lords were scheduled to arrive. Last week, they decided to do a joint meeting with the remaining lords, considering this problem would affect them equally. Maeve and Duncan confirmed with the other two lords who had already requested meetings that they also received similar threats. They had one more meeting scheduled later this week and were waiting to hear back from the remaining three to see if everyone received the threats.

Maeve didn't want to tell Duncan because it would worry him too much, but she was beginning to suspect that news about her pregnancy was the reason for the spike in unrest. If her child bore the mark, it would keep her bloodline in power for another generation, making it harder for the insurgency to win over her people.

In her heart, Maeve hoped her child would be born free from the burden she faced. She wanted them healthy, plump and happy. Her life was never as glamorous as people thought it was. She was hidden from the moment she was born, kept away from the world, and surrounded by disciples. After the age of five, her days consisted of lessons that taught her about the kingdom, their needs, their troubles, and how to control her gifts. The energy needed to exert her gods' given authority over her people usually left her weak and vulnerable. Her dragon was powerful and hard to control. It sometimes raged at her to kill anyone who opposed them, and sometimes, Maeve was tempted to do the same.

All these thoughts went through her head as their advisors updated them on the latest issues across the kingdom. Duncan could feel her distraction and yearning, and could guess what was going through her mind. He felt a bit guilty for bringing up his foolish dream of living in the countryside alone with her, before a difficult day. He knew it was a fool's dream that they usually reserved for those long talks, cuddled in the middle of the night when the moon was out and all things seemed possible, only to never mention it again in the daytime, because the dream was an impossibility.

Maeve was the queen, marked by the gods to lead their people. He was lucky to have been chosen to be by her side and allowed to love her.

Duncan did his best to answer all the questions directed at them, allowing his mate a reprieve from the day's burdens. They broke for lunch, and he was thankful to see her returning to her strong and confident self again.

After lunch, they entered the great hall again to find the three lords and their mates sitting and talking amongst themselves.

"Thank you for coming here today, my lords," Maeve began, quieting the conversations and guiding them all to sit at a table to the side of the hall, where they could better talk with their small number. "There has been some disturbing news lately and I wanted to check in with all of you."

"Three other lords have been receiving threatening messages. One has escalated to threats against their family. Have any of you received any threats of similar nature?" Duncan asked.

Two of the couples nodded in unison, and all heads turned toward the silent couple.

"Lord Cameron?" Duncan prodded, his eyes focusing on the teary, terrified ones of the man's mate. In his mind, this was answer enough.

Chapter Two

The room was silent as they waited for an answer until Lady Heather burst into tears.

"They took our son. Two nights ago. He is only five, my king." She sobbed. "They are threatening to kill him if we don't relinquish our title and our lands."

Lord Cameron's jaw ticked. "They sent us one of his fingers within the last note."

"No," one of the lord's wives whispered and gripped her mates' hand tightly.

"Why didn't you reach out to us before it got to this point?" Maeve asked, her eyes hard, but Duncan could feel the worry running through her.

"We didn't think you would help, Your Majesty. W-we helped them. We fought against you. We thought you would turn us away."

"Lady Heather, I would never turn my back on my people. No matter their past transgressions."

"I will have a team dispatched to your lands to begin looking for clues. Did you bring the note with you? I would like to see the stipulations requested for the safe return of your son," Duncan asked.

Lord Cameron pulled out a blood-stained note and passed it to Duncan with a shaky hand.

"The finger was wrapped in a cloth on top of it," he said by way of explaining the blood on the parchment.

You have forced our hand, and so we will force yours. You have two weeks to hand over your lands before more body parts arrive. In addition, you will leave your cellars full and your coffers intact, or we will return your boy alive but without significant limbs.

Something struck Duncan, and he looked at the other two lords.

"Did you bring your notes?" he asked them.

"What are you thinking?" Maeve asked her mate, when the notes were passed along. Duncan's only response was a grunt that told Maeve he was trying to piece together some connection. He grabbed all the letters and spread them out before him, his eye movement rapidly roaming the notes as he processed all the information in his head. Without another word, he got up and pulled a parchment scroll from the side, and spread a map of the kingdom on the table. He grabbed paperweights and placed the notes on top of their corresponding land.

"They asked for oil and weapons from Lord Frederick here." He pointed to the northeast of the kingdom. "They want cellars stocked here." He pointed northwest, then pointed at the three notes on the south. "They only want your coffers here, and here. Lord David was also asked to relinquish the coffers, while Lord Gavin was asked to give up the lands and hospital supplies," he explained, finishing by pointing back to the north.

"They are attacking from the north, making sure the lands they pass by are full of the supplies they need in case they can't take the castle," he said, leaning back with a frown. "I think we have little over two weeks before that happens, considering the timeline they are giving Lord Cameron."

The room was quiet as everyone took in his words. Only a decade had passed since the last war ended. While the land had healed, the memory of loss and blood was still fresh in everyone's mind. Maeve put a hand to her stomach as she became lost in thought. She wouldn't be able to shift in another month. Not safely. She would be too far along in her pregnancy to do so. If the rebellion wasn't stopped in time. If it came to their door and she was unable to use her full powers, she wasn't sure what would happen to her family.

She felt Duncan's hand squeeze the hand she lay on the table, and she snapped out of her thoughts.

"You need to prepare to leave and evacuate your people. We'll be sending over a small contingent of soldiers to look for the insurgents and ensure you're safe, but if we're unsuccessful, you need to make preparations in case they fail," Maeve told Lord Cameron. "I will let the others close to the north know. We'll send another set of people with you two. Your lands appear safe, but you might need to evacuate yourselves, unless you're turning over the coffers."

The thought of giving up their hoard was more than a few dragons could bear, and any lord worth his salt cared for their people and would refuse to give up the coffers their people and lands depend on in order to thrive.

"If we give them what they want, will they leave us alone? We have children, Your Majesties," Lord Gibson said worriedly.

"I cannot say for sure."

"Where would we stay?" Lady Heather asked.

"We will find a place for you."

The mood was somber after everyone left, and the queen and king took their dinner in their private chambers, where they were quiet and lost in their own thoughts. Duncan could feel Maeve's worry like a palpable presence in the room. Eventually, when he noticed she was only pushing the food around on her plate, he grabbed her, hauled her onto his lap, pulled her plate toward them, grabbed a spoonful of the food and brought it to her face.

"Open up, My Queen." Maeve gave a small smile and allowed her mate to feed her. Once both bowls of stew were empty, he kissed her neck while his hand went to her stomach. "We will be okay. I won't let anything happen to either of you."

Maeve buried her face in his neck, showing the vulnerability that only he would ever see.

"If they attack after I can't shift, I will be mostly useless." Her words made Duncan chuckle.

"You think I would have let you anywhere near the battlegrounds while you grow our hatchling? Shift or not, I would tie you to the bed and keep you away."

"I'm the queen. It's my—"

"You're the queen, and you have an army ready to protect you and the kingdom. You're MY queen, and I will never let anyone get near you."

"I'm scared something will happen to you. There are too many unknowns, and I have a bad feeling growing in my heart," she murmured. Duncan didn't know how to answer that. The truth was, he had a bad feeling too, but he didn't want to worry his mate more. It wouldn't be good for their hatchling.

"I survived the first war without any issues. I will survive this one, too," Duncan tried to reassure her.

"You weren't the king then. You didn't have a target painted on your back because you were my mate," Maeve argued.

"And, I didn't have a reason to live before, either. I'm a stubborn motherfucker, my love, don't discount me just yet."

"I am scared, Duncan." The fear and vulnerability in her eyes broke his heart.

"I know. I'm not saying it won't be hard. You need to trust that the gods put us in this position to succeed. You are the rightful heir. They won't abandon us. We will make it through this."

"I hope so," was all she said before they got ready for bed. Maeve fell into a turbulent sleep, but Duncan continued to stare at her, one hand possessively against her stomach, thinking about the next few weeks. He needed a plan to protect her, and all the subjects she loved so much. If it was up to him, he would grab her and leave it all behind, but he didn't think she could do that and still be happy with him.

By the time she awoke in the morning, Duncan had a plan in place, and they spent the next week putting everything in place. The first of the lords showed up the following week. They were staying in small houses around the palace. Displacing five families to accommodate them was not something they could do, but they rented some barren land, and through some contacts that Maeve made through the years, they contracted a witch to magic the buildings into existence.

Duncan already dealt with three complaints from the lords and expected more when the remaining lords arrived. After the last lords and their people were escorted to the outskirts of the palace city, Duncan sent conscription notices to the queen's army after the volunteer notice had yielded little success. Soldiers began to wander into the barracks to start training, a lot of them still quite green in the teeth.

Over the last week, Maeve's pregnancy wasn't able to be hidden anymore. Her belly had popped almost overnight, something the doctors were quick to say was perfectly normal. What pissed Duncan off more than anything was the worried looks the lords had given to her stomach, before giving some tight-lipped congratulations. As if it was Maeve's fault their shitty decisions led them to be blackmailed months after the couple had chosen to start a family. None of the smaller lords faithful to the true heir had been run out of their homes. No threats given.

Duncan sent half of the queen's army toward the north and half toward the south, just to be sure. He kept his elite squad within the castle, acting as guards or staff. They were always hovering around Maeve's vicinity, making sure she was safe.

Meanwhile, Maeve was a mess. On the outside, she was the calm, composed queen she was born to be, but in the quiet of the night, when her mate finally succumbed to sleep, she spent hours memorizing his face. The furrow of his brows as he dreamt, the way his lips moved when he expelled a breath, the way his hands always pulled her closer when he was having a bad dream and the way he felt against her. The times she could sleep, she was plagued with nightmares of losing her mate, and she was beginning to wonder if her dreams were a vision or a portent of what was to come.

For the first time in her life, Maeve was distrustful of everyone around her. There were too many new faces, and she couldn't tell which were friends or foes. The lords and their staff made the castle their home, despite being provided with adequate lodgings. There was always a lord or lady demanding more from her; bursting into her meetings when told they needed to make an appointment; harassing her staff with ridiculous demands that Duncan and Maeve never made. While she was hopeful that Duncan and the plan he'd put in place would be enough, in the dead of night, she began to pray.

She prayed to the goddess Morrígu, the goddess of fate, to be victorious. She prayed to Athena, the goddess of wisdom, to help her make the right decisions through the war. She prayed to Frigg, to protect her family. And finally, she prayed to Set to keep her family together through the upcoming chaos. She prayed every night in the hopes that someone was listening to her pleas.

News of the first attack reached them quickly two weeks later. They struck at night. The army managed to push them back, but the casualties were high, a fact that broke Maeve's heart.

A few days later, they attacked again. This time they were more prepared, but there were still heavy casualties. No leader had presented themselves yet, and when Duncan called the army back to the second line of defense, he called back half the squadrons protecting the south to the north before he flew out to meet them, hoping to draw out the leader of the insurgents.

Chapter Three

"Leave me," Maeve ordered her now constant companions from her room. Edgar hesitated, before nodding to his fellow guards, and they exited the queen's personal chambers. He was one of the ten elite guards still assigned in the castle, five in plain sight. Duncan had left specific instructions to make sure Maeve was never alone and vulnerable. Her window and any other above the first floor were sealed with magic to prevent an attack. There was only one way in and one way out of her chambers now, so Edgar felt comfortable enough to leave the queen alone with her thoughts and fears.

This wasn't the first time Maeve requested to be alone, and though she tried to be quiet, she knew her guards could hear her cry at night. She was due in a month, and Duncan had been gone from her side for over five weeks. The attacks were coming quicker now, and Duncan was always at the front line. He ensured he sent word to her every day, but it didn't stop the worry, or the hurt in her heart. A few words didn't replace his heat in their bed or his comforting embrace. Loneliness crept up on her throughout the day, and at night, it suffocated her.

Maeve always prided herself on being strong, but it was hard to be strong when she was pregnant, with her hormones out of whack; surrounded by lords, ladies and their bratty children that only took and took from her, without the man she loved at her side. Duncan was her rock and the way she recharged before meeting another day head-on. Maeve felt like she had been starved of love and serenity without his arms at night. Her emotional energy was at an all-time low, and these days, she couldn't even get out of her clothing by herself.

Bridget walked in at the same time today as she did every day. She was another one of Duncan's trusted crew, and as one of the few women he trusted, Bridget was kind enough to come in and help the queen change into more comfortable clothing for the night.

She was in awe of the queen. Bridget was a mother herself, with a little one that she made sure was far away from all the fighting. Her son was staying with her sister in the south, near the portal to Andosea, the neutral zone between realms. If things got bad, she knew where to go, and knowing that her little one was safe gave her the strength and calm to protect her queen. How the queen managed to handle the prospect of giving birth in the middle of a war, while the king was away with such grace, she didn't know. Her own mate was part of the guards left behind by the king, and she was grateful they could comfort each other in the darkness of their suite, where they were not warriors in the middle of a war, but simply lovers.

Every night, when she helped the queen remove the stuffy clothing the court dictated she wears to present an image of strength and confidence, she felt like she was helping the queen remove the layers of caulk she put around herself each morning. Each item she removed revealed the cracks in her heart and her facade until she left her bare and exposed. Some nights, she could see the tears gathering in her eyes before she could exit. She pretended not to see them, respecting the queen's privacy and the validity of her emotions by giving the queen a single squeeze of the hand, before she walked out, letting her know she didn't think her weak for it.

Alone once again in her suite, Maeve wondered how she managed life before Duncan and how she would survive without him again if anything happened to him. Her dragon roared inside her; frustration coursing through the both of them at being unable to shift and help. It already occurred to her more than once that the timing of this war wasn't a coincidence. The insurgents had known she was pregnant before they made the announcement and planned to keep her on the sidelines. This was the reason she allowed Duncan's people to be around her while he was away. There was a traitor in the castle, and she trusted no one right now.

Maeve crawled into bed and let her tears run free, knowing with a little shame that this felt like her routine over the last few weeks. Once she felt spent and her tears dried, she sent up her daily prayers of protection for her people and the man she loved, and willed herself to fall asleep, back to the turbulent dreams that terrified her and left her more afraid than the previous day.

Maeve woke up a few hours later, panicking when she saw a shadow climbing into the bed. She screamed, her hands shifting to claws to defend her hatchling in any way she could. A hand clamped over her mouth, and blue eyes glowed down at her.

"Shhh. It's okay. It's just me, my love." Duncan's voice reached her ears, and her scream turned into a sob. She withdrew the claws she'd dug into his arms as he gathered her into his arms and rocked her, whispering words of comfort and love, soothing her soul like only he could. Her sobs quieted, and Duncan was finally able to bend down and kiss her with all the love he'd missed giving her while he was away. Their kiss turned into a flurry of hurried motions as they removed their clothing, desperate to reacquaint themselves with each other.

Duncan kissed Maeve, swallowing her moan as he thrust into her in one powerful snap of his hips. He was careful not to hurt her, but she was testing his resolve as she panted and begged for more. Five weeks was too long to be away from her. He'd flown as fast as his dragon's wings would go.

"I missed you," he whispered as his thrusts became more urgent, swiveling his hips the way he knew Maeve loved, earning him a moan from her lips, that he felt penetrated his soul. He leaned down, his fingers finding her swollen nub of nerves, and worked towards coaxing his favorite sound from her. He felt the fluttering of her channels and pinched her clit before delivering a few strong thrusts. Her head fell back, and her mouth parted as her orgasm crashed over her.

"Duncan!" she cried out, her scream breaking the last vestiges of his control and he catapulted over the edge with her.

"What are you doing here?" she asked sleepily, their bodies wrapped around each other as their heartbeats began to calm down.

"Are you not happy to see me, My Queen?" he teased.

"I'm over the moon, but is everything okay?" she asked.

"For the moment. We'll talk about it more in the morning. Sleep, my love. I just want to hold you right now," he said, pulling her back until she was flush against him, one hand firmly on her stomach, which jumped under his touch. Maeve smiled, her eyes fluttering closed while Duncan's filled with emotion.

"Our hatchling missed Daddy," she whispered before her breath evened out, and she was fast asleep moments later.

Duncan remained awake for a while before sleep finally claimed him, knowing tomorrow would be a trying day for both of them, but unable to break the peace that settled over his mate tonight. He owed both of them this much.

"Okay, now tell me," Maeve demanded, while they ate breakfast in their chambers. Duncan sighed, and pulled out a small roll of parchment from the duffel bag he dropped inside their door when he arrived last night. He handed the note to his mate and continued eating his breakfast as he watched the emotions cross her face. He expected most of them, rage, incredulity and pain, but he did not expect the laughter that bubbled out of her when she was done reading the demand letter.

"This person is delusional!" She continued to laugh loudly, while holding her large belly; he was beginning to worry about her sanity while he had been away.

"They seem pretty serious to me," he raised an eyebrow.

"Oh, I see that, but the fact that he thinks I'll do any of this is ludicrous," she answered, wiping a tear off her face. Duncan shrugged.

"It is an option," he countered. Maeve's laughter died down immediately when she realized he was serious, and rage began to build within her.

"Are you telling me you came home to tell me to leave you and give up my child?" she asked in a deathly calm voice.

"I'm sure that's their starting proposal. You could probably convince them to keep our child."

Maeve stood, breathing hard and staring down at the pain-filled eyes of her mate. She knew that the insurgents were playing dirty, and it was costing them lives, but she never thought him a coward before. Acting on pure hurt alone, her hand flew, and his head snapped to the side as the slap connected with his cheek. His eyes snapped back and focused on hers, but she couldn't look at him anymore. She marched right out of their suite, snarling at him when he tried to grab her, her claws extending and her eyes glowing with rage. He let her go, unwilling to risk her losing control and shifting in her fit of rage; hurting their hatchling.

Duncan took to the sky, releasing his roar of pain, regret and anger. The last few weeks were some of the worst of his life. He watched the dirty tactics of the insurgents for the last five weeks and was worried for his people, but mostly, he was concerned for his mate. She was at her most vulnerable right now, and if they were determined, he now believed they could find a way through the masses and into the castle to hurt her. Hell, he already believed there were insurgents within the castle walls. As he watched his fellow soldiers die to the traps and ambushes they set for them, without an ounce of scruples or honor of combat, all he could think about was what they might do to the love of his life and their offspring. When he discovered explosives had been placed under their dead so they would explode as soldiers tried to move them to burn them with honor, he knew they would stop at nothing to get what they wanted. He suspected the use of witchcraft, because no one could explain how the explosives got there.

Duncan couldn't lose Maeve or their hatchling. It would be so much worse than when he lost his family. He knew he would not survive losing them, but they could survive him. The letter gave him that option; to sacrifice himself so that his mate and hatchling could have a chance to live. He knew it would be hard for Maeve to consider taking another mate, even if only in name, but he thought he needed to try. He would give his life for them.

He did not expect the rage that coursed through her when she realized he was willing to do anything to keep them safe, including give up his life.

He caught a dragon attempting to catch up to him, calling his attention and flagging him down to fly back toward the castle. When he landed and shifted back, Bridget's husband rushed toward him, and his words almost made his legs buckle under him.

"Your Highness. We heard some screams coming from the queen's office. When we arrived, the guards at her door were unconscious, and we can only hear silence from within. We're trying to break down the door, but we've yet to be successful."

Duncan was running before Ronald even finished. Fear and anger fueled him forward. He barreled through startled staff and visitors, who were looking upward toward the commotion of the guards trying to break through.

"MAEVE!" he shouted, pounding on the door and then backing up to ram his shoulder. The door didn't even wobble. He and two other of his men rammed into it but a wall would have moved more than the door. He couldn't understand it, but he continued his desperate attempt to get to his mate while shouting her name. He would have felt if she was dead; his beast would be writhing in pain and despair if she had, but that didn't mean she wasn't in pain or worse, and it told him nothing about his hatchling.

He rammed against the door, roaring in pain as his shoulder dislocated from the impact. He started sprinting toward the open window at the end of the hall before he remembered all the windows above the first floor were spelled to prevent attacks. He eyed the door and started running at full speed, his good arm poised to destroy the door, one way or another.

His eyes widened when the door opened and he was a few feet from the door. He saw his mate at the entrance, a stoic expression on her face and a hand on her stomach. He was trying to stop, but his speed was so great that he knew he'd plow right into the love of his life. Ronald was the only person who moved when he realized the king would harm his mate, so he rammed into him, and they collided, crashing against the wall.

Duncan's dislocated shoulder was now more askew than before, but the pain barely registered as he stood and ran to his mate, checking her over for injuries while he pushed her into the office and looked for any intruder.

"What are you doing?" Maeve asked as he checked every nook and cranny in her office. "Who was in here? What happened? Where are the guards? Gods, are you okay?"

"An hour ago, you asked me to give you up. In what world would I be okay?" she asked, an eyebrow raised and that same deadly calm she exuded in their suite. Duncan turned to the people in the doorway.

"Leave us," he ordered. The door closed as the last guard exited, and Duncan led a reluctant Maeve to the couch. They stared at each other for a while, neither one talking, before Duncan took a deep breath and said the words he never thought he would say.

"I'm scared, Maeve." He saw the way her face softened at his words, and he continued, "I've never been scared before. I have always been sure that I could protect you, no matter what. I will do everything in my power to protect you until my last breath, but I'm scared it won't be enough. You are the most precious thing to me, and if something were to ha-happen to you..." He couldn't continue, and he looked away, ashamed of the tears he could feel stinging his eyes. Maeve's anger drained from her body at the sight of her powerful mate like this. She grabbed his hand, and he turned to look down at their connected hands before looking back up at her. "I can't lose you."

Maeve crawled onto his lap, wrapping him as best as she could in her embrace.

"It's all going to be okay. We just have to trust that it will all work out." Duncan hugged her tightly, trying his hardest to believe her words, but as he did, he groaned, causing Maeve to pull back. "What happened to you?"

"That's what I asked you," he answered with a chuckle but sobered up as he remembered why his shoulder was injured. "What happened?"

"What do you mean?"

"We've been ramming the door to your office for the last half an hour. The guards guarding it were unconscious, and where is Bridget? She's supposed to be your shadow."

"I sent her to nap. She looked tired, and I needed to be alone," she said, standing up. "I'm not sure what's going on with the door or the guards, I've been working my anger off all morning." She motioned to the desk, which was littered with parchments. Duncan furrowed his brows, confused.

"You didn't hear anything?"

"The door didn't even wobble," she explained.

"Something's going on. Maybe this was a warning. Maeve, I need you to keep Bridget next to you anytime I'm not with you. We can't take the risk anymore." Maeve kissed the worried lines between his eyebrows.

"I won't send her away again, but Duncan, you can't give up on us. I can't do this without you. It's not worth it without you." Duncan crashed lips against Maeve's pouring his love and devotion into the kiss.

"Never," he said, pulling back, and resting his forehead on hers.

"I don't want you to leave anymore, not until after the delivery. Promise me. I need you here."

"I won't leave," he assured her.

In fact, Duncan moved a desk to work from Maeve's office, between the rounds he made to the barracks to check on the queen's army and training after he talked to Bridget, and she didn't seem to remember anything from the morning. He wasn't sure what was going on, but Maeve's nonchalant response to it was troubling him.

Chapter Four

"Faster! Your reactions can't be this slow. We are in the middle of a war. Sluggishness will only get you killed. If you want to see battle and hope to live to see the end of it, you need to be faster. Do it again," Duncan instructed the new recruits. They arrived two days after he sent the conscription notices when he returned from the front lines. He's been training them for two weeks now, and he didn't want to send them to their deaths.

They were too young, too green, and their enemy was devious. Duncan was doing his best to help on the front lines from where he was. He was working with some of the brightest minds he knew to ensure they kept the upper hand, and contracted a coven of witches to prevent more ambushes. It was a difficult and expensive decision. Magic generally rolls off a dragon's hide, so they were pretty useless in the middle of a fight, but Duncan was using them to prevent deaths outside of battle. They could safely detect traps and sense an ambush when transporting supplies. They were costing a pretty gold coin, but Maeve agreed the lives of her people were worth it.

Once Duncan dismissed the trainees for lunch, he went to the office he was now sharing with Maeve. He could hear people talking as he approached and stopped just short of being seen as he heard the voices begin to rise.

"It's your duty as queen to put an end to this war."

"And I'm trying. As you well know, war doesn't have an expiration date. The leader of the insurgents hasn't even come forward. He's hiding like the coward he is, letting his misguided followers die for his stupid crusade."

"How's that different from what you're doing? My son has still not been returned!"

"If you had come to me BEFORE he was taken, you would have your son at your side now! And I would give anything to be out there protecting my people, but I can't shift. What's your excuse, Lord Cameron?"

"And the king?" the asshole countered instead of answering her.

"He's here for the same reason as you. He's a target, and that makes everyone around him a bigger target. Having him here protects the insurgents from attempting to kill everyone to get to him. We have two weeks. The king will not move from here until I deem it necessary."

"So you would put us in danger, but not the soldiers? Isn't that what they are trained to do? Handle difficult situations?"

"There's an army, and half a kingdom, between the insurgents and the palace. You are safe. Unless there's something you know that I don't, My Lord?" The quiet way she asked the question made Duncan wonder if Maeve knew more than he did. He had a few people tracking all the lords, but there were too many people to cover. Aside from the harassment being inflicted on his people, they had come up empty-handed so far. Duncan continued to listen. Lord Cameron's silence was condemning enough in Duncan's eyes, and for a moment, he wasn't sure if the man would answer at all.

"Of course I don't, Your Highness. I only know the information you provide us, but we have a solution and you refuse to take it. Countless lives, including my son's, could be safe if you would see reason."

"You would sacrifice my famil—"

"To save the kingdom? Yes!"

"Would you sacrifice yours?"

"I'm not queen!"

"And I'm not only a queen. I'm a woman, a mate and soon a mother. If all you wanted was to ask me to sacrifice my life for yours, My Lord, you may go."

"If you don't put this stop to this madness soon, the kingdom will make your decision for you."

"Are you threatening Her Majesty?" Bridget asked.

"Of course not. I'm simply advising her that the kingdom doesn't want another war, and will demand a solution if one is not provided soon."

"Because the queen was hoping for a fucking war while she was pregnant." Duncan broke his silence and entered the room, a tight smile appearing on his mate's face and relief flashing in her eyes. "You're dismissed, Lord Cameron."

Lord Cameron's eyes glowed as his dragon tried to push forward, but when Duncan's eyebrow rose, daring him to say anything more, Lord Cameron turned on his heel and exited out the door, stomping away like a petulant child who was told he couldn't have a cookie before dinner.

Maeve slumped back in her seat, and Bridget left them alone at a nod from her king.

"You should be resting. You're due any day now, My Love. The last thing you need is more stress than is already on your shoulders."

"I still have a good week or two to work."

"You *think* you have that long," Duncan corrected her.

"I'm fine, Duncan." Duncan sighed and pulled her up, embracing his stubborn mate for a moment.

"At least kick that asshole out, and I'll deal with him if he comes up here to harass you like that again?" he pleaded.

"I will do my best," Maeve answered, and knowing that was the best response he would get out of her, Duncan led her down to the dining rooms to eat. He was a stickler for making sure she was eating enough during her pregnancy, knowing how hard she worked for the kingdom.

The dining room is in full lunch rush, and they walk toward their table, both of them noticing Lord Cameron talking to the other lords in a very agitated manner. Maeve sighed and pulled her mate along when she felt him trying to steer them toward the lords.

"Let them whine. I'm never giving you up," she whispered to him.

"They should never ask you to."

"You did," Maeve challenged, sitting down and resting a hand on her stomach. Their little hatchling was active right now, and Maeve was trying to soothe them into giving her bladder some rest.

"Baby…" Duncan still regretted having suggested anything of the sort. It took days for Maeve to sleep with any relative ease. She woke up from nightmares several times a night and wouldn't talk to Duncan about them. He wished he could go back in time and tell his past self to shut the fuck up.

"I know. I know. Just let it go. Please. You're the one that said I shouldn't have so much stress."

"Okay." Duncan leaned over and kissed her lips gently. They ate lunch and went to their shared office to continue their day. Bridget, Edgar, and another guard were standing just outside their door, though he made sure they all had a chance to eat and took breaks. These people became his family over the years in the army and through all of this shit. He trusted no one else but them and his mate.

He focused on his paperwork until something shattered against the open window, startling them both out of their concentration.

"What the fuck!" Maeve screeched, a hand on her stomach as they watched the remnants of a volley sliding down the spell protecting the window. The three guards burst in while Duncan was trying to lean out the window to see who attacked them. There was nothing. He couldn't even see what propelled the volley into them.

"Take to the skies. Figure out what the fuck just happened and call a damn witch!" Duncan roared at them. All three turned to leave, but Duncan stopped them. "Bridget. Stay with Maeve," he commanded before walking to his mate and pulling her into his arms. "Are you okay?" he asked, one of his hands traveling to her stomach automatically. She nodded and motioned for him to go. He pressed his lips to hers in a fierce kiss before running out of the office to find out what he could about who and what attacked them.

Bridget sat quietly in the chair she'd permanently placed by Maeve's side as another two guards were placed at the entrance of the office, one of them her own mate, before the door was closed. Maeve scooted in a little closer to her.

"Just another week, I think," Maeve whispered.

"You need to tell him, Your Highness," Bridget whispered back.

"I can't. I'm not allowed to, and you know he wouldn't believe me."

"He won't understand what's going on. He'll fight every step of the way."

"I know, but he'll have to. Have you told your mate?"

Laughter threatened to bubble out of Bridget. "How would I even begin?" she huffed. Then a little more guiltily, she added, "I was kind of hoping you would explain to them when the time comes."

Real peals of nervous laughter left Maeve, making the guards outside open the door to check on them in bewilderment before closing the door behind them again.

"Do you think he will hate me?" Maeve asked, more serious this time.

"His Majesty?" Maeve nodded, bracing herself for the answer. It was Bridget's turn to laugh.

"Your Majesty, forgive me, but if you think that man could ever be mad at you, your hormones are certainly fucking with you."

Maeve chuckled and sighed. "I hope you're right."

An hour later, Duncan walked back into the office with the rest of the guards. The worry visible on his face confirmed Maeve's fears. They didn't catch whoever tried to hurt them.

"One of the witches will arrive tonight, but we couldn't find anything. They hit our office and our suite, but there's no sign of where the fucking volleys came from. There was no one in the air."

"They know I'm close," Maeve mumbled.

"What?" Duncan turned around, and Maeve realized she said the words out loud.

"They have to know I'm close to giving birth. They'll attack when I go into labor. That was probably just a test of our defenses."

"Which we failed spectacularly."

"We got another note today," Maeve confessed, unable to keep it from her mate any longer. All day she'd wondered if she should tell him or not. Duncan whirled around and stalked toward the note she was holding up.

The note stipulated new demands. They wanted the queen to give up their hatchling if it was born with the mark. If they refused, they would take the hatchling anyway and kill them both and anyone else in their way. Duncan roared, his dragon threatening to take over. The guards all circled around the queen, ready to usher her out if Duncan lost control and shifted inside the office, but Maeve pushed through them and grabbed his face, making Duncan's beast look into her eyes.

"They won't touch us," she whispered, resting her head against his, despite the fact that it was beginning to shift. Duncan's breathing slowed, and after a few minutes, he reined his beast back in. He ordered the number of guards around the queen be doubled.

For the next week, no one was allowed around the queen but his most trusted people. Duncan declared the queen to be on maternity rest and would not be able to see anyone. He took on all her meetings and paperwork, while her bedroom was guarded by a witch and half of the guards. Bridget was her shadow, even inside the chambers. Only when Duncan was there himself could Bridget get a break.

Duncan was in protection overload, especially after he found out the note was found within the castle grounds.

"This is ridiculous. If the queen is not in labor, we demand the right to see her. Our people are dying."

"And you will be one of them shortly if YOU DON'T GET THE FUCK OUT OF MY FACE," Duncan roared at Lord Frederick, causing the man to pale and then flush with anger.

"You are not the one chosen to command me."

"I was the one chosen to protect her and that is what I'm doing. Are you going to be the one to challenge the task the gods have given me?" Duncan challenged.

The spectacle was happening in the dining room, where Lord Frederick hoped to shame the king into an audience with the queen, but his plan backfired, and he didn't know how to back out without losing face. The staff in the castle loved Maeve and hated all the lords for the way they treated them. He looked around to find the other lords who promised to back up his demands had slinked away when they saw they had no support from anyone.

"My mate may be the queen, but she is still a person, and she needs the rest. Ask your mate if giving birth was exhausting to her." With those last words, Duncan grabbed the plates of food one of the staff members prepared for him and his mate and walked away without another look at the lord, while the guards stink-eyed him before following behind.

Lord Frederick glared toward the lord's table and left, most of the lords swallowing hard, knowing repercussions would come, but they weren't sure at this point if they should fear Lord Frederick or the king. One of the soldiers under cover caught the glances between the lords and followed Lord Cameron when he made his way out of the castle an hour later. The female guard was carrying a fake hatchling swaddled in her arms, so when Lord Cameron turned to check to make sure he wasn't being followed, all he saw was a mother walking back to her home. He rounded the corner and entered through the back door of a bar.

Marcie got as close as she could, listening through a half-closed window.

"How the fuck are we supposed to get her alone when we can't even get close to her? I needed all of you, and you just left me standing with the noose around my neck." Lord Frederick's voice flowed furiously through the gap.

"I took the last fucking one when I tried to convince the queen to give up the king. If I was part of it again, my head would have rolled."

There was silence for a moment, then a sigh.

"Are we sure we can do this? Every day, I feel like more and more things are going wrong. They are too strong. Perhaps we need to let the will of the gods be." Lord Cameron's voice reached Marcie, uncertainty and fear evident even without seeing his face.

"This whole thing was your idea. If we pull back now, all the money we've invested will be lost. Will you be paying me back? The other lords? We're too fucking close. She will pop at any moment."

"And how the fuck will we even know that when she doesn't leave her chambers?"

"We'll figure it out. Tell the others we're meeting in two days' time. It's time to stop fucking around."

Marcie ran away before she could be discovered, but just as she rounded the corner, something heavy hit her in the back of the head, and her whole world went black.

Chapter Five

Two days later, Duncan was pacing around the office. Marcie was missing, and he didn't know which lord was responsible. It was forty-eight hours since she let Edgar know she was following one of them but failed to mention which one. He stationed guards at the entrance of their floor now. Maeve had been off for a few days now, and while the doctor said it wasn't time yet, she was sluggish and uncomfortable, and he felt helpless, feeling the need to protect her from the pain, but knowing that was an impossible task.

Everyone was on tenterhooks. No one but the guards had seen the queen in the last week, and the doctor's arrival at the castle was a sure sign that the hatchling was almost here. There was guarded excitement among the staff, tense anticipation from the guards, and a sense of urgency for those with tasks to complete.

Maeve was worried and knew Duncan was hiding something from her but was too uncomfortable to ask. Overnight, she began having small shooting pains. She knew the time was coming, but now that she was facing not only the prospect of giving birth, but the possibility that she would be attacked when she was the most vulnerable was daunting. She could only hope that all the preparations that were made would be enough.

The thought of things going wrong and losing her family was something she hadn't allowed herself to think about, but now that the moment was close, her nightmares had returned with a vengeance. She was actively trying not to think about how the pains were becoming sharper and closer together. She did her best not to react when they came, so Bridget and Duncan wouldn't call the doctor back, and hoped she was just freaking out.

Sometime during the afternoon, Maeve felt herself begin to sweat as her pains intensified, but she was determined to ignore them. If she didn't think about it, it wasn't happening, right? Another shooting pain went through her body, and she winced. Immediately, Duncan got up, cursing.

"I knew it. You've been acting weird all day. You're having contractions aren't you?" he asked, almost shaking Maeve as she tried to breathe through the pain.

"If you could stop shaking me," she answered through gritted teeth, and Duncan was instantly contrite.

"Since when, Maeve?"

"They started last night, I think," Maeve answered, to which Duncan felt like a shit mate. How did he not notice until now?

"I'm getting the doctor."

"No! Please," she begged.

"He needs to check you! You're in labor."

"I don't trust him," she finally admitted, making him stop and kneel in front of her.

"Explain."

"All these attacks and problems began shortly after we discovered I was pregnant. We never told anyone what my due date was. Not even the guards, though they eventually figured it out through our planning. Only the doctor and the two of us knew how far along I really was. The fact that everything escalated right after I couldn't shift anymore; the timings of the attacks and the letters." Maeve sighed. "I have no proof, but my gut and my beast don't trust him, and I don't want him near me through the labor."

Duncan looked into Maeve's pleading eyes and ran a hand down his face.

"Okay, but we need to get you someone to help."

Maeve looked over at Bridget, who fidgeted slightly under the king's suspicious eyes.

"My sister is a midwife. I snuck her in here a few days ago, Your Majesty. She delivered my son."

"So you two had already planned this?"

"A little after you left," Maeve said sheepishly. Duncan sighed.

"Why didn't you tell me?"

"You had so much to worry about, including all of my shit. I didn't want to worry you!"

Duncan huffed and walked away from where she was sitting. His back was to both women, and they looked at each other with a bit of unease, until his laughter reached them.

"We need to communicate better, My Love. I've had people looking everywhere for the leads on who is attacking us, and you guys had a pretty strong one already. Don't you talk to Ron, Bridget?"

"Our assignments are separate, Your Highness. We take them seriously and with the privacy they deserve," she answered, with a slight flip of her chin.

"Well, I wish you were just a teensy bit less honorable. Now we're out of time. I have one soldier missing and nothing but suspicions. Go get your sister, and whatever happens today, just make sure Maeve and our little one make it out." There was something desperate in the way he said the last part, clenching Maeve's heart. The small sting of tears pricked the back of her eyes, and she blinked them away.

Giving birth to their first hatchling was supposed to be a joyous experience. This entire pregnancy should have been celebrated and rejoiced. Instead, it had been filled with fear, secrets, and hushed plans. She knew insurgents and plots to take the crown were nothing new for a queen, but Maeve felt robbed. She loved her people and did her best to be their queen, but over the years, she'd begun to realize most of them only demanded. They were selfish and only thought about their own needs, not the needs of the whole. They expected their queen to meet all their wants, selfish or not, and to sacrifice her own life when most weren't willing to do the same.

She knew, instinctively, that it wasn't all of them, but it was enough. The queen's army was generally a voluntary position, but when the attacks began, a missive was sent for more volunteers. When the return was abysmal, Maeve was forced to send out conscriptions. The act tasted like bile and felt like betrayal in her heart, and over the last few months, as she struggled to keep the enemy back while her people only demanded more from her, she began to feel the resentment she had over having to fight for her birthright, festering. Over the last couple of months, as she felt that Duncan and she were alone against this threat, that festered resentment began to turn into rage.

Maeve heaved a deep breath as another contraction hit. She slowly released her breath as she worked through the pain, and a few seconds later, she felt Duncan take her hand.

She looked into his blue eyes filled with love and concern, and she gripped the hand of the man beside her, not from the pain but from the fierce protectiveness that was coursing through her and her beast. Once the contraction passed, she pulled Duncan to her and kissed him with all the love she had in her heart for him.

"We'll be okay. Things are going to change," she promised when she pulled back, resting her head against his. His eyebrows furrowed in confusion, but before he could ask more about it, Bridget entered along with another young woman. The familial traits were strong between them, and Duncan stood to shake her hand.

"Your Highness, this is my sister, Norma," Bridget introduced the two.

"A pleasure to meet you. I'm eternally grateful to have you here to ensure my mate and hatchling are being looked after." Norma's shocked look only confused Duncan more when he saw the smug look on Bridget's. "What did I say?"

"N-nothing, Your Highness. The pleasure is all mine. I will take good care of them."

Maeve's contractions were still far apart enough that everyone settled in for a long wait. Evening came around, and dinner was brought in for everyone. They ate quietly, and Norma was great at making sure that Duncan was helping his mate through the contractions while he could, a small smile forming at the thought of how the king would react when she was actively pushing. Over her years as a midwife, Norma had seen some of the most caring and tough men faint and cry during deliveries, despite not feeling a thing themselves.

By the time the first rays of sunshine began to appear in the sky, Maeve's contractions were three minutes apart, and she was six centimeters dilated. Duncan was pacing the room after every contraction, much to the annoyance of his mate and the amusement of Bridget and Norma.

"Would you just sto-aahhh," Maeve's next contraction began and Duncan was immediately next to her, letting her grip his hand until the worst of it passed. "Thank you," she whispered when it was over, her eyes watering.

"Always."

Shouting from outside interrupted their moment, and Duncan looked up, straining to hear.

"I'll be back. Stay here. Bridget, you know what to do," he said, kissing Maeve fiercely and whispering how much he loved her, before he stood and walked out the door. Maeve looked at Bridget, the fear and worry reflected in both women.

"It's starting," Maeve whispered, and Bridget nodded, heading toward the bathroom and preparing, even as the shouting from the stairs leading to the floor intensified.

Duncan hurried toward the stairs, listening to the diatribe of one of the lords demanding to be let through.

"What's the meaning of this, Lord Bouras!" Duncan demanded, surprised to see him there. He was one of the quieter lords, always letting the rest speak for him.

"We demand to see the queen," he said, a slight tremor to his voice. Duncan wondered who this "we" was, as he only had a couple of his personal guards with him.

"The queen is otherwise occupied. As I've mentioned before, she's getting ready to deliver our hatchling and requires rest."

"This war needs to end!"

"Agreed," Duncan said slowly, holding in his anger. "If you have a solution, I'll be happy to set up an appointment with you to discuss it on another day. The queen will not be available until after she's given birth."

"It's too late for that. The army showed up outside the city walls. They razed my lodgings on the way and kidnapped my mate. They are demanding to see the queen or they will kill my family." Duncan looked over at Edgar, who nodded curtly, letting Duncan know he'd already confirmed the lord's story.

"I will go speak with them."

"They wanted the q—"

"And the queen is indisposed. I am the king! I will meet them." Duncan hesitated only a moment before he turned to Edgar. "Stay here. The orders haven't changed."

"Your Highness, you should take a few—"

"The orders haven't changed," Duncan said, his tone giving no quarter. Edgar stood to attention and nodded. "Let's go." Duncan turned to the man, who was still blocking the stairs. The man hesitated, but seeing no other choice, he turned and walked back down.

Duncan shifted and flew out to the edges of the city, following the lord. He saw the queen's army standing guard over the walls and gates and was surprised to see all the lords standing at the gates, waiting for him. He thought they would have hidden and run like the rats they tended to be.

He took in the man in front of the insurgents' army as he descended and shifted back. Something about him felt familiar, but he knew he'd never met this man before. He was holding Lord Bouras' mate by the neck at his side.

"Your Highness, how about you come closer where we can talk?" The man called out, and Duncan's beast shifted slightly to land a few hundred feet from the man. He heard the gates opening behind him, soldiers coming closer in case they were needed to protect their king. The man let go of the woman when the king landed and bowed overly dramatically before him, giving Duncan the urge to roll his eyes.

"I'm a bit busy. If we could get through the assholery and tell me what you need. What is even the point of all of this? Your army is small. You know the queen will never give you what you seek. The gods won't allow you to rule."

"Won't they? But you're right. I've had to change my goals."

"And what are your new goals, exactly?" Duncan asked.

"Well, at first, I thought I would just ask the queen to take me as a mate. In name only, of course," he said mockingly as if to placate the king. "I need to be king. I was raised to be king. I couldn't care less about the rest. Hell, you could have stayed as a side piece for all I cared." He smirked, and Duncan fought the urge to punch the smirk off his face. "Then I realized she wouldn't agree to it. So I thought I'll take the next heir, kill the both of you, rule and make her mate with my own heir."

Duncan's beast roared with protectiveness, and the man's smile widened, knowing he was getting to him.

"But, it's been impossible to get near her to know when the damn whelp will be born," he continued.

"But now..." he said, looking at Duncan with a shit-eating grin. "Well, now I have adjusted once again."

"Who even are you? What right to the throne do you have?"

"Oh! Where are my manners? My name is Julius Cameron." At his name, Duncan recognized the similarities to the man he'd come to loathe.

"Lord Cameron's boy? The one he said was kidnapped and five years old?"

"No. That would be my little brother. Who I did technically kidnap, I guess, but he's fine. I never actually cut his finger off. It was someone else's." He shrugged. "We needed to make it look good. I was promised the hand of the mark bearer even before she was born. It is my right to rule. I came back from training with every intention of wooing her, but she met you and refused to entertain me. It was a kick to the ego, sure, but that's life and I adjust well." We stood there in silence for a moment before he asked, "Don't you want to know what my new goal is?"

"Whatever it is, I'm sure it will be just as shitty as the others."

"For some maybe," he admitted with a nod of his head. "But, I'm afraid some won't have the happy ending they want."

Duncan was done playing his games. If he wanted to go on an evil villain monologue, he could ask and answer his own damn questions. He crossed his arms, waiting for Julius to continue. When Julius saw that Duncan wasn't biting anymore, he huffed.

"Man, you're no fun. So, here's what I was thinking. I know the queen is probably pushing a whelp from that sweet cunt of hers right now, and I know that you have all your most trusted people on her. So, what I thought I would do, is lure you out here, kill all of your people in there, take the whelp, and then take the queen as mine, and once that cunt is nice and tight again, make another batch of heirs."

"You don't have the army to do any of that," Duncan seethed, his eyes glowing, about to lose control of his beast.

"Don't I?" Julius smiled and snapped his fingers. Screams rose into the air and Duncan turned slightly, keeping one eye on Julius while he watched as his own soldiers killed their own fellow soldiers. The lords were by the gates, surrounded by their own, and a portion of the queen's army shouting orders or otherwise looking at Duncan, with a smile that told him how much they would relish to see him die.

"It's amazing what you can buy with the right amount of gold coins, including half an army willing to kill their fellow comrades," Julius said gleefully as he watched the massacre before him.

Duncan shifted and roared, and the smile faltered from Julius' face for a moment before he also shifted, unable to avoid the full brunt of Duncan's dragon slamming into his side, sending them both rolling.

Chapter Six

Thunder and lightning shook the heavens as Duncan took to the sky to battle Julius and the lords. He dodged their fire, wings, and claws as his dragon unleashed their power upon the fight below in an effort to help his soldiers.

From the palace walls, the sounds of battle were drowned out by Maeve's screaming as Norma urged her to push.

"Your Majesty, you need to push. We can't delay anymore." Bridget hated to rush the queen, but there was a sequence of events that couldn't happen out of order if they hoped to make it through this day unscathed.

"I'm tryyyyyiiiiinnng," Maeve screamed as she pushed, feeling the way the walls trembled and the door shook with the force of the insurgents trying to make it inside.

"One more. One more big push, Your Majesty," Norma urged from between her legs.

"It's almost time. His Majesty is becoming overwhelmed." The words brought urgency and determination through Maeve and her beast, giving her all the motivation she needed. She would not lose her family.

Maeve held onto Bridget's hand, wishing it could be Duncan's she was gripping, hating the people that robbed her of yet another event that she should have been sharing with her mate, and pushed. She felt the searing pain tearing her open, and another scream threatened to fall from her mouth, before she heard the words she had feared for months.

"The king is falling. Do it NOW!"

Outside, Duncan dove to catch up to Julius after landing a heavy blow to the dragon's face. He was tired and had multiple injuries, but he kept pushing through the pain, determined to win this battle, as it would decide the fate of the kingdom. Just as he was about to reach Julius, a set of claws ripped through his wings, forcing his beast to divert from its course to try to slow its descent. A volley of fire hit the belly of his beast, sending Duncan hurling toward the ground, stopping any progress they had made to prevent his crash. Duncan's only thought as his dragon was forced to shift back in mid-air, his eyes closed and bracing for the impact, was his mate, his hatchling and how he wished he would have gotten to meet it and be able to tell them how much he loved them. Dust and wind swirled through the air, thunder made the ground tremble, and lightning whipped through the sky as Duncan crashed into the ground with a sickening crack.

The painful, mournful roar of the queen's dragon could be heard. The thunder stopped, the wind and lightning ceased, and the fighting wound to a halt as both sides waited for the dust to settle. The figure of a dead man with red hair was visible as the fog of dust diminished and Julius' beast roared triumphantly.

What remained of the queen's loyal army set their weapons down and kneeled. The king was dead. The fight was done. The queen's dragon would be too weakened to fight. The war had been won.

Julius took a triumphant breath and incinerated the king's body before flying toward the crowning glory of his new kingdom. He walked into the castle, seeing the bodies of the guards who had protected the queen until their dying breath littering the halls. He ascended the stairs and sauntered over to the royal chambers. Bridget lay in a pool of her own blood, her glassy eyes staring at the wall with her throat slit. Norma was huddled in a corner. She would look peaceful and thoughtful if not for the lance that perforated her chest and anchored her to the wall.

Maeve sat in the middle of her bed, the sheets still stained with blood and fluids, her eyes looked cold and haunted, and she was holding onto a bundle in her arms. She looked up at the man who entered her chambers, the only sign of acknowledgment she could muster.

"Your Highness," one of his men came forward, but Julius held up a hand.

"The hatchling, was it a girl? Does she have the mark?"

"It was a girl, but the king died, and the queen was unable to give birth in time. The pain of losing her mate complicated the birth and the whelp did not survive."

Julius tsked, removing the blanket covering the bundle in the queen's arms to confirm.

"Well, that's unfortunate, but don't worry, Your Highness, I'll ensure you birth the next heir soon enough."

Maeve didn't respond. The fight was gone from her, her beast, nowhere to be seen behind her eyes. Julius smiled, the death of the king and hatchling had broken the queen, clearing the last hurdle in his path: her resistance. He grabbed Maeve's chin, ensuring she could see and hear him. "You have three weeks to mourn for the life you knew. When the time is up, you will make me your chosen mate unless you want the blood bath to continue." He snarled when she didn't react. "Say you understand."

"Yes." The single word left the queen's mouth, and Julius released the queen's face and looked at the guard.

"Make sure that she's never alone, not to bathe or relieve herself unless you've removed anything she could use to take her own life. If she dies, you and your family will know torture like you've never known before."

The guard nodded, and Julius left the chambers. The lords were all seated in the court waiting for their new king, with Lord Cameron sitting pompously front and center with his mate and five-year-old son; hugging his mother tightly after the months of separation.

Julius walked in and sauntered toward the throne. He sat there, taking in the people around him. Years of planning had almost been foiled when the queen fell pregnant, yet the results were better than he expected after having to adjust their plans.

"Have the members of the court loyal to the king and queen been dealt with?" he asked.

"Most of them, Your Highness. We're hunting down the remaining members as we speak."

"Any prisoners?"

"The remnants of the queen's army surrendered. We're awaiting orders as to their fate."

"They will be stripped of any position in the army, or within the palace walls. I will not make the same mistake as my predecessors." Julius' sarcastic smile had the lords chuckling.

Over the course of the next two weeks, Maeve didn't leave her chambers. The guards removed anything that she could use for self-harm. They removed the enchantment on the windows and added their own, sealing the grieving, nearly catatonic queen, who remained in her bed most of the day, in her chambers.

Slowly, she started getting out of bed. It started with a shower, then a walk around the grounds. Most days, though, the castle staff often saw her looking down from her window. They wondered if she would jump if she could, but she only stared at them as they continued working on their chores with a dead look in her eyes. It made them uncomfortable and guilty, and they began to avoid making eye contact as much as possible as they prepared the courtyard for the crowning and mating ceremony Julius decided to have.

Two days before the ceremony, Maeve showed up at the now private dinners Julius had in the castle. The lords and ladies would return home the day after the ceremony, their pockets lined with more gold than they could ever hope to spend.

"My Queen! How good of you to join us," Julius barked out when she entered the dining room. Maeve's face was stoic and cold, as it'd been since the day her mate died. She looked each and every lord and lady in the eye, making them shift and look away uncomfortably as she did.

She walked forward with her head held high, forcing Lord Cameron to urge the rest of the table down in order to seat the queen next to Julius. Dinner was brought out and everyone tucked in, except Maeve. She watched with the same detached look on her face as everyone ate the food presented before them. Food too extravagant to warrant an everyday meal, but which the lords had demanded every day since they came to live in the castle. When dinner came to an end, the staff served dessert—a sampling of delicacies that everyone greedily devoured. As the last crumbs of the pastries were practically licked clean, Lord Cameron began to flex his hand with a frown.

One by one, each person around the table began to struggle. Their limbs felt heavy and numb, and they were slowly losing control of them. Julius tried to stand, only for his knees to buckle under him and land him back in the chair. He looked over at Maeve, who was still looking blankly at the wall.

"What did you do?" he snarled.

Finally, Maeve looked over at Julius and a smile graced her face.

"You're asking the wrong question, *Your Majesty,*" she spat. "The correct question is, what is going to happen to you?"

Maeve stood up and pushed the chair containing a struggling Julius to the side, so that she could once again stand at the head of the table. She heard a few lords trying to call for their guards, but outside of the noise from the few servers she had chosen herself for the night, the entire castle had gone eerily quiet.

"Before I leave here today, every single one of you will be dead. Your insides melted from the inside out. Don't worry, the poison works slowly at first. Long enough for me to tell you how foolish you were for underestimating your queen and the will of the gods," Maeve informed the panicked lords.

"You can't kill us!" Lord Frederick struggled to get the words out as his tongue fought to work.

"Why can't I?"

"Vachum," he struggled to say.

"A power vacuum? You mean like the one you wanted to create by killing the king and myself? The vacuum you wanted to create when you threatened to kill my hatchling before she could even have a chance at life?" Maeve's hand went to her now flat stomach, her eyes glowing as her beast made itself known to them for the first time since the battle.

There was a sudden noise coming from the right side of the dining room, then an oval portal appeared. A man stepped out, making Maeve smile.

"Beta Patrick. Thank you for being on time," she greeted the man as one would a close ally.

"Of course, Your Majesty. Alpha Owen sends his apologies. His mate has gone into labor and he couldn't bear to leave her side. He hopes you understand. The rest of the castle is asleep until morning."

Tears threatened to sting Maeve's eyes as she thought about how she was forced to birth her daughter without her mate. She blinked them back and smiled again.

"He has his priorities in order. His presence, while welcomed, is not required tonight. I'm quite happy for your help. Are they here?" she asked, unable to keep the hopeful tone from her voice.

Patrick smiled kindly at the queen, and stepped aside, revealing another person waiting to enter the portal. Maeve had to hold back a sob as she watched Duncan step through the portal, a tiny bundle in his arms, holding their daughter, Savannah.

Maeve walked toward him quickly, grasping the back of his neck as she kissed him fiercely, before resting her head on his for a moment. If the lords could move their faces, their eyebrows would have disappeared into their receding hairlines.

"N-no. I kil-l-led," Julius tried to roar, drool spilling from his mouth as he attempted to fight the debilitating poison. Maeve stiffened at his words, fury like no other threatening to overtake her, feeling like she was being robbed of this reunion, just like so many other things these people had already robbed her of having.

"You thought you were one step ahead of me the entire time, didn't you?" Maeve spat. "You never were. You can't be steps ahead of the gods."

Two Months Ago

"How can he ask me to give him up?" Maeve raged in her office, tears streaming down her face. Her hand still stung from the slap she delivered on her mate's face. The reminder of his words pierced her heart again.

"He's just worried, Your Majesty. He loves you." Bridget tried to console the queen.

"Not enough to fight for us!" she raged, throwing a trinket across the room, hearing it shatter as she closed her eyes against the onslaught of pain coursing through her heart.

A sudden noise startled her and she opened her eyes, as Bridget pushed her against the wall when a portal opened in her office, putting herself protectively in front of the queen. Two men stepped through, one quickly darting to the door, casting some sort of spell on the door, just before the doorknob rattled and shouts for her began to be heard. A thud was felt on the door, but the door didn't give. Bridget wanted to attack, but she didn't want to leave the queen vulnerable and unprotected, and she couldn't guarantee the mage or warlock in front of her wouldn't attack them if she attacked the other man, so she remained calm, a sword in front of her, her body covering the queen's.

The noise from outside the room was suddenly muffled, and the man by the door turned and nodded to the man standing by the portal. The man was handsome, and you could feel his powerful aura surrounding him.

"Your Majesty, my name is Alpha Owen of the Silver Haven Pack. This is my Beta Patrick, a warlock-wolf hybrid. We've been sent to help. Do you mind if we sit?" He motioned over to the desk. Bridget turned to look at the queen for instructions. Maeve nodded, her beast sensing no real danger from these men, and curious about their statement.

The two women carefully made their way to the other side of the desk and sat.

"Silver Haven Pack? I've never heard of them," Maeve said, though something about the name tickled the back of her mind.

"We are a relatively new pack established in the human realm," Alpha Owen explained, piquing Maeve's curiosity. Most shifter packs were here in Exury. She had only heard about one pack being allowed to live in the human realm. A small pack that had disappeared from Exury over a decade ago was found to have been enslaved and forced to perform for a circus to entertain the humans there a few years ago.

"The pack that was kidnapped to the human realm?" Owen nodded at her words and Maeve finally noticed the scars caused by the silver around his neck. "Who sent you?" Maeve asked.

"You should know, Your Majesty. He said you've prayed to him for weeks." Owen smiled ruefully.

Maeve returned the same rueful smile. "I have prayed to many gods in the last few weeks, Alpha Owen. You're going to have to be more specific than that."

"Set," he answered and Maeve paled, the god of chaos answering her prayer was never a good sign.

"Then that means..."

"*Your enemies are too many, and your people have become too greedy, and easily corrupted. You will not win this war,*" *Alpha Owen said, sympathy clear in his words as he watched a tear slip from Maeve's eyes and her hand go to her swollen stomach.*

"*The gods chose you for a reason, and they still have plans for you, Queen Maeve. That is why they sent us,*" *Alpha Owen said, a kindness to his voice that Maeve had not heard from anyone other than her mate in years.*

"*What plans?*"

"*I'm afraid we're too low on the food chain to be privy to the plans of the gods,*" *Alpha Owen chuckled.* "*We are only following instructions. Pawns, just like you. Our pack was given a second chance, and while the fate that awaits your kingdom is not avoidable, yours is.*"

"*What's going to happen to my kingdom?*"

"*You have seen it already. The dreams. I can see the knowledge in your eyes,*" *Beta Patrick finally spoke.*

"*They weren't just nightmares then?*"

"*No, they were warnings sent by Set.*"

"*How can I save my family?*" *Maeve finally asked.*

"*By granting your mate his deepest wish.*" *It took Maeve only a few moments before she knew what he was referring to.*

"*You want us to run away? Leave my people to suffer alone?*" *Conflict warred inside her as she asked the question.*

"*Your people need a lesson, one that can be painfully carved into their souls to remind them of the gods' power for a few generations, and it's not one that you can spare them from learning. Whether you agree to our help or not, the gods will teach that lesson.*" *Maeve thought long and hard over the words Alpha Owen was speaking. She felt the bile rise in her throat at the thought of abandoning her people, but she knew better than anyone that most of her people's priorities were skewed. They wanted power and wealth over peace and growth. They treated anyone they felt was beneath them worse than animals. If they were going to lose this war so the gods could teach their lessons, why should she sacrifice her family, when they were being told by the gods they didn't deserve the same fate? Hadn't she sacrificed enough already? She looked over at Bridget, who gave her an encouraging nod.*

"*How?*" *she asked.*

"*It will be tricky, but Set has gifted Patrick additional magic to complete this task. When the time comes, we will escort you out of the realm and into the human realm via a portal. We've spent a few months procuring some land for you, your most trusted people and their families," Alpha Owen answered, giving a small nod toward Bridget, who was taken aback at the knowledge that she would be spared. "Some will be transported earlier to avoid everything being left to the last minute, but we have to leave in a way that no one is aware that you're still alive. If they think you're alive, the dragons will hunt you down until you return to lead them."*

The door shook violently but thankfully didn't give, however, Maeve could now hear Duncan screaming for her from the other side. Alpha Owen and Alpha Patrick stood.

"We'll be in touch. Set has given us the list of people who will join you, so we will begin extractions soon. It is imperative that no one outside of this room knows."

"My mate..."

"It's better that he doesn't know. He has a part to play, and it will be better if he isn't aware he will survive," Alpha Owen's face grew full of sympathy, when he saw the ashen face on the queen at his words, then turned to Bridget.

"Your son will be one of the first to be transported. Your sister will remain here and assist the queen in giving birth. We'll take you both when the time comes. Please send word to your sister that Luna Lily will pick him up in a few days. She's my mate. Your son will remain with us until you and your mate are able to join him." A wistful smile appeared on the man's face. "My Luna is expecting. It will be good practice for us."

"Thank you, Alpha Owen," Bridget answered, relief flooding her system.

"We should go. Your mate is about to dislocate both of his shoulders trying to get to you. Once we leave, remove the herbs on the doorway, and the spells will break," Beta Patrick said, turning to Alpha Owen, who nodded in affirmation.

"Wait! Can you put Bridget in her room? If both of us are here, Duncan will never believe we didn't hear anything."

Beta Patrick began murmuring under his breath and a new portal replaced the current one. "This should be it. Pretend to be napping. Tell them you don't know anything that's happened all morning. They can believe witchcraft was involved but without any leads. I had to put the guards outside the doors to sleep while I put the spells on the door."

Bridget stepped through the portal with a nod from her queen.

"We will see you soon, Your Majesty. Stay safe." Alpha Owen said before stepping into the new portal Beta Patrick created.

"I've known from the very beginning what you were planning. I've known thanks to Set that you would all betray me. And it is Set, who has spared my family and me while dooming the kingdom to reap what you've sown." Maeve explained. She needed to hurry. She could see the discomfort beginning to appear on a few faces. "I knew you would attack when I went into labor. So we prepared..."

Two Weeks Ago

Duncan ran out to see what the shouting in the hall was. The moment the door closed, Maeve had Bridget bring the spelled totem she was given and had hidden in the bathroom, and broke it in half. A portal appeared in the corner of the room, and Alpha Owen and Beta Patrick appeared.

"Are you ready to do this, Your Highness?" Beta Patrick asked, looking at her with some concern. Maeve laughed.

"I don't think I can stop this little one from coming out for very long, Beta Patrick."

"Once your mate goes to meet Julius, we will begin." Alpha Owen stood by the window, out of sight from anyone who might see him from below.

"How are you going to get the rest of them to follow you without explaining?" Bridget asked, making Alpha Owen smile widely.

"'Follow' is a strong word. We'll take them the same way the warlocks took us," he answered, motioning over to Beta Patrick, who was blushing furiously with a guilty look on his face.

"I have the power to put people to sleep," he answered.

"Are you that boring, Beta Patrick?" Maeve managed to crack a smile through all the stress and pain. Alpha Owen barked a laugh, and the two other women chuckled as Beta Patrick blushed even harder.

"The king is flying. Let's begin," Alpha Owen said, moving away from the window but almost jumping out of his skin when a contraction hit Maeve, and she couldn't help the elevating scream that suddenly ripped out of her.

"Your mate is pregnant with your first pup, I'm guessing?" Maeve asked with some humor when the contraction started to lessen. It was Alpha Owen's turn to blush and nod. "Better get used to the screaming now. Can't be jumping every time she gets a contraction."

Beta Patrick opened the door, and moments later, Maeve heard two thuds, a few startled yells and more thuds hitting the ground. Alpha Owen came back into the room carrying two unconscious guards.

"Handy," Maeve muttered.

"A little." Alpha Owen laughed. "Patrick is setting up the mud golems that need to be killed in place of the guards. It will take a few minutes."

An hour later, Beta Patrick's mud golems outside of their chambers had been slaughtered by the traitors trying to get inside her chambers. Maeve was trying to push as hard as she could while she could hear her mate fighting for his life outside. Beta Patrick's spells were holding firm and were giving her hope that he would be able to save her family.

"One more. One more big push, Your Majesty," Norma urged from between her legs.

"It's almost time. His Majesty is becoming overwhelmed," Alpha Owen called from the window.

Maeve felt relief when she heard her daughter's first cry, but she didn't have much time to bask in her joy when Alpha Owen took in a sharp breath behind her.

"The king is falling. Do it NOW!"

Beta Patrick opened and left through the portal, reappearing moments later with an unconscious and bleeding Duncan floating onto the bed next to her.

Maeve called on her beast, allowing her face to shift, and she let out a roar that she would have felt if her mate had been killed for all to hear.

Beta Patrick created an exact replica of the king and slid it into place on the other side of the portal.

"Can you wake him? I need to explain," Maeve begged Patrick after he conjured another portal to take them all back to the human realm. He nodded and his lips moved silently. Duncan stirred, then sat straight up, trying to figure out what happened.

"It's okay, my love. You're safe. We're safe." Maeve cooed, motioning to their daughter, currently in her arms. Duncan's face filled with wonder for a moment before the thumping against the door startled him and he finally noticed the strange men and portal in his

chambers. Maeve grabbed onto his hand to call back his attention. "We don't have time. They're friends. We need to trust them."

"What's going on, Maeve?"

"We can't win this fight," Maeve said quietly, tears flowing freely down her face. "I would have lost you."

"I know," he said. Self-hatred at his failure crossed his features and Maeve pulled him down until they were eye to eye.

"You didn't fail. We weren't meant to win. The gods are punishing them. We got caught in the crossfire," she said firmly, unwilling to let her mate leave believing he had failed to protect them. "These people will explain the entire thing later, but right now, you need to trust me when I say we can trust them. Can you do that?"

"I would do anything for you, Maeve, and her," Duncan said, before looking down at his daughter.

"Savannah. That will be her name," Maeve told him, handing over their daughter to him, swallowing a sob, knowing she wouldn't get to hold her again for a while.

"Hi, Savannah. I'm your daddy." A triumphant roar from the battlegrounds ruined the tenderness of their moment.

"You need to go."

"Go? Go where? Where are we going?" Duncan asked wildly.

"Go with them. Trust them. I will meet you later."

"What? No. I'm not leaving you! Maeve you just g—" Duncan tried to argue, but Maeve interrupted him, knowing there was only a little time left.

"You have to. They think you're dead. I need to stay and play the part. I promise I will meet you soon," she sobbed.

"When?" he asked, pain etched into his face as he watched from the corner of his eye as Beta Patrick created two golems that looked like Bridget and Norma, then escorted the real ones through the portal.

"Just a little while. Take care of our daughter. Give her so many kisses for the both of us," Maeve whispered, trying to hold in more tears and be strong for all of them.

"No! Maeve—"

"Please, I need you safe. I won't be able to do this until I know you're safe. Trust me. Trust them," she begged.

"You better come back to me soon," Duncan growled and kissed her fiercely before he turned and walked through the portal before he could change his mind. Beta Patrick and Alpha Owen were the only ones remaining.

"We'll come back in a few hours. They just need to see you destroyed. Patrick has a potion that will numb your emotions. They need to believe you would kill yourself," Alpha Owen said quietly as he respected the grief on the queen's face when Beta Patrick gave her a small bundle enchanted to look like a deceased baby.

Maeve shook her head, reminding herself that this was not her daughter. Her daughter was safe and sound in the arms of her mate. At the thought, the fire came back in her eyes, rage bubbling at having had to witness both deceased forms of the people she loved the most in this life. Making up her mind, she turned to Beta Patrick, who resisted the urge to take a step back at the rage he could see in the queen.

"Give me another totem to summon you. I have things I need to do first," Maeve asked.

"That's not part of the plan." Alpha Owen's brows furrowed with concern.

"It is now. Set wants chaos, a lesson. I will set it in motion for him and get justice for what they've taken from me," she said, squaring her shoulders angrily.

Alpha Owen hesitated, but he thought she had a right to serve her justice and nodded at Beta Patrick, who produced another totem with a whisper, and handed it to Maeve, who hid it under her pillow.

The two men left through the portal, and the Norma golem removed the enchantments to the doors of the queen's chambers, allowing the men to burst in and kill both golems before taking in the sight of the queen on the bed. The queen buried her beast deep in her mind as she heard the man who almost took her family from her approach.

"You can't beat the gods, and now all of you will pay. Your children will know what it's like to lose both parents, just like you wanted my daughter to lose hers. You wanted the kingdom for them? They can have it or what will be left for them after every faction fights for power and the throne. I'm taking my daughter far away from here, where she doesn't have to live a life surrounded by your greed and betrayal. Your children will grow up watching the kingdom plunged into chaos without anyone leading it. I doubt many of them will survive," Maeve told the table as they all writhed in pain; their eyes, nose, mouth and ears bleeding, as the poison destroyed their organs.

Maeve nodded at Beta Patrick, and a deceased replica of the queen appeared next to Julius, seemingly affected by the same poison. Duncan drew in a sharp breath, seeing before him what could have been, and having a hard time making his brain comprehend that it was all a lie. A hand on his cheek made him turn from the image of his mate, dead before him, and Maeve smiled at him, reminding him that she was alive, and at his side.

The group left again through the portal, leaving the castle to wake up to a new day to discover that every person in power was dead.

Chapter Seven

Six Months Later

"Your Majesties. Alpha Owen and Luna Lily have arrived." Bridget came out of the main house, knowing the king and queen enjoyed spending time on the little patio porch near the edge of the forest. Duncan chuckled.

"We're not king and queen anymore, Bridget. It's been six months, you need to get used to calling us by our names."

Bridget smiled and shook her head.

"You will always be my king and queen, but I will try."

"She's just finishing up. Please let them know we'll be there as soon as she finishes eating," Maeve said, looking down at her daughter as she suckled from her breast.

It was a struggle at first, getting her to take the breast after drinking formula for almost three weeks, but now Savannah was happy to suckle her mom's milk.

Duncan kissed Maeve's temple, and they watched their daughter until she was drunk on milk and released the nipple. Duncan took her in his arms, placing her against his shoulder so she could burp while Maeve righted her clothing, and they walked back into their new home.

Alpha Owen had set them up in the north of Scotland. Their new territory was large, and the population was low. It allowed them to shift during the night and let their beasts take to the sky without risking exposure. It was far from an ideal situation, but the king and queen and everyone who was rescued were grateful for the peaceful existence they had been able to achieve in the short time since they had arrived.

They walked into the big house Alpha Owen had constructed for them. He said it was in the style of a wolf's pack house, since their dragon clan was now less than forty strong. No one but those loyal to the king and queen during the turmoil. Once inside, they headed to the living room which was full of people chatting animatedly with wolf shifters that were slowly becoming family, thanks to Patrick being allowed to retain the ability to create portals. Visiting from Paris for the wolves was as easy as opening a portal and taking a few steps through it. They visited often, helping the dragons adjust to life in a place where magic was thought to be a myth.

"Lily, Owen. It's so good to see you. Where's Patrick?" Maeve asked, taking Lily's boy in her arms happily. At her voice, Patrick came into view from the kitchen with a beer already in hand. His face lit up when he saw little Savannah was still awake. He put the beer down and grabbed the little princess from Duncan, making the couple chuckle when their daughter began to coo.

"You're so good with kids, Patrick. You're going to end up with a whole soccer team of little pups." Duncan laughed.

"Uncle Patrick needs to find a mate first, doesn't he, Savannah? Doesn't he?" Patrick talked to the baby in a higher pitch, making the rest chuckle.

Lily and Maeve went into one of the bedrooms a few hours later to put the kids down for their nap. Maeve looked down lovingly at the two babies, a question in the forefront of her mind.

"Do you know if Set really needs us, or does he need them?" she asked. Lily sighed, a hand caressing her sleeping baby boy.

"I don't know. I worry about it sometimes, but we all know we can't escape the will of the gods for long. Owen trains the pack to be strong so that when we're called for whatever purpose we were recruited for, or they are, everyone will be ready." Lily looked up at Maeve and smiled. "It's no use worrying about it too much. Live your life in the moment. We were all given a second chance, and I intend to live it fully."

Maeve finally cracked a smile back, a mischievous glint in her eyes. "Trust me, I won't be missing another minute of it," she answered, her hand going to her flat belly, wincing as Lily shrieked in happiness.

Acknowledgements

Special thanks to Marc, Vicki, Chloe for helping proof read these stories.

Thank you to Michael for all the help with graphics.

Thank you to Pamela K. Isley for allowing us to debut her story. You're wonderful and creative and this story proves that. We look forward to reading more from you.

About the Author

Vera Foxx

Once a dream became a reality a few years ago after covid hit. Vera Foxx's children were growing, and she realized she needed to claim herself once again. She began writing her first book, Under the Moon, which opened up a new world and subsequently began a hot animal with shifters, faes, vampires and orc books. Most of her men are rugged, sexy, obsessive and controlled by a mate bond like no other.

Vera Foxx hates cheating tropes. You won't find any leading man treating her woman badly. You will find obsessive, morally grey, spicy and extra growly on the side who know how to treat a woman right. *Wink*

When she's not writing, she takes care of her husband and children, along with her dog and two cats. She loves reading, swimming, hiking and DIY house projects around her home.

Pamela K. Isley

Pamela is a new writer, dipping her toes into the world of fantasy romance. She has many decades long background in both video games and tabletop roleplaying games to fuel her own worlds; as well as plucking from the pool of long thought, but never played characters to fill them with. Strong females, rich worlds, and happily ever after... eventually... guaranteed.

Emm E. Goshald

Emm E Goshald is a Mexican Canadian Author who specializes in Paranormal Fantasy Romance. She began her journey on a serialized reading app and has since transitioned into printed books.

She enjoys making her readers anxiety spike and adding minorities and different cultures in every book. Her most popular series, Their Aztec Wolves, immerses the reader in Mexican and Mexican-American culture and Aztec Lore.

Becoming an author has brought her into a world of social media, and while daunting for her socially awkward penguin butt, she loves interacting with everyone and appreciates every reaction to her books that she gets.

Emm lives in Canada with her husband and their two dogs. As an introvert and hermit, she enjoys the peace and quiet of living in a small city.

Aside from writing, Emm loves reading, cooking, playing video games with her husband and watching Horror and Pixar movies.

If you want to follow along as she writes, you can find her on Patreon and Inkitt where she shares a platform with Avalina P. Cox and Isa Rinner called Smutty Tea for Thee

Stephanie Light

Stephanie Light is a Mexican American author best known for The World of Ivory Series, featuring The Silent Alpha and The Gold Queen.

After months of writing for herself, she published her debut novel, The Ivory Queen, on a serialized reading platform, and continues bringing new stories to life.

She creates dark fantasy worlds with villains you love to hate and characters whose courage and strength know no bounds. Her books contain original legends and tales of werewolves, witches, dragons, vampires, faes, and everything in between, mixed with plenty of spice.

Isa Rinner

Isa Rinner is a fantasy romance author born and raised in Austria, where she studied linguistics and later technical writing. When she isn't creating fictional worlds, she is working as a Technical Writer. She started her journey as a writer with creating short stories first, before writing her first full-length novel for the reading app Dreame.

Isa specializes in fantasy, paranormal and shifter romance novels, and likes to write stories with healthy relationships and strong yet relatable characters, with a bit of steam and humor to them too. She likes to add her own twists to the genre and create her own fantasy worlds for her readers to dive into.

Her Silverlake Wolves series, currently consisting of five books, was published on Amazon and for KU.

Allie Carstens

Allie is a fantasy romance author with two full-length books under her belt, "The Alpha's Pen Pal," and "The Beta's Blind Date."

Allie loves to put her own spin on popular tropes in the fantasy/werewolf romance genres, and loves unexpected plot twists. Her male leads may make mistakes at times, but they love their partners fiercely and aren't afraid to tell or show them. Her females aren't afraid to stand up for themselves and others, and don't usually let their love interests off easy when they make those dumb mistakes they're bound to make. Allie mixes humor into her stories as well as real-life, heart wrenching moments that have you reaching for your tissues. And no matter what, she will almost always deliver a happily ever after.

Avalina P. Cox

Affectionately known as Chicken, I am an indie author from the UK, with mild insanity and a wild imagination. Creating worlds to get lost in is my passion. When I am not writing, I am plotting the next adventure to take my readers on.

I am a nurse, mother of two young teens and a caregiver. Writing is something I am passionate about. It gives me so much joy (and also a little stress at times) but I love making the pages come to life with words.

Having started as a platform episodic writer for Dreame, under the pen name Parched Chicken, hence my nickname, you will find my very first works available there in very raw form! As I gained confidence with my writing, I moved from YA and contemporary romance, to fantasy, and wrote my first shifter book duo, The Scafell Series.

Enjoying immersing myself in the world of fantasy, I decided to write a high fantasy book, and Guardian of the Fae was born. Guardian of Fae was my first release on Amazon, and my next release will be the second book in the series. However, I love to explore different species and world building so in the future I will be working on different projects.

Writing in all genres, I like to write what comes naturally at the time. Often, I think I know what I am going to write next, but I am usually wrong, and my brain tells me so! Don't forget to join facebook group Chicken's Nuggets, or follow me on Insta, Avalina_P_Cox, where I post regularly with what is going on in my world.

All my future works will be available once complete and edited, on Amazon and Kindle Unlimited. In the meantime, if you want to support me, for a small monthly fee you can follow me on Patreon or Inkitt under the name Smutty Tea for Thee.

There I have joined two other incredible authors, Emm E Goshald and Isa Rinner, so you get three authors' works for one monthly subscription. Our patreon and Inkitt give you the first look of all the projects all of us are working on and you can read them (unedited) before they are released to the general public, and we post everyday between us so you don't have to go a day without a new chapter.

Authors' Works

Whispering Castell

Songs of the Wolf

Allie Carsten

The Alpha's Pen Pal
<u>Coming February 2024</u>
The Beta's Blind Date

Stephanie Light

<u>Dreame</u>
The Gold Queen
The Ivory Queen
The Silent Alpha
<u>Inkitt</u>
The Earth Witch
The Ivory Throne
A Wolf in the Game of Dragons

Avalina P. Cox

Guardian of the Fae

Christmas Countdown

Dragon Foundling

Sacred Fate

Emm E. Goshald

Unexpected Alpha Standalone Series

The Replacement Alpha

The Order of Abaddon Series

Awakened to the Shadows

Their Aztec Wolves Series

His Hunted Aztec Luna

The Aztec God's Redemption

Coming Soon to Their Aztec Wolves Series

The Aztec Beta's Assassin – Feb 14, 2022

The Aztec Heir's Genius – March 15, 2022

The Broken Aztec Princesses – Apr 21, 2022

Isa Rinner

An Omega for the Lycan Prince

A Female Alpha for the Lycan Prince

A Mysterious Slave for the Lycan Prince

A Chance at Love for the Twin Alphas

A Broody Werewolf Mate for the Human

Vera Foxx

Under the Moon Series

Under the Moon

The Alpha's Kitten

Finding Love with the Fae King

The Exiled Dragon

Under the Moon: The Dark War

His True Beloved: A Vampire's Second Chance

Alpha of her Dreams

The Broken Alpha's Princess

Twinning and Sinning: From Mutts to Mates

Under the Moon: God Series

Seeking Hades' Ember

Lucifer's Redemption

Poseidon's Island Flower

Under the Moon: Orc Series

Thorn: A Steamy Orc Rom-Com

The Iron Fang Fang Series

Grim

Hawke

Bear

Made in the USA
Columbia, SC
12 February 2024

6aee4732-e5b5-4510-a221-595f34abab1aR01